The Shadows of Kiln

Hidden From Destiny
Book One: The Shadows of Sorban

The Demon's Curse
Book One: The Shadows of the Amazon

Short Stories
Hiding in the Open
A Shadows of Sorban Story

The Lost Breath
A Shadows of the Amazon Story

Release Me
A Shadows of Time Story

Rules to Kill For
A Shadows of the Assassin Story

Independent Short Stories
Murder For a Friend

The Demon's Curse

The Shadows of Kiln
Book One: The Shadows of the Amazon

Micaela Fischer

Published in the United States by Nightfall Publications.

ISBN 978-0-9837204-5-4

Printed in the United States of America

www.nightfallpublications.com
www.micaelafischer.com

Book design by Amber L. Campbell
Cover Art by Gary McCluskey
Cover Design by Tiara Lynn Agresta
Back Cover Description by Vincent Costa

Never let the inner demons win

For Junebug

Chapter 1

"I am not going in there." Cora's declaration echoed around her. She pulled her head out of the large, dark hole. "It's not at all acceptable. It smells worse than any tavern you've taken me into the three years."

The alley the group stood in stank of stale alcohol, rotten food and urine. The summer heat did not help. Glancing around her, Cora found she was still unhappy with how close the walls were. Windows were closed against the night and, she felt sure, the smells as well. A drunkard, who had been sleeping in the cleanest spot of the alley when they arrived, stared at her.

A wooden disk had covered the entrance to the sewer. Cora did not know if other cities put their sewer entrances into false buildings, with the actual hole in a wall, like this one, but she felt sure there had to be a better way to reach their destination.

She put her hand on her hip and glared at the man next to her, pleased to see his frown. For Cora Rylannes, princess-mage of an Amazon nation, second to the throne, making tasks difficult for Percival "Black Hand" Riesun always made her smile. Though he led their mercenary group, she did not feel it necessary to follow his orders without question. He was their leader only as long as she allowed it. What kind of Amazon would she be to let him think he could give her orders?

Percival stared at her. "You can't be serious. You're refusing to go because of the smell?"

She nodded, twice. "That, and it looks closed in and tight. I cannot have the muck touching me."

"Oh, don't be such a princess, Princess. We'll just take a bath in the ocean when we're done." Tylina, the other mage in the group, laughed as she made her way into the sewer shaft.

Behind Tylina, Nimbly and Brolin stepped forward to take their turn. Nimbly opened his mouth to laugh as well, but Cora's glare Cora silenced him. Instead of reacting to the exchange, Brolin disappeared down the hole.

"That's a good sign, right? If Brolin fits, there should be plenty of room for you, Cora." Nimbly tried to comfort her.

She lowered her spear at him. His face paled and he scrambled into the hole.

Realization lit Percival's face. "Cora, you can't let this stop you."

"I have no idea what you're talking about." She set the end of her spear onto the ground.

Too late, she remembered where she had found the spear. Judging from the way Percival's jaw clenched when his gaze flicked over the rune-carved shaft, he remembered as well. She should have left the spear at the inn. Better yet, she should have stayed there with it and used the damn thing to bar the door.

Percival sighed. "Yes, you do. You have to get past this. This is the only way into the underground city."

He turned to guide Kalik, their blind warrior, to the hole. Though he had lost his sight as a child, Kalik had learned other techniques for making it through his daily life. His sense of hearing, smell and touch were so acute, he often knew things were out of place before the sighted members of the group. He frequently surprised Cora, and she wondered if any Amazon ever had to deal with his disability. She grinned when he pushed Percival's hand away, sliding into the hole easier than anyone else did.

Percival turned back to her. "Cora, for three years, I have kept you from harm. But I cannot let the close proximity of these sewers keep you from our task."

They had met three years earlier, shortly after she and her bodyguard, Satina, had arrived in Glenys from the Amazon islands. He had come upon her and Satina when a small group of thieves tried to steal from them. Percival and his patrol helped the Amazons, even though Cora did not ask for help. That first argument had ended with her rude dismissal of the large warrior. How dare a *man* presume he could protect an Amazon princess!

For a year, their chance meetings had seemed destined by a celestial being, or at least the interference of one. When Percival left his military service at the end of the year, he searched for her, determined to travel with her through Man's World. Though Satina's displeasure with his presence was never in question, Cora accepted his company after she forgave him for his decision to help her in their first meeting.

"I can stay here. Keep anyone else from using this entrance," she offered.

"King Kennan asked all of us to go. You agreed. You can't back out now." He reached to take her hand, but Satina placed herself between them, pushing his hand aside. "I'll be with you. I won't let anything happen to you. We need you to do this with us. You know it is always easier for me—us—with you near." Percival looked away from her.

Cora studied him for a moment. Recently, he had been making comments like that more often. Satina's shoulder blocked most of her view, but she still saw his eyes, and the need she saw in them confused her. She pushed this aside for now. She already had enough to deal with. Stepping around her bodyguard, she peered down the hole again.

"That *man* should never make demands of me. Especially considering his family's connection to my islands."

"What?" he asked, surprised.

"You should know, Black Hand. You are one of his men, after all," Satina declared.

"I don't—" he started.

"Having your *protection* is not important or even the issue, Black Hand. The enclosed area that will collapse on me is the problem."

Cora tried to straighten, but gravel crunched behind her. Before she could turn, hands pressed against her back, pushing her into the hole.

"Kalik! Catch Cora!" Percival's shout rang through the

tunnel, followed by a scraping sound of metal on metal.

Cora fell through the shaft, moaning in disgust at the feel of slime against her skin. The darkness closed around her, squeezing the air from her chest. She couldn't breathe, couldn't think... couldn't scream.

A sudden flare of light illuminated Kalik, his arms outstretched to catch her. She pushed away from his grasp. She fell to her hands and knees. Her breath came in rugged gasps.

She stared at the ground, seeking a focal point in the darkness. Her hands. She could see her hands.

Someone grabbed her shoulders and lifted her from the floor. Where he touched her, her skin felt as if thousands of needles pierced her flesh, though it brought no pain. She lost sight of her hands.

She needed to find a new focus. A lit torch appeared in front of her. Then Percival's face blocked the light.

* * *

Percival shook Cora, gently at first, then with more urgency when she started going limp in his grip. Where his hands touched her, his skin tingled, the sensation pleasant despite his concern.

He had not expected her reaction to be so severe.

A year earlier, the group had been hired for a task that required them to enter a castle. Even though they found what the item quickly, they chose to look for abandoned treasure. Their search led them to the dungeon, where a trap had separated Cora and Percival from the others. Her claustrophobia made her believe the walls were closing in on them, but he had been able to pull her out of it by forcing her to focus on him.

He hoped it worked again.

"Cora, look at me." He forced her gaze to meet his again by lifting her chin.

There! A sigh of relief escaped him. She kept her eyes open and locked her gaze on him. Her blue eyes. Percival pulled her against him, wrapping his left arm around her waist in a firm embrace. The tingling flared, and then returned to its previous level of intensity. He grabbed her left hand with his right and placed it on his chest.

"Breathe with me, Cora. Match your breath to mine." He hoped she heard his whispered words through her panic. Her breath slowed and the fear left her eyes. "That's right. Take it slow. I'm right here."

He knew she was all right when she pulled away from him, eyes blazing with anger. The warmth of her body faded from his skin and he realized... he wanted it back.

"You're welcome." He reached up to wipe a splash of muck from her cheek. Her eyes widened in surprise and she slapped his hand away. "If it wasn't for me, you'd be unconscious from your fear."

"If it wasn't for you, I'd be on the surface and that wouldn't have happened," she snapped.

He watched her take a deep breath, but her attention left him when Satina tried to brush away the muck from Cora's skin.

She slapped Satina's hand away. "Get away from me!" Her order echoed in the sewer.

Percival laughed, then choked it back when Cora turned to him, her eyes narrowed. She extended a hand toward him, blue lightning crackling over her fingers. He pushed her too far this time.

"Arcanum..." she began.

Percival held his breath. He knew that spell. She would not miss.

Before she began the second word, Satina slapped Cora's spear against her palm. Slowly, Cora wrapped her fingers around the wood. The blue lightning jumped from her hand to dance over the wood, until it dissipated.

"You pushed me, Black Hand, knowing how I felt!"

"You agreed to help find the princess, Cora. Imagine how *she* feels!" Percival growled.

"I don't have to imagine! I already know!" she shouted. Her cheeks reddened.

Percival stepped back, his eyes widening. "What?"

"The two of you are pitiful," Tylina interrupted. She laid a hand on each of them and whispered a word of magic, instantly cleansing them both. "For a moment, the two of you were in harmony, breathing as one. Now you're fighting, worse than any man and wife I've ever seen. You must figure this out, but do it somewhere else, at another time, when a little girl's life isn't in danger."

Percival stared at their friend, then backed away. His skin

tingled from his contact with Cora and the movement of her hands on her arms told him she felt it as well. "Point taken."

Percival pulled a map from a pouch and snapped it open. He stared at the parchment. He would have to deal Cora once they found the younger princess. She had never come so close to using magic on him before. If he hadn't laughed, she might not have done it. Maybe she felt that was the only way to fight against a perceived insult.

Taking a deep breath, he pushed his anger away and focused on the map. He squinted at the others. There was only one passage for them to follow and he stood there, staring at a map. Damn that stubborn Amazon.

Putting the map away, he took a step down the passage. "This way."

Chapter 2

Cora relished the silence surrounding her while the group walked through the sewers. The smell proved worse than the alley. Here all manner of refuse was collected, until the city workers sent buckets of water to wash everything to the ocean. Cora did not understand the layout of the system or the lack of a constant flush of water through the sewers. The waste, when it flowed, passed through a depression in the ground, shooting off into smaller, side sewers.

Percival had shown her the map before they left the palace. They were looking for a side passage that would take them to an older part of the sewer system.

She watched Percival's muscular back in front of her and hoped he felt her anger. He was too free with her, speaking to her inappropriately, especially for a man. She must have confided in him too often, gotten too personal during the three years they spent together.

He glanced back at her and she averted her eyes.

Continuing to travel with him was a mistake.

Finally, the tingling in her skin disappeared, but she found it hard to push the sensation from her mind. She wanted to feel it again.

It was inappropriate for her to have such feelings toward a man, but she knew the first time she saw him that he was the one she was searching for. The vision that brought her to Man's World had proven correct.

She had spent some time learning the magic about visions and premonitions. Despite her rapid progress in that school, she had stopped, without explanation to her mother or her mentor. Every spell she cast showed one constant vision. She saw a man—a warrior—being consumed by fire from within. His left hand, where the fire started, was black from his fingertips to just past his wrist. The blackness writhed as if with a life of its own. The swirls of the red tattoo on Cora's leg and stomach matched the black swirls on the man's hand.

She told no one of her vision – except Dekart. It was his idea to come to Man's World, to find the black handed man. After arriving on the mainland, she learned the man from her vision was Captain Percival "The Black Hand" Riesun.

The first time they touched, the magic within Cora reacted to a magic within Percival. The sensation shocked them both. She knew the magic she wielded, but had never heard of anything like the tingling she felt where her skin touched his. After that, they tried to avoid all contact, though there were times Cora wanted—needed—to feel it again. She even went out of her way to make him touch her "accidentally".

She wondered how he felt about it.

Stone broke apart under Cora's boots. They reached a part of the tunnel that no longer received moisture of any type. They traveled at a constant downward slope and she felt the earth above her, the weight pressing on her shoulders. Trying to keep from panicking again, she recited the words Percival used to calm her.

They found the entrance, a hole in the wall crumbling from age. Darkness hid the area beyond the wall. Nimbly lit another torch and the bright light blinded Cora momentarily.

The new tunnel continued on until Cora felt sure the end would never come. The tunnel ceiling felt like a weight on her shoulders, pushing her breath out in gasps. Forcing one foot to move, then the other, she bumped into Satina's back.

"Why did you...?" Cora began then looked up to see the group stood in a large, cavern. Darkness hid the other side. Green algae glowed through the area, but revealed nothing of what waited for them.

After a moment, Percival turned to her. "Cora, can you light it up?"

"Of course." Ignoring Satina's whispered protests, Cora stepped past him. She held her hand out, level with the ground, trying to keep it from quivering with her fear. Letting him see how scared she was, how the earth above her scared her, would not do.

Cora pulled energy from around her, channeling it through her body. Turning her hand, palm now up, a small glowing ball formed, growing larger until it was the size of an orange. She flung it toward the ceiling of the cavern and watched as it ascended, growing to the size of two large pigs and stopping before it reached. "That should do."

The light from the ball revealed a city in the middle of the cavern, abandoned by its builders centuries before. An extensive wall surrounded it, and the parts they could see had not failed in the passing years. The wall made it difficult to see many of the buildings. Deep in the city, its spires reaching for the rock ceiling above them, stood a modest sized temple.

"Did anyone expect us to go this far underground?" Nimbly's voice echoed through the cavern.

Cora studied him, unable to remember the elf ever having issues with being in tight places. The group knew him to be a thief, but he rarely used his talents to steal. Instead, he used his abilities to help them through locked doors and gather information. He always wore leather dyed in dark blues and black to blend into the shadows of a city street easier. Much of their success came from his abilities.

Cora turned away from the elf, her attention drawn to Kalik. Tylina held his hand, moving it through the air in front of him as she described the scene. Kalik's softened leather breeches and riding boots, as well as his beaded leather vest, were clean. Tylina must have used her magic to clean everyone before she took care of Cora and Percival.

Cora sniffed in disgust. She never used her magic in such a trivial manner.

She returned her attention to Nimbly and Percival's discussion about the path they would take to the city gates, until the men turned to the rest of the group. "Are we ready to continue yet?" she asked.

"Yes, Nimbly will lead, looking for traps." Percival gestured for her to follow the elf, but she waited, putting her hand on her hip.

With a huff, Tylina and Kalik went first, pushing past Cora. The muscles in the Black Hand's jaw worked as he tried to stop his retort. Giving him a smirk, Cora started walking, her steps slow. She watched him shake his head before turning to the path in front of her. From behind her, she heard his footsteps on the ground.

Their footsteps echoed around them, their boot soles of hardened leather disturbing the stones on the ground. Though she noticed a hollow sound with each step, Cora remained quiet until one of the stones sank into the dirt.

"Percival..." she whispered. The group stopped and turned to look at her. She gestured at her foot.

Satina closed the distance between them, grabbing Cora's hand and pulling her from the place where she stood frozen.

"No! You idiot!" she cried out, reaching out to support herself from her bodyguard's abrupt decision.

Percival's chest stopped her fall, and his hand held her steady. "Are you all right?" he whispered.

Cora nodded, but Kalik interrupted her with a tap of his staff on the rocks.

"Something is coming." He lifted his unseeing gaze to the ceiling, drawing the gazes of his companions with his.

A large rock fell toward them, showering them with dirt and pebbles. The group separated, trying to avoid the stone as it crashed into the ground. Percival grabbed Cora's hand, pulling her with him. Cora cringed as the stones shifted under her feet.

More stones fell from the ceiling. The previous inhabitants had protected their city well.

"Get into the city!" Cora barely heard Percival's order over the crashing stones, but she saw him gesture toward the city. He pushed her toward the gates and stopped running, releasing her hand.

He intended to stay until the others had passed him. Cora paused, prepared to tell him to run.

"Go, Cora. I will be right behind you," Percival assured her.

She felt her heart beat hard, but continued her run. From behind, someone pushed her unexpectedly and she stumbled over the uneven terrain. A moment later, Satina appeared next to her.

She heard Percival shouting at the others behind her, repeating his order to get to the gated area. The cobblestones ended before the gates, a welcome respite from the trapped path. Cora reached the wall and stepped onto the different stones of the city. She leaned against the wall to watch the progress of her companions.

After the others were past him, Percival ran to the gates. One of the last stones to fall clipped his shoulder. The force made him stumble, then fall into Kalik. The two men slid into the gateway arch, past Cora, Tylina and Nimbly. Brolin rushed to their side and pulled Percival off the other man. Nimbly helped Kalik up.

"The previous occupants had ingenious ways to keep their city safe," Cora observed while Brolin tended to Percival's shoulder.

"I wonder how many of their traps still wait to be triggered," Tylina mused. She checked on Kalik, but he pushed her hands away and stood.

"Thank you, Brolin." Percival stood, stretching his arm. "We'll deal with them as we come across them. Unless you can find them, Nimbly. Let's move."

They stood close to the wrought iron gate, allowing space between them. Cora stood behind Percival, her customary position, and studied the gate. The metal bars showed signs of rust. Despite the decay, the gate stood strong. The design was practical, straight bars without extravagance. She watched Percival lift the latch and push. The gate stood firm in the grip of the wall, remaining in place no matter how hard he pushed.

"Excuse us." Brolin pushed past Cora, Kalik behind him. They added their strength and weight to Percival's. A loud screech tore through the silence as the gate opened.

Brolin turned back to Cora and nodded. The priest always maintained a somber expression, no matter the situation and rarely found humor in anything.

The group waited for Nimbly to step through the opening first. He glanced around the area, running his fingers over the gate and wall. Past him, Cora noted a passage riddled with numerous small holes. The three men in front of her followed the elf into the passage when he signaled all clear.

She had not seen Nimbly touch anything, but it was his specialty and he had made very few mistakes in the year he traveled with them. Still, his quick search for traps did not instill confidence in her.

Tylina pushed past Cora. Satina followed Cora. A loud clicking sound coincided with her servant's second step into the passage. A sharp intake of breath hissed through Cora's clenched teeth. The hum of an arrow flying through the air drowned out the sound. She heard, and felt, the tearing of her flesh as it embedded itself in her shoulder. Arrows flew free from their rusty homes. The clunking of their release repeated throughout the passage. More arrows penetrated the flesh of the companions, who rushed to exit the kill zone. After the initial release, the barrage ceased, the ancient ammunition spent.

"I thought you checked for traps, Nimbly." Percival's sarcasm brought a small smile to Cora's lips. It did not last, the arrows protruding from her arm and thigh proving more important.

"Traps protected or enhanced by magic are more difficult to—" Nimbly attempted to explain.

"I don't want to hear it," Percival cut him off. "How much magic is still functioning in this place? How can it still be effective?" He turned to Cora, his disbelief reflected in his eyes.

She shrugged, adjusting her capeshal so Satina could tend to her wounds. "It is possible, if the caster placed the spell as the city was emptied, or if they made it permanent. A specific trigger could set it off as well."

Cora watched Brolin move amongst them, removing the arrows and bandaging the wounds. Before he turned to look at Cora, the unexpected and undeniable sound of retching reached her. They turned toward the sound, and found Tylina doubled over in obvious pain, away from the rest of them. Cora tried to take a step toward her friend, but a wave of dizziness stopped her.

"Something was wrong with those arrows," she whispered, increasing dizziness forcing her to close her eyes.

"Cora, open your eyes!" Satina's voice sounded muffled, as if from another room.

She tried to do as Satina ordered, but keeping her eyes closed against the spin of the world was more enticing. She slid to the ground, her back against the wall.

"Brolin, they've been poisoned!" Nimbly's voice reached her through the haze. She heard clay vials clink together. "Take care of Cora. I'll give these to the others."

No, I'm fine. I just need to sleep for a bit. We'll continue after a short rest. Cora thought she spoke aloud, but when she tried to ask him if he understood, her mouth would not move. Darkness filled her sight offering a comfortable break from the torchlight. She felt nothing, other than the pain from her wounds.

Pressure from hands, one on her chest and the other on her stomach, disturbed the rest she wanted. Brolin's deep voice invoked the power of his deity. The power of his prayer and spell flowed from his hands, into her body, filling her with warmth.

His magic did not affect her like the touch of the Black Hand. Brolin's touch never brought anything but the warmth of his healing to her. Right now, the warmth felt good.

Her thoughts jumbled together, changing from one to another quickly. When the warmth left her body, Brolin removed his hands.

"Feel better?"

"Yes, thank you." It was easier to open her eyes now, the need to sleep having disappeared with the poison. "Is Tylina all right?"

"Yes, she was only sick. No one else became ill. Nimbly was able to give everyone an antidote while I took care of you." There was no disapproval in the priest's voice and no accusation in his eyes. "We will be fine."

"Thank you, again." Cora waited for Brolin to leave her side. She took a sip from her water skin, then rested her head against the wall. Percival stood near the entrance to the courtyard, watching her.

Nimbly retrieved several of the arrows that lay broken on the ground, examining them before returning to Percival. "The poison is old, placed on the arrows when the trap was last set. Victims would only get sick now, or in Cora's case, want to sleep. Contact with blood must have—"

The howl of an animal from further in the city interrupted the elf, answered seconds later by a second howl. A third, and fourth called and then three others followed these. The group exchanged concerned glances.

"Seven," Tylina said.

"Now what?" Cora stood, taking her spear from Satina. She positioned herself next to Percival. "What is it, Black Hand?"

"I don't know." He glanced at her and grinned, but his posture remained stiff. "Sounds like dogs. Maybe it's just a pack that lives down here, away from the people above."

"So there must be another way into the cavern and the city, given that the traps were still in place at the main entrance." She looked at the others, then back to Percival. "The others are ready. We should move in case this proves to be more than just a pack of dogs."

Percival nodded in agreement, gesturing for everyone to follow him.

Chapter 3

Percival led the way deeper into the city, his thoughts unspoken. The city was larger than expected. The animals continued to call to each other while the group explored. He sent others into the buildings to look for the princess, but always kept Cora outside with him. They waited for their friends in silence.

Percival did not understand why the others were not affected like Cora. Nimbly told him he did not think the poison had much potency left, so why did it hurt her more? Something tickled in his mind, emotions that did not feel like his own. He felt impatience and concern, which he could justify as his, but when the poison had affected Cora, he felt pain and a tiredness he could not account for. These new feelings had been flooding him since he helped Cora out of her claustrophobic panic.

He felt Cora watching him, her stare making him uncomfortable. He turned to look at her, and she slipped into a posture of indifference. At least that had not been affected by what happened.

"Is there an issue, Cora?" Conversation was not necessary, but he did not like the silence.

"You know how I feel about this area, coming through the sewer, or at least you think you know how I feel. I do not understand why the king sent us. You're no longer a member of his army, and we have taken on the role of mercenaries for the kingdom."

"I don't think that is an issue for him. We have worked for him and he has appreciated everything we've done for him. It makes sense to me that he asked us to do this." The others left the building they were searching, looking to Percival for instruction. He gestured for them to continue down the road. Satina stood still, watching him and he had to suppress a sigh.

"Of all the places to take the princess, she is brought here, an ancient underground city, with magical protections that are still effective. If she had come here as often we were told, don't you think some of these protections would have been expended?" A howl interrupted Cora, but she continued after only a brief pause. "I do not believe your explanation of wild dogs. That would be too easy and something tells me, this isn't as easy as it looks."

The others came out of the next building and waved at them, their own impatience to return to the surface obvious.

"We need to join them."

Cora scoffed at his statement. "As usual—"

Percival held up his hand, cutting her off. "I know, you think I'm ignoring what you've said. I'm not, but like you, I'd like to get this done and as you can see, so would our companions."

She stared at him, then nodded. Her hand waved out toward him, but he shook his head. "Of course. I go first." Sarcasm filled her words.

Percival followed her, keeping an eye out for the animals that continued to howl. He was sure she hated him, by the square of her shoulders and her stiff movements. No matter what he did, she was unhappy. He tried to be respectful and it made her even more upset. Sometimes he wondered why he even bothered.

Finally, the group stood at the edge of the town square. The water that once flowed over the now dusty fountain had left behind stains on the aged marble. Broken furniture, wooden boxes, barrels and wheels cluttered the area.

Percival examined the area, looking for the cause of his sudden unease. The group spread out on either side of him, also surveying the scene before them.

Across the square, spread out as if to flank them, five dogs waited for them.

Chapter 4

The creatures did not resemble any dog Cora had ever seen. In her research, she had never come across any pictures of the creatures either. There was no fur on the hounds. No skin covered the flesh. Muscles and red tissues shined in the light. The white of bone made a stark contrast to the blood red of the flesh. A lipless sneer exposed their teeth.

Satina positioned herself in front of Cora, her short sword and shield held in a defensive posture. Cora glanced at the others as they also took defensive stances, weapons drawn. She breathed deep and held it while she studied the hounds.

"What are they?" Cora's curiosity finally got the better of her.

"Demon dogs," Tylina's answer came out in a whisper.

"I've heard of them, but I've never seen any." Percival glanced at Cora. The fire in his eyes, always there when battle was imminent, burned strong. "They are summoned by mages to protect important items, or destroy enemies."

She wondered if there would ever come a time when that fire would burn out of control. Cora felt anger grow within her, but could not explain it. Her emotions were calm.

"I assume they can be killed like everything else?" Determination and fear filled Nimbly's voice.

"We're about to find out." Percival's voice sounded hoarse.

While they talked, the five dogs advanced. Percival met them, sword ready. Brolin followed close behind. Placing himself between the creatures and Tylina, Kalik moved to the sounds around him. One step took him in front of Cora. Satina, in an effort to protect the princess-mage, pushed against him.

"Satina, now is not the time. Let Kalik be," Cora ordered, flexing her fingers on her spear.

The other Amazon looked back, but Cora fixed her glare on the woman. "Do as you are ordered, Warrior."

Satina paled and stepped away from Kalik, just as the animals reached them.

The dogs circled them, forcing the group to place their backs toward the center of their small circle. The largest beast looked at one of the others and growled. The second beast leaped forward, liquid fire dripping from its fangs. Another dog soon followed.

* * *

The tension built within Percival. The first of the two beasts came close. He stepped out to meet the dog. His blade sliced across the creature, cutting into its flesh. The two advanced toward each other. The fire from the dog's mouth dripped onto Percival's foot, burning the leather. The second dog slowed its advance, and appeared to be waiting for others to join it.

A sheet of ice formed over two of the animals, then fell, shattering on contact with the dogs and the street. The yelps of pain from the creatures distracted Percival. Steam rising from the skin of the dogs washed over him, the smell of blood gagging him. He took a moment to wipe his forehead as a cone of snow engulfed the animals, their howls of pain echoing in the cavern.

A human voice, crying out in frustration and pain, came from behind him. He turned, pulling his attention from the dogs completely. He knew that voice, because he rarely heard it raised in pain. Why wasn't Satina protecting Cora?

Cora held her spear in both hands, across her body. She fought with the sixth dog, pushing it back. Fire dripped at her feet. The dog snapped at her, narrowly missing her hands. Satina faced the seventh, her bare skin red from burns where its fire had landed.

Before Percival could move to her defense, Cora lifted a

finger from the wooden shaft of her spear. A long knife of ice formed at her fingertip. The ice knife grew until it pierced the dog's head. The animal fell.

She turned to look at Percival. Her eyes grew wide and she dropped her spear to the ground. She lifted her hands and her lips moved. Snow flew from her fingertips past Percival. Whipped by the cold and wind of the spell, he turned to see another dog jump at him. He swung his sword, cutting into the dog. Two pieces of the animal fell to the ground behind him.

The lead dog started circling Percival. It kept a safe distance from his dripping blade, intelligence shining in its eyes. The two circled each other, neither acknowledging the dead creatures they stepped over. Not even the sound of a dog falling to Satina's sword drew their attention.

Liquid fire dripped from the dog's mouth, melting the cobblestones beneath it. Percival charged into an attack on the dog at the same time icicles rained upon it. Tiny ice knives pierced and sliced open the dog's flesh. He sliced his blade down, severing the creature's head.

* * *

As the last creature fell to the ground, Cora leaned against Satina, her strength drained by her magic use. The tingle of the magic still flowed through her body and blue sparks crackled from her fingertips. The use of magic always left her weak. The more magic she used, the weaker she felt.

Many mages, priests and even minor users of magic used the same method as Cora, and she had heard of deaths attributed to the magic. Druids and rangers, as well as nature priests, manipulated the magic in almost the same way, but they drew it out of nearby animals and plant life and if they were not careful, they could kill everything around them. Cora had also heard of casters using the same method as the naturists, only they pulled all the magic from around them until everything died. She knew all types of casters from her training, yet she always preferred her casting method, despite her weakened state afterward.

She felt someone watching her and glanced up, her gaze meeting Percival's. His eyes still blazed with the fire she had seen so often during their travels together. Normally the fire dimmed when combat was over. Not this time. Did he still sense something?

Chapter 5

Percival's senses remained heightened, something he usually experienced only if he needed to be wary of an unseen danger. Cautious, he glanced around the town square, his gaze stopping on a building across from where they entered the area. The entrance appeared as if it had been torn down, then patched back up.

"Kalik, come with me." He straightened his back. Gesturing for Cora and the others to stay where they were, he walked across the square with the plainsman behind him.

Drawing closer to the building, Percival recognized the bars commonly used to block the jail windows. Within the building, a deep growl echoed from an unknown animal. He glanced at Kalik, who already had his weapon ready.

Before they reached the building, the patched wall exploded in a burst of dust, bricks and wood. Another hellhound jumped from it. The beast landed on the ground in front of them and glared at Percival with three sets of eyes, one for each of its heads. It jumped again, over the men and toward the rest of the group.

Percival turned, taking in the beast's appearance before charging in. After the attack by the smaller dogs, he wanted to be sure what he and his friends faced. Broad shoulders supported three heads. The animal stood as tall at the shoulder as a heavy warhorse and as wide as three horses. The creature's speed and grace surprised him, but it was its direct movements toward the two Amazons that shocked him.

A sudden fear filled him and he ran toward the group again. "Cora!"

He saw Satina glance up at the sound of his voice. Recognizing the danger, she pushed Cora away from her and out of the path of the animal. The bodyguard met the rush of the animal with her shield pushing against the middle head. The right head bit at the woman, her skin turning blue from the bite.

Ice. Like Cora.

Before Percival could move closer, the left head snapped toward Cora. Despite the other Amazon pushing against its middle head, the creature tried to pull the rest of its body toward the victim it obviously wanted.

The shield Satina pushed against the creature began to crack from the pressure. Saliva dripped from the dog's mouth onto the metal. Smoke rose from the shield. Percival watched her shove her sword up through the bottom of the animal's mouth. She backed away, dropping the shield and leaving her sword in the beast.

If the right head had ice, and the middle acid, then the last must be the one with the fire. In response to Percival's thought, liquid fire dripped from the head that still struggled to reach Cora.

The head in the middle fought against the blade forcing its mouth shut. The amount of acid increased, until the head exploded, spewing the green gunk everywhere. Everyone covered their heads, trying to protect themselves.

Percival pulled himself onto the large creature's back. The dog turned its ice head and tried to bite him. He swung his sword and batted the head away.

Blue lightning coursed over the flesh. Percival's legs tightened on the dog as it shook. He grunted, expecting pain from the lightning. Instead, his skin warmed. From in front of the dog, he saw Cora fall to her knees, opening herself to attack from the head of fire. She brought her spear up, but the dog had learned from Satina's attack and pulled its head away from the weapon.

Ignoring Percival, both heads continued to snap at Cora

while trying to avoid the spear she held in a weak grip. Ice crept over the spear. Percival leaned up over the remaining heads in time to see Cora successfully penetrate the fire head with her spear. The ice head butted her, throwing her back and ripping the spear out of the fire head. The head hung limp, dragging on the ground.

Growling, the animal stalked toward the prone mage. Shouts from the others, as well as weapons and rubble thrown at the creature failed to pull its attention from Cora. The last head spit ice at its intended victim.

Percival dug his hand into the muscle at the nape of the creature's neck to support himself as he cut into its back. The monster turned its attention on the warrior, snapping at him. Failing that, it snorted shards of ice at Percival.

He avoided its attacks to pull himself further up its neck toward the last head. He straddled the large neck to drive his sword through its skull. Before he could strike, the head turned toward him again. He plunged the sword into its eye, feeling the scrape of bone on the metal. Thick bone halted the blade's progress. Percival stood, bracing his feet and put all his weight onto the sword. Finally, the weapon pushed through the skull with a loud cracking sound.

The dog collapsed to the ground, all heads dead. Percival rolled away from the corpse to absorb the impact. Standing again, he dusted his breeches off. He pulled his sword from the last head and surveyed the area around the group.

Brolin already tended to wounds. Cora sat away from the others, watching Percival in turn. She was pale, despite the tan of her skin, and her hair that normally seemed to have a mind of its own lay limp on her shoulders.

He no longer felt any immediate danger in the area and the rush of battle had left him as soon as the dog died. Concern for Cora, knowing her magic use would leave her weak, replaced the rush he felt. She had cast too many spells, too close together.

He stepped toward her, but stopped when he heard Satina yelling at Brolin.

"I do not need assistance from you!" Satina's difficulty with the trade language did not prevent her from expressing her anger. She pulled her arm from Brolin's grip.

"I am not asking you, Satina. You need healing before we

continue. How can you protect Cora if you are so injured you cannot fight?"

Satina pushed her chest out. "I am Amazon warrior. I will protect my Princeesa until my death, as the queen has instructed me to do. You will tend to her before me."

The three turned to look at Cora. She shook her head and waved her hand at them. "I just need to rest. Brolin can do nothing for me." She looked at Percival. "I'll be fine. Just give me a few moments before we continue."

He nodded. "We can wait."

Chapter 6

Cora was grateful for a few moments rest, though she wouldn't give Percival the satisfaction of telling him. Finally feeling like she could stand without seeing the area around her spin, Cora addressed Percival, "We may continue, if the rest of you are ready."

"But we were wa—" Tylina started, but stopped at Percival's shake of his head.

He gestured toward the remains of the prison. "The big one came from there. It must have had a reason." He led the way, Cora following close behind. The others fell in step behind her.

Stepping over the rubble of the wall the dog destroyed in its escape, Cora surveyed the small building. Light from her magical globe in the cavern entered through a hole in the ceiling.

Looking toward the ceiling, Cora stopped walking. Somewhere in her mind, she felt the others push past her, but her attention remained focused on the hole.

The crumbling walls faded from her vision, replaced by the rock of a small cave. The light from the globe became the yellow of the sun she knew she would never bask in again.

Her breath caught in her throat. Pressure weighed on her chest, crushing her. How could she be in the cave again?

She glanced around, struggling to find anything of the prison she should be standing in. The others were gone. Only the stone of the cave that had been her prison remained.

The smell of a dying fire filled her nose and choked her. The hole at the top of the cave did little to clear it from the cramped area.

Her mother would come to save her soon—right? She had only taken three days the first time. The queen would know where to look this time. Cora should be home—safe—before another night passed.

No—not this time. Her mother was nowhere near her. Cora was stuck in this cave and there was no way out. Shoshona had won.

Panic built up in Cora's chest and her struggle to breathe increased. Darkness overwhelmed her vision and she felt her legs weaken.

"Cora!" Percival's voice reached her. The sudden grip of his hand on her arm jolted her back to the prison.

"But... the cave..." She looked around at the mess of the ruined prison. "What happened?"

"That's what I want to know," he whispered harshly in her ear. "You're getting worse."

"I most certainly am not!" She yanked her arm out of his grip. "I don't need your assistance, Black Hand. I have everything under control."

"You don't look like you have it under control." He turned away at the sound of banging—metal against metal. "We will discuss this later. I want to know about the cave."

"You will not question the Princeesa as if you were her equal, Black Hand." Satina pushed between them. "Your mark matches her tattoo. Slaves do not question their masters. It's time you learned your place."

Percival stiffened, sucking air through his teeth in a hiss. Anger coursed through Cora and she tightened her grip on her spear.

"Satina, step away," she ordered, trying to push past the warrior.

Percival's eyes burned when he turned to glare at the Amazons again. "I am not *her* slave. I may be enslaved to this thing—" He held up his left hand. "But Cora is not my master."

Cora stared at him, her words caught in her throat from shock. He narrowed his eyes, looking past Satina to Cora. "Do you understand, Princess?" he demanded.

She nodded. With a growl, Percival stormed away.

Clearing her throat, Cora pushed Satina out of her way. "Shae take you, Satina. Must you always force our beliefs down his throat?"

"He has been disrespectful ever since we arrived," Satina defended herself.

"Actually the way he has acted could be considered as nothing but respectful in his culture," Cora said. "You understand nothing about his world, even after three years. Tattoos do not mean the same thing here as they do on the islands." Cora pushed a finger into her bodyguard's chest. "Do not mention it again, Warrior. I have had quite enough of your insolence over these years."

Satina dipped her head and slumped her shoulders. "As you command, Princeesa."

Cora waited a heartbeat to ensure Satina understood her command, then turned away. From further in the building, down a short hall, she saw shadows moving and could hear the voices of the others. She hurried toward them, leaving Satina behind.

A single torch burned within a cell, lighting a small area in the hall. Spent torches littered the floor outside the cell, and a pile of unused ones waited inside. Tylina stood over Nimbly who was working to open a lock on a chain that hung midway down the cell door. A child huddled against the far wall of the cell. Through the dirt, grime and disheveled appearance of her clothing and hair, Cora recognized Princess Stepha Kennan.

Just as Cora stopped next to Percival, the lock fell to the ground, followed by the chain. Nimbly stood and turned to grin at them.

Behind him, Tylina pulled the door open and cautiously stepped into the cell. "Princess, are you all right?"

The girl nodded, tears streaming over her dirt-covered face. She watched the rest of the group enter the cell, then threw herself into Tylina's outstretched arms.

While Tylina comforted the girl, taking her out of the building, the others began to search the cell and the other rooms. Within the cell, Cora found four saddlebags in a corner. Two of which held food, with water skins underneath them.

The other bags held a blanket, and a few items the kidnapper must have thought the girl would want; a book of nursery rhymes, parchment, quill and ink and toys.

With a casual eye, Cora glanced over the items and prepared to close the bags when a bright colored cloth caught her attention. She pulled the cloth from the bag, careful to hide it from the others. The colors were similar to that of her clothing. She rubbed the material between her fingers. Material that only Amazons wore. It was never traded with the mainlanders.

Within the material, wrapped in a second covering of softened leather, she found an arrow with a small piece of the shaft still attached. The arrowhead was painted in a forest green with matching feathers tied to the wooden shaft. A mixture of colors used by one of the tribes of the Amazon islands. In the time she had spent in Man's World, Cora never saw another group use colors to decorate spears, arrows or clothing like the Amazons.

And now an arrowhead in Amazon material was left with the child. A child left in a building, so similar to the cave Cora had been held in when she was younger.

"What did you find, Princeesa?" Cora's stomach knotted at Satina's whispered question in their native language. The warrior had silenced her approach, or Cora had been too focused on the items in the bag. Either way, she was thankful it had not been one of the others.

"An arrowhead. This isn't right." Cora assured herself no one else listened to their conversation or looked at them. "Someone was very intent on leaving a message for me."

"Only Amazons know how this would affect you. None of us would ever consider doing such a thing, just to send you a message," Satina insisted.

Cora showed her the arrowhead, and nodded in satisfaction when Satina's eyes grew wide. "She would."

"Your mother would kill her if she did this," Satina gasped.

"My mother isn't here." Cora slipped the cloth, arrowhead and fletching into her pouch and let her fingers caress her spell plates. "Black Hand, I will wait outside for you. I need a few more moments to regain my strength," she called out in the Trade language.

He grunted in acknowledgement as she left the building.

Chapter 7

After allowing Brolin time to ensure the little princess was without injury, and giving Cora a little more time to rest, Percival led the group farther into the city.

He kept an eye on Cora, concerned with her growing weakness. Even though Satina tried to help her, she continued to stagger. Color had not returned to her complexion, despite the rest. He could see her fatigue increasing, but he chose to keep moving. Everyone was tired, but he felt sure there was another way out of the city. The group had set the traps off protecting the city, but not the hellhounds or the kidnapper.

Two hours after starting their search, the group found a break in the outer wall. The hole was large enough for the three-headed hellhound to fit through easily.

Finally, outside the walls of the city, opposite where they entered, Nimbly found a worn path. They followed the path to the edge of the cavern, arriving at another tunnel connected to the sewer.

"We missed the obvious when we came through. The map was inaccurate and we accepted the information without question." Percival paced in frustration when they stopped to rest at the entrance to the sewer.

"If the Princeesa had been leading us, as is appropriate, she would have found this entrance in the beginning," Satina spat her displeasure.

"Quiet, Satina!" Cora hissed. "No one missed it, Black Hand. It was not obvious, or we would not have missed it," she continued, her words filled with weariness.

He snapped his gaze in her direction, his concern suddenly renewed. She sounded worse. Cora waved Satina away and he took the opportunity to kneel in front of her.

"You need to eat something, drink some water," Percival whispered, controlling the urge to check her cheeks for a fever.

"I do not need you telling me what to do, Black Hand. Just get me out of here," she snapped, her eyes focusing again.

"As quickly as I can." Percival stood and walked over to Tylina. "Let's keep going."

Their return journey to the surface took longer than it did to reach the city. Frequent stops for both Princess Stepha and Cora delayed their progress. Though the others grumbled in frustration, Cora remained silent and Percival forced a slower pace for her. He hoped it would help Cora regain her strength faster.

He wanted to stop and have Brolin do something—anything—to help her, but his last whispered conversation with the priest did not reveal any way to relieve her fatigue. Either Brolin was not as experienced as he claimed, or he did not know how to deal with the fatigue induced by Cora pulling magical essence through her.

With no map to lead them, Percival had to guess which route would return them to the surface. Only the upward slope of the sewer gave him any indication they were on the right path.

Finally, they came across a wooden door in the wall. A handle was on their side of the door, as well as hinges. Percival put his hand on the handle, turned it and pushed.

"You're taking too long, Black Hand. Just open the door!" Cora pushed at him, determined to be the first out of the sewers.

"Patience, Cora. We will all get out." He stepped aside, allowing her to exit, then followed her, hiding a small smile.

"Not fast enough." She stood in the alley, her head lifted toward the stars. A breeze brushed her hair behind her, and her capeshal fluttered around her arms and body. "This feels so much better. I feel like we've been down there for years."

He smiled and stood to the side of the door to allow the others to leave the sewers.

Don't be so happy, Black Hand. Give me one day alone with her and I will kill her. Neither of us will have to deal with her anymore.

Percival looked around, though he knew no one else could hear the voice. *Quiet, Stromas. The time for me to deal with you is not here yet.*

But when it comes, I won't make it easy. I've been waiting three years to get at her. I will not be denied forever.

But I will deny you for as long as I am in control.

Chapter 8

Percival's delay in opening the door to the surface frustrated Cora. He claimed to understand how she felt, but his delay made it questionable. She breathed deeply of the warm summer night air. Being out in the open was so much better than being in the sewers.

Glancing back at Percival, she expected him to make her move and not allow her time to enjoy the open air. He looked distracted. His eyes burned with the same battle fire as during their last encounter.

Cora looked toward the sky. A nearby light dimmed the starlight in her eyes somewhat. The closeness of the ocean kissed the warm air with the fresh smell of the water and the taste of salt. She could stand there all night, but her fatigue returned too quickly.

"Let's go, Cora. The sooner we get back to the palace, the sooner you can bathe and get some real rest." Percival's quiet voice broke through the serenity she felt coming over her.

She felt his body next to hers, close, but not touching. Opening her eyes, she saw Satina stepping toward her, to get between them, as usual. She raised her hand to stop the bodyguard. "I'm ready. If you hadn't promised a bath, I would stay here."

He smiled at her, the fire gone from his eyes. He gestured for her to go first, and surprise filled his expression when she nodded and started walking out of the alley.

She led the way to the palace, Percival and Satina on opposite sides of her. Tylina helped the little princess until she stumbled from fatigue. Before Percival could pick her up, Kalik lifted the princess and let her rest her head on his shoulder.

At the palace, the steward instructed a page to take them to rooms and took Princess Stepha from Kalik's arms. The king had given them half the floor to use, a shared common area for their rooms at the end of the hall. The page stood in the center of the common area.

In the middle of the room, a sitting pit was filled with pillows and floor cushions. A table and two chairs sat in front of a window that ran from the floor to the ceiling. Double doors, more glass than wood, revealed a balcony that ran the length of the common room. Another window was on the other side of the double doors, a matching table and chairs in front of it as well.

"Baths have been prepared in each private room." The page waited for them to each choose a room, then left the area.

Instead of waiting for the others, Cora chose one and shut the door before Satina could follow her. Leaning against the wood of the door, she sighed. Finally, a few minutes alone.

A large bed occupied the middle of the longest wall, a small table on each side with a lamp on each table. A dresser with a mirror stood to her left and an armoire was on her right. Another table and chairs sat in the area in front of a window past the dresser. The shutters on the window had already been closed for the night. A small hall indicated the presence of another room. Dropping her capeshal on the bed, Cora undressed quickly and followed the hall to the privy and bath.

The bath waited in a bronze tub, a stack of towels on a table nearby, as well as soaps and scented oils. After smelling each bottle of oil, she chose one that reminded her of the wild flowers on her island and poured half of it into the water.

The warm water soothed sore muscles and helped to relax her. Cora lay back in the tub, closing her eyes, then sat up abruptly. She needed food and rest, not just a bath.

She washed the dirt and grime from her skin, massaging her legs, arms and shoulders while she did. The large towels made it easy to dry herself quickly. The material was fluffy, like she imagined clouds would be if she could ever touch them, yet absorbed the water with ease.

Returning to the main part of the bedroom, Cora searched the dresser. In one of the drawers, she found four nightdresses of different materials. After making her choice, she slipped the gown over her head and admired herself in the mirror. The gown covered her to her ankles and felt like silk against her skin. Picking up a light blanket to take with her, she returned to the common area.

Opening the door, she hid a smirk. The Black Hand, clean and in fresh clothes, sat on the floor cushions, facing the door to her room. He still protected her, even in the safety of the palace. Despite the way she treated him, he tried to make her see him differently. She wondered if there would ever be a time that she no longer felt forced to stand separate from him.

Cora closed the door and stepped down into the sitting area. "When will food be brought? I would like to sleep soon."

Percival nodded. "I understand. The page came back while you were still inside your room. He said it should be very soon. Sit down and rest until it gets here."

She nodded and sat down across from him. After arranging the pillows around and under her, she curled up with the blanket and allowed her eyes to close.

Chapter 9

Percival watched Cora sleep, reassured that she would finally get the rest she needed after their combat and travel. This was the first time she had ever fallen asleep under his watchful gaze, without Satina to keep watch over him. The bath did not appear to have helped her much. He hoped sleep would help more. He understood she had performed quite a few spells in a short span of time, but she had never been so weak for so long before.

The page returned, four other servants with him. The servants laid out trays of mutton, chicken, fruit, cheese, and tarts on the tables throughout the area, as well as plates, mugs, and pitchers of ale and wine. Each bowed to Percival, then left the common area.

The page gestured at the food and drinks. "Is there anything else I may provide for you at this time?" he mumbled.

Percival looked at the boy, trying to remember if he had ever seen the boy before. He knew the page wasn't afraid of him, but didn't know who he really was afraid of. "Is there something wrong, boy?"

The page shook his head. "No, sir." But he glanced at Cora's sleeping form.

"Go. She won't hurt you, and I will make sure the other one doesn't even look at you." The boy nodded, and turned to run down the hall. Percival shook his head, suddenly remembering

Satina yelling at the page before they had left to find Princess Stepha.

"Let's eat!" he called out.

The others came out of their rooms, greeted by the aroma of the food filling the area. Satina stepped into the sitting pit and woke Cora with a not too gentle shake of her shoulder.

"Let her sleep. We can save food for her," Percival suggested.

Satina leveled her gaze at him and shook Cora again. He shook his head. The princess could handle her bodyguard herself.

Cora opened her eyes and glared at her bodyguard. "What?" she demanded.

Satina gestured at the food, but before she said anything, Percival interrupted. "Food is here, Cora. You need something to eat. Then you can go back to sleep"

She nodded, stood and wrapped the light blanket around her shoulders. With practiced ease born from wearing her capeshal, she filled a plate with food without dropping the blanket or spilling the food. He stood as well, and filled a plate of his own, then returned to his pillows.

Percival waited until Satina took her food to her own room, before turning to Tylina and Brolin. "I don't understand what is happening with Cora. She has cast powerful spells before, several during combat, but she has never been affected like this."

Tylina nodded. "Her spells were quite powerful. I've never seen anyone create a sheet of ice like the one she did. And that ice knife she did from her fingertip...no semantics, no components, no incantation. That is a new one for me and it must have taken quite a bit of strength to do. She did more in a short period of time than usual."

"She uses a different type of magic than I do, Percival. I do not completely understand how it works for her." Brolin folded a slice of meat in his mouth. After he finished chewing and swallowed, he continued. "From what I have been able to learn from the church, she pulls the magic essence through her, manipulates it and then it comes out as the spell effects we see."

Percival felt a knot form in his stomach. "Will pulling the magic through her like that hurt her inside? In a way we can't see?"

"I have never heard of it happening, but anything is possible, Percival." Tylina's attention turned to Kalik until he sat on the pillows next to her. "I can do some further research if you would like."

Percival nodded. "When you are able, I would appreciate that. I would like to know more of how this affects her and if she could be hurting herself permanently."

As he finished speaking, the palace steward came into the common area and cleared his throat. "Please excuse my interruption. I have spoken to King Kennan and he has advised that he will be unable to meet with you until after the celebration for the gladiators. He appreciates your assistance, but is unavailable until then."

"Thank you. We understand his commitments. We will be ready to meet with him when he is available." The steward bowed at Percival's words and left them to finish their meal.

Chapter 10

The next morning, Cora woke before her companions. After a quick bath, she stayed in her room with the door open while she waited for morning meal to arrive. In the mirror, she could see purple bruises that discolored the skin around her eyes and the luster of her hair had faded.

She needed more rest, but didn't want to spend the whole day in bed if the group was expected to meet with the king. She already felt ridiculous putting a nightdress back on.

A door opened next to her room and footsteps sounded in the hall until they stopped in her doorway.

"The king isn't available to meet with us until after the gladiatorial celebration tomorrow night, Cora." Percival's voice had the morning roughness Cora was not willing to admit she liked. "Why don't you get some more rest? You still look a little tired."

She knew he was trying to be nice by not saying how bad she really looked. "I am not sick. Staying in bed is for the sick and invalid." Cora stood from the bed, the sudden movement making her vision swim. She grabbed the bedpost to steady herself.

Percival rushed to her side and guided her back to the edge of the bed. "Don't be so stubborn, Cora."

"Don't tell me what to do, Black Hand." But she remained in his steadying grip. "Don't you have something else you can do today, besides irritate me?"

He smirked, then sat next to her. "Since we have to wait, I have all day to hear about the cave."

She lifted her chin. "I have no idea—"

"I'm getting very tired of your denials, Princess," he interrupted.

"And I have long grown tired of your constant questions and attempts to make me as weak as the women of your world. No man on my islands would dare speak to me like you do—not even Dekart." She shifted away from him.

"I don't know who Dekart is, but you seem to have forgotten— again—we are not on the islands." Percival stood from the bed and placed himself in front of her. "And, I'm even more tired of you treating me like a slave."

"I most certainly do—" she started.

"You do—the way you talk to me, the way you act around me, the way you treat the others. Either attempt to be more accepting of the equality most of us have in my world, or go home." He stared down at her, his eyes narrowed.

"You're right, Black Hand." Cora stood from the bed again, slower this time. Despite her vision, she would not continue arguing with him. He didn't need her. And she certainly did not need him.

She pushed past him, careful not to touch his skin. Fear knotted her stomach when she stood in front of the dresser, the emotion washing over her.

"What are you doing?" he asked, his voice a hoarse croak.

"Packing. I've been away from home too long. It's time I return," she answered, but she struggled to make her hands react to her mental commands.

"Cora, I wasn't serious. I don't want you to leave. I was just trying to make you realize we aren't on your islands."

She could feel him standing behind her, his heat radiating against her. "I know where we are. I am reminded every day I wake up in some place other than my own bed," she whispered.

Fingers traced a line down the middle of her back. Surprise jolted through Cora and she spun to face him. Her back pressed against the dresser, the wood biting into her flesh.

"Tell me about the cave, Cora," Percival persisted. He brushed his hand on her arm and retreated from her.

"Telling you won't help me."

"It might."

Cora shrugged her shoulders in defeat. He wouldn't leave her alone. Better to tell him—briefly—or he will persist in his questions.

"I was kidnapped when I was younger, younger than Stepha, maybe one—two—summers. I was confined in a small cave. I only had enough room to walk ten steps. I had food, water and a minimal supply of torches, exactly the same as Stepha. A large boulder blocked the cave entrance." Cora felt the familiar grip of fear tighten around her throat, constricting her breathing.

"My—" She cleared her throat and tried again. "My only source of fresh air was a small opening in the cave ceiling. I have suffered from claustrophobia ever since."

Percival's surprise filled his face. "Did you know who your kidnapper was?"

"Of course. My mother punished her and threatened her with exile if she should ever try to harm me again." She turned back to the dresser. "Now, if you don't mind, I need to finish packing."

* * *

Cora pulled out two capeshals before Percival reached out to stop her. His hand warmed when he touched her, but the material of her gown prevented the tingle he expected.

"You don't need to pack, Cora," he whispered.

She stopped, but did not move away from him. "You ordered me to go home."

He blew a breath out through his teeth. "I already said I didn't mean it." He squeezed her arm. "I don't want you to leave."

She stood still under his grip, until she finally nodded. "Please leave me alone, Black Hand. Like you said, I need to rest more."

Percival released her, then left her room. He shouldn't have told her to leave. He knew Cora didn't know the nuances of his sarcasm, but he did it anyway. Her reaction should not have surprised him.

Humans. Always so emotional.

Percival shook his head. *Not now, Stromas.*

Chapter 11

The night of the celebration, Percival stood on the balcony of his room, looking out over the city before going to the banquet hall. Torchlight from the battlements surrounding the town of Glenys flickered on the armor of the guards walking their patrol. He used to walk those same paths when he started his military career. Nights like this always made him curious about what happened during the parties. Tonight he would finally find out.

He could see torches lighting the streets of the city and imagined the light driving the shadows away. Campfires outside the city walls attested to the many camps for the gladiators who participated in the contests for the last two weeks. He knew he could have won his contests if he hadn't gone after Princess Stepha. Kalik, Satina and Percival had given up the renown those contests would have given them.

The sounds of boisterous celebrations filled the streets and the musical sounds of all the different bards and musicians performing in the taverns reached him. The heat of the summer night finally drove him inside and he closed the doors to the balcony.

Turning to the door of his room, he stopped in surprise. Cora stood inside the doorway, watching him. "Is it time to go down, Cora?"

She nodded.

"Then let's go. Unless you want to stand here, staring at me longer."

Her cheeks reddened. "No, not especially, Black Hand." The tone of her voice did not match the denial of her words.

Smiling, he followed her through the common area of their rooms and to the others who waited in the hall for them. The page who had helped them upon their return with Princess Stepha led them to the banquet hall. Within minutes, they stood at the entrance.

The celebration Percival had heard from his balcony quieted as he walked into the banquet hall. The nobles were too subdued and boring to celebrate properly. The group made their way through the crowd of tables and people until they reached their place below the dais where the royal family sat.

Percival sat, noting with regret that Cora placed herself at the end to his left. Satina and Brolin sat between them. Nimbly, Kalik and Tylina sat to his right. Cora's efforts to avoid him had become more obvious since they spoke in her room the day before. She had even refused to eat with the group, ordering Satina to bring food to her room.

King Kennan stood, silencing the crowd. Percival heard him speaking, but still let his mind wander. The group of competitors for the gladiatorial games clapped and shouted approval at the king's words.

Percival watched the nobles. His chest filled with laughter he fought to keep under control at their forced applause. Only their loyalty to the king and greed brought them to the gathering. He turned his attention to King Kennan when he saw Princess Stepha join her father at the front of the dais.

"I have one final announcement before we begin the festivities." The king waited until the commotion faded before continuing. "Four days ago, my daughter was kidnapped by an unknown individual. Captain Percival Riesun, also known as The Black Hand, and his companions were able to rescue Princess Stepha. The Queen and I are extremely grateful for their assistance." Both he and the queen bowed their heads toward the group.

The announcement received shocked silence. The king's advisors had done their job well for no information to get out about the kidnapping. Percival studied the faces staring at the king. When the news sank into the thoughts of the gathered nobles, he could not find any looks of disappointment to reveal the kidnapper. His glances were met with approval.

The gladiators again filled the large room with exuberant cheering. Percival's focus on searching the room made him miss what King Kennan said, but he did not miss the nobles whispering amongst themselves while appraising those at the front of the room.

Across the room, a large man wearing a leather mask stared in the direction of the group. Exar was their final member. Instead of joining them in the princess' rescue, he refused to leave his competition. Because of his refusal, even though Exar had won his competition, the king did not allow him to sit with the others at their table. Percival had to admit he did not miss the larger man. Something about Exar made him uncomfortable.

After the guests had eaten their fill, King Kennan summoned a troupe of musicians and escorted his queen onto the open floor between the banquet tables. They danced alone for the first part of the song, then others began filing onto the floor to join them. Percival smiled as Tylina convinced Kalik to dance with her and Nimbly relieved a lady-in-waiting of her chair and spun her around the floor.

Percival watched in silence. Finally, after the third song ended and the fourth began, he glanced down the table to Cora's chair. For two years, he had tried to convince Cora to dance with him. He intended to succeed tonight. He had pushed back his chair when Brolin sat back, revealing the empty chair at the end of the table.

"Damn her," Percival cursed in frustration. He stood and stormed from the banquet hall.

Chapter 12

Cora strolled through the silent keep to the garden. During the three years she and Satina traveled in Man's World, she had slowly become accustomed to living in a male dominated society. Still, she found many things difficult to understand.

Her vision showed the Black Hand needed her. But why should she care if a man needed her help?

She cared because she saw him as a way to get away from her mother. The fact that he was a man meant nothing to her. She felt the same about Dekart.

Cora smirked. Maybe she was a little attracted to him. For a man, he was good-looking. And she enjoyed telling him how difficult she found it to adjust to his world. It was not really that hard for her. She just liked his frustration when he tried to explain his world.

When she reached the garden, Cora pulled a leather falconer's glove from a large pouch and fit her hand inside. She glanced around to ensure she was alone. The floral scent of the garden surrounded her, sneaking into her nose and forcing an unexpected sneeze. She whistled loudly, holding her hand up. The call of a bird answered her, followed by the sound of flapping wings. She let a sigh of satisfaction escape as her hunting falcon landed on her protected wrist, dipping its head to look at her. She lowered her arm, bringing the bird closer to her chest and smoothed the feathers on its head.

"Reyna, how are you, my lovely?" Cora whispered, bringing out a small piece of meat for the bird to eat. Reyna took the meat in her claw and jumped to the bench her master stood near. Cora sat next to her feathered companion as the bird began to eat.

As she listened to the sounds of the night and Reyna eating, Cora's thoughts turned to recent events, her concern rising anew. An Amazon or someone working for an Amazon left the arrowhead with the girl.

A chirp from Reyna refocused Cora's attention to the area around her. The bird cocked its head to the side and looked in the direction of the palace. Cora followed Reyna's gaze, trying to find the source of the bird's agitation. A shadow progressed down the main path of the garden. She stood, calling to mind a spell that would defend her and distract the shadow long enough for her to get back to a better guarded area of the palace grounds. She pulled a strand of magical energy from around her, pooling it in her hand. The shadow came closer, moving through a patch of light from a nearby torch. Reyna spread her wings, then settled, returning her attention to her food.

* * *

Percival stood gazing at Cora and her falcon. Since he first saw her, almost three years earlier, she had become an even more beautiful woman. At some point, she decided to wear clothing similar to Satina's. He liked the short top and skirt and knew it was both functional and appropriate for her sense of decency.

Tonight, Cora wore a long white loincloth and top with gold and blue embroidered through it. Her blue capeshal, a hybrid between a cape and a shawl, draped over her shoulders and covered her legs. Around her neck, she wore a gold necklace with a single swirl that matched her tattoo.

The first time they actually spoke did not go well. He and his friends interposed on the Amazon's behalf and frightened bandits away, only to turn around and receive a tongue lashing from the sixteen-year-old Amazon princess-mage. When he tried to explain his actions to her, she dismissed him. After that, he never intended to see her again. But the next time he saw her, he tried to explain his actions once more. His multiple attempts at calm conversation with her met only failure.

After they started traveling together consistently during the last two years, they met the rest of the group. Though Satina constantly reminded everyone she thought Cora should lead the group, Cora always quieted the other woman. It seemed she preferred his leadership to doing it herself.

"One day, you will dance with me, Cora." His announcement received a small smile.

"Not likely, Black Hand." She turned back to her bird.

He shook his head in resignation. "What are you doing here?"

"I came to feed Reyna. I haven't seen her since we went after the princess." She straightened her back defensively.

"You know you shouldn't go anywhere without Satina, myself, or one of the others."

She sighed at his over protectiveness. "I know. You keep telling me that, but I have yet to see you proven correct. I am capable of defending myself." After taking the last piece of meat from her hand, Reyna flew away. They watched until she disappeared in the night.

Percival nodded, looking around the garden. "Yes, I know you are. But, we both know that if anything were to happen to you, Satina would never rest until she had carried out your people's version of justice. That is not something I wish visited upon this land."

She nodded as well. "I can remember my mother quite vividly, even after almost three years away from her. She would sit on her throne, dealing out justice to the men we held as slaves. My mother entrusted Satina with my safety, swearing a painful death if anything happened to me. If Satina is unable to handle the problem alone, she is to return to the island and bring back the Sea Wolves, the Amazon nation's protectors and mercenary band. The Sea Wolves are sailors for the most part, though a large portion of the force is also land-based. They patrol the shoreline of the islands and bring the queen any men who try to use the islands as a haven for their pirating activities. The men are held as slaves, both menial and personal." Cora glanced down at her hands. "My father was a shipwrecked sailor."

She looked at him again. "You're right. We do not want Satina to return with the Sea Wolves. Let me sit for a moment longer. The scent of the roses and the silence of the garden are calming after such an active evening."

"All right," he whispered.

She leaned back to admire the stars. She had never told him so much about her people before. Maybe her ease with him was increasing.

Percival let his gaze roam over her figure, entranced by the moonlight playing across her skin. A tan from her love of the outdoors still colored her skin and her white hair contrasted with it beautifully. She was muscular, enough to bring an attractive definition to her figure, with the natural curves of her body accentuated by her change in clothing. Her long muscular legs hung over the bench, her booted feet touching the ground. Her hair lay around her head, having grown to a length that touched the middle of her back when she stood. At her full height, she stood a little taller than his shoulders and she had to look up just a bit to see eye to eye with him. Her green eyes seemed to penetrate his soul when she looked at him.

He smiled. The bruises had healed and her complexion was no longer pale. Her healthy looking hair again flowed around her in the breeze.

A sound from the bench caught his attention.

"What are you thinking about, Black Hand?" Her quiet question surprised him.

He shook his head, embarrassed she caught him staring at her. "I was just thinking about everything we've been through since we met."

She rose from the bench to stand in front of him, close enough that he could feel the heat from her body. She scrutinized him, as if trying to read his thoughts. After a moment, she sighed, giving up on the attempt.

"I'm going to bed. Reyna has been fed and I am still weak from our journey."

He nodded, then turned to watch her walk away from him. He stood in the garden a moment longer, breathing in the scent of the flowers. No perfume lingered. She did not wear any. Finally, he turned and walked back into the castle.

Chapter 13

The next day, after finishing midday meal in their common room, the group received notice that King Kennan would meet with them. The page had not given a specific time, just asked them to be available.

Percival stood on the balcony for the common room, trying to control his patience. Usually he had to counsel Cora on the importance of patience when dealing with the king, as well as other male authority figures. Today, every moment that passed felt like a noose tightening around his neck.

"How much longer do you think he is going to make us wait?" The impatience in Cora's voice grated on Percival's already irritated nerves.

He turned a glare on her. "If you're so impatient, then maybe you should go find the steward yourself."

Her stunned expression did nothing to improve his mood. Percival heaved a deep breath. *Why did I do that? She did nothing to deserve that.*

Our time draws near, Black Hand. You know your temper rages out of control the closer it comes.

Stromas, you damn demon. Leave me alone. It's not time yet. Stop antagonizing me. Percival caught Cora staring at him "What?"

She shook her head. "Nothing. You're just more irritable than normal. Are you feeling ill?"

"I feel fine. I don't—" Percival began.

"I beg your pardon, but if you are ready to see His Majesty, I will take you to the throne room," the steward interrupted their conversation, no remorse in his voice.

Percival turned his glare on the man. "Of course, we're ready." He pushed past Cora and the steward and stomped into the common room. "The king is finally ready to meet with us," he announced to the others as he continued through to the hall.

The steward rushed to get in front of Percival, acting as though he had been in the lead the entire time when he finally was. When they stood at the double doors to the throne room, the steward stopped and straightened his clothes.

"I will announce your arrival. Please stay behind me," he instructed.

"This is ridiculous. The Princeesa should not have to follow behind a man," Satina protested.

"Satina!" Cora spun on her bodyguard, a dagger in her hand suddenly. "I told you the last time you acted like this that it would not be tolerated. Return to our rooms and wait for us there."

Percival stepped up behind Cora, trying to keep his face neutral. Satina had become more vocal in her hatred for Man's World recently. He wondered how much longer Cora would tolerate it, or if the other Amazon would force Cora to return home soon.

"Princeesa, I must stay with you, to protect you from these men," Satina protested.

"I don't need your protection right now." Cora glanced at Percival. "If I need to be protected, the Black Hand will do it. He will do what you are not able to."

Surprise burned in Percival's chest, but he felt sure it didn't match the shock on Satina's face. Behind him, the steward cleared his throat.

"His Majesty is waiting. Are you ready?"

"Go, Satina. I do not want to see you waiting for me when we are finished." Cora turned away from Satina.

Percival waited until she also turned away, then he followed the steward and Cora into the throne room. Several servants, busy cleaning the statues and armor throughout the room, looked up at their entrance.

Sitting in his throne, on the dais, King Kennan smiled at the steward's announcement of their arrival. "Come forward, Black Hand, Princess Rylannes, Tylina Orenda, Kalik Riverwind, Brolin Tourrados, and Nimbly." He named each one, as if trying to memorize their names. "I want to thank you all for finding my daughter. Her mother is happy to have her returned to her arms and I am happy she was found safe."

"It was our pleasure, Your Majesty. We are grateful she was unharmed." Despite having made them wait, Percival knew taking his anger out on the king would not accomplish anything. He bowed, followed by the others in turn, except Cora. She tilted her head in acknowledgement.

"Your Majesty, if I might ask, how often has your daughter traveled to that underground city?" Cora's question drew looks of surprise from everyone in the group, as well as the king.

"I never go to the city," Princess Stepha's soft voice came from behind the king's throne. She stepped out and climbed into her father's lap, gracing everyone with a pout. "That was my first time there."

"Then why were we told you liked to play there, Princess?" Cora approached the throne.

"Her nanny told me that is where she played, though I am not sure how she could have gotten down there without help." King Kennan held his daughter closer.

"Where is her nanny now?" Percival closed the distance to Cora's side. Hearing her voice calmed his temper, almost as if she could drive Stromas away.

"Missing, since you were asked to retrieve Stepha." The king stood, placing the girl in his chair.

"How long was she the princess' nanny?" Cora asked in a strained whisper.

Percival turned to study her, confused by the fear he heard in her voice.

"A little less than three years, shortly after the time you arrived here, Princess Rylannes." King Kennan descended to the main floor, stopping in front of her. "Why do you ask?"

"Doesn't it seem a little unusual that a woman would come here, take on the duty of being your daughter's nanny, then disappear after the princess has been kidnapped after telling you and the rescuers a lie about where the girl likes to play?"

"Yes, it does." The king's voice increased in volume with every word. "Do you know who she is?"

"No, I do not. I suggest you do a thorough check of the city and those who are leaving now since the gladiator games are finished, to find your missing nanny. Let your best judgment guide you from there." Cora squared her shoulders and lifted her chin in renewed confidence against the growing frustration in the king's face.

Percival knew she was hiding something from them, but the king would have to deal with her secrets on his own. Percival was more concerned about what she hid from him. His temper returned to its previous level, the calm he felt from Cora's voice gone.

The king stared at her a moment longer, then nodded, stepping away from her. "I shall have my people do as you suggest. I will also make sure whatever information we find that may be important to you and the others is passed along." He waited for Cora to bow her head again. "Now, as for your reward. My steward has for each of you a sizeable amount of money. You should be quite comfortable for several months."

"Your Majesty, instead of the gems, I would like to have a meeting with your mage," Percival requested.

King Kennan studied him, his expression thoughtful. After a moment, he nodded. "Of course, Captain Riesun. Arrangements will be made for you to meet with him tomorrow."

"Thank you." Percival bowed again.

The king nodded, then waved his hand, dismissing them. He returned to his throne and picked up his daughter playfully.

Percival followed the others out of the throne room. The steward waited for them on the other side of the door, with their page and a silver tray filled with pouches.

"I will deliver the pouches to your rooms, if that would meet with your approval," the steward announced.

"Thank you. I'm sure we all have things that need to be tended to before the sun sets." Percival waited until the steward and page departed, then grabbed Cora's hand as she tried to walk past him.

Color filled Cora's cheeks and her eyes darkened with anger. Finally, Cora broke through the building tension. "What do you want, Black Hand?"

"Why did you ask the king those questions? Do you know something about the kidnapper or nanny that the rest of us need to know?" he demanded, keeping his voice low.

"Not that I'm aware of, but if I learn something, I will share it with all who need to know." A small smile lifted the corner of her mouth.

"You frustrate me, Cora. I never feel like your answers are as informative as they should be." Percival released her hand and flexed his fingers.

"I'm so glad. Trust me, the feeling is mutual, Black Hand. You often frustrate me and leave me questioning my decision to travel with you." Cora turned and left him standing in stunned silence.

Percival watched her leave, then stormed down the hall after her.

"Percival!" Tylina's voice chased him.

"Not now, Tylina. Not now!"

Chapter 14

Leaving his friends in the rooms the king provided for the group, Percival chose to see the king's mage. He still debated the intelligence of the request. What if the mage couldn't give him any answers?

The lanterns shining sun lit the part of the room Percival stood in through the opened windows. He could just make out a wooden desk at the edge of an unnatural darkness. Light did not penetrate the dark corner of the room.

"His Majesty tells me you have some questions." The mage's voice reached Percival from the other side of the dark desk.

Steeling himself with a deep breath, Percival nodded. "I have long suffered from an affliction I believe you might be able to help me with."

"I am not a cleric." The sound of a book slamming shut filled the room. "Perhaps you should have asked to speak to the king's private healer instead. I understand the cleric you travel with is still inexperienced." The mage stomped into the light, displeasure evident on his face.

"I don't need a cleric. The priestly magic cannot heal the curse inflicted by wizardly magic." Percival held his black hand up for the mage to see.

The mage studied him for a moment, then realization brightened his sour demeanor. "You are the Black Hand,

Captain Percival Riesun. Your father was a wizard of great renown, years ago, until his greed and insanity destroyed him" He circled the younger man, studying him. "Or so the rumors say."

"Yes, that describes the man who sired me." Percival let his bitterness fill his words.

"I understand that your father somehow combined your life with that of a creature from another plane," the mage said casually.

Percival glared at the mage, but before he could question the other man, he continued speaking. "The king has known of your *situation* since the day you started in his service. Many of us in the world of magic have tried to understand and even duplicate what your father did to you. It has not been accomplished by anyone else, which I believe is a good thing." The mage completed his path in front of Percival, his eyes gazing at the man before him. "You need to make a journey to find your true self and to find the one thing that will set the demon free. Journey to the Tower of Winter and seek out Arch Mage Wintress. He should be able to help you further." The man disappeared into the darkness again, leaving the room in silence.

Percival stared at the empty room around him, then turned to leave. The meeting had been a complete waste of time.

I could have told you that, Black Hand. You will never be free of me. And if I ever do release you from our little arrangement, it will be because you are dead and I am free in your world.

Percival's heart raced with the demonic laughter filling his mind. "Enough, demon. I will do whatever it takes to be rid of you."

Not without losing your life.

Chapter 15

Three days after the celebration, Cora finally freed herself from Satina's ever watchful gaze. She sat in the garden again, studying the arrowhead. So far, she failed to convince herself that the arrowhead belonged to someone else. Her mother's enemies had found her. Worse, the woman who kidnapped Cora as a child led the hunt.

Silk slippered feet drew her attention from the arrow and to a young page that stood nervous in her scrutiny.

"Yes?" She tapped her finger on the arrow, impatient with the boy's silence.

"I apologize, milady. Duke Orenda requests your presence at his estate. Your horse has been saddled and your companions are waiting for you at the stable." The page stammered out his message, his expression panicked in his nervousness.

She stared at him for a heartbeat, then realized why he acted the way he did. Every time Cora and the others stayed in the palace, the boy had the misfortune of being their page. The first time, he tried to help her with her saddlebags and accidentally touched the princess. Satina struck the boy for his inappropriate gesture, though Cora did not feel he had done anything wrong. Ever since, the page feared the two Amazons.

Cora waved her hand, dismissing him. She stood and glanced around the garden, not surprised to see Satina waiting for her on the path. Once the arrow lay securely hidden in her backpack, the two Amazons made their way to the stables to meet their companions.

Arriving at the stables, Cora noticed that Exar was not with the others.

She could feel Percival's attention on her. He watched her, like Reyna watched her prey. Cora didn't like the feeling of being hunted. He waited for the others to mount their horses first, then mounted his own. After looking around to make sure everyone was ready, he led them from the stable, across the courtyard and into the city proper.

They rode through the city in silence, the sounds louder than Cora's thoughts. They turned down a road leading to the noble sector and continued until they arrived at the Orenda estate.

The manor looked like all the others, with brown brick throughout both levels. Yard keepers worked in the gardens full of blooming flowers. Guards patrolled the well-kept grounds. The guards stopped the group at the gate, then allowed them to pass when Tylina identified herself. They directed the group to the stable, then a guard showed them into a receiving room where they were told to wait for Duke Orenda to send for them.

Finally, before Satina's pacing wore through Cora's limited patience, the Orenda's steward appeared in the archway and bowed.

"Duke Orenda will see all of you now." He bowed again and started walking down the main hall.

Cora looked around the study before entering. Dark wood bookshelves lined one wall, filled with books of varying ages and sizes. Opposite the door they entered, a large window revealed a rose garden. A thin, blue lace covered it, with a darker blue lace pulled into a bundle on each side. A small table stood to their right with four chairs surrounding it and a couch only large enough to seat two. The duke's desk waited to the left of the door, cluttered with parchment and an oil lamp on the right hand corner. Two chairs sat in front of the desk. The group separated and sat in the available seats. Cora took one of the chairs in front of the desk, Satina standing behind her. Percival took the chair next to her.

Before they could get comfortable, the door to the study opened again and Duke Orenda entered, smiling at them. He took Tylina's hand in his, and kissed her fingers. With an even bigger smile, he walked around the desk to sit in his own chair.

A painting of a beautiful elven woman rested on the wall behind the duke. A brief moment of study and Cora realized the woman's features closely resembled Tylina's. Tylina's long hair blended the dark of brown and the light of blond colors and the painting showed her mother's hair as a lighter shade than her mix. The family shared the trait of blue eyes, but Tylina's facial shape resembled her elven heritage. Her eyes were not as slanted as her mother's, just as her ears were not as pointed. Her figure was slim and attractive, more curvaceous than her mother's and where the other woman's painting showed a beautiful silk dress, Tylina chose to wear clothing more suited for her life on the road; leather boots, softened leather breeches, and a shirt dyed in the colors of nature.

"Thank you for coming on such short notice." The duke cleared his throat before continuing, drawing everyone's attention to him. "As I'm sure you are aware, questions are circulating in the court regarding your companion, Exar, also known as Fenris the Hunter." The group looked at each other.

Cora could see by the expressions on the others faces that she was not the only one surprised by this announcement. But they appeared to know who this Fenris was while she didn't. She looked at Percival. He should have told her about this Fenris person.

"By the gods, don't tell me you didn't know he was a bounty hunter." Disbelief filled Duke Orenda's voice.

"No, we knew he was a bounty hunter, just not that particular one. But since he has been with us, he has not taken a bounty that we are aware of." Percival defended his friends, his vehemence strong.

"I see, Captain Riesun. Are you also aware that the bounties he takes are usually for elves and half-elves?" His glance at Tylina left no doubt as to his meaning. "The world is filled with societies and individuals who harbor a hatred for the elven people. Exar comes from a country where a man is measured by the number of his victims. He is known to associate with people who put a price on the heads of others, even their own. The trophies he takes are the severed ears of his victims. He likes to beat women and has no problem with forcing himself on any female he wants."

"We will keep your daughter safe, Duke Orenda, as we have always done." Kalik's quiet voice rose over the silence Duke Orenda's words created.

"I know you will, Kalik. That is really the least of my worries." The duke shuffled through the parchments on his desk for a moment, then belatedly removed the top sheet from the stack and handed it to Percival. "Exar has accepted a position with a merchant caravan traveling to Jonquil. My concern is this— my wife is there and her family, as well as the largest elven community in our part of the continent. I want you to watch him, to make sure he takes no actions against any of them."

The others nodded in agreement, but Cora remained still. Behind her, she felt Satina stiffen at Duke Orenda's request.

"We will handle it, Duke Orenda." Percival pushed his chair back in anticipation of the conclusion of their meeting.

"I have made arrangements for all of you to be in that caravan. But before you go, I have something else to discuss with you, Captain Riesun, as well as Princess Rylannes." The duke nodded in Cora's direction.

She raised her eyebrow at him, surprised, then glanced at the others. Did he know about the arrow?

The duke studied her a moment more, then glanced at Satina. The others, who had stood to leave, seeing Satina standing in place, returned to their seats. Sighing in resignation, Duke Orenda cleared his throat again.

"Cora, everyone in the court knows who you are and where you come from. Since the day you arrived in Glenys, my people have been watching you."

Cora bristled at his words. "Why is that, Duke Orenda?"

"Because of our concern that some might try to use you against our people." He pointed at Satina. "Your bodyguard can protect you to some degree, but it seems that someone has let it be known they want you to walk in a different plan of existence.

"Princess Kennan's kidnapping was planned, from what we have been able to learn, specifically to place you in danger. The nanny told the king about the kidnapping and strongly recommended we approach you to find his daughter. She suggested offering you whatever it took to get you to go. After making such a strong recommendation, the nanny disappeared before you returned." The duke watched her as he revealed this information.

Cora sat back in her chair, studying Orenda's face. With this information, her fears were confirmed. A great weight dropped on her shoulders, like a tight box closed in on her. Her usual confidence shattered.

She took a deep breath, straightened her back and smiled, employing her mother's technique to mask her emotions. "I'm sure I have no idea what you're talking about, Duke Orenda." Her voice remained calm. Good for her. "Surely I would know if someone wished me harm."

The duke remained silent, watching the group of people in front of him. She felt sure he had seen a momentary flash of fear on her face. From the corner of her eye, Cora could see The Black Hand struggling to control his anger.

"Yes, Your Highness, you're right. I assume that you would know if anyone wished you harm." The duke stood and offered his hand to the Black Hand. "If that is what you wish for me to know, then I am not in a position to push the issue further. Once again, I appreciate your coming to hear me out and I wish you safe journeys in the days ahead. Please let me know whatever you find out about Exar and his actions."

Percival took his hand, giving it a brief shake, then turned to Cora as he waited for her to stand. The Amazon princess looked at the duke, nodding slightly, then turned away from the men and sauntered to the door. The duke held Percival back before he left away, allowing the others to follow Cora out of the room.

Cora stopped outside the door while the others continued past her. Crossing her arms, she waited for the men to finish their conversation.

"Keep a watchful eye on her as well. The last thing we need is a war with the Amazon nation because we let their princess come to harm. Our trading on the sea would be adversely affected by that," Duke Orenda advised, still trying to keep his voice quiet.

"Aye, milord. I will be ever watchful of her safety. I will find out exactly what is going on."

Cora heard Percival's anger in his voice and knew he no longer held it in check. She peeked around the door jam at him, noting the fire in his eyes again. Had she finally pushed him too far?

Duke Orenda nodded and escorted him from his study. She turned away from the door, letting the two men get in front of her. She waited for the Black Hand to say something, but he remained silent, lost in his own thoughts. The duke's guards led them to the stable, where their horses waited. The group rode in silence through the city.

Cora watched Percival's body move in sync with his horse and found herself staring at him longer than she intended. Far too often, she found herself too easily distracted by him. Even admitting to herself that she liked him holding her close in the sewers was a distraction.

Thinking about a man like that was inappropriate, she reminded herself, letting her eyes drift over his back, the muscles rippling under his shirt while he looked around for anything that might present a danger to them. Instead of his usual banded and chain armor, he wore a white shirt, black leather breeches and matching black riding boots. His handsome, rugged features had matured since she first met him, and his body had grown even more to accommodate his muscles. He let his hair grow longer, but kept it short enough to not touch his shoulders. She liked how he kept his facial hair trimmed neat and short. The fire in his dark eyes had grown brighter over three years, but she knew it burned brightest with strong emotions—anger, fear, displeasure, during combat and once a month when he left the group for the night. He never explained to them why he left.

Whenever he looked at her, she felt a tickle and tightness in her stomach. The flush it gave her was almost as intense as the tingling she felt when he touched her or when magic was used around her. Worse, she didn't know how to deal with these feelings.

When she agreed to travel with the Black Hand, Satina questioned her decision to let him lead the group. Cora defended herself by saying he knew the area and the lands better than the Amazons did and he could be trusted. But since then, she questioned if she agreed to his leadership because he reminded her of Dekart and how safe he made her feel. The Black Hand sought her counsel often and accepted it when offered without sarcasm.

A hand on her leg interrupted her thoughts. Satina reached up to help her from the horse. "Are you all right?" Her question in the Amazon's native language brought a frown to Cora's face.

Despite the frown, she nodded, pushing aside the offered hand and swinging her leg over to jump down from her horse. The two Amazons guided their mounts into the stable behind the others.

A strange shiver raced across Cora's skin. She turned, assuming the source was the Black Hand. He stood too far from her to have caused the reaction. Instead, standing beyond the gate to the courtyard, a man or at least a man-sized creature, stared at them. A dark cloak covered his body, the hood pulled down to cover his face. From within the hood, Cora could see a red glow. His shoulders appeared bigger than would be normal.

She released her reins and took a step toward the man. A hand on her arm stopped her, sending a jolt through her. She glanced back to see Percival holding her arm, but when she turned back to the man at the gate, he had disappeared.

* * *

"Where are you going, Cora?" Percival glanced toward the gate to the courtyard, but could find nothing that should have pulled her away from the group.

"I thought I saw... Never mind." She yanked her arm from his grip. "What do you want?"

"We need to talk." The anger he had held in check as they rode through the town filled his statement and pushed toward her.

She stared at him. He saw her own anger growing in her expression—the tightening of her jaw muscles, the clenching of her fist and the narrowing of her eyes. "Don't presume to order me, Black Hand. We've had this conversation before. I do not order you as my mother and our people would have me do. You do not order me as if I were a woman who does not know her own worth."

He stepped back, surprised by her words. Either she was truly angry with him or whatever she saw scared her. Or... she was worried the time she spent with him was affecting her in ways that would be seen as improper by her people. Percival felt the fire in his eyes increase, and forced a calming breath to bring it under control. He bowed slightly, and with one step, backed away from her.

"Fine, Princess, we'll talk when you come back from getting your supplies, after evening meal."

She nodded, then strode past him. Satina rushed to match her angered stride. Percival watched Cora until she disappeared through the gates, back the way they had come. He followed, turning in the opposite direction from her.

He stopped and turned to find Cora's retreating form. He needed to go in the same direction to see to his own needs.

Chapter 16

The group met at evening meal, in the common room for their suites. Cora avoided the conversation during the meal, lost in her own thoughts, but she heard enough to know it revolved around the journey that waited for them on the morrow. Exar accepted the news they would be joining the caravan without comment, only saying he had also looked into the caravan and agreed it would be a good job for them to take. It surprised her that no one pressed him further or mentioned they already knew he joined the caravan. After his announcement, the conversation immediately changed to other topics.

The ongoing conversation only served to irritate Cora more. Satina had spent the entire afternoon questioning her decision to stay in Man's World—again. Cora wanted to punish her bodyguard for arguing with her. At least follow through with the threat to send her back to the islands. They did not speak to each other the rest of the day.

After the page stoked their fire for the second time, Cora stood, leaving the comfort of the cushions she had been relaxing upon. She passed her wine glass to Satina, as well as her plate of half-eaten food.

"I'm going to my room to study." Satina stood as if to join her, but Cora shook her head. "I want to be alone and I definitely do not want *you* around."

The older Amazon returned to her pillows, her anger following Cora into her room.

* * *

Percival waited until Cora shut the door behind her, then stood as well and excused himself from the conversation. Again, Satina stood, determined to stop him.

"She said she wanted to be alone." The Amazon's anger came out in full force against him.

"She will answer my questions before we leave in the morning, or she won't be going, Satina." Percival turned on her, his own displeasure burning in his eyes. "If *you* want to stay here, that's fine with me, but we benefit from having *her* with us."

Satina stared at him for a moment, then shrugged her shoulders. "She will remove you from her presence if she wishes." She returned to her cushions and swallowed the last of her ale, dismissing him with her refusal to acknowledge him any further.

Percival stood in silence. Normally he would force the argument, but this time he decided it would be more productive to direct his focus on learning who was after Cora. He crossed the distance to her room.

* * *

Cora jumped at the knock on her door, the bronze spell plates she had been studying dropping to the floor. With a sigh, she stooped to pick them up, and returned the plates to the pouch she kept them in, on her waist. She took her time opening the door. She knew Percival stood on the other side, and hated him for being so persistent. Things weren't right between them. Anger tickled at the edge of her mind again, but it still was not hers.

She opened the door just a hands breadth, and gazed at Percival.

"Are you ready to talk to me now?" Percival pushed the door open further to step into the room.

Cora stepped back to avoid the door. "Well, come in, Black Hand. By all means. Would you like to sleep in the bed as well?" She allowed her indignation to fill her words.

"Just tell me who is after you, Cora. Tell me why you haven't said anything about this before and what I should expect." He pulled the door from her control and slammed it shut, then stormed across the room to the window.

She took a calming breath before turning toward him. "We both harbor secrets, Black Hand. That is something we have always known about the other. Why is it a problem now? Just because a man has said something to bring it to your attention more than before?"

"Because the duke made sure I knew that the king knows. Because your stubbornness has left me unprepared for what is to come. And someone kidnapped a little girl to get the chance to kill you." His voice increased in volume with each word, until he was shouting at her. "Your secrets are going to cause a war between our people."

"I have nothing to tell you, Black Hand." Her voice remained quiet. "However, I'm glad to see concern for my safety is the least important of your worries."

In three steps, he crossed the distance between them and grabbed her arms painfully. "Tell me!"

She studied him, feeling his breath on her skin. She felt bruises forming on her arms from his tight grip, but his touch made her stomach clench. She wanted him to hold her closer, instead of yelling at her about... What was he yelling about again?

The contact of their skin reignited the magic between them. It coursed through her arms, warming her skin where his hands touched her. The world around her had melted away as they stood together, his hands on her arms only intensifying the feeling of them being the only people in the world.

They had been alone in the world when he held her in the sewer. It felt natural to be in his arms, against his chest, while they breathed as one. She wanted to feel that way again. She wanted to run her fingers through his hair, to feel his lips pressed against hers and on her neck as his hands touched her with tenderness instead of the anger he felt right now. She wanted to turn his anger aside, to make the fire in his eyes burn because of desire instead of anger.

Chapter 17

Percival watched the emotions play across Cora's face and eyes. He never expected to see desire in her face when she looked at him. Everything he saw said she wanted him to hold her. He took a deep breath. He agreed with her. He wanted to hold her. He wanted to be the first to kiss her lips—lips that had yet to feel the touch of a man.

The many different things he wanted to show her and teach her flowed through his mind. If only she wasn't so stubborn because of her upbringing. If only his own secret didn't keep him from fulfilling his own needs.

His secret always kept him from ever being with a woman for more than a few weeks at a time. The feelings he had for them never grew beyond just short term lust, fulfilling the needs of the moment.

When Percival left King Kennan's service, he searched for Cora. He had already learned his anger seemed less intense when she was near. He breathed in the scent of the oils she had bathed in earlier. Wild flowers. He didn't understand why he felt this way, but he was connected to her, somehow. This connection drew him to Cora, whatever it was.

Her movements reluctant, Cora backed away from him just as his grip loosened on her arms. "All right, Percival. I'll tell you what I can." Her voice was strong with the desire she could not hide from him. She walked past him, closer to the window.

He struggled to control his breathing. She called him Percival. She had never used his given name before. His hands dropped to his sides. If he touched her again, he would act on his own desire. That could be a serious mistake.

"I'm listening." Emotions filled his voice. He breathed deep again.

"My mother wasn't the heir to the Amazon throne. She won it in a contest, as our traditions demand when no heir survived from the last queen. Her greatest competitor was Shoshona. The battles they fought were intense, many of them coming very close to death for my mother or Shoshona. The combat was so fierce, my people feared there would be no victor and no survivor. Both had held positions of great importance. My mother was the captain of the personal guard for the previous queen, while Shoshona was the captain of the Sea Wolves. They had been the closest of friends until the competitions started. Then they became the strongest of enemies. I was but a babe when this occurred, the second of my mother's daughters. When my mother won, Shoshona swore that she would have the throne, that she would be the death of my mother and her heirs." Cora's voice grew in strength as she gained control of her emotions again. She turned to look out the window. "Shoshona must have found someone amongst her followers willing to come to your world and hire mercenaries to find and dispose of me. The nanny must have been a member of Shoshona's tribe."

"Has she tried before?" His question came out a little above a whisper. He stood behind her again, almost touching her, the golden skin of her shoulders begging for attention. He closed his eyes, and pushed his emotions deep.

"The cave," she whispered.

"How can you be sure she's here?"

"Because no one else wants to hurt me like Shoshona. And," she paused, taking a deep breath. "I found an arrowhead with her tribe's coloring and feathers." She stopped again, looking outside. "Aren't you angry I didn't tell you about it?"

"Yes, but you finally told me." He wondered how much more she still kept from him.

She turned from the window, stepping back before she bumped against him. "I can't tell you what to expect. I have never dealt with Exar's type before, the bounty hunters who will take a person's life for money or the mercenaries who take those kinds of jobs. That is something I expect you to know."

He nodded, looking out the window. On the battlements, across the garden, Percival could see the silhouette of a figure, lit by the torches of the city. In the area of the figure's head, he could see a red glow beginning to spread until the entire figure glowed. While he watched, two more figures joined the first, also glowing.

It appears someone has finally come to rescue me, Black Hand. Will you be able to protect your little princess when my followers attack you both?

Stromas, you are more confident than normal. But I am still not in the mood to listen to your bantering. Shut up. Percival reached around Cora to close the shutters, their closeness making her suck in her breath. "I do not know what kind of tactics they will use, but I will keep my eyes open for anything out of the ordinary that might cause you harm."

"Now it's your turn, Black Hand." She took his blackened hand in hers.

A painful jolt shot through his arm at her touch and they both gasped in pain and surprise.

Chapter 18

Percival yanked his hand from hers. "What was that?"

"That's never happened before." Cora stared at her hand. "Tell me about your hand and why you have to leave us every month. Maybe I can figure out why we react so…" She let her voice trail off, not wanting to put words to their reactions.

"That is something that you do not need to concern yourself with." His abrupt answer surprised her.

"Yes, it is. If you are going to designate yourself as my sole protector, even though I already have Satina, then I am in danger when you leave the group. I want to know what is so important that you would leave me open and vulnerable to attack in your absence." She could not hide her sarcasm. A man could not possibly protect her from one of her own people. Not even this man. But the idea of having his protection made her feel safe.

Everything she felt conflicted with her upbringing.

"Damn it, Cora." Percival looked toward the ceiling. "I fight for control of myself during the black moon. I have the displeasure of dealing with something that wants me for its own purposes." He pointed at the pouch that held her spell plates. "Maybe when you are more capable with your magic, we can find a way to help me win the war completely. Until then, and only after you've made the decision to help, I will fight each battle on my own." He walked to the door and opened it. "Good night, Princess."

She watched him leave her room and realized it was sooner than she would have preferred. The fear in his eyes at her questions about his hand kept her from following him. Moreover, his insult about her magic, though it sounded reflexive, still cut her. Rubbing her hand where she had touched him, she realized her flesh still tingled. That jolt was unexpected. The only difference was that she touched his hand with her primary casting hand. She could not remember if she had ever done that before. She still felt him, just as if they were still touching. Shaking her head, she turned back to the window, opening the shutters.

"What did he see out there?" Cora had seen Percival's reaction to something in the night before he closed the shutters earlier, but nothing out of the norm was visible at the moment.

She would learn more about his problem and if possible, she would help him defeat whatever inner demons he fought against. But she feared she would lose herself in her vow—forever. The light from the moon drew her eyes to the golden orb.

Percival always left the group when a black moon darkened the night sky. His temper grew shorter as the cycle drew closer, while during the full moon his temper did not seem to control him. The black moon was just days away. They would be on the road when it happened.

What changes would the black moon bring to her life?

Chapter 19

The next morning, as the sun broke over the horizon, Cora and the others joined the caravan. The Black Hand spoke to the captain and the merchant paying for the transport while they waited.

When Percival finished, he rejoined the others. "We have two wagons toward the end of the caravan. We will be guarding the wagons, not driving them. He has drivers already."

They helped with final preparations though Cora repeatedly had to yell at Satina to keep working. At high sun, the caravan left Glenys and began its two week journey.

With a long road ahead, Cora relaxed in her saddle and studied her companions. Each joined the group for different reasons, or more accurately, joined her and Percival, Satina being the third by default. She found their companionship comforting at times, especially when she argued with Satina. The diversity of each person intrigued her, and how it was reflected not only in their background, but also in their stories and appearance.

Kalik Riverwind rode his horse bareback, his sightless eyes scanning the land around them. Tylina rode beside him, and a comfortable silence settled between them. Kalik's efforts to protect Cora and Tylina continued to surprise the Amazon princess.

To the right of their group, Nimbly rode in a scouting

position. He waved at her. His usual cheerful demeanor made Cora uncomfortable. Despite that, she could not imagine their group being as successful without him

Cora shifted on her horse so she could see the people behind her. Brolin Tourrados, priest of Garen, rode his white stallion in silence as he studied a small book, the symbol of Garen burned into the leather cover. The symbol was a hand, palm out, wrapped in a white chain with a blue ribbon laced through the links. Brolin matched Percival in size as well as strength, though he had chosen the path of religion over that of a warrior. Though he lived the life of a priest, he always threw himself into battle like a warrior. He did not often speak about his life before joining them, but did occasionally mention a calling he received and that it led him to the group. As if he could hear her thoughts, Brolin looked up, nodded at her, then returned his attention to his book.

Next to Brolin rode the most mysterious member of the group—Exar. His only obvious features were his size and his voice. Exar stood larger than Percival in height, weight and width and his voice had the sound of a sandstorm in the middle of the summer season. He always wore black, hardened leather with spikes that covered his entire body, from the top of his head to his feet. Over his face, he wore a black mask made from the same leather and no one had ever seen him remove the mask, even to eat. Cora could not recall ever having seen him eat. He always took his meals in his room when they stayed at an inn or in his tent when they traveled.

When Exar did sit with the group, he rarely spoke, keeping his comments to as few words as possible. The man remained a constant source of tension for Percival. He constantly left the group and refused to join them on jobs. Cora did not understand why the Black Hand continued to tolerate his insolence.

Cora continued to look behind her, her eyes drawn to a group of riders that followed the caravan. The riders, three of them, each wore the same style dark cloak as the one she noticed outside the palace courtyard the day before.

She returned her attention to Percival, surprised to see that he had also turned to look at her. "Black Hand, a group of three people are following the caravan. I think I recognize one of them from Glenys."

He nodded, his attention shifting to the group in the distance. "I see them. They have been there since we left. I don't like it."

"What are we going to do about it? Should we tell the caravan master about them?"

"If they continue to follow, yes. But for now, I want you to be on watch with me." He pulled his horse back so he rode next to her.

"That's ridiculous, Black Hand. If you are not worried about them, then it should not matter what watch I am on." She scoffed at his suggestion.

"I told you, I will do whatever needs to be done to protect you. You will be on watch with me, period."

Cora felt her nerves tighten at the order. "I am growing extremely tired of your orders!"

He took a deep breath, closed his eyes, then looked at her again. "Cora, please, I don't want to argue with you. Let me do this. How many times do I have to show you that your safety is important to me?"

Cora also took a deep breath, and worked to soothe her anger. "Fine, Black Hand, as long as it is one that will allow me to rest and still be prepared the next day."

"We will take first watch."

Chapter 20

The third night on the road, after their watch started, Cora took her customary place next to the fire, journal in hand. Percival sat across from her, watching her for a short time, then with a sigh, he stood and began his walk around the camp.

He hoped their watch went well and the time passed quickly. He did not want to leave Cora alone, with the others asleep, while he dealt with Stromas.

Yes, your delay is beginning to annoy me, Black Hand.

Percival stopped, facing the camp so he could see Cora silhouetted in the glow of the fire. *You are beginning to annoy me, Stromas. I tire of our constant battles.*

You could always give up, quit fighting me.

Not while there's still life in my body. Percival continued around the perimeter, keeping his attention between Cora and the path he walked.

He paced the perimeter for most of their watch, unsure he could control Stromas while near her, but their watch was ending and he wanted to return to the fire before waking Tylina and Kalik. He finally made his way back to the fire and sat across from Cora again.

Neither said anything until Percival broke the silence himself, coughing. He heard her sigh and hid a grin as she laid her quill between the pages of her journal and gave him her full attention.

"Yes, Black Hand?" Resignation filled her voice.

"What are you writing? For over two years, I've watched you write in those journals. I've seen you buy new books and supplies. Yet, I have no idea what you write about." He waited for her to answer, watching her expectantly.

"The journals are for my mother, about my journey in your world and the many things I have learned." Another sigh lifted her shoulders.

"But why?"

She stared at him, her eyes wide in surprise. "I've told you this before, Black Hand. To prepare my islands in case your people should ever try to take our freedom from us."

"I don't believe that is your entire reason for being here. I think something else brought you here." He studied her through the firelight. Did the fire hide his battle to keep Stromas under control?

She continued to stare at him, then a genuine smile lit her face. "My father's ship crashed and he washed up on the shores of our island with several others from his crew. I don't know why my mother took him for herself, but I am glad she did. Dekart and I are close—closer than my people deem appropriate for an Amazon and her father. He used to tell me stories about his world—your world. I guess curiosity got the better of me. As soon as I turned sixteen, I requested and received permission to come to your world." She pointed at him. "Again, now it's your turn. Tell me about your family, Black Hand."

He sat in silence for a long time, staring at the fire dance between them. Finally, he stood and walked to her side of the fire. He sat next to her, surprised she didn't move away from him.

"My father was a mage, like you. His greed for power got the better of him, and after cursing me with this hand, he tried to kill me. My mother saved me and we left him. I don't know if he is still alive. Mother died when I was twelve…" His voice trailed off.

Turning, he scanned the forest. "Did you hear something?"

"No." They stood together, both facing the perimeter of their camp. She stepped closer to him. "What did you hear?"

He breathed deeply, his arm warmed from the closeness of

her body. "Probably nothing. Go wake Tylina for watch. We're done."

Percival's gazed followed Cora to the wagon Tylina and Kalik slept near. A feeling of calm settled over him. She did not push him to give more information about his father. She had to know he did not tell her everything. Cora was a smart woman. He was sure she heard the evasiveness in his answer.

Kalik approached him, his staff sliding over the logs as he walked. "Anything going on tonight, Percival?"

"Not really. I thought I heard something, so I am going to walk the perimeter one more time before I get some sleep. I will let you know if I find anything." Percival did not wait for an answer, but turned from Kalik and entered the trees.

As he traveled, the area around him changed. The dark was replaced with a gray sky, brighter than the night. The terrain changed to a desolate, rock strewn valley. Large boulders filled the area.

In front of him, a demon stood waiting, his large arms crossed. Two large horns protruded from his head and large wings sprung from his back. Five fingers on each hand ended in black nails, while his feet resembled cloven hooves. He wore only a loincloth. The demon stood at twice Percival's height and he watched the man who confined him with eyes of burning embers.

"Who are the three following us, Stromas?"

"Which three?" The demon's voice echoed throughout the area around them.

Percival shifted in surprise. "There are more than just the three in black cloaks following us? Who do you have following us? How were you able to contact them?"

Stromas laughed. *"You misunderstand the situation, Black Hand. I don't have to answer your questions. I just need to find a way to free myself."*

With a growl, Percival pulled his sword from its scabbard and charged the demon. Stromas uncrossed his arms, lifting his hands to defend himself. Percival swung his sword, pushing Stromas' left hand away. He brought his sword back around and slid the blade into the belly of the demon.

"How many more times can you win before you are too weak to fight against me?" Stromas' laughter surrounded Percival

again as his image faded.

"One of these days, I will kill you for real, Stromas."

"Are you sure you want to?"

Chapter 21

In the morning, while Cora prepared her horse, she felt Percival watching her. She turned to return his look, but Satina stepped between them, her anger coming in waves.

"What do you think you are doing, Princeesa?"

"I am saddling my horse, Satina. Have you been blinded overnight?" Cora straightened, giving the bodyguard her full attention. Behind Satina, Percival stepped closer and Cora gave him a slight shake of her head.

"You understand exactly what I mean, Princeesa. You spend too much time with the Black Hand. You have become too comfortable with him. I heard you talking to him last night about your father." Satina pressed closer to Cora, closer than the princess normally allowed anyone. "You speak about your father as if he is a man worth noticing. You are behaving inappropriately for an Amazon, especially our Princeesa."

Cora's breath caught. Satina had never been so bold as to admit she had been spying on her princess before. "You are speaking out of place, Satina. I will not tolerate this." Cora placed her hand on Satina's shoulder and pushed her back. "Get away from me. I am not in the mood for your insubordination—Warrior."

Satina stared at her, her nostrils flaring in anger. Finally, she bowed her head. "As you wish." She spun away and went to her own horse, glaring at both Cora and Percival.

Cora knew she was going to have another confrontation with Satina. The warrior would not easily back down. But she should not question Cora. She looked up to see Percival still watching her. He raised an eyebrow in a silent question.

"I am fine. I do not need you to stand in my defense against one of my own people."

He shrugged and mounted his horse. "Get mounted. The caravan isn't going to wait on us." He rode ahead of the first of the wagons their group was responsible for.

Cora's legs and back were sore from spending every day for the last week on her horse. Her bedding did not feel soft enough to relieve the pain and even salves did not help. She did not think her backside could handle four more days in the saddle.

For the most part, the travel remained peaceful. Percival's tension while they rode continued. At night, he refused to begin conversations with her that kept him from concentrating on the area around them. His only response to her questions was to not worry—not much of a comfort.

Their travel this morning had started as the sun crested the horizon. As usual, the caravan broke camp quickly and continued the journey.

Cora rode between Satina and Percival. They passed through the old trees of the forest, the green bringing warm memories of home to her mind.

Behind her, she heard the chatter of Nimbly and Tylina's conversation. She glanced at Percival throughout the morning, his position to her left making it easy for her to do so. Watching their surroundings, he appeared more distracted than usual. A peace knot no longer locked his sword in the scabbard, the leather strips hanging loose.

She looked behind her, a long curve in the road letting her see the end of the caravan. She had not seen the three strangers following them recently. But she knew they were still there, somewhere. She felt their eyes watching her.

* * *

Percival glanced to his right when the feeling of being watched became overwhelming. He forced a brief smile at Cora, his eyes roaming over her features and her shapely figure, barely concealed under her long, flowing capeshal. Looking at her, he felt his heart race and his stomach tighten. The memory of the look in her eyes when he held her the night before they left still haunted him.

He gripped the leather reins for his horse tight, trying to control the urge he felt to reach out and take her hand in his. He grinned, the tension in his face relaxing for the moment.

He opened his mouth, prepared to ask what she was thinking. The distinct humming sound of an arrow flying through the air caught his attention. Movement entered his line of vision. His gaze locked with Cora's at the soft thudding sound of the arrow hitting its target. Her eyes grew wide with surprise, and her hands grabbed at the arrow protruding from her throat.

"Cora!" Percival shouted, jumping from his horse and grabbing her as she fell from her own.

Cora gasped for breath through the blood in her throat, tears pooling in her eyes. A cry from above, then the sound of something landing on the ground drew his attention. "Reyna," he whispered. An arrow also protruded from the bird. Regret gripped him as the bird's struggles to stand ended quickly and she lay dead in the dirt.

Satina appeared next to him. Without a word, she grabbed Cora from him, pushing his hands away. "Find who did this." She hissed the order, and gently resting Cora on the ground.

His rush of anger toward the Amazon disappeared quickly, replaced with the burn he always felt in combat. Another arrow flew through the air, embedding itself in his armor. He turned from the women, mounted again and spurred his horse in the direction of the attack.

He felt the bloodlust burning within him and knew his eyes glowed red with the fire that scared so many. His sword slipped naturally into his hand. Rushing to the trees, he followed Kalik, who had already headed in. They broke through the line of trees, pulling their horses to a stop.

Percival watched Kalik while the other man's sightless gaze searched the trees. After a brief moment, his hand came up and pointed to a tree a short distance from them. Without hesitation, Percival charged the tree, moving to stand on his saddle. He grabbed a branch as his horse galloped under it. Pulling himself up, he came face to face with the would-be assassin.

Tight fitting, green clothing covered the man Percival faced. He was thin, slightly muscular and pale skinned. A short sword hung from his belt and he held a shortened bow in his hand. He returned Percival's stare briefly. A heartbeat later, the other man jumped from the tree and landed with a crunch of leaves.

"Kalik!" Percival shouted as he jumped to the ground as well. Turning to give chase, he stopped when a large shadow moved through the trees. The sound of something flying through the air again followed the movement. The loud crunch of cracking bones echoed around him as he began to run after the escaping assassin.

Exar appeared behind him, both reaching the prone man at the same time. The bolas Exar had thrown bound the man's legs together, though one leg lay bent at an unnatural angle. Exar worked to disentangle the bolas while Percival dragged the man to his feet. Kalik joined them and the four returned to the caravan.

Percival found Nimbly before going to look for the caravan captain. "Nimbly, check for others. Kalik will show you where this one was found."

Chapter 22

When Nimbly and Kalik left to find any other attackers, Percival turned his attention to his prisoner. The longer he looked at the man, the angrier he became. He glanced toward Cora's rider-less horse. Percival directed his horse away from Exar, his mouth dry from the mix of emotions within him.

"Hold him until the caravan captain gives us a place to put him, Exar," Percival ordered.

The black leather clad man grunted in response, then pulled the man with him. A grumble of laughter reached Percival.

Trying to regain control of his emotions, the Black Hand rode his horse through the caravan line, meeting its captain midway.

"What happened, Captain Riesun? I am told someone was attacked," he asked, looking past Percival.

"Yes, Cora Rylannes was attacked We captured one person, but I believe there may be others," Percival explained.

The caravan captain nodded. "I will have someone take your prisoner. We have a cleric or two with us as well, if yours should need assistance."

"Thank you, Captain. We will let you know if we need anything. May we have the night to attempt to stabilize her?" Percival knew the night would not be enough, but he doubted the captain would allow them more time.

"I can give you the night, but anything more than that will cause a delay the merchant won't tolerate. Money is his concern, as I'm sure you are aware." The captain turned his horse toward the front of the caravan. "Meet with me in the morning so we can discuss matters further. Maintain your watches." The man rode away.

Percival stared at the man's back, took two deep breaths, and returned to the wagons his group protected. Nimbly and Kalik waited for him by the tree line.

"As far as I can tell, there were two others, but they seem to have disappeared." Nimbly's report did nothing to calm Percival. "We'll need to be cautious until they're caught."

Percival nodded, distracted by shouting suddenly coming from the closest wagon. "Of course we'll be cautious, Nimbly. That would only make sense." He looked back at the two. "Thank you. Keep your eyes open for anything else. Let me know if you see or hear anything."

Climbing into the wagon, he was not surprised to find Satina was the one shouting.

"Do not touch her again! I will not tolerate the lack of concern you are showing for the Princeesa!" Anger and frustration had changed Satina's face to a bright red.

"What is going on in here?" Percival demanded when she stopped for a breath.

Brolin looked at him and shook his head, returning his attention to the motionless form in front of him.

"He is hurting the Princeesa. I will not allow him to continue." Satina glared at Percival, her eyes widening when he returned her expression.

"You will allow Brolin to do what needs to be done to heal her. I will not allow her to die because of your stubbornness," he retorted.

Again, Satina glared at him, but she closed her mouth to hold her comment. Percival knelt next to Brolin just before the cleric placed his hand on the arrow.

Cora's body arched with pain. Her eyes opened, but she did not focus on anything around her. Pain coursed through his own body, as if it were an echo of the pain she felt. Why would he feel her pain? He pulled Brolin's hand from the arrow, his body and Cora's both relaxing, free of pain for the moment.

"Please, Brolin, stop. Just for a moment. Even the slightest touch is hurting her," Percival whispered. He knew Brolin needed to heal her, but her pain was overwhelming. He breathed deeply to control the memory of the pain.

Cora looked paler than when she had overused her magic in the underground city. Blood reddened her lips as if she wore lip stain. It covered her throat and upper chest and fresh blood flowed from the wound in a slow, steady stream around the arrow shaft. Brolin laid his hand on her throat again, the arrow between his thumbs and softly whispered words to call upon his deity's power to heal. As he spoke the last words, his hands glowed with a pale golden light that left his hands and surrounded the wound in Cora's flesh. Under his hands, the flow of blood ebbed slightly. Brolin looked at Percival and Satina, who maintained a silent vigilance.

"I have to remove the arrow. Doing so will tear the flesh worse. I need one of you to hold her down, the other to pull the arrow while I heal the wound. It has to be done right or she could bleed even worse and we put her at an even greater risk of dying." He waited only a moment, then reached out and grabbed Satina's hand. "We don't have time for a drawn out discussion, threats of what will happen to us if she dies or to even think about it. Satina, you pull the arrow. Percival, you hold her."

Satina turned her glare on the priest, yanked her hands from his, then calmed herself. She went to her knees and prepared to remove the arrow, her hands steady.

Percival found a blanket and carefully laid it over Cora, tucking it under her, then gently placed his upper body over her middle. He ensured her arms were under him and positioned himself so he could watch her face. Where he touched her, his skin tingled, and pain seeped into him. Again, the touch intensified a connection he didn't remember having with her before. Was it possible it had been there since the first time he helped her in the castle?

"Are we ready?" Brolin asked and received quick, positive answers from both. He again placed his hands around the arrow, allowing more room so it could be pulled out. The words of his spell filled the wagon. Nearing the end of his casting, he nodded to Satina.

At his command, Satina ripped the arrow from her princess' throat. Cora's body arched again, against Percival's weight, her mouth opened in a silent scream. Percival coughed against a sudden increase in pain in his throat, coming from Cora. The golden light from Brolin's hands flowed over the wound, closing it only slightly. A moment later, her body relaxed again as she slipped into what Percival hoped was painless oblivion.

He concentrated for a moment, then shook his head. No, not completely painless.

A glow from Brolin's hands and warmth in Percival's throat drew his attention back to the priest's ministrations. The wound closed a little more, but fresh blood still colored the jagged edge. He sat back and looked at Percival, careful not to look at Satina.

"My healing abilities are almost spent and her wound is barely healed. I will use my last spell for the day, bandage the wound and then begin my meditations. Did you find the person who did this?"

Percival nodded, lifting his head to see Satina examining the arrow. "We found one of them. Exar and Kalik have him until the Captain can provide more guards. But, Nimbly says there were two others they couldn't find. How long do you think it will be before you can heal her completely?"

Brolin shrugged, surprising Percival. "I am not sure. I would like to examine the prisoner's possessions to determine what he may have used to cause the wound to be so bad."

"We can arrange that. I'm sure they have removed all his possessions."

"Good. The arrow was deep. I do not know if she will be able to speak, even after she has been healed. See what you can get from the prisoner. I will tell you when I am done so someone can stay with her." He returned his attention to the young woman in front of him, dismissing the two without another word.

Percival stood, following Satina from the wagon.

Satina waited until he stood on the ground in front of her before brandishing the arrow at him. "If she dies, Black Hand, the queen will be very unhappy."

"I think that was the plan, Satina. Don't you?"

Chapter 23

After the sun set, Percival returned to the wagon. He had seen to burying Cora's bird, saving some of the feathers that had fallen out in her distress. He wanted to give them to Cora when she recovered in case she felt a need to keep them. It was a sentimental gesture and he did not know if she would understand. He just wanted to be with her when she woke.

So far, Satina had not allowed anyone to sit with Cora. The bodyguard needed to rest, or else she would be useless. He needed everyone alert in case there was another attack.

Satina glanced up from the spear she was sharpening when he lifted the flap that served as a door. "What do you want, Black Hand?" Her question came out in a growl.

"I am going to sit with her for you, so you can get some rest." He sat next to Cora, opposite the bodyguard and examined the dressings. "Brolin did good work on the bandages."

"For a man, he has done acceptable work. I do not need you to relieve me. I will sit with the Princeesa until she recovers." She returned her attention to the weapon.

Percival heard a tone of dismissal in her words, but chose to ignore it. "Stay tonight, but tomorrow you will share the duty with the rest of us." He caressed Cora's cheek, a gasp escaping him. He pulled his hand away.

Emptiness. He felt nothing. It was like she was a husk. He

touched her cheek again, this time resting his hand on her skin. Inexperienced with this strange connection, Percival struggled with understanding what he felt. No, he did feel her, deep inside. As if she was lost.

Of course she's lost to you, Black Hand. Even if she were to awaken from this state, she will not be the same. Just let her body rot. It would be easier for you. You can do nothing for her. Stromas' laughter filled his mind.

Shut up, demon. I don't need to hear from you right now. You had your say days ago.

Obviously I have more to say and I am no longer happy with our once a month conversations. Won't it be grand when I am in complete control?

Percival ignored the demonic voice in his head. Looking up, he found Satina's red, angry face inches from his.

"Are you purposely ignoring me, Black Hand?" Her eyes narrowed with her demand.

"I was thinking. I thought I felt her move when I touched her."

"Then I will repeat myself. Remove your hand."

Taking a moment to look past the Amazon's angered expression, Percival realized that she crouched in a ready position, her spear gripped tightly. She intended to fight him because she thought he ignored her.

"Do not presume to order me, Black Hand. You are only a man."

He stood slowly to ensure Satina did not misunderstand his movements. "You travel with us because of Cora, and through her command, you are a member of this group. I require everyone to be alert and if you refuse to rest, you will be of no use to Cora or anyone else." He lifted the cover to the wagon again, then glanced back at her. "You refuse to follow my orders, that's your choice. But you *will* have to answer to Cora for *your* actions. Don't expect me to follow your orders, though, just because I am a man." He exited the wagon, his angered step on the running board shaking it.

On the ground, he tried to walk away from his frustration, but Tylina cut him off. He stopped abruptly, his hand on his sword before he realized he held it.

Tylina rested a hand on his chest. "Calm, Percival. How is

Cora?" Her musical voice reached him through his emotional haze.

"She has not woken." He lifted his hand from his weapon, flexing his fingers to calm himself.

"Is Satina being obstinate?" Tylina laughed softly.

"Of course. She is worse than Cora is. At least Cora is willing to talk, to listen, to try to see things differently. At least she is…" He stopped at the grin on Tylina's face. "What are you smiling about?"

"Nothing really. When you are angry or fighting, your eyes burn with an intense fire. But when you talk about Cora, and even when you look at her, your eyes glow with a different fire, no less intense, but it doesn't scare me as the other does." Her answer came quietly as she reached to touch his arm. "And then, there was that moment in the sewer, when nothing else seemed to matter to you but her."

'*Nothing else seemed to matter to you but her.*' He repeated those words, silent in his contemplation. He returned his attention to his friend.

"Try to relieve Satina some time tonight." He patted Tylina's hand, removed it from his chest and strode away.

Walking through the small camp, Percival made his way to the cooking fire. He found a log to sit on, on the opposite side of the fire from the wagon, so the glow was between him and the wagon. Sitting, he rested his head in his hands and tried to block out the sounds around him.

He didn't understand how Tylina could see something in him that he had missed. Maybe he refused to see it. He always made sure he took care of Cora's needs before his own. He made sure she wanted for nothing. Unless it put the others in danger, then he would take the time to explain his decision to her when he wouldn't do that for anyone else. Was it just because of who she was? Was he afraid of what she could bring down on the kingdom?

He liked the challenge of finding ways to take care of Cora without insulting her. Even when they argued, he still enjoyed her company. He didn't think he was denying feelings for her. He thought about that night in her room again, the sewers and the castle when he first held her against her claustrophobia.

May he knew it, but kept silent, waiting for her to realize it.

He lifted his head to study his blackened left hand. He had searched for a way to reverse the curse ever since he was old enough to know the cause. Dread filled him every month when he had to deal with Stromas. Despite this, he stayed with King Kennan for almost six years and traveled with Cora for three. He had never committed to anyone else like that.

The curse made his temper shorter. It became worse as the black moon approached. Without even realizing it, he was giving Stromas more control.

Cora's injury affected him in ways he was not expecting. Even though he had already faced Stromas for the month, his anger felt stronger and more intense than before the confrontation. If he hadn't turned her would-be assassin over to the caravan guards, he knew he would have killed the man with his bare hands. The overwhelming desire to kill the man for what he did to the Amazon princess washed over Percival again, like lava flowing from a volcano. His need to find the person who ordered the attempt tempered the emotion into a finely honed blade.

Pulling his thoughts back to Tylina's words, it was easier to accept that he wanted to hold Cora and take her pain away. He felt as if he betrayed her trust with his inability to protect her. Even now, he wanted to go to her.

Struck first by doubt, then the realization of his need to be with her, he looked past his hand, at the wagon she laid in. He wanted to love her openly and for her to love him in return. But would she be able to do that? The emotions had been with him, though he did not know when it began. He knew he felt incomplete when they were separated. But he wondered if he would be able to make her truly happy. Could she have feelings for him despite the demon within him? Maybe he could show her a new way to live. He pushed away the doubt he felt and stood, determined to not let Satina keep him from Cora.

Heat from behind hit him in the back, forcing him forward. Turning, his hand going to his sword, he found the three individuals that had been following the group. Their hands glowed brighter than the rest of their bodies. The glow reached toward him, as if it were a hand or weapon.

Percival tried to retreat from the glow, drawing his weapon. "What in the hells do you want?"

A growl next to him distracted him momentarily. Exar stood next to him, his own weapons in hand. Together, the two attacked the wall of heat trying to engulf Percival. Their weapons slid through the heat without affect.

Percival brought his sword up to strike again, intent with moving closer to the individuals trying to hurt him. Instead of obeying his mental command, his sword arm remained at his side. *What? Why can't I move?* He tried again to move his arm and to take a step closer to them, but could not move any part of his body.

See, Black Hand? I am getting stronger and you are becoming weaker. It won't be long before I am in total control. Stromas' laughter filled his mind.

"Let me go!" Percival spoke aloud. The three individuals glared at him. They sent a gush of heat at him again, then disappeared. When the last of the heat disappeared from his skin, he regained movement and control of his body.

"What in all the hells was that about?" Exar demanded.

"I don't know, Exar."

"Well, you better figure it out before I get killed because of your ineptitude." Exar stormed away, not giving Percival the chance to respond.

Chapter 24

In the morning, while they packed their supplies, the caravan captain came to the group and pulled Percival aside. "What happened last night? I understand that your group was attacked again."

"No, I was attacked," Percival clarified.

"Black Hand, I agreed to your coming with us because of Duke Orenda and your service to the king. None of that will matter if the problems with your group continue. One more incident and I will be forced to separate you from us. You are already delaying us and I cannot allow it to become a problem." He turned away from Percival. "I will try to keep a slower pace, but if the merchant wants us to travel faster, then we will do it. Do I make my position clear enough?"

Percival nodded. "Yes, Captain. Perfectly."

The caravan continued its journey to the city of Jonquil. Percival received small comfort from the fact that the prisoner had been taken farther up the line of the caravan and now rode a horse that he had also been tied to. Satina insisted on driving the wagon Cora rested in, but Percival rode next to it, despite her complaints. He would not allow her to keep him from Cora.

Percival caught Satina glaring at him from time to time. Instead of returning the look, he favored her with a smirk. Her surprised expression made him smile even bigger.

The day passed by uneventful, a fact that again brought no comfort to Percival. Things were too quiet and they were being followed by too many people for the calm to be a good sign.

When darkness fell on the land, the caravan stopped its travel and made camp for the night. After helping the others setup their tents and taking time to eat evening meal, Percival returned to the wagon and climbed inside. Satina stared at him, her emotions poorly concealed.

"She is no different now than she was at mid-meal."

"I've come to relieve you for the night. It's time you got some rest." Percival removed his sword belt and laid it on the floor.

Satina's face filled with hatred. She stood, taking a step toward him. "I will rest when I feel it is necessary. Until then, you will mind your own."

"You will let me see her, Satina. She needs more than you can offer." He stepped to her left, going to his knee next to Cora.

Reaching out, he touched her cheek again. She still felt lost within her own mind. He had never experienced anything like this before. How could he help her find a way back to them if he didn't understand what was happening?

Unsure of what to do, Percival imagined a light in his own mind that traveled through his right hand, and into the darkness of Cora's mind. Maybe that would help her.

He stood and faced Satina. "I will be back at the end of first watch. Be prepared to leave when I return."

Without waiting for her angered response, he retrieved his sword belt and left the wagon.

Chapter 25

Darkness surrounded Cora. She felt weightless, as if she floated in water. *Where am I? How long have I been like this?*

She didn't understand how she arrived here. The last thing she remembered was being struck by an arrow and Percival holding her on the ground. He had looked so scared, just for a moment, then his eyes burned with fire and he left her.

That should not bother her, but it did. He left her when she needed him. At least he proved to her quickly that he could not be counted on. Only took three years and one promise.

A light brightened an area of the darkness and she turned in its direction. Something about the light drew her to it. Swimming through the darkness made it easier for her to move toward the light.

White light combined with gold. *Two lights, different colors, but so close to each other. Will one of them take me back?*

Cora swam closer to the white light. Pain gripped her, contracting her limbs, forcing her eyes closed. Instinct curled her into a ball, her knees tight against her chest. Thoughts became lost in the pain and she drifted through the darkness uncontrolled.

Cora floated until the pain began to decrease and she

could open her eyes. *I've moved away from the light some. Maybe if I try—* She tried to pull magic from the darkness around her. Magic coalesced within her, but the energy felt less, weaker. *What's happened? I can't feel Reyna or draw my magic.*

Cora looked toward the white light. *The gold light, it's changed.* The gold light, still next to the white light, changed to blue with red edges. The two lights hovered close to each other. *Is that my way out of this? Is that why it's a different color? If so, why is it so close to the one that causes me pain?* A small, silent laugh escaped her. *Because coming out of this means I have to face the pain of the wound that put me here. But I can't stay here.*

With her mind, she pushed herself toward the blue light. Pain ripped through her body again. She made one more desperate thrust toward the light before she crushed her knees against her chest. Closer to the blue light, she felt herself pulled into it.

Pain clouded her vision when she opened her eyes. She screamed, but no sound came out. The darkness was gone, replaced with the light of a lantern.

* * *

Placing another log of wood on the campfire, Percival prepared to begin his walk of the camp when pain tore through his throat. He swallowed against it, painful gulps that did nothing to relieve the pain. "What in Shae's name is this?" he gasped, swallowing again, this time clearing some of the pain away.

He took another step. Pain again raged through his throat and his chest. Then a sudden 'waking' sensation washed over him. Cora was awake!

Percival ran to the back of the wagon, throwing the cover aside to step inside. "Cora!"

"Leave us, Black Hand! We do not need you here." Satina kicked her spear up into her hand and swung it around. The tip landed against his chest.

"Move aside, Satina," Percival demanded. "I'm done with this."

"And I am done with you, Black Hand. You hold no control over me," she growled at him, pushing the spear against his skin more.

Percival glanced at the spear pressing into his flesh. He looked at her again, slowly letting his anger rise in his eyes. When their eyes met, hers grew wide. He saw his fire reflected in her eyes. She set her feet firm though and kept the spear level. The tip pierced his skin, a small drop of blood forming on the metal.

"Are you sure you want to do this, Satina?" False calm filled his voice. He knew he had to reach a real calm or the anger would take control.

The two stared at each other. The silence in the covered wagon grew heavier with each passing moment.

A knock on the wood behind Satina broke the tension building between them. Together, they looked away from each other to find the source. Cora lay on her left side, her expression filled with pain.

She closed her eyes for a heartbeat, then opened them again and glared at Satina. Mouthing the words, "Get out," she waved at the back of the wagon.

"But, Princeesa, I am…" Satina pulled her weapon away from Percival, protesting the obvious order from her princess.

Cora knocked on the wood again. She waited a moment, her eyes closing once again. Opening her eyes, she repeated the order for her bodyguard to leave.

Satina returned Cora's glare, then stormed out of the wagon. Percival waited for the flap to settle before relaxing his anger with deep breaths.

"She won't be happy when she returns, Cora." He finally sat next to her.

She nodded and shrugged her shoulders, relaxing in the cushion of her makeshift bed. Extra blankets from their friends and other members of the caravan had been used to make the floor of the wagon comfortable for her.

"You left me," Cora mouthed, flashing Percival a brief look of anger before pain marred her beauty again.

"What? I didn't leave you," he protested.

She closed her eyes and for a moment, he thought she had lost consciousness. However, she opened her eyes again and nodded.

"After attack. You left me."

He tried to recall what he could have done to make her think he left her, then realization filled him. "Only for a few minutes. I had to find the one who attacked you. Didn't Satina tell you?"

She shook her head.

"I couldn't let them get away. Kalik and I found one, but there were two more. We didn't find them." Not finding the others still angered him, but he didn't want her to see how much. "I will find them, Cora. I promise."

Percival gently brushed her hair from her face. She was hurting herself, trying to talk to him. "You need to rest, stop trying to talk."

She lifted one of her shoulders, then shifted, moving closer to the warmth of his body. Percival breathed deeply. To keep her quiet, he would have to do all the talking tonight.

"You asked me why I leave every month. A demon is confined within my body. That is what I fight every month. My father placed the demon there. He made me a slave to this demon. Stromas, his name is Stromas. Because of this slavery my father forced me into, I deplore the idea of slavery, seeing anyone enslaved, just slavery overall." He glanced at her when he felt her move.

She tried to say something, her hand going to her throat.

"No, don't talk. Don't even try. You can wait to say whatever you want until you are healed." She pointed at her chest. "Yes, I know. Your people keep slaves, male slaves. You and Satina have made that quite clear over the time we've been together. But that doesn't change the way I feel about it." With a gentle touch, Percival smoothed her hair, rubbing several strands between his fingers. "Why did you come here? To learn about Man's World, and the way we live. There have been some things you've adopted, I've seen it. You do not treat me as you did at the beginning. You allow me to be who I am and do not require that I bow to you.

"I've enjoyed my time traveling with you. The trouble you cause me isn't always bad, and even when we argue, I still enjoy it." He admired the smooth skin of her cheeks, her beautiful eyes. "I'm not expressing myself well enough. I would like us to be more than just friends and traveling companions, if you have any feelings for me. I care about you, Cora, in ways I never felt possible."

Her eyes widened and she started mouthing words so quickly he could not understand her. He placed a finger against her lips, stopping further protests.

"Cora, I can't understand you. Rest, we can talk about it

later, after you are better."

She nodded, closing her eyes again.

She didn't move away from him. He waited for her to adjust her position, pressing her back against his side. Stretching out, he tried to get comfortable for the night.

Chapter 26

Cora laid in the pre-dawn darkness, and listened to Percival breathe. The tension in his face showed in the flickering light of the dying lantern. Even in his sleep, he fought for control of his temper and his body. She wondered what images played in his dreams.

His announcement had shocked her. Amazons did not take mates out of love. What if she was wrong and that wasn't what he meant?

She had made so many changes to her way of thinking since she met him. She wasn't prepared for the person or problems he presented. Her vision had been so vague of details. And she didn't expect something like this to happen. Was this a step she was prepared to take?

The memory of how she felt when they touched returned to her. Being near him now was a comfort. She didn't know when it happened, but she'd come to depend on him to always be close by, protecting her. That did not help against the men who hurt her though. Maybe she had become too dependent on him and changing their relationship would be a weakness that could kill them both.

But if she denied the way he made her feel, would she be able to live without him? Of course she knew she could, but would she want to? How could she return to the more restricted life of an Amazon now that she had lived away from it for so long?

Still unsure of how she felt about Percival's words, Cora repositioned herself carefully on her makeshift bed. Uncertainty filled her as she reached out and rested her hand on his chest. The tension in his face relaxed a little and his breathing slowed more.

Why did her touch affect him like that? Even through his shirt, she felt his warmth and the electricity of her reaction to him. Surely a demon could not be soothed with just a touch.

Unless the demon had a desire of his own.

Chapter 27

Cora's injuries hindered travel. To keep from jostling her, the caravan captain agreed to slow their pace. Though he and Percival had come to an agreement, the merchant made sure everyone knew of his displeasure with the delay.

While they traveled, each member of the group took turns driving the wagon. Percival insisted on taking the longest shifts. He knew the others would drive carefully, but he trusted his control more.

A quick glance in the back of the wagon revealed Cora still slept. At least he hoped she was sleeping.

Satina rode next to the wagon. She glared at anyone who even glanced in her direction. Every time Percival wanted to sit with Cora, Satina argued with him. For almost two weeks, she kept the anger burning. Percival looked over at the Amazon, confirming she still wore a scowl. He shook his head in disbelief. Only Shae understood how she had the energy.

Invoking the name of the war god, even in his thoughts, did not bring Percival the peace it normally did. He never told Cora they worshipped the same deity. She had been so angry the first time she went into one of the god's temples after they started traveling together. She took the image of the god as a man as a personal insult.

Movement from the wagon drew Percival's attention again, and he handed the horse's reins to Tylina, who sat next to him. "I will be right back."

She nodded, repositioning herself. Percival climbed over the seat and into the wagon. He knelt next to Cora, touching her hand. The thrashing that had drawn his attention to her stopped at his touch.

She had gotten worse despite Brolin's healing. The wound resisted all healing cast upon it. Percival swore he had even seen it get worse instead of better. He adjusted the blanket covering her chest. Red streaks traced through her flesh, from the wound and around her neck, down her chest. Since the night he told her how he felt, she had barely been able to stay awake longer than a few moments at a time. She was too weak. If they didn't figure out what was wrong soon, he was afraid he would lose her.

"Percival!" Tylina called for him, her voice filled with excitement. "I can see Jonquil. We're almost there."

Percival returned to the driver's seat and sighed in relief at the sight of the walled city they approached. "Finally."

The afternoon sun burned above the caravan upon its arrival at the walls of Jonquil. Percival could not be sure how long they traveled around the city to reach the warehouse district. He waited for the wagons in front of theirs to go through before reaching the city guards.

When their wagon approached the guards, the men bowed their heads to Tylina. "Lady Orenda, your message was delivered to your mother and our captain. We have arranged for a cleric to meet you at your mother's estate. We hope this meets with your approval."

Tylina nodded, smiling at Percival. "That is wonderful. Thank you."

Guiding their wagon through the warehouses, Percival continued to follow the caravan wagon. When they arrived at the warehouse, he left the wagon with Satina and went inside. After finding the merchant and the caravan captain, he prepared himself for their anger.

"Captain Riesun, I am not happy with the delay your group caused me. I'm sure it will affect my sales in the market." The merchant was the first to speak, his anger pouring from his words.

"And I apologized for the delay numerous times. It was not something we expected. However, I'm sure your goods will sell, in their entirety, before the season closes."

"What makes you think that? You know nothing about the market, the prices, or the season."

Percival struggled to control his rising anger. "You have thrown this tirade every day for almost the last two weeks. It changes nothing. You are four days later than you expected. Nothing I can do will change that." The merchant balked. Before he had a chance to respond, Percival continued, turning to the captain. "I can't put her on a horse, you know that. If I could use the wagon, at least to get her to the Orenda Estate or a temple, I will be sure to return it to you as soon as I can."

The captain nodded. "Take it. Return it when Cora is better. I am in no rush. I will not need it for several weeks, until the end of the season." He ignored the huffed breathing from the merchant, leading Percival away. "Don't worry about him. I will handle it. Smoke bird has been sent to Duke Orenda as well. If we have any further problems the Duke will take care of any compensation he feels the merchant is entitled to."

"Thank you, Captain." Percival shook hands with the man and returned to the wagon.

With their business complete, and money paid to the group for their work, Percival led the others from the warehouse. Before he could direct the wagon onto the main road, a gilded carriage stopped in front of him, blocking his path. A beautiful elven woman in a green gown stood next to it. Tylina jumped from the wagon and ran to the woman, embracing her. After a moment, the half-elf turned to the group.

"This is my mother, Lady Elsena Orenda."

Percival drove the wagon closer to the two women. "It is a pleasure to meet you, Lady Orenda. Cora needs attention. Can we take the pleasantries to your estate?"

"Of course, Captain Riesun. I have arranged for a cleric to meet you at my home. Please follow me." Lady Orenda ascended into her carriage, pulling Tylina with her. The carriage began to move, the others following with Percival coming last.

After leaving the warehouse district, they traveled through

the merchant district, avoiding the main market place. Percival ignored the city around him, intent on keeping Lady Orenda's carriage in sight.

When the carriage slowed, he pulled back on the reins and looked at the estate in front of him. Flowers grew in a controlled fashion. Decorative spires reached for the sky, an attempt by its elven mistress to bring her culture's influence into the design. Ivy crept over the walls and trees grew in positions that would provide the most shade to the house on a hot summer day.

Percival drove the wagon onto the estate grounds, the sound of the horse's hooves clacking noisily on the cobblestone. Two horses waited in front of the double doors leading into the home. A servant was tying the reins to a post. When he finished, he ran to help Lady Orenda from her carriage. Tylina left without assistance and walked over to Percival.

"I will be back in a moment with help."

Percival grunted, then left the wagon when she entered the house. He paced the cobbled driveway next to the wagon. After glancing at the house three times, he changed his path and tromped toward the front door, his impatience winning out.

Tylina stepped out of the house, followed by four servants and a carrier for Cora, lined with blankets. She gestured at the servants. "They can carry her easier with this."

He nodded, stepping back, out of the way. Satina refused to follow his lead. Percival cringed at her tone as she gave instructions on the best way to move Cora from the wagon and into the house.

Despite Satina's interference, the servant's finally carried Cora into the house. Satina followed closely, with Kalik, Nimbly and Tylina behind her. Before Percival followed, Exar blocked his path.

"I am leaving," Exar informed Percival. "Good-bye, Black Hand." Without waiting for a response, the large figure turned, mounted his horse and rode from the estate.

Percival watched him leave, unable to stop him. He couldn't follow Duke Orenda's directive if Exar wasn't with them.

A light touch on his shoulder drew his attention. Lady Orenda stood behind him, watching Exar leave the estate as well. "Do not worry, Captain Riesun. Exar is not stupid enough to stay in my home, especially without knowing how much I know about him." Lady Orenda tried to comfort him. "I will ensure he is informed of when you are leaving and make it quite clear he is to leave with you."

Percival stared at her as she returned to the house, then followed her.

Chapter 28

While the estate in Glenys showed more of the duke's influence, this home held more of Lady Orenda's culture. The interior of the house held paintings of Duke Orenda's family. Gold candlesticks rested upon shelves and fireplace mantles. Books filled a sitting room and lace curtains covered all windows. Inside the front door, a large staircase led to the second floor and Percival could see the others waiting outside the room he assumed Cora had been taken to. He made his way upstairs to join them.

"Where is Nimbly?" he asked, searching the hall for the elf.

"I sent him to keep an eye on Exar." Kalik whispered.

"Good." Percival rested a hand on Tylina's shoulder, then walked into the room.

Lady Elsena stood next to the door and looked at him when he entered. Before he could close the door, she took it from his hand and left the room. He heard her whispers before the door closed behind her.

Satina leaned against the wall next to the bed Cora lay in, opposite the door. She glanced at him, scowling. Two men also stood near the bed, whispering to each other.

"Why are you standing around? Shouldn't you be doing something for Cora?" Percival's anger filled the room.

"We are discussing the best way to do it. The wound has

mended, on its own, actually quite a bit, but not necessarily in the correct way. That is why she is still unable to speak, or would be, if she were conscious. The red streaks lead me to believe she was poisoned. Do you still have the arrow?"

Percival nodded, pulling the tip of the arrow from his pouch. Cora's dried blood crusted the metal, and flaked off in his hand. He had never heard of a poison affecting a victim like this one did.

"I will have to check this. I believe they must have used something that would work against the magic we would use to heal her, if she should survive the original attack." The older of the two men examined the arrow tip. "I'm surprised your cleric didn't try to cure poison when he saw the red streaks."

"Me too." Percival glanced toward the door. He would have to ask Brolin why he didn't try to neutralize the poison. "Will that work? Will getting rid of the poison allow you to heal her?"

"I have more experience and more powerful spells than your companion, Black Hand. I'm sure I can cure the poison and heal her. She will still need time to heal though. This is a lot of stress for her body and throat to handle. I suggest you wait to continue whatever journey you may have planned until she is completely healed."

Percival nodded. "Nothing we are doing is so important that we need to put her at risk. We will wait."

Satina pushed off the wall toward them. "Do something for her now, Old Man. Your delay is annoying me." Her demand tightened the cords of muscles in Percival's throat.

"Satina, calm yourself or you will have to leave." Percival interposed himself, sure Satina would try to hurt the old priest. "The sooner you do this, priest, the happier we will all be."

"Of course. Give us a few moments more to prepare." The old man turned back to his companion and began whispering again.

Percival sat on the bed opposite Satina and took Cora's hand in his. The magic tingling he always felt when he touched her felt weak against his skin, barely a tickle. If the cleric didn't heal Cora, she would probably die. What would he do if that happened? He reached out with his mind, trying to touch her through their connection again. Pain overwhelmed him, clouding his vision. He placed a hand out to catch himself as he started to fall forward. Releasing her hand, the connection was lost. How was she still alive with that kind of pain?

"You will leave, Black Hand." Satina's sharp words cut into his thoughts.

He glanced up, hiding his emotions. The Amazon could not know how that statement affected him. "I've told you, Satina, you will not give me orders. I will do what I want and I will only leave if Cora says she doesn't want me here."

A light touch on his leg called his attention to Cora. Bruises discolored her eyes and the flesh had sunken in, making her cheeks more prominent. The usual deep blue of her eyes had faded to a sky blue. Her face was still pale and her tan had begun to fade. Despite the pallor, he still found her beautiful.

With weak movements, slowed more so by pain, Cora gestured at Satina. "Both stay, or you go," she mouthed the words to Satina, forcing her bodyguard to make the decision. Her eyes closed again, her strength spent from her effort. Her hand remained on Percival's leg, a weak grip keeping the contact.

Percival sneered at Satina in triumph, and repositioned himself so the cleric could reach Cora easily. The older Amazon glared at him in return, her hands clenched in white knuckled fists. Sitting on the bed, she took Cora's other hand in hers.

Finally, the cleric separated from his assistant and clapped his hands once. "I am ready to begin." He took a step toward Satina, hesitated, then bustled past Percival to place himself next to Cora.

Magical words filled the room as the cleric began to cast his spell to remove the poison from Cora's body. The flow of magic that went into her warmed Percival's hand. A golden light enveloped the priest's hands and cascaded over Cora's neck.

Percival watched the wound, wanting to see an improvement. Instead, the red streaks that wrapped around her throat started to recede.

"Now, I will heal the wound itself," the cleric whispered.

Again, the golden light enveloped his hands, this time flowing into the wound. His words increased in intensity. Cora's body arched, her grip tightening on his hand.

Percival rested his black hand on her leg, his normal

reluctance to touch her with it forgotten in his concern. He caressed her while whispering words of comfort. Though he knew she couldn't hear him, he felt better talking to her.

After what felt like hours, the cleric straightened. He nodded to Percival. "She should be fine. Let her rest. She will need to give her throat time to recover and remember how to speak again. Delayed healing such as this can often be more stressful than the initial injury." He shook Percival's hand, looked as if he would try the same with Satina, but must have decided against it. With a wave and a smile, the two men left the room.

Percival and Satina stared at each other in silence until a knock on the door broke the growing tension. Without an invitation, Lady Orenda entered the room.

"His Holiness informs me Cora will be fine." Percival nodded. "Good. You are all welcome to stay here while you attend to your business. I will enjoy my time with Tylina." She rested a hand on Cora's foot. "Food has been prepared. Please come downstairs and eat."

He watched the elven woman leave, then turned to Satina. "Go ahead. I'll sit with Cora while you get something to eat."

"I will send Tylina to sit with her." Her tone left no room for argument—or so she thought.

"Satina, this is ridiculous. Cora has already told you I can be with her in your absence." He sighed. The anger he normally felt at the Amazon's stubbornness did not fill him. He just wanted to be left alone with Cora.

"The Princeesa does not know what she is doing when you are near her. You muddle her mind with thoughts and ideas an Amazon should never have." Satina released Cora's hand and stormed from the room before he could respond.

He sat in silence, then skirted around the bed to the empty chair. Leaning forward, his head resting on his arms, he watched Cora sleep.

Chapter 29

Percival sat on the bed rubbing Cora's legs, the same thing he had done every night for five days. Since the first night at the Orenda estate, he sent positive thoughts through their connection; first asking, then demanding Cora wake up. Every night since their arrival, he had argued with Satina about sitting with Cora. He just wanted her to wake up longer than just the few minutes it took to sip two spoonsful of broth.

"Would you stop that? It hurts." A hoarse voice, barely a whisper, reached him from the head of the bed.

Looking up, he found Cora elevated on one elbow, gazing at him through half-closed eyes. "Cora?" He released her leg, and grabbed her in an embrace. "Finally! We were so worried."

She returned the embrace, then pushed him away. "I'm hungry."

"Of course." He left the room and rushed to find Tylina.

She sat in the tearoom with her mother, both looking up in surprise when he stormed into the room. "Really, Percival. It isn't necessary to run through the house."

"Yes, Cora is awake. Do we have anything—?"

Lady Orenda stood, interrupting Percival. "Of course. I will have the cooks prepare a thicker soup for her. It will be easier for her to swallow and give her something more substantial in her stomach. I'll send some more broth until the soup is done."

Percival watched her leave the room, then turned to Tylina. "Would you bring the others to Cora's room? I think it's time to explain a few things. I'll be the first. Maybe Cora will follow my example."

She nodded and left the room to find the rest of the group. Percival returned to Cora's room, a servant from the kitchen behind him with a small bowl of broth and bread. He took the tray from the servant and set it on the table next to the bed.

"Lady Orenda is having a thicker soup made for you, but I think she wanted you to have something, even something small, while you wait."

Cora accepted the bowl and bread after positioning pillows behind her and sitting up. "Thank you."

Her voice didn't sound any better. How long was it going to take her voice to return to normal?

Before he could answer, Satina came into the room. "Princeesa, finally you wake."

Cora nodded. "Yes." She glanced at Percival, scrunching her eyes at him, a one-sided smile lifting the corner of her mouth. "Supplies. Retrieve what I need," she forced her strained voice to speak.

"But..." Satina bowed her head. "Of course, Princeesa. I assume you will need the usual items." Again, Cora nodded. "Then I will return before sunset." She turned, glared at Percival and left the room.

"Rest your voice, Cora. Don't overdo it." He stood at the foot of her bed. "The others will be joining us soon. I want to make sure everyone understands what we are facing."

She opened her mouth to speak again, but the door opened again, interrupting her.

Percival watched the others settle into chairs while Tylina sat on the bed with Cora. He began to pace the room, his chest and face flushing with embarrassment and nervousness. Finally, he stopped and looked at Cora again

"Since Cora has been attacked once already, and we know two others are still out there, as well as someone who is trying to kill me, I feel it's time to tell you what I face every month. I want you to know on the chance I am not there during the next attack." He took a deep breath.

"When I was a little over one summer old, my father

attempted to summon a greater demon. It was more powerful than he realized. It threatened to break free of his restraining spells. In an attempt to keep it confined, my father put me into the summoning circle, then cast a spell that threw the demon into me. I am like a living container for the demon. Until I was thirteen summers, the demon was too weak to do much. That summer, he tried to break free. I was able to remain in control, but now I fight him on a monthly basis. His power is strongest during the black moon, weaker during the rest of the month. When I leave you, I am fighting to keep the demon under control and within his restraints created by my body. The longer I wait to do this each month, the weaker I become." He studied his hands, then wiped them on the legs of his breeches.

"Being a greater demon, he is short tempered and that affects me. When the demon entered my body, my left hand started turning black—a sign of the curse I'm forced to live with. It has grown over the years to what you see now. My father tied my fate to something dark and I don't know what will happen if I lose control." He waited for a reaction.

The group sat in silence, staring at him. He felt their scrutiny—their judgment—with each breath.

When the silence continued for more than two drops of the water clock, he cleared his throat. "Did you understand me?" he asked, cautious.

"Yes, Black Hand." Cora spoke for the others, despite his warning. Her voice cracked over the words. "Why would your father use you, instead of releasing the demon from his summons, back to its own world?"

"Please, Cora, stop talking."

Her shoulders lifted in a frustrated shrug.

Percival shook his head, then continued. "My father hungered for the power he thought the demon could give him. To release the demon would be to admit defeat in controlling a superior creature." Percival turned toward Kalik. "Can I count on you, Kalik, to protect Cora and the others in my absence?"

"Of course, Black Hand. There should never be a question." Kalik's voice indicated there should have been no doubt.

"Good. In two days, I meet with some of the local mages to find out if they know of any way to remove or banish the demon. Will you come with me, Cora?" Percival wanted her with him, but worried it would be too soon.

Cora nodded, choosing now to close her mouth tight.

Tylina smiled and stood from the bed. "I hope the mages have something useful for you, Percival. I am going to check on the food my mother promised Cora."

"Before you go, I have one further thing. I have already been told about a mage who may be able to help me, Arch Mage Wintress. His tower is in the Winter Forest. If the mages here have no answers, will you join me on that journey as well?"

"We have joined together in a common cause, Percival. We have no reason to leave you now," Brolin spoke up.

Kalik nodded. "I'm sure Nimbly will agree." He turned to Cora. "We will go now. Cora still needs to rest, especially if we want to leave soon." He and Brolin followed Tylina from the room.

Percival waited for the door to close, then walked over and sat next to Cora on the bed. "Are you feeling any better?"

She nodded.

"I have something to give you." He reached into one of his pouches and removed a folded cloth. "I am so sorry I was not able to do anything for her. I buried her, though." Opening the folds, Reyna's feathers lay in his hand.

Cora stared at the feathers, then reached out to touch them. "Oh, Reyna," she whispered.

"We can attach them to your spear, that way she is always with you. I will help you."

Cora nodded, folding the feathers back into the cloth. She took the cloth from him and set it on the table next to the bed.

Percival cleared his throat. "I need to know if you have ever felt a connection between us, Cora."

She squinted, her forehead furrowing. "What?" she mouthed.

"Ever since we were in the sewers, after your claustrophobic incident, I have felt something in my head, like a tickle, or a bird stuck in a cage." He breathed, trying to find the words. "But since your injury, I have been able to feel some of your pain. I knew when you woke up. I could feel when you were lost in the darkness before that. I feel connected to you, through something that has to do with the magic we seem to have together."

She stared at him, then nodded again. "I have felt something, too. I don't know what it is, but I feel it," she croaked.

"We will need to find out, especially if you don't want…"

Cora's hand on his stopped him. "I want a bath."

He nodded at her whispered request, reached out to touch her cheek, but stopped himself before contact. She had not agreed to be more than his traveling companion. He didn't want to push her away.

"I will get the servants to bring up water for you." A knock at the door surprised them both and he stood abruptly from the bed. "Come in."

Servants came in with buckets of water and filled the tub in the corner. The two watched in silence, until they finished. When the servants left, after ensuring Cora had clean towels, soaps and lotions, Percival returned his attention to Cora.

"I guess Tylina beat me to it."

Cora nodded, throwing the blankets off her. Percival looked away, but not before he saw her legs. She wore only a shirt – a man's shirt. He didn't remember her buying the shirt, or having one before. He felt his cheeks flush, remembering the way the shirt exposed more of her chest than he expected.

She touched his arm. "A little unsteady. Help me?"

Even in a whisper, her voice was still beautiful. "Of course." He turned back to her, put his arm around her waist and helped her walk toward the tub.

When she stood next to the tub, he rested her hand on the edge and retreated from her. "I'll have Tylina come in to help you and send Satina to you as soon as she comes back."

"You're leaving?" She reached for his hand, grabbing his arm instead.

"Yes, Cora. Right now, you need to take care of yourself. We can talk later." He removed her hand from his arm and left the room.

When he stood on the other side of the door, Percival dry washed his face, giving his beard a scratch. Walking away from Cora proved more difficult than he expected. And the image he created in his mind of her bathing would definitely stay with him until he saw the real thing.

If he ever did.

Chapter 30

Two days later, after midday meal, Cora and Percival stood in front of the mage tower. The building reached for the sky, its stonewalls sprinkled with windows. No flags flapped in the weak breeze. Nothing to indicate they were expected.

Lady Orenda had expedited a meeting with the mage council for Percival, though he had not asked for it. Cora had not been in the room for their conversation, but he told her he had only asked for a name. Maybe he didn't want her to know he gave in to desperation.

A boy greeted them at the door, a silent nod his only acknowledgement of their introductions. He ushered them into an entryway, then gestured for them to wait.

Once the boy returned, he gestured for them to follow. He led them to the first floor council room. The chamber appeared larger than the tower could accommodate, the ceiling twenty feet above them. The room stretched into darkness beyond Cora's ability to see and their footsteps echoed in the expanse. A long table stood in front of them, approximately fifteen strides from the entrance. At the table, four men waited, their hands crossed on top of the wood. When the door closed behind the two, the men stood in greeting.

"Welcome Captain Riesun, Princess Rylannes," the tallest of the four spoke first. "Please have a seat."

Two chairs appeared in front of the table. Cora and Percival crossed the floor to them, when the mage gestured for them to approach. Once they were seated, the room remained silent as the two groups studied each other. Finally, the one who had spoken cleared his throat noisily.

"We understand you are seeking information on an affliction you suffer from. Your father is known to us, as well as what he did to you. We have completed research for you. What we found indicates you need to go on a journey, a painful one, but you will find the answers you seek if you keep your eyes open." He pulled a map out and pushed it across the table toward Percival. "This map has detailed directions to the Tower of Winter. Mage Wintress should be able to help you further, or at least guide you better toward any item that will help against your affliction."

"That's it?" Percival stood in frustration. "Do you mages find it amusing to only give me information in the form of riddles? You give me partial answers. Don't you realize what I suffer from, how long I've tried to find answers?"

"Yes, we understand. We've seen what happens to others who have been forced to endure what you have suffered since infancy. No one else has survived as long as you have. You should feel some form of satisfaction in that. At least you live today to continue your search." Another mage defended himself and his companions.

"You've done this to others?" Cora could not contain her shock. Maybe her mother was right. Maybe men really were as destructive as she said.

"Many mages have tried to duplicate what Mage Riesun did. As cruel as it may seem, it was an attempt by some of us to understand the process so we could free the captain as well as others that may be forced to endure the same," a third mage responded.

"How nice of you. You expect us to believe you did that to help him? Or more likely, you did it to help yourselves? Or did you do it to try to gain the power for yourself?" Sarcasm filled Cora's words. "Now that you've discovered none can survive but Percival, does your experimenting continue?"

"No. The pain and death it caused was too high a price. Percival must discover his catalyst on his own. Perhaps you can help him. Now, please take the map and continue your journey. We have our studies to return to." The fourth and final mage dismissed them with a wave of his hand.

Percival planted his feet, his determination to stay evident.

"No, Percival. These men are useless and don't deserve the power they were born with." Cora pulled on his arm. "We will find another way."

He stared at her, his anger lighting the fire in his eyes. Instead of answering, he turned away from the mages.

"Princess Rylannes, that was uncalled for," the first mage declared. His companions nodded, their faces flushed in embarrassment.

The man's words stopped Cora from following Percival. "You are quite right. It was uncalled for."

The mages nodded again, their faces smug.

"Your apology is accepted, but only because we know how difficult it is for an Amazon to apologize to a man," the first mage said, waving his hand in dismissal again.

Cora raised her own hand, her magic responding to her mental summons instantly. The man's hand stopped moving and his mouth fell open in surprise.

"You misunderstand me. You are quite right that your careless dismissal of Percival was uncalled for. Even worse, to treat me so poorly only proves you suffer from a lack of a strong sense of self preservation." She closed her hand into a fist, the flow of magic increasing as the mage's hand began to turn white.

"What are you doing to him?" one of the other mages demanded.

"Making my point quite clear." Cora looked pointedly at the mage she held in her grip. "I *have* made my point, haven't I?"

Before the mage could respond, his companion slapped the table with his palm. "You have only proved Amazons are as violent as we thought!"

"Silence, fool!" the first mage ordered. "You obviously don't understand the power we're dealing with." He returned his attention to Cora, dropping his eyes in deference, though she could see the pain he felt. Pain she caused.

"My apologies, Princess-Mage Rylannes. Your point is very clear. I did not realize who I was being so disrespectful to," he said, his words humble.

Cora opened her hand, stopping the flow of magic. The mage gasped and held his injured hand to his chest.

"You apology is accepted." She turned away from the mages and bumped into Percival. "We can leave now," she advised him.

Percival nodded and allowed her to take him from the room. Once outside, she took his hand in hers and made him stop.

"Don't worry, Percival. We will find a way to rid you of this demon. I promise."

"Thank you, Cora, but if I put you in danger, if your life is in danger from me, I want you to leave." His hand moved to her cheek, but he clenched his fist without touching her. "I don't want to hurt you."

Instead of questioning him about the touch he resisted, Cora chose to act as if she had not seen it. "I'm sure you won't hurt me."

"I won't mean to, but I might. Physically, emotionally—I don't know. I may not do it myself, but I will be the cause of it. I couldn't live with myself if I hurt you." He grabbed her shoulders

She struggled against his grasp, uncomfortable with his intense emotions. "Percival, let me go." His grip loosened. Cora looked around, trying to find a distraction. A crowd of people bustled past the two, toward the market. "I want to go to the market. I want to do some shopping."

He nodded, then released her. After composing himself, he led her down the street to the market square.

While they strolled through the market, she could feel his eyes on her. She easily avoided the merchants, stopping only at carts selling goods that interested her. Eventually, they arrived at a cart filled with wooden carvings.

Cora picked up a carving of a horse, her fingers caressing the smooth wood. The carver watched her expectantly, dry washing his hands. She studied the artistry with a critical eye, impressed with what she saw.

Percival glanced over the many carvings, searching for a particular piece. He picked up a budding rose, its petals stained red. After passing the carver several coins, he turned to Cora.

"Cora," he whispered, handing her the rose.

She stared at the wooden carving, absently placing the

horse back on the cart. Without a word, she grabbed him in an embrace, then kissed him.

Cora pulled away from him, noting the surprise on his face. She could not believe she just did that either.

Percival's surprise was pushed aside by a more serious expression. He placed his hand on the back of her neck, gentle in his touch, and pulled her to him. Their lips touched again.

Passion washed over her. The intense magic she usually felt when they touched flared like a newly ignited fire. The fire grew the longer he held her.

The kiss continued a heartbeat longer, then they separated. Her cheeks warmed in embarrassment. Instead of looking at him, she stared at the rose in her hand.

"Thank you, for the rose, Percival." She refused to look at him, convinced he could hear her nervousness.

He cleared his throat, stepping away from her. A small smile curved his lips and lit his eyes when she spoke his given name. "You're welcome, Cora. Shall we continue?" He gestured toward the line of carts.

She nodded, then slipped past him. He placed his hands on her elbow, and her breath caught in her throat. Such a brief touch, yet her heart skipped a beat and her knees became unsteady. How was it possible for him to affect her like this? This was not what she expected when she chose to follow her vision.

He walked next to her, his embarrassment a wave of warmth washing off him. He had said he cared for her, but did he regret that now?

They continued through the market, avoiding each other. When the sky grew dark as night drew near, they returned to the estate.

Chapter 31

When Cora and Percival returned to the Orenda estate, evening meal had already been served. Instead of going to the table, Cora prepared a plate of food for herself. She wanted to go outside and sit under the stars—to think about what happened in the market.

"Won't you be joining us, Cora?" Lady Orenda asked, laughter in her voice.

Cora turned back to the table, not surprised to see Percival on the other side of the room, avoiding her. "I thought I would eat outside."

"Of course. Please let the servants know if you need anything."

Cora nodded and continued outside. After finding a bench in the garden to sit on, she set the food aside and gazed up at the stars.

What was she doing? She came to find the man from her vision, not fall in love with him.

She removed the wooden rose from her pouch. There was no way she could have known what would happen when she found him. But her vision couldn't be wrong. She just didn't understand why she should care about saving a man.

The leaves of the bushes rustled, demanding her attention. She reached for her spear and realized she had left it in her room. Her second movement brought her hand to her dagger. She stood as three figures stepped out of the bushes.

"Who are you?" Her question slipped out before she could stop it.

The figure in the middle jumped at her. Cora tripped in her rush to get over the bench. The rock of the bench scraped her legs. Clenching her jaw against the sudden pain, she finally made it to the other side, away from the figure.

"Soola lancium." She completed the magical phrase and the ice lance she favored appeared in her hands. Swinging it low, the cold tip cut into the hand of the figure in front of her.

The figure's roar of pain pierced her ears. Cora dropped the ice lance, and covered her ears. The sound of a thousand voices crying out in pain assaulted her ears.

The figure reached out and grabbed her arm. Burning pain ripped through her flesh, digging into her bone. Her own scream joined the voices.

"Let her go!" Percival's voice broke through her scream.

Releasing her, the figure turned toward him and raised its hands. Streams of fire shot out toward Percival, creating a wall between them.

Satina stood next to Percival, concern for her princess more important than her hatred for the man. Others emerged from the house, joining them.

"We aren't done with you, Princess." The creature closest to Cora returned its attention to her. "We'll finish what we started, one way or another." Lifting its arm, it and its companions disappeared in a flare of fire.

The fire wall disappeared with the creatures, allowing Percival and Satina to reach her. Cora tried to push herself off the ground with her right hand. Pain still raged in her left arm.

"Cora! Are you all right?" Percival's concern washed over her. He pulled Cora to her feet by her left hand.

"Uhhh! Stop!" Yanking her hand from his grip, she pushed away from him.

Percival reached out and took her hand again, gentler this time. "What is it?" He studied her arm. "How did this happen?"

"One of them grabbed me by the arm, and burned this mark into my arm." She breathed deep. "It feels like it's burned into my bone."

"If it wasn't for the Black Hand, you would not have been injured. This is the second time you were attacked by whatever these things are," Satina accused from behind Percival.

"How is this because of him?" Cora glared at her guard.

"Because of who he is… *What* he is." Satina stood tall against her princess' glare.

"Go inside, Satina. Now!" Cora ordered, her patience at an end. The Amazon warrior stormed into the house, followed by the others. "Do you recognize the symbol, Percival?"

Careful to use his right hand, Percival's fingers floated over the symbol. "It resembles the symbol I have seen on Stromas. I don't know why they would put this mark on you."

They stared at the mark for several heartbeats before Cora took a deep breath. "I want to go to my room."

Percival nodded, picked up her plate of food and guided her into the house. Instead of leaving her in the dining room, he followed her to her room. Standing at the door, Cora looked at him, confused.

Percival cleared his throat. "Can I come in?" he asked, gesturing at the door.

She stared at him for a moment more, then opened the door and led him inside. He glanced down the hall in both directions before shutting the door behind him.

"Percival, thank you for staying with me while I healed." Her voice held a nervous tremor as she struggled to find something to talk about.

He blushed, something she had not seen often. "Of course, Cora. It felt… right… to sit with you. I wanted to do it."

"Satina is very upset with us. She does not understand having a man as a friend. I can't say I even totally understand why you felt you needed to be with me," Cora whispered.

"Because I feel better than my best day when I'm with you. You make me forget what the demon wants. You help to keep the anger away that the demon perpetuates. Do you feel nothing between us, Cora? Will you always only see me as a friend?" Percival asked, reaching out to touch her cheek. "As just a man?"

"I don't know what you mean, Percival. Today we kissed. Is this really something that we should do?" she whispered as he pressed closer. She heard the denial in her voice and fought to control the uncertainty she felt surfacing. How could she want to be with him one moment and then want to stay away from him the next? Did either of them really know what they wanted?

"I think it is. Are you willing?" He leaned closer, his lips brushing hers. "You would be an Amazon who chooses to be with a man because you want to be, instead out of necessity." His lips roamed over her neck and to her ear. "Together, we can accomplish anything. We have a strength no one can defeat. Together, we can forge a new way of thinking for your people."

She closed her eyes. His breath warmed her skin and made her shake as a shiver coursed through her. "Right now, I don't care what my people think," Cora declared breathlessly. She turned into his lips and returned his rough kisses.

Percival guided her toward the bed, kissing her neck as they moved. His hand rested against the small of her back while his other hand caressed the exposed skin of her stomach. The tingling of their contact exploded, increasing the sensitivity of their caresses.

Cora gasped with the intensity of their contact and put her hands on his chest. "Percival…"

"Let yourself go, Cora. It won't hurt us. Nothing can hurt us. Your mother can't control how you feel. Only *you* can stop yourself from loving me." He continued his caresses when she did not move away from him.

"But I am…" He pushed a finger against her lips, then kissed her.

"I know."

Later, as the moon began its descent in the sky, Cora squirmed under Percival's gaze. He smiled, pushing hair out of her face. His fingers traced a path down her body, then caressed the lines of her tattoo.

"I love you, Cora," he whispered, his breath cool against her sweat soaked skin.

"I don't really know what that means, Percival."

He nodded. "I will show you by loving you and we will learn together how an Amazon can love." Percival lifted away from her, pulling the blankets down for them to crawl under. When they were covered, he pulled her close, his chest against her bare back. He kissed her shoulder softly until they both fell asleep.

Chapter 32

Cora stayed in Percival's arms, his breath moving her hair while he slept. She rested her head on his chest, listening to his heartbeat. Not once since they had started traveling together had she ever heard him sleep so quiet. Usually, his sleep was restless—a constant turning and changing of positions. Now she assumed the usual disturbances were caused by his demon. She breathed softly against his skin, glad that for one night he would sleep without his normal tension.

The door to her room opened and Cora opened her eyes slightly to see Satina standing in the doorway. The light from the hall sconces filtered into the room, washing over Cora and Percival. The older Amazon stood in silence for a moment, studying them. Cora watched Satina's chest move with angered breaths, before she shut the door again. She made no indication she knew Cora watched her.

Though she knew Satina would be difficult to deal with in the morning, Cora snuggled closer to Percival, breathing in the scent of his body. A sense of peace flowed over her as she let sleep take her again.

"We shouldn't have come here, Princeesa," Satina announced the next morning, refusing to look at Cora.

"It's too late. We're here and I plan to stay." Cora closed

her journal and rested it on top of the other journals she had written over the last three years.

Percival still slept upstairs, where Cora left him. Instead of waking him, she chose to deal with Satina alone.

"You are not thinking clearly, Cora. You are letting your time with this *man* affect your thinking—the way you act." Satina jumped from the chair Cora forced her to sit in while she finished the journals. Pacing the room, Satina continued the argument in their native language. "You are not acting like an Amazon—like an Amazon *princess*. You are falling in love with the Black Hand and abandoning your upbringing."

Cora stood, warmth washing over her from embarrassment and anger. "Satina, you overstep your station with me."

"I am trying to protect you! That is my obligation to your mother! That is what I was sent here for," she yelled at the younger Amazon.

"I am trying to live my own life! Why are you and my mother so intent on controlling that?" Cora raised her voice, but held herself from shouting in return.

The door opened, and a servant peeked in. With an angry wave of her hand, Cora sent the man away.

"Your mother will not be happy. She will demand you return home and that you forget the Black Hand. You will be punished if you refuse, and he will be killed," Satina said, smugly crossing her arms over her chest.

"I will not be returning home." Cora sneered in return, shoving her journals toward the other woman. "These hold all the information I've gathered over the past three years. Give them to my mother. Travel safely, Satina. May Shae guide and protect you in your journeys."

"You are sending me to my death." Satina grabbed the books from her hands and stormed from the room.

Cora followed her to the second floor, returning to her own room when Satina entered hers. Standing in front of the window, the princess enjoyed the morning sun reflecting off the dew on the ivy below her window. As she watched, Satina left the house, retrieved her horse from a groom who stood waiting for her and rode away, without a backward glance.

"What's wrong, Cora?" Percival's sleepy question surprised Cora as she let the curtains fall to cover the window again.

"I ordered Satina to return home. She was beginning to wear on me." Cora removed her robe, then returned to the bed, moving against him to warm herself because of the morning chill.

"All right," he yawned, pulling her close and caressing her arm. "Good for her."

"Not really. Since she is returning home without me, my mother will be extremely angry. Satina said my mother will kill her for this failure."

Silence filled the room, then Percival sat up, pulling her with him. "She will kill Satina if you don't return with her?"

"That is what she said."

"And what will your mother do to you?" Fully awake now, Percival held her away from him.

"If she comes after me, or if I were to somehow return to her, she would demand I explain my actions toward you and the other men. If I returned, I would be punished. I would be forced to choose between the true Amazon ways, or exile. I would never see my islands again. Letting Satina return without me gives my mother free reign to make her own assumptions, no matter what I have written in my journals." The worry building in Percival with each word was obvious, intensified by the shadows from the morning sun peeking through the curtained windows.

"Explaining yourself I can live with, but Cora, we've finally realized we want to be with each other…" He stopped, his eyes narrowing. "You do want to be with me, right? You understand I can offer more to you than children and servitude, right?"

The uncertainty in his voice reflected her own. Was he more afraid of rejection or being made a slave? Reaching up, she caressed his cheek. Her fingers tingled with the touch, as well as his short beard.

"Are you trying to push me away? Haven't we already talked about how different this is for me? These feelings are new. I need to make them a part of me, but if you are going to be worried all the time about my upbringing, you aren't giving me the chance to learn."

He shook his head. "I am not trying to push you away." His doubt still echoed in her ears. "Do you want to go home, Cora?"

"No. I want to stay with you."

Percival took a deep breath, his shoulders lifting and falling. "That is all I need to know. I will not let your mother take you back. I will go to the Amazon islands themselves to bring you home if I have to." He returned her caresses, pushing a strand of her cloud white hair behind her ear. "I've noticed you call me by my given name more. Are you comfortable with that?"

"It is your name, more so than the Black Hand. Since I know the reason behind your hand, I cannot, in good conscience, call you that again." Her fingertips touched the length of his left hand. Blue sparks trailed behind her caress, evidence of the magic between their touches. "The Black Hand may have formed our group, but Percival Riesun leads it, at least he has recently."

"Not everyone sees me as Percival,' he whispered, watching her hand as well.

"I know. We will get past that as well. Together, right?"

"Together." He pulled her into a kiss.

"Treame. My mother named me Treame. That is the name I go by in private with my mother, sister, and occasionally Dekart." She glanced away. "And now you."

"I will protect it, as I protect you," he said, solemn and sincere in his promise. She felt the tension that held his body tight just moments before leave with another deep breath. He pulled her close again, easing her back under the covers. "With the morning, those you didn't wake in arguing with Satina will be rising soon. Let me hold you for a while longer before they come to interfere."

Cora relaxed in his embrace. Her mother saw allowing a man to comfort her and loving a man as a weakness. She still had to work to keep her mother's beliefs from interfering, but she felt sure she had chosen correctly in staying with Percival and in taking the chance to love him.

Chapter 33

The day after Satina's departure, the group of companions gathered supplies, packed their horses and prepared for the journey to the Tower of Winter. Cora joined Percival at the front of the estate while Tylina embraced her mother.

Lady Orenda turned to the two after kissing her daughter on the cheek. "Be careful. I don't know much about where you are traveling, but with everything that has happened to you already, you need to take precautions."

"We will, Lady Orenda. Thank you for your hospitality." Percival took her hand and bowed over it, placing a kiss on her knuckles.

With a blush, Lady Orenda waved them away. "Travel with Crystalline's blessings," her musical laughter filled her words.

Cora allowed Percival to help her onto her horse, resting her spear along the length of the beast. The day before, she had tied the feathers Percival had saved from Reyna to the shaft, below the spearhead. She fingered the feathers while waiting for the others to mount up. The constant companionship and friendship from the bird would be missed.

"Are you ready, Cora?" Percival asked quietly. His hand touched her thigh, drawing her attention.

She nodded, swallowing against a lump in her throat. Gesturing to the others, Percival led the group off the estate and down the road. Cora guided her horse close to him.

Traveling through the warehouse section of town, they passed the Hemisphere Flyer, the inn Exar had stayed in while they were at the Orenda estate. The large man stood outside the building, looking down the street in their direction.

When they drew closer, Percival raised his hand. "Greetings, Exar. Are you joining us today?"

"Yes," Exar snapped. Without another word, he mounted his large horse and fell in behind the others.

Percival breathed in relief. Cora smiled. "Lady Orenda told you she would make sure he left with us."

"I know," Percival agreed.

During the first days of travel, Cora reveled in the freedom she experienced without Satina. Despite Percival's happiness, she watched his temper shorten with the shrinking size of the moon. Apprehension filled her with each day that passed.

Percival was going to have to deal with the demon soon. They would not make it to the next city before the black moon heralded the confrontation. Cora glanced at the cloud-darkened sky. The weather grew worse with each day as well, as if nature felt the coming confrontation. The rain-heavy clouds made the summer heat oppressive.

A week after leaving Jonquil, during their watch, Percival came to stand next to Cora after completing his perimeter check. "I'm going to need tomorrow to handle Stromas. Don't follow me. Just let me be alone. I will return when I am done."

Cora glanced at him, the undercurrent of anger in his voice concerning her. "All right, Percival. We will wait here," she advised him.

She watched him walk away without comment. She had almost allowed the happy man he was a week ago to wipe out the memories of how angry he became during the black moon. Had he left so abruptly to keep her from seeing how difficult it was for him to control his temper?

The night creatures quietly going about their business filled the air around her. When Percival returned from another perimeter check, Cora woke Tylina and Kalik for their turn at watch and went to the tent she agreed to share with Percival. She lay against his back, holding him until he fell asleep. Sleep avoided her, enhancing the worry she felt over his confrontation the next day.

The next morning, Percival left the camp. Cora followed him until she reached the perimeter. Eventually he was lost in the plains grass, while she stood in silence. Tylina appeared next to her.

"Cora…" Tylina began when rain abruptly broke free of the clouds. "Let's get back to the tents. He'll be back as soon as he's done."

The two women ran the short distance to the fire pit in the middle of camp. Cora glanced at the sky as darkness fell on the area. Before she could say anything about the unusual change, Cora went to one knee. She grabbed her forearm above the scar she received in Jonquil. Pain raged through her left arm and into her chest.

"Cora!" Nimbly shouted through the sound of thunder.

She looked toward the elf, but three glowing figures near the fire pit drew her attention instead. Recognizing them from the Orenda estate, Cora forced herself to her feet, still holding her arm.

"What do you want?" she demanded.

The one who had grabbed her arm that night bared his teeth. "You are the only thing keeping the Black Hand in control of his emotions and body, Amazon. Your death will set Stromas free."

"I don't think so," Cora declared. Raking her hand through the air, she whispered, "Arcanum misi."

Three blue missiles streaked toward the demons. One struck each demon in their chest, opening wounds that instantly cauterized.

Next to her, Tylina also sent three red missiles toward the demons. Identical wounds opened on their chests.

"Soola lancium!" Cora cried, gripping the ice lance that appeared in her hand. Throwing the lance at the one who burned her, another magical phrase controlled its flight. It struck home, embedding itself in the demon's belly.

From behind her, a dagger flew through the air, sticking into flesh next to the ice lance. Tylina and Cora again struck out with the arcane missiles, until the demon sank to the ground.

"We will return, Cora. His death does not affect our goal."
The demon on the right sneered at her, then the surviving two
demons disappeared.

Reaching out to steady herself, Cora gripped Tylina's
shoulder. "Persistent, aren't they?"

Before Tylina could answer, movement from the edge of
camp drew Cora's attention. "What is he doing back so soon?"
Cora asked, releasing her friend's shoulder and taking a step
toward Percival.

Percival plodded toward them, his hand on his sword. Even
from her position near the fire pit, Cora could see the fire
burning in his eyes.

"Do you see it, Cora?" Tylina asked.

"Yes. Something is wrong."

Chapter 34

Ignoring the rain, Percival walked until the familiar darkness surrounded him. Though he knew the actual terrain never changed, in his mind it appeared as a desolate, rock strewn valley. Large boulders filled the area.

Perched on the largest boulder, Stromas waited for him. Two large horns protruded from his head and large wings sprang from his back. Five fingers on each hand ended in black claws, while his feet resembled cloven hooves. The demon wore only a loincloth and the red of his skin was so deep, it blended with the darkness around them. Even crouched on the boulder, Stromas was still twice Percival's height. He watched the man who confined him with eyes of burning embers.

"You know your fate, Percival. Every time I make you angry, I gain a little more control over you. One day, I will be in total control. I will be free and have full access to your world through you. No one will be able to banish me." Stromas flashed Percival a toothy grin.

"The anger does not come as easily as it once did, Stromas. I have found happiness with Cora and she helps me to control the violent emotions that feed you," Percival responded, confident, leaning back on another large boulder.

Running his tongue over his leathery lips, Stromas' grin grew wider. *"Ah yes, she is such a tasty morsel. I am so pleased we finally started taking her to our bed."* He lifted his hand in front of his face to study it. *"I've so enjoyed our time with her."* A brief, distant look came to Stromas' eyes, then he focused on Percival again. *"The feel of her skin as you—or more truly—we caress her. Have you never wondered where that passion comes from? Do you even possess the depth of emotion to feel like that? Or in those moments, am I truly in control?"*

Struggling to maintain his composure and temper, cords of muscle quivered in Percival's jaw. A bead of sweat dripped from his forehead, and a sliver of doubt flashed through his stomach.

"Yes," Stromas gloated, inhaling deeply. *"Now you begin to see that maybe it has been me who has been bedding your pretty little plaything."*

"I'll kill you!" Percival shouted, launching himself at the demon. He pulled his sword free of its scabbard. Anger replaced the calm he felt just moments earlier.

Stromas jumped to the ground and stood tall, drinking in Percival's anger. *"That's right! Let the anger take control!"*

Before he could swing his sword, pain shot through Percival's left arm, starting at his fingertips and going up his arm. Pressing his arm against his stomach, Percival struggled to maintain a grip on his sword. "What are you doing to me?"

"Expanding my control." Stromas made a fist with his left hand and the pain in Percival's arm increased.

Percival raised his sword, prepared to charge Stromas, when a frigid cold wrapped around him. Stromas turned to look behind him, his pleasure at Percival's pain replaced with anger.

"How dare she interfere with this!" Stromas growled. *"When I am free of you, Black Hand, I will make her mine. You will be unable to stop me."*

In the next moment, the darkness lifted from around Percival. Stromas disappeared, as well as the desert terrain they stood in. Percival glanced around him, surprised to find himself back at the camp. Cora, her hands raised to cast a spell, stood closest to him, her face filled with fear. Tylina stood behind her, hands also working the semantics of a spell. To Percival's right, Kalik and Nimbly advanced toward him, weapons prepared for an attack.

"What happened?" Percival asked. This was the first time his reality had ever been affected by the confrontation with

Stromas. Was the demon right? Was he actually losing control?

Cora balled the energy she had been accumulating between her hands and quashed it between her palms. She glanced at Tylina who made the same gesture. Stepping toward him, Cora's movements were slow, evidence that reabsorbing the magical energy was more difficult than she made it appear. "You walked back into camp, sword in hand. Your eyes burned with a brighter fire than we have ever seen before. Before I cast a spell on you, it appeared you were going to attack us."

Percival looked at the sword in his hand, then slammed it back into the scabbard. He waited for her to step closer, pulling her close to his body in a tight embrace when she came close enough for him to grab. He buried his face in her hair, breathing deeply of her scent. Was it his love for her or Stromas' lust that made her touch feel like a relief to his pain?

Deep in his mind, he heard Stromas' laughter booming maniacally. His embrace became tighter and he felt his body begin to shake.

"Percival, you're hurting me," Cora whispered against his shoulder. He loosened his grip, but did not release her. "What happened with Stromas?"

"He tried to make me angry. Something about how the anger gives him more control over me. Nothing you need to worry about. I'm in control." Percival released her, putting his hands on her face and kissing her.

She looked at him in surprise, and allowed him to wrap his arms around her again.

"Do you believe I love you, Cora?" Percival asked, fear and doubt strong in his voice.

She nodded. "It's new, but I do not doubt it. Should I?"

"No. I just need to know you believe me. Everything is easier when you believe in me, when you trust me."

Cora placed her own hands on his cheeks, this time starting the kiss herself. "Of course I do. You have allowed me the chance to learn about this at my own pace, without forcing me. Now, let's get in our tent. It's late and the rain is getting worse."

Percival put his arm around her waist, his hand tingling where his skin touched hers. He could not allow Stromas to take over. Cora must never become one of the demon's victims.

Chapter 35

Travel continued for another week. Cora watched Percival closely, the end to his last confrontation still fresh in her memory. Nimbly left them often to scout the area as they traveled. When he returned, she waited while he spoke with Percival alone, then they continued their journey.

After seven days, the small town they had been traveling toward appeared on the morning horizon. By midday meal, the group arrived at the town. Nothing Cora had ever seen while traveling with Percival and the others had prepared her for this town.

Throughout the town, slaves followed masters who carried chains and ropes. Even the Amazon islands did not have as many slaves as Cora saw walking through the town. Groups of slaves waited near a stage, while others on the stage were auctioned off.

The slaves wore minimal clothing, the women barely wearing more than the men. Each wore a collar around their neck and manacles on their wrists and ankles, with either chains or ropes running from ankle to ankle, wrist to wrist.

Next to Cora, Percival stiffened at the sight of the slaves, increasing the pace of his horse past the large group at the stage. After passing smaller groups of slaves, they reached the largest inn within the city.

The horses were stabled and Kalik made sure the stable boy understood what to feed them before Percival paid for the animals' care.

Cora stayed close to Percival as they entered the inn, slipping her hand onto his arm when he stiffened again. Only a few empty tables were available in the cramped room. A bard tried to entertain the crowd with a song that barely drowned out the low conversations in the room.

Percival pulled Cora to the closest empty table and waved for service. A girl came over, wearing the chains of slavery as well as only a loincloth, like the other serving girls in the room.

"Percival, what's wrong?" Cora whispered after they ordered food and drinks.

He shook his head, his attention focused on the bard. When the music ended, he turned his attention to the others.

"Where do we go from here?" Exar asked, his gruff voice easily heard over the other conversations.

"We travel to the Winter Forest. It should take us almost two weeks to get to the Tower of Winter. Once there, we will speak to Mage Wintress, see what information he can offer, then we will decide where to go," Percival answered through clenched teeth.

Cora's concern grew each time he tightened his jaw—every time a slave walked by their table. She rested her hand on his thigh and he shifted his leg closer to hers.

After finishing his meal in silence, Percival stood and placed some gold near Cora's hand. "Pay for the meals, and get some rooms. I need to get out of here for a while."

She nodded, trying to keep the emotions from her face. He gave her a small smile, then turned and left the inn.

"Cora, what's wrong with Percival?" Tylina asked when the door closed behind him.

"I think it's the slaves. I'll talk to him when he gets back." Cora stopped when Exar stood, throwing his chair back with his weight.

"Whatever his problem is, I'm no longer involved. I left Jonquil because I had no choice, but I am done with you and him." Exar pointed at Cora and Tylina. "Figure out what you're going to do on your own. I don't care." He waited a heartbeat, then the large man left the inn as well.

"Think he figured out we know who he is?" Kalik asked.

Nimbly laughed. "Not that we will really miss him. He was always going off on his own without a thought for us. We're better off without him."

"Let's get some rooms and rest while we can," Cora suggested dismissing Nimbly's glib comment. She made her way to the bar and returned shortly with room keys.

Passing several to the others, Cora noticed a cloaked figure enter the room. She felt drawn to the individual and at the same time, repulsed.

The figure surveyed the room, its features lost within the depths of the hood. Its search complete, the figure continued through the crowded room to the only table available in a darkened corner. Cora watched until the individual sat, then returned her attention to her friends.

"I'm going to take a bath. I've given instructions to the barkeep to give Percival a key when he returns. I will see you in the morning." She smiled at Tylina, left the remaining gold on the table and went upstairs after picking up hers and Percival's saddlebags.

The young Amazon opened the door to her room and pulled the bags inside. She kicked the door shut and put the bags to the side of the door. Removing her capeshal, a sense of freedom filled her as she watched the thin material float lazily to the ground.

A knock sounded at the door and she spun in surprise, grabbing the dagger she kept on her thigh. Breathing deeply, she released the weapon and reached to open the door.

"I didn't expect you so…" Cora began, expecting to find a servant on the other side with water for her bath.

Framed by the door stood a woman taller than Cora, with long black hair. A green-feathered band held her hair back from her face. She wore clothing similar to Cora's, though the top covered more of her abdomen, in stiff leather, more appropriate for the warriors of the princess' island. Instead of the spear typically used by the Amazons, the warrior had two swords attached to her hip. A dark, forest green cloak flowed around her legs, and Cora recognized her as the cloaked figure that had entered the inn before Cora went to her room.

"Shoshona," the princess whispered, stepping back from the

door. Her hand returned to the dagger on her leg, then dropped, the familiar paralyzing fear gripping her.

"Princeesa, I see you didn't return with Satina as you should have. That makes it much easier for me to finish my plans." Shoshona stepped into the room, closing the door behind her.

Cora felt her limbs go numb as the older woman sauntered through her room. The fear she had told Percival about regarding Shoshona returned to her, paralyzing her and making her unable to defend herself or force the woman to leave.

"What a pity. I see you are still unable to do anything to stop me." Shoshona stopped in front of the window and gazed outside. "I've gone to great lengths for you, Cora. Hiring assassins to find and remove you from this constant fear. Sending one of my own Amazons and forcing her to live in this hell for three years until just the right time when she could get rid of you. All of this and you appreciate none of it. All of this and yet… you still live." Shoshona turned to glare at Cora. "Why? How have you been able to survive everything I've thrown at you?"

"I don't know, Shoshona," Cora whispered, struggling to control her breathing. "I have friends who have helped me." She slid to her knees, her breath uncontrolled gasps. The room began to darken around her until only Shoshona remained.

"Yes, your friends. They have proven to be quite a nuisance themselves. I have spoken to Satina about your friends. She was very upset when she informed me that you had taken one of them to your bed. The Black Hand, I believe is what she called him. Your mother will be most upset." Shoshona's words echoed with laughter. "I will wait for this Black Hand and once we are together, I will make sure the three of us have a grand conversation before I kill you."

Cora stared at her in shock, before her fear overwhelmed her and she finally lost consciousness.

Chapter 36

After retrieving the room key Cora left for him, Percival wearily trudged through the inn. He had found a group of off-duty guards outside the city. After exchanging stories of war and adventures, they agreed to a few rounds of mock combat with Percival. He trained with them until he was exhausted. When the sun dipped behind the horizon, leaving the land in the grip of impending darkness, he returned to the inn and found that the others had gone upstairs to their rooms already.

While he walked, Percival struggled to close his mind to the sight of the working slaves and tried to think only of the time he had spent with Cora. The memory of her laughter, the light touch of her hand on his and the soft touch of her lips helped to block what he did not want to see.

Stepping through the door to the room he would share with her, he stopped at the sight that greeted him.

Cora lay on the floor, her capeshal several feet from her. In front of the window stood another Amazon, older than the two he traveled with. They stared at each other in silence, both waiting for the other to make a move.

"Who are you? What did you do to Cora?" Percival asked, breaking the silence. He shifted his hand to his sword and unlatched the lock that held the blade in place.

"I am Shoshona," the Amazon answered, her commanding

tone indicating her response should be all he needed. "I have only reminded her of the place I hold in her life."

"From what she has told me, you are the reason for her fears, her inability to be in closed in places. I will not allow you to do that to her again," he informed her.

"How gallant of you. Come to the defense of your woman. Next you'll tell me how you've convinced her to bear you a dozen children and that she's learned how to bake bread," Shoshona sneered, laughing at him. "Typical man, to take a strong Amazon woman and demean her to the point of slavery."

"I have not made her a slave," Percival growled, advancing on Shoshona while drawing his sword.

She drew her own swords and met his initial attack. "I have come to finish what I started years ago. And I will not allow a man to stop me."

The two retreated, then lunged forward again, Shoshona's second sword slicing under Percival's. He spun away from the blade, bringing his own down across her body. Neither weapon hit flesh as the two experienced combatants situated themselves for the next attack.

Again, they stepped forward, their blades ringing in the room as they hit. Percival arched his shoulder away from the second blade, but not before it cut into his shirt. For the second time since leaving Glenys, Percival did not wear his armor while facing an Amazon. He wondered if he was losing his edge. He pushed the thought aside as Shoshona's first blade slipped from the block he put up and slashed across his chest. Percival's shirt fell open and his flesh burned from the fresh cut. Hissing, he forced his mind back to the battle instead of the distraction he created for himself.

The two continued to exchange blows, Percival cutting Shoshona in return for the wounds she gave him.

Chapter 37

Cora woke to the sound of battle. She forced herself to her hands and knees, struggling to keep her breath calm as the clashing of swords echoed in her ears. Finally, she sat back on her heels and watched Shoshona force Percival back several steps, pushing her attack.

Suddenly the room felt too small for three people.

Cora knew Percival was capable of defending himself, but Shoshona was an Amazon warrior. She had dedicated her life to the art of war, as required by all the warriors of the Amazon nation. Having seen what the Amazons went through for training, new fear gripped Cora. His death was an outcome she did not want to face.

She cringed as the number of wounds increased on the two combatants, most of them on Percival. Shoshona was playing with him, trying to tire him. Cora could see the usual fire that filled his eyes when in combat, but would the hidden strength granted to him by the demon be enough to help against the Amazon warrior?

Cora stood. "Arcanum misi linge." Her hand traced an arc in front of her at the height of the spell, five blue lines trailing the movement of her fingers. Five identical lines appeared on Shoshona's chest.

She fell back from Percival, allowing him an unblocked

attack against his surprised opponent.

Growling, he lunged with his sword. Cora gasped when his weapon slid into Shoshona's stomach, the sound covered by the woman's cry of pain.

In a last attempt to kill him, Shoshona stabbed with one sword, forcing it through Percival's flesh. A wound identical to hers tore into his abdomen. Her other sword sliced toward the ceiling, into his armpit.

Percival staggered back from her. His sword opened the wound more as it left her body.

"Percival!" Cora cried, covering the few steps to his side.

He turned to her, his pale face filled with shock. His hand opened, letting his sword fall to the floor. Blood seeped from the wound in his arm, covering the right side of his body. He grabbed his stomach with his left hand and tried to staunch the flow of blood.

"Let me help you," Cora whispered, guiding him to the floor. She reached for her capeshal, and pressed it against the wound under his arm, trying to staunch the bleeding.

Percival nodded, resting against the wall.

"I need to get Brolin, Percival. Stay awake," she pleaded.

He nodded again, putting his head against the wood and closing his eyes.

Glancing at Shoshona's still form, Cora ran from the room, down the hall to the room Brolin shared with Nimbly.

"Brolin! Come quickly!" She pounded on the door until Brolin opened it. He stared at her through partially closed eyes. "We were attacked. Percival's been hurt!"

Brolin nodded, pushed past her and rushed to her room. Cora followed him, Nimbly close behind.

Brolin pulled towels from the dresser to press against Percival's wounds. Tylina and Kalik arrived soon after with three members of the city guard.

"Cora, the barkeep sent a message to the city guard. They want to know what happened," Tylina explained before helping Kalik around the others to assist with Percival.

Cora nodded, stepping outside the room to speak to the guards. She glanced back, surprised to see Nimbly behind her.

"What happened here?" the tallest of the city guard asked, his voice gruff.

"I came up to my room and a warrior from my islands was waiting here," Cora began.

"Were you expecting her?"

She shook her head. "When Percival came in, she attacked him. They fought, and he killed her, but not before she injured him."

She knew only Percival understood how Shoshona affected her. The guards would never understand.

"We will take her body to be handled by the city. Unless you have an objection?" Again the same guard spoke.

"Not at all. But first, let me see if I can find anything to explain why she came here." The guard nodded, gesturing for Cora to return to the room.

Cora went back inside, and searched through Shoshona's travel bag. After removing items she knew would displease her mother if they were in the hands of men, including weapons and clothing, Cora allowed the guards to take the body.

"The barkeep can send for another cleric if needed, to help," the guard advised.

"Thank you." Cora closed the door behind them, then turned to the bed to see Brolin straighten from his position over Percival. "Brolin?"

"The wounds are deep. I don't think she hit anything serious, but I am unable to heal either wound." Brolin's frustration filled his words.

"What do you mean you're unable to heal him?" Cora hurried to the opposite side of the bed and sat next to Percival. She reached for his hand, at the same time reaching out with her mind to touch the connection Percival had told her he used to reach her.

In her mind, a red wall of flame raged in front of her. *Stromas?* The wall fluctuated in response to the demon's name. *Why do you insist on blocking me?*

"The wounds are bad, his blood loss is severe, but he appears to be resisting me. Cora, who was that woman? Maybe she did something to cause this." Brolin's voice pulled her back to the room.

"That was Shoshona, an enemy of my mother's. I think she was the one who hired the assassins. I also think the nanny who kidnapped King Kennan's daughter was from her tribe."

Cora took a deep breath and touched Percival's pale cheek. "She wants to kill me." Cora paused, correcting herself. "*Wanted* to kill me. She does not know magic. I don't believe she could do anything to prevent the healing. Shoshona was a strong warrior, but what the assassin did to me with the arrow is not something she could have concocted alone."

"I will try again, but if I am unable to heal him, we may need to seek further help. Percival will be lost to us if that proves useless." Brolin gestured for her to leave the bed and returned to his work.

Chapter 38

Percival stood in a land barren of plant, animal or any other form of life. Even the typical boulders that peppered the terrain when he normally dealt with Stromas were missing.

Stromas stood in front of him, his arms held up, with his hands gesturing toward a wall of fire. The demon turned to look at Percival.

"Beautiful, isn't it?" he asked, indicating the wall.

"What do you want, Stromas? It isn't time for us yet. You push too soon." Percival ignored the question, asking his own.

"True, but your injuries give me strength while you are weakened." The demon pointed at the wall. "I will resist the healing Brolin uses on you so that you will continue to weaken. I will then take control of you."

"I won't allow that, Stromas." Percival tried to draw the sword he always had with him. Pain tore through his arm. The weight of the weapon pulled his arm down, the point driven into the dirt at his feet.

"Your injuries in your reality affect you in my reality. Can you fight me for your life now, Black Hand?" Stromas laughed, reaching out to grab Percival's throat. "This will be so much easier than I expected."

"I will not fall to you, Stromas," Percival gasped.

Percival! You need to hear me! Cora's voice, above a whisper, sounded over Percival's struggle for breath.

Stromas dropped him, turning to look around them. ***"Where is she? How can she do that?"***

Percival rubbed his throat. "I don't know, but I'm not going to question it." He stood and rushed toward the wall of fire.

Chapter 39

Two hours after she left Brolin with Percival, Cora looked up to see the priest walking down the stairs into the common room. She watched him without saying a word, her fear increasing at the defeat in his expression.

Brolin sat at the table. For the first time since he began traveling with the group, he poured himself a mug of ale from the pitcher and drank it. "I have only been able to do minimal healing spells. Anything stronger and he resists it. I have also felt some kind of a backlash in the magic. I don't understand what is happening, but, Cora, I think you need to see if you can find out."

Cora stared at him while he finished his ale, then excused herself. This fear was new, just like her feelings for Percival. She never thought she would concern herself about the health of a man.

Or care if he lived or died.

Even after her vision and finding Percival.

She reached her room, closing the door softly behind her. Taking a moment, she was surprised to see Percival clutching the sheets of the bed, his back arched against… pain? Or perhaps something else she could not comprehend. His chest lifted in shallow breaths, and his mouth contracted in a soundless grimace with each one.

Cora crossed the room and sat on the bed next to him, careful in her movements. "How do I find out what you are doing to keep the healing spells from working?" She caressed his arm with her fingers.

"Everything is so new. I have never known the love of a man, other than my father. But you already know that. Do these new emotions make me weak? Will being loved by a man, and loving him in return, change who I am?" She leaned back, placing herself against the wall.

"I did not come to Man's World to just learn about the tactics and the people. I had a vision about a man. A man with a black hand. I could... feel that I needed to find him, though I didn't understand why." Cora looked down at him, stroking his sweat-drenched hair out of his face.

"I know now. I came here to find you. You are the reason I am in Man's World." His lack of response frustrated her and she stood, grabbing him by the shoulders. Lifting him off the bed, she shook him—once, twice. "Percival! You need to hear me!"

The tension left him immediately. His eyes fluttered, then opened. "What did you say?"

Cora laughed, relief filling her. She wrapped him in an embrace, releasing him when he gasped in pain. "I said you are the reason I came here. I came to find you."

Percival coughed, then gave her a weak grin. "I told you we were special together."

She laughed again. "No you didn't." She leaned over, kissing him. "I am sure of one more thing, Percival. I love you."

His smile grew stronger. "I love you too." He tried to look around the room. "Where is she?"

"The city guard took Shoshona's body. Thank you for freeing me from my demon that has haunted me for so many years." Just speaking about Shoshona, even for such a brief moment, reminded Cora of the pain the older Amazon had caused her, and now Percival.

"She was going to hurt you." Percival coughed again, closing his eyes for a moment from the pain. "You would do the same for me."

Cora nodded. "I *will* do the same for you. We will find a way to rid you of Stromas, but for now, you have to allow Brolin to heal you. Do you know why you are resisting his spells?"

"Yes. Stromas wants to keep me weak. It seems the demon and his followers are going to take extreme steps to free him."

"I won't allow that. I will be with you until you are healed." She dipped a cloth into basin of water on the side table and used the damp towel to wet his lips. "As you said, we've just found each other. I'm not ready to lose you yet. Together we are strong."

He stared at her, then nodded. "Get Brolin. Let's try again."

Cora leaned over and kissed him, then rushed downstairs. "Brolin, would you please try again? I know what the problem is. We think we can beat it."

He nodded and followed her back upstairs.

Cora returned to her place on the bed next to Percival. She held his hand while Brolin cast his spells. She could feel the magic flow through his body and through the wall Stromas had placed in Percival's mind.

She would have to try to lower the wall with her own magic. She brought to mind the words of a spell that would lower resistance, and cast it toward the wall. Through her connection with Percival, she felt the wall weaken and the magic Brolin sent into his body grow stronger.

Then the wall disappeared completely.

Percival's wounds closed as the priest's magic took effect. Both Cora and Brolin breathed a sigh of relief when the second spell he cast took full effect. She wanted to question the disappearance of the wall, but thought better than to question their good fortune.

After casting one more spell, Brolin examined Percival's wounds and nodded. "They appear to be healed, as best as can be, considering I wasted so much of my healing capability at the beginning. I will return in the morning and finish. Keep him from moving too much tonight. I don't want anything to tear open again."

Cora nodded in agreement, not watching him as he left the room. Shortly after Brolin left, two women from the inn came in to change the bedding. Cora returned Percival to the bed when they completed their task. Using water and cloths left by the women, she cleaned the blood from his skin before allowing him to lie down again.

"You need a proper bath, Percival. I can't get all of it like this," she tried to tease him, but he failed to acknowledge her attempt. "Get some rest. Brolin will finish healing you in the morning, after he has had a chance to rest."

Percival nodded, sleep already pulling him into its bosom.

She used some of the water to wipe the sweat from her own body and took a shirt from Percival's saddlebag. After rubbing her cheek with the material, she pulled the shirt on and climbed into the bed next to him, exhausted from the activity of the day.

Chapter 40

At Cora and Brolin's insistence, the group remained in town the next day to give Percival's wounds additional time to heal. When the sun started to set, despite his obvious pain, Percival renewed his argument with Cora.

"I can't stay here. We need to leave now." Percival shouldered his saddlebags and reached for the door.

"Percival, one more night is not going to hinder our journey. You need the rest." Cora pulled the bags from his shoulder, dropping them to the floor.

"You don't understand, Cora. I can't."

She looked down. "Percival, Exar is no longer with us. He left yesterday."

"And this is supposed to encourage me to stay? We were asked to keep Exar from getting close to Orenda's wife and her people. Even though he came this far with us, he can just as easily travel back." Percival picked up his saddlebags again and opened the door. "We can send a message to Orenda on our way out."

The others stood waiting in the hall. Cora shook her head slightly, disappointment filling her when their expressions fell from hopeful to resigned. Percival pushed past them and down the stairs.

After retrieving their horses from the stable, the group of

friends made their way to the city gates. Just inside the gate, a building with a sign that announced a messenger service caught Cora's attention.

"Percival, we can send the message from here."

He nodded, leaning forward over his horse's neck. Cora beckoned to Tylina and the two mages walked inside after passing off the reins of their horses.

The storekeeper gestured toward one of the standing desks as the door closed behind the women. Stepping up, Cora passed quill, ink and parchment to her friend.

"Pen a message to your father, Tylina. We need to make sure he knows that Exar is no longer with us," Cora instructed.

While Tylina wrote the message, Cora paid for a messenger to travel to Glenys. When the half-elf finished, the two women rejoined the group and continued their travel in silence.

When they stopped for the night, only a couple of hours distance from the town, Cora confronted Percival. He still looked pale from losing so much blood. On top of that, Cora was concerned about Brolin, who was still weak from casting so many spells in such a short time.

"Honestly, Percival, we should have stayed. Brolin needed to rest after casting those healing spells. And, you are not up to full capability yet," she insisted, refusing to release his arm when he tried to pull away from her.

"I needed to get away from the slaves." Unfamiliar desperation filled his voice.

"Percival, they are not you. You can free yourself from the demon."

"I told you I abhor slavery of any type. Stromas holds me as a slave. To see it on such a large scale makes me sick." He stopped when he felt her grip.

"I understand. I promise no one will do that to you. We will free you of Stromas." She leaned forward and kissed him on the cheek.

He smiled at her, then left to help the others set up camp.

Chapter 41

The next morning, after breaking camp, the group continued their journey. Frustration kept Cora silent and the others took the nonverbal cue from her. Percival rode in front while she watched him for any signs that his healing was incomplete.

With the sun setting, before Percival called a stop to their travel, arrows flew into their midst again, narrowly missing Cora. Two men appeared in the plains around them. Tendrils of magic floated away from them.

With a shout, Percival raced toward the men, followed by Kalik and Nimbly. Cora and Tylina turned their horses, raising their hands in intricate gestures. Cora felt the magic flow through her, gathered it in her hands and waited. Percival and the others were too close to the attackers.

One attacker circled around the men, making his way to the two women. Cora watched him move closer, then sent the magic she held at him. A bright colored bolt of lightning streaked from her hands, wrapping around him. His movement stopped, restricted by the lightning crackling over his skin. Tylina sent her magic at him, a stream of ice encasing his body. Another bolt of lightning slammed into the man. Smoke filled the air around him. When it cleared, he lay on the ground, a hole in his chest. His flesh sizzled from the lightning bolt.

Cora dismounted, holding onto the reins of her horse for

support. Her knees shook from the strain of the magic she had used. The lightning required more energy than the ice spells she normally used. She staggered toward the body, but the return of Percival and the others returning stopped her progress. She flinched at the frustration marring their faces. "Did you get the other one?" she asked.

Percival shook his head. "He bit into something that created smoke in his mouth and then killed him. We weren't able to get any information."

"We accomplished nothing," Kalik repeated.

"At least all the assassins are dead now," Cora tried to fill her words with encouragement.

Nimbly shrugged. "We don't know who ordered it."

"Yes, we do." Cora straightened, fighting against the weakness left from her magic. "When we rescued the princess, I found items that made me believe Amazons did it. Duke Orenda confirmed my suspicions." She gestured in the direction of the town they left the day before. "The woman at the inn was Shoshona. She is the one who wanted me dead."

Kalik pushed the end of his staff into the dirt at his feet. "You should have told us sooner. How can we help you if you don't tell us?"

"She is aware of that now, Kalik. Cora is still trying to learn our ways. Give her peace," Percival came to her defense, stepping between them.

"I do not wish to return to the islands. I am trying to learn a new life," Cora explained, stepping closer to Percival, her hand on his back. Was she really allowing a man to defend her? Did her love for Percival make her a weaker woman?

"We know, Cora. They are just frustrated with the different attacks we've been faced with." Tylina squeezed her arm. "Just be sure to tell us in the future what we should expect, please."

Cora nodded, and smiled at her friend before Tylina walked away with Nimbly and Kalik.

The rush of excitement from the fight left her and Cora again felt the magic she used to kill her would-be assassin. She stared at the body. She couldn't believe she had killed him. She fell to her knees, her stomach reacting to her thoughts and threatening to reject the food she ate at midday. Trying to control the nausea gripping her, she felt the ground tear into her hands and knees.

She was raised to defend her people with her magic. She should have no issues with killing—especially a man.

"Are you all right, Cora?" Percival knelt next to her and tried to pull her close.

"I've never killed anyone with my magic like that. I've injured them, and you, Kalik or one of the others struck the finishing blow. Tylina and I killed that one, purely with our magic. It doesn't matter how my mother raised me, I feel tainted." She leaned into his chest, his warmth calming her shaking.

"You'll be fine. It just takes time to get used to the idea. You had to do it to protect yourself. I wasn't here. If you hadn't done something, he would have hurt you. You would be dead instead of him." He held her tighter.

"I hope I never get used to the idea of taking someone's life. It doesn't feel natural," she whispered into his chest.

They sat together until Nimbly came over to them. "I'm sorry, Percival, but we need help burying the bodies. Brolin is insisting on giving them a proper burial." Sarcasm echoed in his words, making Cora laugh.

Percival nodded. "Stay here until you are calm, Cora. I will help with this."

Cora nodded as well. "I will be fine."

She waited until he left, waving her hand at him when he glanced back at her.

She stared at the ground, forcing the shaking from her hands and body. Deep breaths helped, and though she still felt the weakness, which she dealt with routinely since coming into her magic, by the time Percival returned, Cora was able to ride again.

"We will ride for another change. That will give us sufficient distance from this place," he explained, walking with Cora to her horse.

"Thank you for giving me the time I needed. I apologize for not helping."

"Don't worry about it. I'm supposed to help with things like that."

She glanced at him, and smiled at the blush of his cheeks. "It's good to see you smiling again, Percival."

He kissed her on the cheek. "You too."

Chapter 42

For nine days, the group continued their journey. Cora found comfort in knowing the assassins sent by Shoshona were dead. More concerning, though, was that the demons had not been seen. Instead of reassuring her, their absence worried her.

While they traveled, she listened to Percival's instruction on signs of spiderkin and giants throughout the countryside. The large footprints of the giants and overturned trees were unmistakable. The spiderkin were more subtle, their presence given away only by the spider webs covering the occasional tree.

Since she had never seen a giant before, Cora accepted Percival's calm explanation that they were far enough away to not cause any worry.

When they entered the Winter Forest, the sudden cold crashed into them. They were not prepared for this and they scrambled to find proper clothing to keep warm. The first night in the forest, after the group had hunted rabbits and foxes for their pelts, Percival gave Cora a pair of his breeches.

She looked at him in surprise, fingering the rough material. "What are these for?"

"You'll freeze in those clothes," he advised, eyeing the very revealing clothing she wore. The red of her tattoo drew his attention and Cora had to clear her throat to make him bring his gaze back to hers. "Please, I can already see how cold you are."

Cora laughed. "You see only the bare skin, Percival." She pulled a shirt from her saddlebag and fitted her arms through the sleeves.

"That's my shirt," he observed.

"Yes, and these are your breeches," she agreed, slipping them over her legs. "This is so confining. How can Tylina wear them every day?"

"It provides better protection than your clothing."

Cora stood and removed the loincloth she wore. Placing the material and chain into her saddlebag, she finished buttoning her shirt. "Will Kalik be able to cure the pelts fast enough for them to be of use to us?"

Percival nodded. "Tylina has a spell of some kind that will do it for him."

"Interesting. I will have to ask her about that. I have never heard of such a spell." Cora slipped her hand into Percival's and followed him to the fire.

Three days after entering the forest, the Tower of Winter loomed before them.

The tower reached for the heavens, the top ending in a large spire with three claws at the points of a triangle. The stones of the walls glowed with a deep blue and magic snow fell within the stones themselves. Approaching the tower, a door appeared at the base.

"Hobble the horses so we can go inside," Percival directed when everyone dismounted.

Kalik tended to the horses. He spoke to them in whispers, in a language Cora assumed was his native tongue. His ability to handle the horses, amongst his other skills, still amazed her especially since he was blind. The others gladly gave him the duty of caring for the horses because he felt they did not understand the animals' needs.

When the animals were hobbled and had feed bags over their heads, the companions approached the door with caution. Before Percival put his hand on the blue wood, the door opened of its own volition.

"Please enter," a voice from within the tower invited them. "Choose two friends. The others can wait outside."

Percival turned to look at his friends. He reached out and took Cora's hand in his. "Who wants to go? I can't choose between you."

Kalik gave Tylina a slight push toward him. "Tylina has magic like Cora. Perhaps the two will be able to understand what the Arch mage has to say better than the rest of us."

With the decision made, the three entered the dark tower. A glowing ball of light waited for them at the base of a staircase that disappeared into the heights of the tower. When they stood near it, the ball ascended the stairs. The three followed without discussion.

The light led them up the stairs, the dark of the tower surrounding them. Cora's legs burned from the climb, and when they finally reached a platform, she stopped in relief. The light waited for them, then it led the way down a long hall.

Looking around, Cora ran her fingers over the stone of the wall, feeling the magic inside. She knew the Arch Mage Wintress used magic to make the outside of the tower appear too small to accommodate the hall they were in. It was magic she did not use. Her mother did not allow the teaching of such 'useless' magic on her islands.

More time passed until they stood in front of a door that opened again without their help. Percival walked in first, followed by Cora, then Tylina.

Warmth wrapped around Cora like a comfortable blanket as soon as she crossed the threshold. Torches burned in sconces on the walls, lighting the room. A fire burned within the fireplace. Cushioned chairs waited for them. In an oversized chair, an elderly woman waited.

Percival stopped in front of Cora, surprised. "A woman? No one said Wintress was a woman."

Hair the color of night with white streaks that reminded Cora of a shooting star hung free around Wintress' face. Her robes were a blue that matched the outer stones of the tower. Smaller snowflakes drifted across the material.

"Considering who you travel with, my being a woman should be the least of your worries." Wintress laughed. "Come in, come in. Please be seated," she invited, waving her hand at the chair. "Make yourselves at home. Tea, wine, mead?" The offered drinks appeared on the table in front of the mage.

The three friends sat in chairs facing the mage, Percival taking the closest one. After taking polite sips of the offered drinks, Cora and Tylina looked to Percival, waiting for him to state their business.

Before he could say anything, Mage Wintress held up her hand. "I know why you are here, Captain Riesun. I have been waiting for you to reach a point in your life when being free of this demon would be important enough to you to seek my help. You needed to find a life you wanted to live."

"What do you mean, you've been waiting for me? You don't even know me," Percival said in agitation.

"I know you better than you realize, Captain. I know that the item you seek to free you is a finicky one. It will only bow to you when you treat it as an equal in all things. I know you must open yourself fully, leaving your emotions and feelings exposed to be hurt and for yourself to be rejected. You must give of yourself completely or the item will not work. I also know the answer you seek is closer than you realize." The mage contemplated Percival and Cora, her gaze intense. "I know the item isn't really an object."

"Finally, I know what the demon has neglected to mention. If you were to die before the demon is released, you both die. So, while he may seem to push you toward your death at times, he can't allow you to die. To do so would mean his own demise. The demon forces you into uncontrollable anger and drives you to fight with a ferocity no other man can match. When you are injured, you are weak. When you are weak, he can take control easier, whether during the black moon or not." Wintress pointed a finger at the ceiling and made a circle motion. A black moon appeared looking as it would during the phase of a black moon.

"If you are ever injured where he can take over, and then you regain control, it will be easier for him the next time. He knows your weaknesses and will use them to make you lose your temper or give up. And then, he will have you." She clapped her hands together and frowned.

"Why couldn't anyone else tell him this?" Tylina whispered.

"The captain's father accomplished something no mage before him could. Many have tried since then, to the sad demise of innocents. No one knows Percival or what was done to him better than I." The old woman frowned again.

"Why is that, Mage Wintress?" Cora asked. She had wanted to ask that question since the mage started speaking, but chose instead to let her finish.

"Because I taught his father everything he knows…"

Percival interrupted her. "My father knows nothing. I suffer because of his greed and lack of foresight," he insisted. "Maybe he's dead. I haven't seen him in years."

"Oh no, my boy. That couldn't be further from the truth." Wintress produced a mirror next to her. An image appeared in the mirror of an older version of Percival, not as muscular, in the black robes worn by some mages. The man sat at a desk, studying a large tome. "Your father is alive and well, and unless I'm mistaken, studying to duplicate what he did to you. But he won't be able to. You have an innate magic that combined with the demon's. The only way to duplicate it would be for him to either have another child or to take a child of yours."

Percival stared at her in shock, his mouth open. Time passed in silence, the occasional sound of the fire popping the only sound to be heard.

"Percival?" Cora broke the silence, reaching out to touch his hand.

"I don't want to think of my father being alive or what he would do to another child." He looked at her, his eyes glowing from the fire within him. "I'm all right." He turned back to the other mage. "Wintress, you haven't explained how you know me so well."

"I know you and watch you, because I am your grandmother," the mage announced with pride.

Shocked silence again filled the room. While the three stared at her, Wintress picked up a cup of tea and sipped it while she waited for Percival to speak. Cora watched her studying Percival, a small smile lighting her face.

"I didn't know," he said finally, lowering his eyes.

"Not many did, including your mother. She did not keep anything from you. I felt it was better to remain anonymous until you were ready to know." The mage continued to sip at her tea. "Now, unless I can do anymore for you, your friends outside are getting cold and you should be joining them. A guesthouse has been prepared for you. Please make yourselves at home for the night. Percival, you may return whenever you want, just be sure to announce your need aloud. I will hear it and will prepare for you."

The three stood and after shaking hands with the mage, they followed the light from the room. Outside the tower, the guesthouse Wintress mentioned stood next to a barn. Cora followed Percival into the guesthouse, both silent, despite the questions their friends asked.

Later that evening, Cora stood outside the guesthouse, watching the magical snow play over Wintress' tower. The others fell asleep earlier, but she had lain in bed listening to Percival's breathing, unable to sleep.

The older mage revealed more information than the mages in Jonquil, but Cora felt there was still more to be revealed.

"I did that with a purpose in mind, Princess Rylannes." The voice of the mage came from the tower, then the woman appeared in front of the Amazon. The two studied each other for several breaths until, with a twitch of her lips, Wintress nodded. "Magic is very strong within you, like Percival, but you use it minimally. You are afraid to use it. You hate the magic, yet embrace it."

"My mother was disappointed when the shamans told her I was destined for magic and not the sword. Though she sees our mages as powerful, in her daughters, she sees only weakness. My magic use was met with disapproval and so I learned to hate it." Cora never told anyone how her mother reacted to finding out her youngest daughter would be a mage. Speaking of it now eased a tension she had not realized she felt.

"That is unfortunate. Had you been my daughter, I would have encouraged the use of the magic, nurtured it and eventually you would have become one of the most powerful mages in the land," Wintress' words increased in excitement as she spoke. "Instead of hiding your powers."

"And, I could have used my ability to enslave my own child, as your son did."

Wintress' eyes widened in shocked surprise, then softened. "A painful point you make, Cora. I do not often concede in a discussion with other mages—especially one as young as you. But, tell me, how will you keep from treating Percival as a slave in the years to come? How will you be any different than his father?"

Cora felt as if the woman had slapped her. She tried to put her upbringing behind her to embrace a new way of life. No matter how hard she tried, would others always question Percival's loyalty and love for her? Would they assume he stayed with her because she claimed him as property?

"No, dear, others will not question you as I have done." Again, Wintress read her thoughts.

"Stay out of my mind, old woman," Cora growled in frustration.

Wintress laughed softly. "My apologies. I am too used to using it as an advantage when dealing with others. And, I questioned you like that because I dislike it when others make a point against me. I am a sore loser."

Silence filled the night around them, each woman lost in their own thoughts. Finally, Cora turned back to Wintress.

"I feel as if you kept information from Percival earlier," she stated her concerns, though she was certain Wintress already knew them.

"Yes, I did. Percival is a strong man, but if he fears Stromas, he may become weak, trying to avoid injury. His fighting abilities help him stay focused and keep Stromas under better control during his battles." She scrutinized Cora. "And I know exactly what he needs to do to free himself from the demon, but he must learn it on his own. No one else can make him see what he needs to free himself. Stromas must realize it as well for his freedom to be complete."

Cora stared at her. There were so many things Wintress could mean, and the obvious seemed too easy.

"The most obvious thing is to love, Wintress, and he loves me, so I do not know what else it could be."

Wintress nodded. "Yes, he does love you…" the mage started to fade like smoke carried away by the wind, "doesn't he?"

Cora watched until the mage disappeared completely. Then she walked back into the house. "More cryptic words and now she wants me to have Percival question his feelings for me." However, as she returned to bed with Percival, she wondered if it was confidence or fear of what he would say that would keep her from repeating what Wintress had suggested.

Or maybe she knew he already questioned those feelings.

Chapter 43

The next morning, the group of friends began their journey again. Warmth surrounded them as they traveled through the forest. Wintress had been thoughtful and gifted them with a globe of warmth while they traveled through her forest. For the first time, Percival was happy that a member of his family practiced magic.

Three days after leaving the Tower of Winter, the group greeted their departure from the forest with sighs of relief from the men and cries of excitement from Cora and Tylina. The extra clothing came off in a rush and Percival watched Cora in appreciation as she stretched her arms and legs. She gave him a shy snicker.

"I feel free now. That clothing was confining," she explained, her cheeks flushing.

He smiled at her embarrassment and glee at her renewed freedom, though he did not share in her happiness. When they continued riding, he rode in silence next to Cora, returning her grin when he caught her looking at him. Though he knew she spoke to him, he heard nothing, and even though her voice normally made him happy, this time it did little to lift his spirits.

Finding his grandmother made up for the lack of information, at least. He learned more about his father, but nothing to help him get rid of Stromas.

Because you can't get rid of me. Stromas' laughter echoed through Percival's mind.

Ignoring the demon, Percival turned toward Cora again. Agitation filled her eyes.

"What's bothering you, Percival?" The agitation echoed in her voice, proof that she had tried to get his attention more than once.

"I'm sorry, Cora. I'm just thinking about what Wintress said. I don't think she really helped me with my quest." He couldn't keep the frustration from his voice.

"You're wrong, Percival. She gave you some very good clues. You just have to figure out what they mean. No one knows you better than you know yourself, no matter how close they are to you. That includes me. Until you know yourself, I can never fully know you." She guided her horse closer to his and reached out to touch his hand. "I can wait. Learning with you is enough for me."

"How can you be so patient, Cora? I have forced such an arduous journey on us. Wouldn't you rather be doing something else? Be someplace else?"

He was pushing her away, but whether for her protection, or his own, he didn't know. Maybe he just thought it would be easier for her to leave if he gave her an opening.

"Like what? I'm happy here. I want to be by your side. I don't want to return to my mother's islands. I will only return to them if I am forced, or if you're dead. Since I do not see the latter happening soon, I am sure you will fight to prevent the former." She smiled at him, her confidence wrapping around him like a warm blanket. "Enjoy the journey, no matter how difficult. Be glad we're together. Isn't that what people in a relationship, and who love each other do? Stand by each other?"

"I'm very glad we're together." He took her hand in his and gave it a gentle squeeze. "Together makes every part of this journey easier."

They continued to ride in a comfortable silence, their occasional words to the other easier. Percival pushed his doubts aside for the time being and tried to enjoy the travel.

Two days after leaving the forest, on a different route than the one they traveled to reach it, as the afternoon crept toward evening, the group found a clearing for the night. Kalik tethered the horses near a tree while the others set up tents and cleared space for a fire. The ground beneath them shook, causing Percival to straighten and pull his sword. The trees next to him and Brolin were suddenly torn from the ground by a large hand. Panicking, their horses tore their tethers from the ground and bolted for the cover of the nearby trees.

"By Shae, a giant," Cora gasped. She retreated toward the middle of camp, away from Percival.

Percival glanced at her, noting her hands moving in the intricate designs of her spell casting. Turning away from her, confident Cora would use her magic to compliment his attacks, he joined Kalik in advancing on the first giant. Over their heads, a spear of ice tore into the giant's chest.

The creature roared in pain and threw a tree into the camp. Arrows joined the ice spear in the creature's flesh. Its wails of pain filled the air around them.

Percival looked up, into the face of the creature he attacked. Its eyes! Glowing red like the demons that had attacked before.

Stepping back, he searched the area before going back in for another slice at the giant's legs. The group was nowhere near the giant's territory. Why were they attacking? A red glow behind the giant caught his attention.

"Demons!" he shouted.

Another giant, its eyes also glowing red, threw a boulder into the camp, forcing the group to move to avoid being hit. Percival changed targets. Advancing on the giant's legs, he cut through its thick clothing.

"Get back, Kalik. Your staff is doing nothing!" Percival ordered, gesturing at Brolin to take the plainsman's place.

Archaic words rang through the clearing. Another ice spear slammed into the second giant's chest. Frustrated, the giant hefted a large boulder in his hands and threw it. Cora's scream matched the thunder of the stone hitting the ground.

Pain tore through Percival, dropping him to a knee. With his empty hand, he reached to his back, feeling for a weapon. Another jolt of pain blinded him, shredding the battle haze that normally clouded his mind.

Silence filled the camp. Percival's vision returned as suddenly as it had been taken. Cora lay motionless in the path of the boulder. Kalik lay next to her, his arm draped over her. The boulder continued away from the two on the ground, leaving a trench in its path.

The two did not move. Blood pounded in Percival's ears. The pain that gripped him had to come through the connection he shared with Cora. Damn their bond!

With a feral growl, Percival returned his attention to the giant. Fear fueled his anger.

The Black Hand pressed his attack, forcing the giant to turn. An arrow buried itself deep in its neck and the creature's howl of pain filled the air.

Percival sliced across the back of its knee, severing the muscles and tendons. The creature howled again. It grasped at the injury, falling to one knee. Percival sidestepped the giant's leg, lunging in to sever its other hamstring.

From behind him, a bolt of energy shot through the air, striking the creature's back. The energy forced it forward, onto the ground. Shouting, his eyes burning with a bright fire, Percival charged the giant's neck. He drove his sword into its flesh. Its lifeblood splattered him and the trees, the liquid gushing from the wound.

He stood next to the creature for a moment longer. Driving his weapon deeper, he glanced up, searching for the demons that had incited the attack. Next to him, the second giant crashed to the ground, arrows in its neck.

"I'm going after the demons," Percival announced, not caring if the others heard him.

Chapter 44

Percival chased the demons, ignoring Brolin's attempts to get his attention. For a brief moment, he wanted Exar's bola to slow the creature's escape. Instead, he threw a dagger.

The demon on the right stumbled when the bladed imbedded itself in its back.

The other demon glanced back, sneered and continued its escape.

Percival pounced on the downed demon, digging the dagger deeper into its flesh. Then, with a grunt, he pulled the dagger out and forced the demon onto its back.

"Why! Why do you keep following us? Attacking us?" Percival demanded, picking the demon up and slamming it into the ground before it could answer.

A coughing laugh escaped the creature. "Just how stupid are you, Black Hand? How many times do you have to be told? The Amazon's death will destroy you. Stromas will be free."

"No!" Percival drove the blade into the demon's chest.

Once.

Twice.

Three times.

With a shudder, the demon's last breath came out in a gurgle.

I don't appreciate you killing one of my minions, Black Hand.

"I don't care, Stromas. I'm sick of you trying to hurt Cora,"

Percival growled through clenched teeth. "How are you doing it? How are you getting a message to them? Why now? For three years you've made no move against her. Why now?"

Because you love her, Black Hand.

Percival roared, slamming the dagger into the demon's chest again. He struggled to control his breath through his rage.

"I won't let you hurt her anymore."

You don't have a choice, Black Hand. You can't stop me.

Chapter 45

Percival returned to the group, still wiping the blood of both the demon and giant from his hands.

Disappointment replaced the spark of hope he held tight as he passed the perimeter of their camp. Tylina and Brolin stood next to Cora and Kalik, both now covered with blankets. They stopped their discussion, looking at him as he approached. Percival slammed his sword into its scabbard and finished making his way toward them.

Brolin stood in front of Percival, slowing his forward motion. "Percival, I will take care of everything. You need to let me handle this."

Percival strained to look past the priest. "Cora needs…" He stopped, shaking his head. His protests would accomplish nothing.

"We all need you right now, Black Hand." Brolin gripped Percival's arm in a gesture meant to comfort the other man. With a nod, the priest returned his attention to the injured members of the group.

Pushing his emotions aside, Percival took a deep breath. "You're right. Use our tent. I will set it up for you." He turned his back on the injured and their caregivers.

Brolin had called him Black Hand. Despite everything with Cora, the efforts she had made to call him Percival, he was still the Black Hand.

After setting up the tent and lighting a fire, Percival waited for news. Time passed while he helped Tylina with moving the corpses of the giants. The half-elf used magic to decrease the weight and the size of the giants, making it easier. Since Kalik's horse was the only one that had not run at the giant's attack, Percival sent Nimbly in search of the others while he and Tylina tied the corpses to the horse to move them.

"Percival, everything will be fine," Tylina tried to draw him into conversation.

"You don't know that, Tylina." He spun on her. He felt his anger pushing at him, urging him to strike out—verbally or physically, it did not matter. "You are only saying that because you hope it will. But you don't know."

"No, I don't, but I am only—"

"I don't care what you are only trying to do. Not right now. Just move the damn bodies so we don't have to smell them!" Percival shouted, unaffected by the way she cringed and took a step back.

Tylina turned away from him, casting another spell on the giant they were trying to move.

Damn! What was wrong with him? She was only trying to help. Percival rubbed his face, trying to relieve the pain he could feel growing behind his eyes. His body ached from the combat, and the constant pain he felt from Cora.

Turning back to Tylina, Percival rested a hand on her shoulder. "Tylina, I'm sorry. I shouldn't have done that."

"No, you shouldn't have. Bring your temper under control, Percival. It doesn't help." She did not look at him, but shrugged his hand off her.

They finished moving the bodies in silence. Once they were done, Percival started a fire for the night. When Nimbly returned, he joined Tylina at the fire. Both sat across from Percival, watching him. Percival felt their eyes on him, following his movements. Fear and uncertainty filled their faces.

Above them, the quarter-moon reached the zenith of its journey for the night. Percival felt his approaching confrontation with Stromas pulling at him, despite the pain he felt at Cora's injuries and his frustration.

A quiet conversation between Nimbly and Tylina drew Percival's attention. He watched her leave her seat and prepare evening meal. Nimbly assisted her and in minutes, the smell of stew came from the pot hanging over the fire. When the food finished, Tylina passed out bowls and the three sat in silence, picking at the food.

The rustling tent flap brought Percival to his feet. His food fell to the ground, spilling into the dirt He watched Brolin walk toward them, his sluggish footsteps evidence of the weariness he felt.

"Sooner or later, I'm going to need to spend some time training in my temple, learning how to draw on the magic from the gods. My current abilities are not strong enough to keep up with the injuries this group receives.' The priest's attempt at humor brought a deep scowl from his leader.

"Worry about that later. How are they?" Percival growled.

"Alive, which is the best I can do at the moment. I can heal the wounds of the flesh, but the bones will take stronger healing than I can do. We need to find another healer, with more advanced abilities soon. I fear the bones will set wrong and healing them with my abilities will cause further damage." Brolin turned to smile at Tylina. "At least I can give you some good news. Kalik did not take the full brunt of the stone. His injuries are not as bad as I first thought."

Tylina's face brightened with relief. When she looked at Percival, her joy disappeared and he felt his glare deepen. She reached for him, but he pushed her hand away. He turned away from the fire, filled with frustration. Finally he stormed from the camp. The sound of his footsteps echoed around him throughout the forest.

* * *

Tylina stared until Percival disappeared, unsure if she should follow him. Behind her, Nimbly cleared his throat and she turned back to him and Brolin.

"How bad are Cora's injuries?" Nimbly asked.

"Her hips are crushed, at least one of her legs is broken and she has some broken ribs. I don't know if even a more experienced healer would be able to help her." Brolin shook his head. "I am just trying to give Percival some kind of hope."

"Why are hers so much worse than Kalik's?" Tylina was not

sure she wanted to know.

She was just grateful Kalik would not suffer like the Amazon.

Shame filled her. The two women were friends. She should be concerned about Cora as well, but for the moment, the friendship was overshadowed by her relationship with the plainsman.

Tylina's parents had not raised her to be so cruel to her friends. She should be more supportive of both Percival and Cora. If she died, he would be destroyed.

Again, Brolin shook his head. "I don't know. When the boulder hit her, it must have bounced or something. Kalik was only hit on the shoulder, enough to crush his shoulder and arm. I'm sure he would be able to function and live without the use of his arm, if it didn't heal properly. But Cora…" He shrugged. "There won't be much of a life for her if the wounds don't kill her."

Nimbly and Tylina stared at Brolin for a moment, then Tylina left them, making her way to the tent Kalik and Cora lay in.

Chapter 46

The fire had already begun to die down when Percival returned to the camp. The missing horses had been found while he was gone and were tethered to a nearby tree. Putting fresh wood on the fading embers of the fire, he stoked the flame until it caught the new supply of fuel. He continued walking to the tent he put up so Brolin could care for Cora and Kalik.

Brolin slept on a bedroll outside the tent. Percival glanced back toward the fire and found Nimbly sleeping with his back against a log next to it. He did not see Tylina and assumed she slept inside. The tent she normally shared with Kalik had been put up, but the flap was open and it appeared empty.

He pulled the tent flap back, revealing the sleeping forms of Cora and Kalik. Tylina sat between them, in a meditative trance, her head resting on her arms on her knees. Percival knelt in front of her, and softly touched her shoulder.

"Tylina, go to your tent. Get some rest. I will sit with them for the rest of the night," he whispered close to her ear.

She looked at him, her eyes clearing after a breath, then she nodded. After a soft kiss on Kalik's cheek, Tylina left the tent, letting the flap fall behind her.

Percival shifted, taking Tylina's position between Cora and Kalik. He leaned close to Cora, wanting to kiss her cheek. Adjusting his weight on his arm, he bumped her hip with his hand.

Cora's eyes opened immediately. Her scream, filled with pain, followed an instant later.

"Cora, I'm sorry," Percival whispered, trying to shush her. "Please, stop. I'm sorry. I'm not touching you anymore."

The tent flap whipped aside and Brolin rushed into the tent, his eyes filled with panic. "What happened?" he asked in concern, kneeling next to Cora.

Rubbing his hands together, Brolin muttered a brief incantation. He moved his hands over her body, not touching her. Cora stopped her screams, slipping back into unconsciousness.

"What did you do, Percival?" Brolin asked again.

Percival pulled back from the glare the priest leveled at him. "I was just trying to be closer. I didn't mean to touch her," he answered. His own distress at the pain he caused filled his words.

Brolin sighed. "It's all right, Captain. You must be more careful though. Each spell is helping her less and less, at least in terms of controlling her pain." He rested his hand on Cora's foot, his touch gentle. He whispered a spell and Percival watched her relax into a more peaceful sleep.

"I'll leave. You and Tylina obviously have everything under control." Percival stood.

"No, Percival, stay. I'm sure she would appreciate having you near," Brolin protested.

"No." Percival left the tent, careful not to shake the canvas in his frustration.

He marched to the edge of the clearing after retrieving his bedroll from his horse. He threw the bundle on the ground, then looked at the area around him. Nothing he did would relieve his frustration. Anything he did would only hurt him and take Brolin's spells away from Cora and Kalik.

It's all your fault, Black Hand. Stromas' voice reached him through the depths of his anger. *If you had protected her better, been more alert to your surroundings, you would have known the giants were coming. You could have gotten her to safety. Instead, you led her into an ambush. You almost killed her. You will do my work for me.*

"Go away, Stromas. I am not in the mood for competing with you for control. If you cared at all for Cora, you would leave me alone," Percival almost pleaded with the demon.

Who said I care for her?

"No one, Stromas. Just go away." Percival tried to force the sound of the demon's voice out of his mind.

Just give up, Black Hand. Let me take control. I will ensure you will never hurt her again. Stromas pushed him. *My time is drawing closer, Black Hand. Be prepared.*

"I just don't care right now." Percival finished laying his blankets out and sat down, watching the camp.

Because of their connection, he still felt Cora. She wasn't lost to him—yet. But she was buried deeper than the first time, too deep for him to reach. He felt emptiness where her warmth used to be. His carelessness had caused the pain she hid from.

He vowed not to touch her again. No matter how much he wanted to, he would not cause her pain. He couldn't hurt her if he stayed away.

Chapter 47

"Percival," Nimbly's whisper woke him from his sleep.

Percival opened his eyes, squinting against the sunlight. "What?"

"I scouted ahead some and I found a village that has an experienced healer that would probably help us," the elf advised.

Percival sat up, fully awake. "How far?"

The rogue gestured at the closed tent Cora and Kalik slept in. "Less than a day, normally, but with them being injured, probably two days if we push it. I've spoken to Brolin. He thinks we should be able to make the trip safely, when you're ready. We can move them on stretched blankets."

Percival nodded, standing and putting his bedroll away. From his backpack, he pulled out a map. "Where is the village?" He stretched the map out.

Nimbly studied the map, tracing an unmarked route. "Here." Nimbly pointed to a spot close to the trees they currently camped in.

"All right. Get packed up. I need to talk to Brolin."

Nimbly nodded, then sauntered away.

After picking up his backpack and saddlebags, Percival crossed the camp. Holding his breath, he opened the tent flap and allowed the bright sun to filter into the darkness.

"Brolin, we are going to the village Nimbly found. He says he spoke to you about it." Percival refused to look at his injured friends—his lover—focusing his attention on Brolin.

"Yes, he went into the village and spoke to a village elder. That's how he found out about the healer," Brolin explained. He glanced at the others, raising his eyebrows at Percival's direct stare.

"I'll get their blankets to make litters to carry them. Nimbly and I will have them ready for you by midday meal." Percival stared at Brolin for a moment longer, then left to finish the needed preparations.

By midday meal, the litters were ready. Tylina woke Kalik enough to gain his help in getting onto the litter. He protested at first, but when he tried to mount his horse, the pain from his shoulder caused him to pass out and they had to wait to wake him again. Though Percival could see Kalik's desire to ride, it brought the captain a brief moment of relief when the other man agreed to lie on the litter.

Once Kalik was in place, Percival carried Cora over to the litter, careful in his steps. Laying her on the stretched blanket, his heart ached with the pain he caused her. She moaned the entire time, and turned her head away from him even though she was unconscious. The pain he felt through their connection was still intense, but it didn't paralyze him like it initially had.

Brolin came up behind Percival and rested his hand on his shoulder. "Percival, we need to get her to the healer. There is no other way to help her," he whispered.

"Why do I feel like you are hiding something from me?" Percival asked, keeping his gaze on Cora.

The priest remained silent for a breath. "I have no idea what you're talking about."

"Don't lie to me, Brolin. You're a horrible liar." Percival straightened, turning on the priest. "Tell me what you're hiding."

The two men stared at each other, Brolin's eyes flicking with nervousness. Finally, Brolin nodded, once. "It's bad. Her hips are crushed. If she doesn't get help from a more experienced healer—soon—she may never walk again."

"Can't you do anything else for her?" Percival whispered.

Brolin shook his head. "I've tried to set the bones that I can. Like I said, my spells will heal the wounds of the flesh, but damage to the bone is beyond my ability."

Percival breathed in deep through his nose, holding it before letting out. "All right. It will take us two days with the litters, without any delays. We need to get moving." He turned to the others, hiding his emotions. "Let's move out," he ordered, his voice again taking on the tone of authority.

The litters were attached to horses, the reins held by Percival and Nimbly. The group began its journey in the direction the rogue pointed.

"Brolin, you need to do something to lessen the pain," Percival demanded, his jaw clenched tight against the pain he felt seeping through his connection with Cora.

"I've used all my spells for the day. And I haven't been able to find any of the plants that could help," Brolin's voice was slow with fatigue and he closed his eyes to the glare the Black Hand turned on him.

"That's ridiculous. You must have found something. Every time we stop, you're digging up roots." Percival kicked at a fresh mound of dirt the other man had dug up just moments before.

"Stop it, Percival!" Tylina interposed herself between them, punching Percival in the arm.

She must have used magic to strengthen her hit, because he found himself actually taking a step back from her. Surprised, and a little embarrassed, he rubbed the rapidly blooming bruise. Reaching for the anger that left him so suddenly, he was stopped by her hand, palm facing him.

"I told you to do something about your anger. I meant it. Get it under control, or we will take Cora to the village and leave you here," she ordered. "Do I make myself clear?"

Percival stared at her for a measured breath—two breaths—and nodded his understanding.

"Good. We've traveled all we can today. Brolin needs to rest." Tylina waited a moment, then stormed away.

Percival waited until she was occupied with building a fire, then he went to his horse to retrieve his tent.

Why didn't you do something—anything—to show her that she should never touch you? Just who does the wench think she is? Stromas demanded, his voice booming in Percival's head.

Pain began to build behind his eyes again, intensified by the demon's angered demands. *She's right. I need to get my anger under control.*

Not while Cora's like this. Her pain feeds your anger, in turn feeding me. I gladly use all of it to fuel my strength. It's a vicious cycle and I love it all.

"Shut up, demon," Percival ordered, drawing Tylina's attention. He shook his head at her. "It's nothing. Just talking to myself."

Knowing Tylina did not need his assistance, Percival sat next to a tree to rest before evening meal and his watch.

After the others had retired for the evening, getting what sleep they could before the next watch, Percival sat next to Cora. He had always liked to watch her sleep, but tonight, her face was contorted in pain. The shadows caused by the moonlight made her look worse. Shallow breathing barely moved her chest, each breath deepening the lines of pain in her face. It hurt him to see that even the most basic of needs increased her agony.

"I'm so sorry, Cora," Percival whispered, brushing her cheek with his fingertips.

She moaned at his touch, turning away from him. His breath caught in his throat when he realized every part of her body must hurt. The force of being thrown to the ground by Kalik and being pushed into the dirt by the boulder bruised everything not broken. No matter where he touched her, he only caused more pain.

"I've failed to protect you, Cora, again. I wouldn't blame you if you left me after this, especially since I seem incapable of keeping you safe." He heard the defeat in his own words, but the feel of her resurfacing through their link distracted him.

"But, Percival, I love you," her hoarse whisper made him cringe.

He glanced at her. Her eyes were open, though he could see the haze of pain holding her in its grip. Without thinking, he grabbed her hand, squeezing it.

From their link, pain washed through him. Gasping, he released her. The pain was more intense than when she was injured by the arrow. How was she keeping it from him?

Again, he felt her bury herself in her mind, hiding from the pain she felt—and him. He moved away from her, distancing himself from her litter.

Chapter 48

Three days after the giant attack, the group finally arrived at the small village Nimbly had found. Percival was unhappy with the time it had taken, which had been slower than expected. Despite their efforts to make Cora and Kalik comfortable, the constant movement had only increased their pain. Brolin insisted on frequent stops to allow the two brief respites and administer healing spells to ease the pain.

Homes made of clay bricks with straw roofs dotted the dirt paths of the village. As the group traveled amongst the houses, farmers came out to meet them.

"Do you have a healer?" Percival asked the first one to approach him.

The man nodded and led the group to a hut at the end of town. When they stopped in front of the squat, thatch building, an elderly woman came out to greet them. The woman wore mismatched clothing, her skirt a faded blue and her shirt was threadbare green. Her gray hair was pulled back in a tight bun. Her face showed her age and her green stained fingers betrayed her work with herbs.

"Can I help you?" she asked, peaking through the horses.

"We have injured." Percival directed her toward the litters with Cora and Kalik. "Are you a healer?"

The woman slipped between the horses to the injured, bending to examine them. After a brief moment, she stood.

"Take them inside. I will give you a list of things I will need to help with the healing." She walked into the hut without looking back.

Percival stood by, allowing Brolin to carry Cora into the hut. He followed, glancing around the small common room. Open windows and candles lit the inside. A cot stood in the corner opposite the area that could be considered a kitchen. Herbs, clay jars and various knick-knacks cluttered the one room hut. A curtain stood ready to separate the single room in two.

"Another cot is out back. Bring it inside and lay fresh blankets on it," the old woman instructed. "Put the girl on this cot."

Nimbly helped Brolin lay Cora on the indicated cot while Percival retrieved the cot from outside for Kalik. After making the injured comfortable, the old woman pushed the others from her hut.

"I need to examine them further. I will speak to you once I am finished," she informed them, shutting the door before anyone could respond.

They stood staring at each other for several moments, then Percival turned from his companions and walked away.

"Percival," he heard Tylina call after him.

He walked ten paces, then stopped, staring at the ground at his feet. What would he do if Cora died? He didn't know how long it would be before the Amazon queen found out. Perhaps it would be faster if he went to the queen and let her punish him for failing to protect her daughter.

"Leave him be, Tylina," Brolin instructed her. "He blames himself. He needs to come to terms with this alone. We can't help him."

Percival started to walk away again, Tylina's next words still able to reach him. "He is too hard on himself. I fear for the damage he may cause if he continues this way."

Maybe they were right. He was being too hard on himself. He could have stopped it all. He should not have dragged Cora into his search for freedom.

Percival continued his walk through the village, stopping at the well. He put his hands on the rock, looking into the darkness. "No one can help me. Because of Stromas, I bring only pain to anyone I get close to. No one can help free me from Stromas. Not even Cora."

Chapter 49

A change of the water clock later, Percival rejoined the others outside the hut to wait for the elderly healer to give them news. The farmer who led them to the healer's hut had found Percival at the well and showed him an empty house near her hut. After accepting his offer for them to stay there, Percival had stabled their horses and carried their belongings into the house.

Before he had the chance to tell the others about the house, the healer exited her hut. "My name is Bethany." She held the door open and gestured for them to enter.

Percival felt her gaze on him when he walked in. He chose a place on the other side of the room, watching Tylina sit next to Kalik, holding his hand.

"Your friends should have been brought here sooner," Bethany chastised, glaring at them.

"We brought them as quickly as we could. We were afraid of worsening their injuries," Brolin defended their actions. "I healed them to the best of my abilities, but I didn't want to do too much for fear it would cause permanent damage to their bones."

"Well at least you were smart enough to think of that." Bethany crossed the room to the cots. "Kalik, he told me his name and the girl's, his wounds are easier to deal with. The bones are bad, but I should be able to take care of them by tomorrow morning. Cora, she is going to take a few more days. I have a list of supplies I am going to need, mostly a specific herb. You," she pointed at Percival, "will get them for me. Kalik told me you were the leader and the one Cora looks to for comfort. The herbs are for her."

Percival nodded. "Get me the list and I'll get all that you need."

Bethany pulled a crumpled parchment from a pocket in her apron. "Take that burlap sack. Fill it with as much as it will hold. The more, the better. The village has an herb garden at the east end. You will find everything there. The herbs are identified with signs. Even you should be able to find the one I want."

"Fine." He picked up the sack

"Well, aren't you a pleasant one?" Bethany's sarcasm brought a deeper frown to his face. "Are you always like this?"

"You know nothing about me," Percival snarled.

"He's concerned about Cora, but trying to hide it," Tylina interjected, standing between them.

"Then going after the herbs will distract you, like I thought it would. Now everyone out, except you." She pointed at Brolin. "You can learn something, perhaps advance your skills."

Percival turned and stormed out of the hut, not waiting for anyone else.

He found the garden Bethany directed him to easily. After identifying the herb he needed, he began picking them per the woman's instructions.

You can't pick herbs right now, Black Hand. You need to deal with me, Stromas insisted, his voice loud in Percival's mind.

"I have to. Cora needs them. I don't have time for you right now." Percival tried to push the demon aside. He bent over to pull leaves from the closest plant. Briefly, he felt Stromas try to exert control over his hand, but he fought against the resistance and plucked the leaves from the small plant.

You don't have time for me? If you don't make time for me, I will make your life miserable, Stromas threatened.

Percival laughed. "'Make my life miserable'? Don't you think I'm miserable enough with Cora on the edge of death? Don't you think you've made my life miserable just being a part of me?"

Not as miserable as I can make it.

"You'll have to wait, Stromas. Right now, I need to deal with this. I can't take a day or so to listen to your babble." Percival continued plucking leaves, dropping them in the sack.

A day away from her won't make a difference to the injuries you caused. Don't you understand that? Stromas pushed, trying to play on Percival's feelings of failure.

"I understand what caused her injuries. You've made that very clear."

You understand that every time you touch her, you cause her pain. The pain she feels is because of you. You only make it worse when you try to hold her.

"Yes," Percival shouted. "Now leave me alone." The sound of the demon's laughter filled his mind, then slowly faded. "Curse you, Stromas." His jaw clenched, gnashing his teeth together as he continued to pick the herbs Bethany sent him for.

For three days, Bethany kept the others from seeing Cora and Kalik. Brolin would deliver daily reports to Tylina and Nimbly, who would then in turn advise Percival. On the third morning, when Brolin returned to the house for morning meal, Kalik arrived with him. Though he was gone two days longer than expected, happiness filled the reunion between the friends except for Percival, who immediately left the house upon hearing Cora would not be able to travel for two more days.

Percival's temper continued to shorten with the passing days. Frustration drove him to a more intense anger and abrupt violence than the others had ever seen in their time with the Black Hand. Bethany's refusal to let him see Cora only served to make things worse. Kalik's return, but Cora's continued confinement, made him hate himself even more than before.

He ate only because Tylina and Nimbly forced him to. Sleep came after long hours awake, practicing his sword technique against any who would volunteer. Not even the innocent faces of youths wanting to be trained in the use of a weapon brought him any cheer.

Exhaustion would finally drag him into the depths of sleep, but relief from his anger and fear continued to elude him. The battle with the giant replayed in his dreams and would always end with the image of Cora's crumpled body being revealed by the rolling boulder. When he tried to move past the scene, his imagination would take the dream further. Instead of just revealing her injured body, it ended in her dying when he touched her, cursing him with her last breath.

Percival continued like this until the fifth day, when Brolin told him he could see Cora after midday meal.

Chapter 50

The morning sun touching her face woke Cora. The pain that had consumed her every time she woke since she was injured had lessened. Until she stretched against the stiffness she felt from lying still for so long. Pain ripped through her body like a knife and she cried out.

"Careful, Cora. While your wounds have healed, you're still bruised, and your muscles are still knitting together. You will continue to have some pain, because your bones heal slower. You may suffer pain from them for quite a while," the woman who had been her caregiver soothed her, holding a wooden cup to Cora's lips so she could drink.

"Who are you?" Cora asked, her voice hoarse. Even though the constant haze of pain lifted for the moment, her memories were still clouded.

"I am Bethany. Brolin has been helping me care for you. I have been able to help him tap into his abilities, though he should seek further guidance at his temple."

"I will be sure to explain that to him when I see him again." Cora hid her sarcasm poorly.

Bethany laughed, bringing the image of an old crone to Cora's mind. "At least you have a better sense of humor than your man."

Cora smiled as well, though Bethany's laughter faded quickly.

She sat next Cora, careful not to disturb the bed too much with her weight. "Cora, I need to explain something to you, so no more interruptions until I'm done." The Amazon nodded, her eyes narrowing. "The injuries to the lower part of your body were extensive. No matter how much healing I give you, things just won't be the same."

"What are you saying?" Cora's voice broke.

"If you were to become pregnant, I feel it would be very dangerous to your health and your life. I do not know that you would be able to carry a baby to birth. And I do not know that either of you would survive the birth, if you were able to carry it any length of time at all." The elderly woman pulled a leather bag from her belt. "If you take this herb every time you are with Percival, it will ensure that you remain sterile. Eventually, your extensive use of this will ensure you are permanently barren and you will be able to stop, but that won't happen for years."

Cora accepted the pouch, her hand shaking. "Are you sure? Isn't there a chance you are wrong?"

"A slight chance, but you will know better the first time you are with him. If it hurts, more than just being bruised, deep inside," Bethany touched Cora's abdomen. "Here, then there is a very good possibility of the problems I described." She pressed Cora's fingers into the pouch. "I have three more pouches ready for you. I have also given Brolin instructions for making more."

"You told Brolin before you told me?" Cora asked in surprise.

"No, Cora, I told him the tea was for something else. He does not know what the situation is," Bethany assured her.

Cora sat in silence, staring at the pouch in her hand. "When can I see Percival and the others?" she asked finally.

Without looking up, she could feel the woman studying her. "At mid-day meal. You can leave tomorrow, if you like. I will perform another healing before you go. Your friends are getting anxious to see you and leave."

Cora nodded, closing her eyes. She hoped the healer would understand she wanted to be alone. Bethany's hand gripped her shoulder gently and squeezed with a touch that reminded Cora of her father.

Bethany stood from the bed. "Sleep until they arrive. I will make sure you all have a meal to share."

Footsteps moved away from Cora. She had tasted herbs in

the water, and her sudden drowsiness made sleep easier to succumb to.

Chapter 51

Percival waited until the sun reached its zenith of mid-day before walking to Bethany's hut, alone. Tylina and Brolin insisted he visit Cora without them. Tylina said it would help Cora's recovery if he visited her alone. Even though he wanted to see her—needed to see her—Percival reluctantly went to the healer's home.

Now he stood outside the door, delaying knocking to advise her of his arrival. Finally, with a deep breath, he knocked on the aged wood of the door.

Bethany answered, glancing behind Percival and to each side of the door for the rest of his group. "Well, come in, I guess, Percival. Where are the others?"

"They said I had to come alone." His voice sounded hollow. Making no effort to see past her into the hut, he shrugged his shoulders. "If you would prefer, I can come back later, or send Tylina instead."

Bethany titled her head to the left and squinted. "Do you want to come back later?" she asked.

Quiet surrounded them for a moment while Percival considered her question. Finally, he shook his head. "No, I don't. I want to see her now."

Bethany nodded, stepping aside to allow him to enter. He pushed past her, looking around the small hut. The curtain hung across the length of the room, making it appear smaller than it really was. Bethany pulled the curtain aside to reveal Cora sitting up in the cot, her face glowing from the sun coming in through the window.

"Good morn, Percival," Cora greeted him, pointing at the chair next to the cot. "Please, sit with me."

He walked over to the chair and sat in it uncomfortably. The couple waited in silence while Bethany brought them a tray of food, resting it on the cot at Cora's feet. The healer patted Cora's foot through the blanket, then left the hut.

"Brolin says you're doing better," Percival muttered after several more minutes of silence.

"Yes, Bethany says we can leave tomorrow if we want." Cora handed him a wooden plate with greens and roasted chicken on it. "How are you, Percival?"

He sat quiet again, staring at the food on the plate. "I failed you. I didn't protect you... again."

"You didn't fail me," she protested.

Percival stared at her, recognizing her attempt to make him feel better and the way her forehead scrunched up when she was thinking. "I feel like I failed you and you look as if you agree."

"No, I don't agree. You didn't fail me. You did everything you could to save me, as well as the others. If it wasn't for the group of you, I wouldn't be alive to have this argument with you," she insisted. Cora reached over and caressed his cheek. "You *didn't* fail me."

He nodded at her repeated words. Inspired, he placed his plate on the floor and reached for her. As he pulled her into his arms, she cried out, pushing away from him. She gasped for breath, gripping the blanket in a tight grip.

"I thought Bethany said you were better." Percival straightened, a mixture of shock and fear gripping him.

"She said I would hurt for a while longer, from the bruised muscles still healing and the bones knitting together," she tried to explain through gasps.

"I don't want to be afraid to touch you, Treame." He knelt next to the cot, resting his head on the blanket, careful not to touch her again.

"I know, Percival. It will get better soon." Cora ran her fingers through his hair. He reached up and touched her fingers with his own. "We're together. It can only get better."

Chapter 52

The next day, Percival purchased a wagon from one of the farmers. Standing outside Bethany's house, he hitched Cora's horse to the wagon while she watched him. He kept his back to her, his movements looked stiff and uncomfortable.

"I don't want to ride in the wagon, Percival," Cora informed him.

"You need to ride in the wagon so you are able to finish healing. I know riding the horse will cause you more pain," he insisted, looking at the horse's flank and not at her. "I can't be the cause of more pain for you, Cora."

Cora watched him, unable to say anything more. She heard the doubt and anger in his words. Sighing, she knew she could not give him the comfort and reassurance he needed. She did not know how to make him stop punishing himself. And he was not the only one who needed reassuring.

Percival helped her into the wagon and drove it to the house where he and the others had been staying. After getting everyone's belongings loaded into the wagon, the group began their journey to Larkspur.

While they traveled, Cora took the time alone to think. Her mother's dislike of Cora's abilities played prominently in her thoughts. The queen always felt Cora incapable of the power to defend herself. Was she right?

Worse, Cora felt Percival slipping away from her. The blame he took created a barrier between them and weakened their connection. Cora had to admit, at times, she laid the blame at his feet too. His promise to protect her had been broken, again. She stared at Percival's back, watching him move with his horse's steps.

She had failed to protect herself, as well, though. By depending on Percival's protection alone, she had not kept herself safe. Their combined strength was needed, not just one.

It bothered her more that he looked at her less often each day. While they traveled, he still told her he loved her. Sometimes, when they were in their tent, before he fell asleep, he told her of his feelings, but he still did not speak directly to her often. She spent one night trying to remember each time he had touched her since they started traveling, again.

She couldn't count more than a single hand of touches.

If he forgave himself, would it be easier for her to forgive him?

A day's travel from Larkspur, Cora sat with her back against the side of the wagon, cushioned by her blankets and those of her friends. Percival sat on the seat, taking his turn at driving.

"Tylina, take these for a moment," Cora heard him say before the wooden seat creaked and he turned toward her.

Cora added a number to her mental tally for the day, chastising herself as she did. This made three times he had looked at her since they started traveling for the day.

"Cora, are you able to take watch tonight? I think we're close enough to the city that we shouldn't have any problems," Percival said, his voice void of emotion.

She glanced at him, returning her attention to the plains they traveled through. "Yes, I'm ready to take watch again," she answered, her voice quiet.

"You're sure you are able to—physically?"

Was that sarcasm or concern in his voice? Cora gave a slight nod. "Yes, I'm fine."

From the corner of her eye, she saw him watching her. Without another word, he turned back to the road, taking the reins from Tylina. The three rode in silence until Nimbly notified Percival of a place for them to camp for the night.

While they set up camp, Cora joined Percival in the area where he was putting up their tent. "Can I help?"

"No, I can do this alone. Go help with the meal," he dismissed her.

Cora stared at him, then turned away. She had asked to help every night since they left the village. And, he sent her away until he finished every time. But he had never dismissed her like this.

Tylina already had the stew in the pot, so Cora sat on a log next to her, waiting for the meal to be done.

Cora ate in silence, Percival eating on the other side of the fire. When she finished, she cleaned her bowl and waited for the others to finish.

Percival stood after cleaning his own bowl. "Tylina, Kalik, take first watch. Cora and I will take second." He walked over to Cora's side of the fire, gripped her arm and pulled her from seat.

He guided her to their tent, his grip tight, but she could feel it was not his intent to hurt her. When he opened the tent flap, Percival gave her a slight push inside, then removed his hand from her arm.

"You need some rest before watch," he informed her.

Cora glared at him. "So do you."

He nodded. "I will lie down in a minute. I want you to get to sleep first."

She stared at him, defiant, then waved her hand at him. He accepted the dismissal with a shrug of his shoulders and left her alone.

Percival's soft, hesitant touch on her shoulder woke Cora at the beginning of their watch. When she moved, he jerked his hand away. Outside the tent, she saw the shadows of Kalik and Tylina moving in front of the fire to their own tent.

"Are you sure you're ready?" he responded his question from earlier.

Cora sighed in frustration. "Yes." She stood slowly, feeling stiff from her injuries and the cold of the night.

Percival left the tent to allow her time to get ready. After wrapping her capeshal around her, Cora left the tent and took to her usual position by the fire. His questioning glance brought another sigh from her.

"I want to go back to some place we can call home," she advised him.

"Home... being with you is good enough for me." Again, his voice was void of emotion. "Once we reach Larkspur, we'll restock our supplies and return to Jonquil."

Cora nodded. "That should be fine, if we are going to call it home."

"Yes, Jonquil should be fine, for now at least. I am accustomed to Glenys, but Jonquil should give you some distance from the Amazons in the capital." He shrugged. "I don't know where to go from here. Everything I've learned has been cryptic. We'll take some time to ourselves, then we can begin our search again after we've had a chance to rest." He leaned toward her, and reached out with his hand to touch her, but stopped himself.

She turned away from him, nodding. "Agreed. You need to be comfortable with that decision. I'm sure you'll get us back safely." She kept her emotions from being heard in her voice.

Guilt darkened his face. "I hope I can."

"I still have faith in you." She studied the fire again.

Cora felt him watching her. She wanted him to hold her, even for a moment. Why did he insist on staying away from her?

Percival stood from the log and walked away. "I wish I could take your pain away, Cora." He stopped, turning back to her, then continued walking. "I'm checking the perimeter."

"I have the camp," she called after him, her routine response coming easily to her lips.

"And my heart." His voice came back to her through the darkness.

Cora waited until she no longer heard his footsteps, then stood. She wanted to talk to Percival without the others hearing. Slowly, so as not to aggravate the healing muscles of her body, she weaved a path through the camp, casting a spell of protection around her sleeping companions. Confident she had done her best to protect them, she left the camp, following in Percival's footsteps.

Moving through the tall grass of the plains, she easily spotted him ahead of her under the moonlight. He stood gazing out at the plains, but turned when the sound of her footsteps reached him, drawing his sword. She stopped her movement toward him, holding her hands up in front of her.

"It's only me," she called quietly.

He released the breath he had been holding. "A more beautiful sight I can't imagine." A brief grin broke through his stoic expression. Sadness filled Cora when it disappeared in less than a heartbeat. His sword hissed as it slid back home. "Camp secure?"

"As secure as I can make it."

He laughed, and she realized how much she missed hearing that sound. "I'm sure it's fine." He paused. "I have faith in you."

She said nothing, moving closer to him, wrapping her arms around herself tighter. He reached toward her, his palm up and waited, his hand shaking. She appraised his hand, unsure if he really wanted her to take it. Finally, she rested her hand on his.

Percival brought it to his lips, brushing her fingertips with his lips. "What's wrong?"

As if he did not know. Cora's body shook with a deep sigh. "I'm afraid you have more faith in me than I do."

He straightened his back, still holding her hand. "You are talented, Cora. I've seen the damage your magic can cause. You are my magic and I am your strength. We will always need your power. It has helped the group many times in the past."

She stared at him, his eyes lighting briefly with the fire she was learning to fear. Stepping away from him, she tried to pull her hand from his. "I didn't come to talk to the Black Hand, our leader. I came here to talk to Percival, the man I love. The man who is supposed to love me."

His grip on her hand tightened as he pulled her back to him. "Have I hurt you so much that you see me as the Black Hand again? You are an asset to the group as a whole and your value to me personally is beyond measure. You are a strength I draw upon to survive day to day. You keep the demon at bay and without you, the emptiness would eat my soul before the demon could even get close."

She tried to pull her hand away again, forcing him to relax his grip.

"That is what bothers me. I don't feel as if I am a strength to you. I feel as if I am a weakness, a distraction, a hindrance..." She gestured with her hand, trying to say more, but she could not make the words come out.

"Why would you ever think that? You bring me strength at the most difficult times. Your faith in me keeps me from giving in to the demon." He put her hand on his chest, over his heart.

Then why not touch her? Why avoid her? Instead of asking the questions she wanted to, Cora pointed at the scar on her throat from the assassin's arrow, then at the fading bruises that she revealed by opening her capeshal. "Proof of my weakness. I do not have the strength. I don't feel as if I can be everything you need me to be. I can't give you everything that any other couple has or wants." She paused, then continued. "The healer said I most likely won't be able to bear a child."

Percival stared at her. Silence filled the air around them.

"I never realized how much I wanted a child with you until now, after you tell me we can't," he finally whispered. "Child or no, I will love you no less. You are what matters." Cora heard his words, but again she heard the doubt that filled them. "I can accept being childless, but only if you are by my side. I don't want to lose you."

"I am not going anywhere, Percival." She pressed closer to him, resting against his chest. She knew there would be pain if he held her, but she *needed* him to hold her.

"Treame," he whispered in her ear. "I've missed you." He brought his hands to her waist, caressing her. His fingers pressed into her flesh.

She gasped, pain shooting through her. He backed away from her, anger filling the space between them.

"Go back to camp," he growled, turning from her and continuing on his patrol of the camp perimeter.

Cora stood watching him, shocked, and tried to control her breathing. When the pain subsided, she returned to the camp, her own emotions raging out of control.

Chapter 53

Percival listened until Cora's footsteps faded, then turned to watch her until she disappeared in the darkness.

He still caused her pain every time he touched her.

She called him Black Hand, just as Brolin had. It had been so long since she called him by that name. He hadn't realized how much he enjoyed hearing his name pass her lips. He must have hurt her in ways he had refused to acknowledge.

You need to touch her, Black Hand. What's holding you back? Stromas' hoarse voice echoed in Percival's ears.

"The pain she still feels, Stromas. I don't want to hurt her," he answered, looking down at his hands—hands that had already caused Cora so much pain.

But I want to touch her, Black Hand. It's been so long since we felt her skin against ours. Lust tainted Stromas' voice, disgusting Percival that he was forced to shared his desire with the demon.

"Go away, Stromas. I know how long it's been." He continued on his path around the camp.

Our time has come and gone, Black Hand. You can't keep resisting me.

"I can and I will. More important things than you occupy my mind right now," Percival snapped. Not for the first time in his life, he wished Stromas were a physical being he could hit.

Oh yes, I'm sure there are. Like, for instance, how you will never have a child. Most unfortunate. Stromas laughed. *Oh well! I was so looking forward to seeing if a child would come out looking like you or me. Do you think Cora will allow you to be with another woman so that I can see what would happen?*

"Enough, demon! I do not want another woman!" Percival yelled.

Then do something about it! Take what you want! Don't hold back, Stromas pushed him.

"Go away, Stromas. You will have to wait. I'm done with you tonight." Percival tried to push the demon's voice out of his head.

You are only making it worse, Black Hand. My next visit will not be so pleasant. The demon's words echoed in Percival's mind.

Percival waited, his angered breath calming with every rise of his chest. How much longer would he have to deal with this demon? He raised his gaze to the star filled sky. "What were you thinking, Father? Why tie me to this demon for your own greed? Did you really accomplish anything?"

Chapter 54

The afternoon sun had begun to sink into the western horizon when the group of companions passed through the large wooden gates of Larkspur. Cora sat in the wagon, silent, while Percival obtained the name and directions to an inn from the city guards.

Cora stared at the crowds of people still roaming the streets at the early evening hour. The citizens opened a path for the wagon without complaint, even waving at the Amazon in greeting. She returned their waves, her gesture hesitant.

The sun set completely by the time they arrived at the inn. Percival and Kalik took the horses and the wagon to the stable, while Cora led the others inside. She nodded without thinking when Tylina suggested she find a table while Cora paid for rooms.

Cora turned toward the bar, taking a moment to look around the tavern. The overcrowded room smelled of ale and sweat and her senses felt suffocated with the strong scents. Gaining the barkeep's attention took patience she did not have. Instead of waiting, she used a cantrip to increase the volume of her voice to call for him.

"Barkeep!" Cora waved when he finally looked in her direction.

He sauntered to her end of the bar and sneered at her. "Yeah?

You looking for me?"

"Only so I can purchase rooms for the next few nights. I need three," she explained, keeping the smirk she felt hidden.

"If you find yourself alone one of those nights, I'd be happy to rectify that," he said with a wink, pushing a book toward her. "Sign here."

Cora signed the book on three lines, then watched the barkeep notate room numbers next to her name. He pushed three bone keys toward her.

"Do you need more keys?" She nodded and he pushed three more keys over. "They are marked with the room numbers," he said with a grin.

"My thanks," she responded, picking up the keys after counting out gold to pay for their accommodations.

She made her way to the table Tylina had found and sat in the empty chair next to Percival. He pulled his chair away from her, just enough that she noticed the increased space, though he did not make a big show of it. Cora glanced at him, then turned her attention to the barmaid who had appeared next to the table to take their order.

While they waited for their food, Cora listened to the conversations from the other tables. Soon after ordering, a bard began playing from a place near the fireplace. His face looked familiar, but she could not remember from where. She turned toward Percival, hoping he would remember.

"Have we heard this bard before?"

Percival looked at her, his eyes glazed, the fire from Stromas burning bright, but he did not appear to have heard her.

"Percival?" She reached to touch him, but he swatted her hand away.

"Yes, this is the bard from King Kennan's celebration," Tylina answered for Percival, favoring him with a wary glance.

Cora stared at Percival a moment longer, then turned away from him, looking at Tylina. Her friend's eyes were filled with sympathy. She opened her mouth as if to say something, but the Amazon shook her head.

The meal passed in silence, the only conversation between Tylina, Brolin and Nimbly. Cora listened to them, but her own thoughts distracted her.

The day before, Percival had made her feel better, telling

her she was strong. And yet, he appeared worse than before, pale, his jaw constantly clenched. He refused to touch her again and she was unsure how much more she could forgive. Looking down, she realized she had not touched her food. Forcing herself to eat, the food tasted bland and had become cold.

The bard stopped playing, begging an ale for his parched throat. When he passed her on his way to the bar, he smiled at her. It was the look one friend gave another, as if he knew the pain she felt in both body and heart. But that was not possible. They had never spoken, even in Glenys. No longer able to sit in silence, Cora finished her food and stood.

With a glance at the bard, who now stood at the bar talking to the barkeep, Cora stretched, lifting her arms over her head, but a sudden burst of pain jolted through her abdomen. A gasp escaped her and she dropped her arms to hold her stomach. Glancing at Tylina and Brolin, she flinched at the concern in their eyes.

"It's getting better," she tried to assure them. She smiled, but it rapidly faded when she looked at Percival.

His scowl had deepened, though he refused to look at her. His knuckles turned white as he gripped his eating knife tight.

Cora set a room key on the table next to his hand. "I'm going to bed. See all of you in the morning."

She turned from their table and plodded to the stairs, her thoughts on how Percival had acted since leaving Bethany's village. She knew he had tried to talk to her before the group reached Bethany in an attempt to comfort her. His efforts to comfort her caused more pain when he touched her, unintentionally.

He wouldn't even look at her now and went out of his way to avoid touching her. Her thoughts continuing to flow through her mind, she opened the door to her room and locked it behind her. The bags that held her and Percival's belongings sat in a pile near the table, having been brought in by the stable boy when Percival stabled the horses.

From one of her bags, she pulled out the shirt she had taken from Percival. She held it to her face, enjoying the feel of it against her skin. Though she slept in it, the material still smelled of him, at least in her mind. His scent was more a comfort than anything else was right now, since it was the only thing she had.

With a small sigh, she carefully changed her clothes, turned the lamps down that lit the room and climbed into bed.

Chapter 55

Downstairs, Tylina sat with Percival, watching him. The others had retired to their rooms for the evening after Cora, leaving the two friends alone. Percival stared into his mug, the ale holding his attention since Cora left, almost a full change of the water clock later. A sudden movement from him startled Tylina and she realized he was ordering a fresh mug from the barmaid as the woman passed their table.

When the new mug was delivered, he drank from it twice, then resumed staring at the liquid. Finally, Tylina could no longer sit in silence with him and she changed to a seat closer to his.

"What's wrong, Percival?"

When he looked up from the mug, his eyes burned with the fire she always associated with anger or when he was in combat. Nothing indicated he was angry and there was no reason to think they were in danger of being attacked in the crowded tavern. The fire burned, intense, for a heartbeat, then faded when he shook his head.

"Nothing, Tylina. Nothing is wrong." Percival took another swallow of his ale.

"I don't agree. You sit here, without Cora, sending her to bed without so much as a touch or look." She rested a hand on his arm. "I've been watching both of you. She is doing better.

Surely you can at least look at her," Tylina voiced only a small part of her concern over her friend's sudden distance from each other.

He pushed the mug away, almost tipping it in his sudden anger. "I look at her."

"Maybe before, but not within the past day. Not since she stood watch with you. I've seen how you looked at her in the past. Even after her injury, you still looked at her like no one else was around for miles. Like no one else was in the same room, or even near you." She removed her hand from his arm. "Remember, you weren't the only one affected by her injuries."

He stared at her, his eyes narrowing, then grabbed the key Cora left for him from the table. "Many things affect me right now, Tylina. It'll be harder to fix than you think." He stood, tossed coins on the table and tromped upstairs without waiting for her to respond.

Tylina stayed at the table, gazing at the empty chair. "If it is the demon, there is nothing I can do to help you, Percival. No one can help you, unless you let them." Adding two more coins to the ones Percival left, she made her way upstairs to the room she would share with Kalik.

Chapter 56

Percival shut the door behind him, careful not to disturb Cora. The lamps in the room burned low, only remaining lit enough to give him light when he came in.

Cora still took care of him, even though he didn't deserve it. And he had to admit—Tylina was right. He barely looked at Cora anymore.

Turning away, he undressed and turned the lamp on the dresser down completely, letting the flame flicker out. He tiptoed over to the bed and pulled the blankets back so he could get in, unintentionally exposing Cora's back. Moaning, she reached behind her, pulling the blankets over her again.

"I'm sorry. I didn't mean to wake you," Percival whispered, leaning over to get close to her ear.

"It's all right," she whispered in return. Cora rolled over, right into his arm and body. She whimpered at the contact and tried to move away from him.

Growling, Percival stood, removing his weight from the bedding, affording her the chance to resituate herself in the bed. After she stopped moving, he sat on the edge of the bed, his back toward her. He heard her move again and he felt her gaze on him.

"Maybe I should get another room," he suggested after a moment of silence.

"No, I don't want you to do that." He felt her move closer and then she touched his back. Percival tensed, mirroring her reacting at this touch.

"I don't want to hurt you, Cora. I've hurt you enough already," he whispered.

"Not intentionally, Percival." She rested her head on his back. His breath quickened as her hand grazed his skin until she touched his chest.

He spun around, taking her into his arms. She gasped at his sudden movement and he felt her pull away slightly, but remained in his embrace. For a heartbeat, he held her, letting the smell of her hair fill his senses. Finally, he pulled away from her, wiping a tear from her cheek.

"Good night, my Princeesa." Percival stood, taking his pillow from the bed and went to the floor, using his bedroll from his pack as cushion and blanket. The room filled with the quiet sound of Cora crying while he remained awake, unable to sleep.

He had never seen or heard her cry like this. And he was the cause.

Return to the bed, you fool, Stromas insisted.

Leave me be, demon.

Your strength against me grows weaker with each day you resist our confrontation and resist your need to be with her. You will lose, Black Hand.

Maybe.

Stromas' demands went silent.

Finally.

* * *

Cora cried until the pain of breathing against her tears forced her to stop. She could hear Percival breathing from where he lay on the floor, but she knew he did not sleep.

She had not cried many times since coming to Man's World, but the pain she felt at her healing injuries and Percival's refusal to sleep in the bed overwhelmed her. The tears came unbidden and freely.

He had not called her 'princess' since confessing his love for her—since they became intimate. And, he never called her 'Princeesa'. The sarcasm she thought she heard in his voice made her cringe with pain in her heart. Physical pain from his touch did not compare.

Percival's breathing had not changed while they lay in silence. Cora knew he had not been sleeping well; the fatigue was obvious in his face and demeanor. Even in falling asleep, they could not agree.

Chapter 57

In the morning, Percival went to the market without Cora. She had refused to leave their room and had turned her back to him.

Tylina and Kalik accompanied him, neither wanting him to be alone. Percival followed the couple, listening to the different cries for attention from merchants desperate to sell their wares.

Despite his blindness, Kalik traveled through the crowded area easily, always keeping within reach. Tylina never wandered far from her companion, often reaching back to touch his hand or arm. Percival knew they had become closer over the time the group traveled together, though he did not know how far their relationship had progressed.

"Percival," Tylina's voice broke through his thoughts. They had stopped in front of a store that sold food and drink. Three small tables occupied the front of the store with chairs at each one. Kalik sat at one table, waiting for the other two to sit.

Percival joined Kalik at the table, after pulling out a chair for Tylina. After ordering food and drink, the three sat in silence. Percival felt Tylina watching him and even Kalik's blind inspection made his skin itch. Finally, Tylina broke the quiet.

"You look tired, Percival. Didn't you sleep last night?" she asked.

"Yes, I slept, but not very well." Percival looked past her at the people walking through the market, hoping she wouldn't push the inquiry.

"Why not?"

He sighed, and returned his gaze to meet Tylina's again. "I slept on the floor. Cora was hurting. I didn't want to aggravate her injuries more."

"Have you spoken to her about how you feel? Have you asked her how she feels?" She held up her hand to stop his response. "I don't mean physically. She's been seriously injured twice since we left Glenys. The demons keep telling her that they want to kill her to free Stromas. Given her upbringing and everything they are taught, don't you think she feels some level of inadequacy?"

Percival opened his mouth to respond, but Tylina pushed her hand toward him again. "I understand that you have your own issues, and I'm sure this isn't easy on you. Everyone knows how much you depend on her for strength during your monthly trial, but you can't continue to ignore her. She needs to know you still love her, despite her injuries. You've got to get past it or you may end up losing her."

Percival stared at her in disbelief. "Do you really think I've done that much damage to our relationship?" he asked in a whisper.

"Yes," Tylina and Kalik said in unison.

"I don't know what to do. I'm afraid of hurting her." Percival lowered his gaze to the table.

The serving girl returned with their food and glasses of wine.

"You will hurt her more if you don't do something. You need to show her you still love her," Kalik advised, his hand skimming the table, searching for his drink.

Tylina pushed the glass closer to Kalik's hand and positioned his plate in front of him. "You should return to the inn. You need to talk to her."

Percival nodded in agreement, gave Tylina a small smile and left the table.

He returned to the inn, and rushed up the stairs to the second floor. Opening the door to the room he and Cora shared, he found her sitting in a chair by the window. She looked outside and did not turn when the door opened.

"I'm sorry, Cora." Percival shut the door and crossed across the room, stopping behind her. Kneeling next to the chair on one knee, he wrapped his arms around her and the chair. He was still mindful of her injuries and kept his embrace loose.

"For what?" She rested her hand against his shoulder.

"I wasn't thinking. I was so worried about hurting you physically, that I didn't stop to think that I was hurting you emotionally with my distance." The closeness of her body excited him and the smell of her hair, still damp from a bath, filled his senses. He breathed deeply to keep himself calm and focused on what he wanted to say. "You don't know what it was like while I waited to find out if you would live or not. Bethany kept us away from you and Kalik for three days. Only Brolin was allowed to see you, and his reports regarding your progress just weren't enough." He moved to the front of the chair, and leaned against her legs.

"When Kalik came back to the group, it was like the giant that hurt you had punched me in the stomach. I hated myself for allowing you to be hurt. My temper became worse, shortening with each day. I didn't want to eat, thinking that I could starve myself. I couldn't sleep." Percival rested his head on Cora's lap.

"Percival..." Cora began.

"No, let me finish." He looked up at her, his pain reflected in her eyes. "My dreams were filled with images of that last battle. And they always ended the same way; you under the large boulder. But instead of surviving, I watched you die every time I tried to touch you."

"I'm so sorry, Percival." She ran her fingers through his hair.

"I miss you, Treame. I want you to know how much you mean to me," Percival whispered.

"I miss you, Percival." She brought his fingers to her lips and kissed them.

He pulled her from the chair, kissing her. "I am so glad you survived—that we survived—together."

"Yes, together," she whispered in his ear, then kissed his neck.

Guiding Cora to the bed, his kisses touched a path down her neck and over her shoulder. With gentle control, he laid her on the bed, letting their emotions and needs be their guide.

Chapter 58

Lying in Percival's embrace, Cora pressed her hand into her abdomen, trying to stop the pain she felt. Bethany's warning returned to her. She held her breath to determine how intense the pain was within her.

Cora felt it deep inside, as the older woman had warned. Looking at her bags, she noticed the top of one of the pouches containing the herbs that would prevent pregnancy. Briefly, she thought about making the tea. She could feel Percival's breath on her shoulder, and as her skin warmed, then cooled with each breath, she knew she could never prevent a child they created together from coming into the world—even if it killed her. Closing her eyes, fear for her decision filled her.

Suddenly, Percival sat up on his elbow. He pulled away from her and she turned to look at him. With a gentle touch, he wiped the tears from her face, concern etched on his face. "Are you all right?" he whispered.

She nodded, turning her head to kiss his fingertips. "Yes. I'm fine. I'm with you. What could possibly be wrong?"

His smile broadened and he cupped her cheek in his hand. Reaching his arms around her, he hugged her, his embrace still gentle. She knew he was still aware of the pain she felt, but he was no longer afraid to touch her. His deep sigh of relief filled the room when she snuggled deeper in his embrace. "I've missed you so much, Treame. I've missed even the slightest touch of your hand on my arm."

She nodded, sleep slowing her reaction.

"Cora, I need to tell you something. I won't be returning to Jonquil with you. I have to face Stromas," he whispered.

"Is it bad this time?" She woke fully, frightened by his words.

"It could be. I've been putting it off for about fifteen days now, because of yours and Kalik's injuries. It's harder to keep him under control with each passing day." A distant look came to his eyes, then he shook his head and returned his attention to her. "In the morning, you will leave with the others and I will see you in Jonquil as soon as I can get there."

"No, we will wait for you here. I'm surprised you would even suggest we leave without you," she whispered, disappointed.

Percival shook his head. "You *will* go. I can't be sure how long it will take or what might happen if you don't. I don't want you to get hurt," he said, his voice filled with desperation she had not expected to hear.

She sat up, turning to look at him. "Don't be ridiculous, Percival. You would never do anything to hurt me, no matter what happens with Stromas."

Before she could react, he sat up as well and grabbed her by the shoulders, his eyes lighting with the fire that seemed to be controlled by Stromas. She cried out in surprise and tried to pull away from him, but his strong grip would not let her go.

"I'm not being ridiculous, Cora. I will not place you in danger again because I can't control Stromas. I don't know what this confrontation will bring and I won't let him get to you if I can prevent it." His grip continued to tighten. "Don't you remember what happened the last time?"

"Percival, stop! You're hurting me." Her words broke through the haze of anger and fear surrounding him.

He released her, disbelief and disappointment replacing the fire in his eyes. His gaze fell to his hands and the red marks on Cora's arms.

"I'm sorry, Cora. I don't know what came over me," he whispered. His voice was filled with pain and he moved away, turning his back toward her.

Silence filled the room for several minutes while each of them tried to calm their breathing and the fear they felt. Finally,

Cora took a deep, cleansing breath and reached out to touch Percival's back.

"Percival, look at me." He turned slightly, self-hatred still in his eyes. "You didn't mean to hurt me. I know that. You're worried about me and the others." She laughed a little. "I'll even go so far as to say I was being my usual argumentative self." Cora pulled him toward her, despite his resistance.

He wrapped her in his embrace again. His rough fingers traced circles on her back while he lifted her long hair over her shoulder.

"We always seem to have one problem or another come between us," he whispered in her ear.

She nodded, then allowed him to pull her back down on the bed. Despite a desire she could feel in his touches, he continued to caress her back and hair. His touch relaxed the tension in her muscles and she let his caresses lull her into a light sleep.

Chapter 59

While Cora slept, Percival took a bath, then dressed. Pulling his bags from under hers, a small leather pouch fell onto the floor. He bent to pick up the pouch, examining it in the fading afternoon light.

"What is this, Cora?" he whispered, turning toward the bed.

He knew she still slept. Her breathing hadn't changed. Instead of waking her, he opened the pouch and poured the contents into his hand. He smelled a mixture of dried herbs—bitter and sweet. With no training in herbs or other medicines, he couldn't identify them, but they smelled like the leaves he had collected for Bethany.

Hoping Cora wouldn't be too angry, he searched through her bag and found two more pouches. The ties on the other pouches were knotted, just like the one he opened. None of them appeared to have been used.

He dumped the herbs back into the pouch, closed it again and placed it in his saddlebags. He would find out exactly what the contents were for after he dealt with Stromas. Leaving a kiss on Cora's cheek, he left to arrange for the group's supplies for their return to Jonquil.

* * *

Later, as the moon rose to shine its bright light on the city, the group of friends met to eat evening meal together. After everyone ordered food, Percival cleared his throat to draw their attention.

"I won't be joining you on the journey to Jonquil," he advised. "My... situation demands my immediate attention. To delay longer will only make it worse."

"Then we will wait. A few days in the city will be fun," Nimbly declared.

Percival shook his head. "No, I want you all to continue on to Jonquil."

"Why can't we wait? We've waited before," Kalik asked.

"I don't know how long it will take, and we all know it will be difficult to keep Cora from following." Cora started to protest, but Percival smiled at her and shook his head. "I'm not complaining. I just don't want you to be hurt again."

"But by the time you're finished, we may be too far away," Tylina exclaimed.

Percival nodded. "I understand, Tylina, but I can't go with you right now." His eyes flared with the familiar fire, much brighter than normal. "I need to stay. I'll meet you in Jonquil." He reached out to hold Cora's hand.

She gave him a small nod, acknowledging his silent cue. "We have made arrangements for fresh mounts and supplies. We leave in the morning. Hopefully no one has anything else to tend to before we go."

Cora did not hide her emotions well. Percival could see her struggle to hold back tears and force a small smile to her mouth. He glanced at Tylina, noting that she too saw Cora's efforts to control her emotions. Squeezing Cora's hand, he continued with his plans for the group's return to Jonquil.

Chapter 60

The next day, after midday meal, the group went outside the city gates to bid farewell to Percival before beginning their journey. The captain stood next to Cora, his hand resting on her lower back while they watched the others make final adjustments to their horses. Kalik joined the group moments later, after checking with the city guard about any reports of problems on the road they would travel.

Percival's hand warmed against Cora's skin. She would be safe with their friends. He had no doubt they would be capable of protecting her until he returned.

"I'm still not happy about this, Percival." Cora turned to look at him, tears in her eyes.

He reached up and brushed away a tear before it could start down her cheek. "I know, but Stromas has tried to confront me three times since your injury and I feel myself growing weaker each day. If I don't face him now, I'm afraid I will lose control and I don't know what will happen. I could lose myself forever. Neither of us wants that. If he gains control of me, there's no way to know what kind of destruction he will cause."

Cora nodded reluctantly. "I know. We'll find a way to solve this."

He wrapped his arms around her and held her close for a moment. After a deep breath that filled his lungs with her scent—wild flowers—he pulled away and gently pushed her toward her horse.

"I love you, Treame," Percival whispered when the others turned their horses away from him and started down the road.

He stood watching them until they disappeared in the dust of the road. When they were gone, he mounted his horse and turned in the opposite direction his friends went. He rode until the setting sun turned the sky red.

Turning off the road, he continued until the red faded from the sky, and then set up camp. By the time full darkness descended on the land, he finished the preparations of his camp. He lit a fire, but felt no desire to cock a meal. Staring at the flames, he felt the familiar descent into the depths of his mind, the prelude to every confrontation with Stromas.

The large demon waited for him in a large cavern. Percival could not remember ever having met Stromas in such an environment before. A fire burned in the cavern, but the familiar large boulder sat on the side opposite of where Percival sat. Stromas sat on the boulder facing him, a clawed hand strumming the rock in impatience.

They sat in silence while Percival resumed his study of the fire. Instead of focusing on what the demon wanted, he remembered the feel of Cora's skin against his before he let her go.

"You are a weak fool, Black Hand." Stromas flung his insult, finally breaking the silence between them. *"Without me, you are weak. I give you the strength to do the things you do. I give you the emotions to lust for that woman. The only emotions that are truly yours are anger, hatred and sadness."*

"Cora helps to keep those away," Percival mumbled.

"And your weakness almost cost you what little sanctuary her love gives you. I turn my attention from you for a moment and look at the damage you've caused without my guidance." Stromas shook his head in disgust. *"I knew I made a mistake when I gave you the emotions to love her."*

Percival jumped to his feet, his anger driving him. "My love for her is my own. You didn't give it to me!"

The demon bared his teeth at Percival. *"How can you be so sure? Have you ever felt this way about any other woman?"*

The Black Hand stared at him, doubt making him scrunch

his forehead. "That's because I never made any effort to love anyone else. I was afraid I would hurt them because of you."

"No, it's because none of them ever intrigued me as much as she does. Her abilities will benefit me when I am finally in control and I am free of you." The demon licked his lips. *"Oh, the things I will teach her when I am no longer restricted by your weaknesses."*

Anger flashed in a wave of heat through Percival, then he took a deep breath, trying to calm himself. "That will not happen, Stromas. I will fight you until my dying breath. Cora will never let you have control of me—or her."

"How can you be so sure of that? How do you know she isn't just using you for the power I will be able to give her? Your father used you. What makes her any different?" Stromas stood, walking to Percival's side of the fire. He slowly circled around the Black Hand.

"Cora didn't come to me because of you. She never sought me out. I am the one who found her. She knew nothing about you until I told her." Percival turned his head to look at the demon. "She is nothing like the man who sired me."

"They are both mages, Percival. I see no difference," Stromas growled, coming to a stop in front of him. *"Have you forgotten her vision? She came here looking for you. There's a reason for that. She wants me."*

Percival stared at the demon, a smile coming to his lips with a sudden idea. "Stromas, what exactly are you trying to do? In one statement, it sounds like you want to keep Cora and me together. Yet, in the next, you try to tear us apart. Do you really know what you want?"

The demon stared at him in surprise. *"I am only trying to make a point. Perhaps she isn't what you think she is."*

"Yet, you would give me the emotions to love someone who is deceiving me and make your own plans to use her. That doesn't seem possible, Stromas." Percival smirked at the demon.

With a growl, the demon lunged at him, raking Percival's chest with his claw. He cried out, trying to move away from Stromas. Percival drew his sword, bringing it up in time to block the next attack.

Stromas reached out, grabbing Percival's left wrist. *"See this! This shows the world that I control you!"*

Percival jerked his wrist from Stromas' grip. "You don't control me!"

Pain shot up Percival's left arm, into his chest, driving the large man to a knee. Laughing, Stromas swung, hitting the side of Percival's head and knocking him to the ground.

"I will control you! And I will show your Amazon what it's like to be MY mistress!" he shouted in Percival's face.

"Over my dead body!" Percival shouted in return.

"Oh no, my stupid human. But you will wish you were." Stromas turned his back on the Black Hand. "Enough for this time." The demon immediately disappeared.

Percival struggled to stand, staring at the spot where the demon had been. The darkness gradually faded, returning him to his camp. He looked around, noting that his fire had died out. Putting his hand next to the ash and half-burned log, he realized the fire was cold and a thin layer of dust covered the remains. The sun must have risen hours earlier because of its close approach to the midday high.

His chest hurt from the slashes Stromas had left with his claw. The pain from his left arm had settled near his heart. Looking at his arm, Percival stabbed his sword into the dirt at his feet.

"What did he do to me?" The black on his arm had progressed to his elbow. Did the progression mean that Stromas could take control easier? Percival looked at the sky. "Will I lose my fight against Stromas?"

Exhaustion threatened to overwhelm him, as if he had not slept in at least two days. After emptying his water skin, he cleared the fire pit, changed his shirt, and packed everything onto his packhorse. He mounted his horse and rode back to Larkspur, struggling to stay awake until he arrived.

He returned to the inn where he and the others had stayed, hoping a room would be available. The barkeep pushed Percival's money back to him.

"Your room has been paid for. The white haired woman you were with, she paid for a room for you, for as long as you would need. I've been waiting for you to return," the barkeep explained. "When you leave, any money left over will be returned to you."

"How many days have I been gone?" Percival asked, shock at Cora's arrangement adding to his fatigue.

"Three days. Where have you been?"

"What about a bath?" Percival redirected the conversation.

"Those have been paid for as well as any food and drink you will need." The barkeep rested a key next to Percival's hand and walked away. "I'll have the water taken up to your room," he called behind him, walking into the kitchen.

Percival ate in his room while the tub was filled. After a refreshing bath and almost falling asleep in the tub, he gratefully climbed into bed.

The next afternoon, Percival left the inn and made his way to the local alchemist. He had slept until mid-morning, recovering from the time he lost dealing with Stromas. The claw marks on his chest had scabbed after he cleaned them in the bath and the pain from the expanding mark on his arm disappeared before he woke. He would never forget how that felt and he knew he never wanted to feel it again.

Percival had the pouch of herbs that he took from Cora's saddlebag in his pocket. Before beginning his journey to Jonquil, he wanted to find out what the herbs were.

He walked into the shop, the different aromas of all the herbs in the room suddenly assailing his senses. An old man looked up at his entrance and smiled, several teeth missing in his grin.

"Can I help you?" The man stepped out from behind the counter.

Percival handed him the pouch. "I would like to know what this is used for."

The old man nodded. He studied the contents while Percival looked on, impatient. A pinch rubbed between two fingers, a sniff of the pouch and a small taste gave the alchemist the information he needed.

"This mixture of herbs is used to keep a woman from becoming pregnant." The old man squinted at the younger man. "Why do you have this? The herb does nothing for men and surely one as young as you should be looking to start a family, not prevent one."

Percival nodded, disbelief and shock keeping him silent. The words spoken by the old man slammed into him like a wave hitting a cliff during a storm. Finally, Percival found his voice again and after thanking the alchemist for his help, returned to the inn.

While he walked, he tried to make sense of all he knew about the herbs. He picked the leaves himself used to make the mixture that would keep Cora from becoming pregnant. That revelation alone had been enough to shock him. Obviously, Bethany had felt Cora's injuries were severe enough to not only warn the Amazon against having children, but to give her the herbs as well.

Cora's refusal to use the mixture surprised him the most. He did not know what would happen if she tried to carry a child to term, but he did not want to lose her to a decision made because she was stubborn. The fact he had not been told about the herbs angered him to the point that he worried if he would be able to control his temper next time he saw her.

For the remainder of the day, until he went to sleep, Percival focused his thoughts on the conversation he planned to have with the Amazon when they were together again.

The next morning, after packing his supplies and possessions onto his extra horse, Percival began his travel to Jonquil.

Chapter 61

For two weeks, Cora and the others traveled. Because of Kalik's meticulous care of their horses, there were no issues with the animals. The group stayed at Traveler's Inns infrequently, despite their availability. Pushing for speed, they passed every other inn.

In the early afternoon sun, on the first day of the third week after leaving Percival, the towers and walls of Jonquil filled the horizon. When they moved closer, they could see a large number of tents outside the city. Flags fluttered above the tents in the light breeze. As the group neared the city, Cora heard the distinctive sound of metal striking metal. Figures strolled amongst the tents and many others were practicing with weapons

Recognizing the most prominent symbol on the flags, Cora felt the warmth drain from her face. With a glance at Tylina, she found her fear reflected in the concern on her friend's face.

"Do you know them, Cora?" Tylina asked.

The Amazon nodded, then took a deep breath. "I need to write a message to Percival as soon as I can. I'm afraid my time here may be over." She pointed at the flag flying from the top of the largest tent, then touched her necklace. The symbol on the medallion was the same as the flag.

Tylina looked at her, confused. Cora sighed.

"My mother."

When they passed the Amazon's tents, Cora pulled her capeshal over her head, hoping to hide from the women watching the road. The group traveled through the city until they reached the Hemisphere Flyer. At the inn, Tylina and Cora held their saddlebags while waiting for Kalik and Nimbly to make arrangements for their horses. When the men joined them, the group entered the building and the sounds and smells quickly overwhelmed them.

Cora glanced around the room, her gaze finally settling on a table filled with female warriors, all well-armed. Tylina grabbed her arm and pulled her into a corner away from the table.

"How did they know we would be here?" Tylina asked in a hushed whisper.

"Satina probably told Reann about how close this inn is to your house. The queen most likely has Sea Wolves at all the taverns in the city, just in case," Cora answered, her voice as quiet as her friend's.

"Write the message quickly, Cora. They do not look patient."

Cora nodded, rushed to the bar and pulled out the items she would need to write a letter to Percival. She wrote quickly, her strokes hurried. Blowing on the ink to dry it, Cora put her items away, then folded the letter. Handing the parchment to Tylina, she glanced toward the table the Amazon warriors had occupied and found two were missing. Glancing around the room, she found them standing behind Tylina. Her eyes widened in shock, and Tylina turned around quickly.

"My Princeesa." The one on the right pushed past Tylina and tipped her head toward Cora. "I am Reesa, Captain of the Sea Wolves."

Cora took a deep breath, forcing her face to become free of emotion. After another breath, she straightened her back, whipping her hair over her shoulder with a flick of her hand. "I know who you are, Captain Reesa. My time here has not affected my memory."

Reesa's face reddened briefly. "Of course, Princeesa. Please forgive me." She glanced at the table still occupied by the other women. "Your mother wishes to see you, immediately."

Cora glanced between Tylina and Reesa, then reached for

her saddlebags. The other Amazon behind Tylina came forward and took the bags from Cora's hands before she could put them on her shoulder. Cora reached to take the bags back, but stopped when she saw the surprise on Reesa's face.

"All right, Captain Reesa, take me to my mother." She brushed past the two Amazons and rested her hand on Tylina's shoulder. "I will be back, after whatever displays of authority my mother wishes to portray are done. I will let you know what she requires." Cora squeezed gently, then led the other Amazons from the tavern.

The princess-mage followed Captain Reesa through the city, with the rest of her Amazon escort behind her. No one spoke to her, giving her the appropriate respect for her station. Only Captain Reesa held enough rank to speak to their princess without her speaking first.

As soon as they left the confines of the city walls, Captain Reesa sent two of the women ahead. She turned to Cora. "Your mother has a feast planned in honor of your return. They will let her know you are coming, so final preparations can be made."

Cora studied the other woman, then continued toward the Amazon camp. She took five steps before the captain followed in silence.

Cora's mind was crowded with thoughts of convincing her mother to let her stay and how Percival would react when he found she was gone. How would she free herself if her mother forced her to return to the islands? She looked up as a shadow crossed her path, reminding her of the companion she lost to Shoshona's hatred.

Cora entered the large tent and stopped at the sight that greeted her. Her mother sat on the pillows that covered the floor, reading a book Cora recognized as one of her journals. Elite guards stood on the perimeter of the tent, their eyes forward but alert to everyone around them.

She expected to see her mother's attendants, but none sat around the queen. Cora was surprised to see Dekart sitting with chains on his wrists and legs, close to Reann. Bruises colored his face and chest. His shoulder length blond hair was unkempt. He wore no shirt, only the leather breeches worn by many of the male slaves of the islands. Cora could not remember the last time he had not worn a shirt like the others. Her father looked up at Cora's entrance and gave his youngest daughter a brief smile. Without returning the expression, confident he would understand, Cora turned her full attention to her mother.

Bringing her hand up in a fist over her heart, she lowered her head. "May Shae bless you, My Queen," Cora spoke the traditional greeting and waited for her mother to acknowledge her presence before returning to a normal stance.

Reann slowly pulled her eyes from her reading to look at her daughter, the child she had come to Man's World to retrieve. Her mother's waist-length hair was almost as white as Cora's and her eyes shined the same bright color. Cora resembled her mother more than she wanted to admit. The queen chose to wear more modest clothing, whether to give herself a more dignified appearance, or to hide the scars she received fighting for the throne, Cora never knew.

"I'm glad you agreed to join us. Please, at ease, my daughter." She patted the pillows next to her. "Come, sit next to me."

Cora bit her lip, trying to keep her angry retort from slipping out. She raised her head and lowered her hand from her chest, not comforted by her mother's change to an informal meeting. She crossed to Reann's side and sat on the pile of pillows. Glancing up when she heard movement from the guards, she gaped in surprise when they began to file out of the tent. A soft chuckle returned her attention to her mother.

"Don't act so surprised, Cora. I do not require the guards to be present when I am with my daughter." Cora watched the smile on her mother's face disappear, to be replaced with the stern expression she wore whenever the princess required discipline. "No reason for the guards to hear what is said—between us— or for them to think you came with us for any other reason than because you were bored and wanted to come home."

Reann's attention returned to the journal and Cora waited for her to continue. "Why, Treame? Why this man, this *Black Hand*?" Cora opened her mouth, closing it again when she realized her mother did not want an answer yet. "Aren't you afraid of his curse? What is it about him that would cause you to abandon the traditions of your people and allow a sister Amazon to return without you?" Reann stopped and looked at her, waiting for an answer.

Cora contemplated her mother, then took another calming breath. "When I'm with him, I feel things I never thought were possible for an Amazon. I'm happy. I feel… complete."

Her mother stared a moment longer, then sat up fully, slamming the journal shut. "That is not acceptable. Treame, you will retrieve whatever possessions you have left with your *friends* and you will come home with us. We leave in the morning." She stood.

"And if I refuse? What then, Mother?" Cora stood as well, her posture confident despite her mother's growing anger.

Reann's face reddened. "Then your attempts to save him and your friends will be for naught. I will send the elite guard to find and kill them all, except the Black Hand. I will have him captured and put in chains as my prisoner. If you still refuse to come home, I will visit upon you the worst punishment I can imagine, but not one of death. You will live with the knowledge that your decision killed your friends and your man. His death I will make very slow and painful. I will bring him to the islands and he will suffer the punishment that our most uncivilized sisters can imagine for him." She pointed at Dekart. "And your father will suffer his fate as well."

The younger Amazon stared at her mother. Behind Reann, Cora saw Dekart raise his head and shake it slightly, defeat in his eyes. She could not fight her mother. To protect Percival and her father, her freedom was forfeit.

Cora turned to leave, but stopped when she reached the tent flap. Shaking with fear and anger, she turned to face Reann again.

"Mother, what happened to Satina when she returned with my journals and not me?" Her voice shook as well, though she struggled to keep her emotions under control.

Reann brushed her hand over her clothing. "As I warned her, if she returned without you, she was killed."

"You can't be serious," Cora gasped in disbelief.

"I am quite serious. I take your safety very seriously and she failed me. Her lack of success forced me to come after you. Perhaps you should have thought about her life before you sent her away." Reann stared at her for a moment more, then sat again and returned her attention to Cora's journal.

"I should have thought of many things." Cora left the tent,

allowing the flap to close behind her. "I am so sorry, Satina. I never dreamed she would follow through with her threat." The princess spoke quietly, ignoring the guards waiting nearby with horses. A moment later, she mounted one of the horses and led the others into town.

"Can she really make you return with her?" Tylina asked in disbelief.

Cora nodded. "She is my queen first, my mother second. She can order me to do anything she wants. And, when she places the lives of my friends and the man I love in danger, she can expect me to do exactly as she orders."

"We can help you, keep you from going," Brolin suggested, bringing nods of agreement from everyone.

"It won't do any good. She has already said she would kill you and torture my father and Percival in the ways of the wild Amazons." She rested her hand on Tylina's. "Please, don't do anything that will bring her wrath upon you. Don't come after me and do your best to keep Percival from following."

"We will do as you ask, Cora, but only because we do not want to cause you any harm," Kalik assured her in his usual quiet voice.

"Thank you, Kalik. Please be sure to give him my letter and this." Cora placed her necklace in Tylina's hand. After forcing a smile to reassure her friends, she turned to leave. She stopped before leaving the room, and glanced at Kalik. "Please tell Percival I'm sorry and that I love him," she whispered, knowing the plainsman would hear her.

Kalik nodded, his expression solemn.

When Cora walked outside the Orenda house, the sound of her friends following her surprised her. Her mother's personal guards waited for her, glaring at the intruders. Nimbly and Brolin stepped forward to help Cora onto her horse while Kalik made sure the animal was not over loaded.

Drawing their weapons, the Amazons and advanced toward the men. The leader of the squad shouted a command in the Amazon language.

"She wants you to stop," Cora translated, brushing Nimbly's hands from her horse. "You need to stop. She won't hesitate to attack you."

Nimbly and Brolin nodded, and backed away from her. Kalik took their place, putting a hand on her leg and lifting his sightless eyes to meet hers.

"Cora, remember who you have become since you came here. Your mother cannot take that from you." His quiet words struck a chord of harmony within her, easing the fear and anger she felt.

Before Cora could respond, the closest guard struck Kalik in his chest with the butt of her spear. He stumbled back several steps, his hands coming up to block another attack.

"*Stop*!" Cora shouted in her native language.

Two more women advanced, their weapons pointed at Kalik's chest.

"Arcanum misi linge!" Cora shouted again, raking her fingers across her chest, creating identical marks on the chest of the first Amazon.

"I said stop!" Cora repeated her order as she prepared another spell. "Leave him alone, or I will kill you."

The elite guards hesitated for a moment, then retreated. Tylina helped Kalik back away from the women. Cora looked down at her friends, tried to smile again, but failed. With a slight wave, she turned her horse and led the Amazons away.

As the sun fell below the horizon, Reann's celebration began. Cora watched everything with a detached expression. When she had stayed an acceptable period of time, she excused herself and went to the tent that had been erected for her.

She sat inside, listening to the music and singing. After midnight the celebration ended, the Amazon camp finally blanketed with the sound of sleeping women. Cora knew in the morning, no matter how much the Amazons drank or how late they celebrated, they would be ready to leave when the queen was. The journey home would begin.

Chapter 62

Percival handed the reins of his horse to the stable boy. "Be sure to wash her down. She's been very good this past month. Give her some extra oats, please."

The boy nodded before Percival turned and exited the stable. He had traveled for a month to reach Jonquil, with time spent to care for his horse when she went lame. One night was lost to dealing with Stromas, and fortunately, he had spent it in a Traveler's Inn. At one point, bandits attacked him, but he fought them off. Now he looked forward to a hot meal, the companionship of his friends, and a warm bath.

But he really wanted to see Cora. He grinned at the thought of the bath and her hands washing his back, followed by a night in a soft bed with her close by to ease the stress of the travel. His pace into the Orenda estate quickened with anticipation.

Entering the house, an unexpected silence greeted him. The servants moved about quietly. Upon seeing Percival, they avoided him, hiding quickly. Finally he found Kalik, Brolin, Tylina and Nimbly in the library.

"Well met! Glad to see everyone made it back," he called to them from the door. He strolled into the room and over to a cart with decanters of liquor. "Kalik, I need you to take a look at my horse, if you would. She twisted her leg and the days I gave her to rest may not have been enough." Percival poured himself a glass of wine while he spoke, then turned to look at them.

The men did not look at him directly, instead mumbling their greetings. Only Tylina met his gaze, her eyes filled with sadness. "Percival, we need to talk. Something has happened."

"What happened?" He sat in a chair facing the half-elf. Concern filled him and he knew he did not keep it from his face as he glanced around the room again. "Where's Cora? Why isn't she down here with you?"

"Cora is gone," Tylina whispered, forcing him to lean forward to hear her.

"What did you say?" he asked slowly.

"Cora is gone," she repeated.

"What?" he exclaimed. Percival stood from his chair. He couldn't believe she acted so nonchalant.

Brolin reached out to pull him back into his chair. "Anger will not solve this, Percival. Listen to what she has to say, then you can do what you want."

Percival stared at Brolin and Tylina, then sat back down, impatient at Tylina's slow path to her point.

"Cora's mother was waiting for us with a small army. She forced Cora to go back with her to the islands. The queen said if Cora didn't go, she would send out a force to find all of us and kill everyone. Cora left to protect all of us. She had no choice Her mother threatened her father, as well." Tylina reached into a pouch and took out a piece of folded parchment. "She left this for you." She handed the parchment to him.

As Percival read the letter, Brolin leaned forward. "She begged us not to go after her, especially the men. She knew we wouldn't be able to stop you, but she made us promise not to go. She wanted us to try to stop you, as if we could. She was scared of what would happen if we followed. But she was very intent on the fact that we were not to go to the islands. *None* of us."

Tylina slipped something into Percival's hand when his eyes left the letter. "She said to give this to you as well."

Percival looked at the item in his hand and found Cora's necklace. He remembered their last night together, how the medallion rested on her chest.

Kalik spoke for the first time. "Before she left, she did say one more thing." The others turned to look at him. "She whispered it, so I was the only one who heard. She said she was sorry and that she loves you."

Percival's eyes went to the parchment again. The hurried strokes of her letters revealed the urgency she felt when she wrote it.

"When did she write this?" he whispered.

"As soon as she saw the Amazons. After we arrived at The Hemisphere Flyer. It was the last thing she did before she was escorted out by the captain of the Sea Wolves," Tylina answered.

Percival searched the letter again, trying to find anything else, anything the others had left out. The anger and fear grew within him and when he looked at the others, the flames in his eyes made Tylina move back in her chair. He could feel Stromas grabbing onto the anger he felt and made it stronger.

"You let her go, without a fight or a struggle or even a harsh word? You've heard her speak about how her people treat the men on their island and you let that determine whether or not you were going to stop a member of our group from returning to a place she hates." He glared at them, his anger reaching full force. "Why would you let her go? Does her safety mean anything to anyone but me?" His shouted words echoed in the small room.

"Her safety meant enough to us that Kalik was attacked by the guards who came with her when she returned to tell us the news." Tylina's angered words surprised Percival. "She in turn attacked the Amazons. It was not an easy decision to let her go. She insisted!"

Silence filled the room. They stared at each other, none of them sure of what to say next. Percival waited a moment more, then stormed from the room, slamming the door behind him. He grabbed his bags from where he left them at the bottom of the stairs and stormed out the front door, slamming it as well.

Returning to the stable, he found his horse still being brushed down. "I'm leaving again. Put her saddle back on, just don't tie it down all the way."

The stable boy stopped brushing her. "But, she's tired. She needs to rest."

"I know. I will walk her. I just need to get her to the inn."

The boy stared at him. Finally he nodded and retrieved the saddle and blanket Percival used. He placed them on the horse loosely. "Be careful with her."

Percival nodded. "Thank you." He took the reins of the horse and guided her from the stable.

He stormed through the city streets toward The Hemisphere Flyer. He pushed people aside, his anger fueling his strength. The people yelled at him in their frustration, but quickly retreated when they saw the fire in his eyes and the dark anger on his face.

When he reached the inn, after giving the reins of his horse to the stable boy and practically throwing coins at him, Percival went into the building, ordered drinks, a meal and paid for a room. He sat in the common room, watching people around him at the other tables while he fumed about the news he had received. His food and drink were delivered and though he was hungry, he barely touched his meal. The first drink disappeared quickly, as well as the second and third that were delivered to his table.

After finishing more drinks than he wanted to count, and more than he had drank since traveling with Cora, Percival finally ate his cold meal. He gave the barkeep an amount of gold, paying for one of the stable boys to refresh his travel supplies. His horse was to be readied for an early morning journey.

With his head aching from his over indulgence in ale, he went upstairs to his room. His plans to retrieve Cora from the Amazons were set within his mind. First, he would get a boat, then find the island, and bring her home by force if they refused to let her go willingly.

The next morning, after eating in an attempt to curb the pain still lingering in his head, Percival guided his horse from the stable. The sight of his friends waiting for him as he exited the building lifted some of the weight from his chest.

"Thank you for coming with me," he mumbled.

"We want to let the Amazons know we don't appreciate them taking Cora from us," Kalik informed him.

"Then we should get going." Percival gave them a brief nod, mounted and led them from the town.

Chapter 63

"Are you telling me you've been intimate with the Black Hand?"

Cora felt her mother's glare cutting into her back, but tried to ignore it while she breathed against the pain cutting through her abdomen. The trees lining the road brought no comfort, especially with the memories of the attack racing through her mind.

"I'm not telling you anything, Mother. I'm in too much pain to tell you anything," Cora groaned. "I don't understand your anger. You weren't much older than me when you took Dekart for yourself."

"This is different, isn't it, Cora? Dekart is my slave. I have never treated him differently. You treat The Black Hand as an equal," Reann stated, her voice lacking sympathy for her daughter's current discomfort.

"Yes, I do. Mother, he will follow me and he will try to bring me back from the islands. You will not be able to keep us separated." Cora could feel the pain decreasing slightly. "I was destined to meet him."

"Why do you say that?" Curiosity lit Reann's face briefly, replaced by the emotionless mask she always wore when dealing with an irritation.

"When I was training in the divination spells." Cora stopped, holding her stomach. "I wish this would stop, even if it's just for a short time."

"Continue," Reann ordered.

"I saw him, Percival, and his black hand, in a vision. I saw us, together."

"And has the vision come to pass?"

"Not yet. But he will come for me," Cora reiterated her warning.

"This does not concern me. Your vision means nothing to me. You know I do not look as favorably upon your magic as I do the combat skills of your sister." Reann huffed in anger. "I will do whatever I feel necessary to protect you and our way of life."

Cora waved her hand at her mother. "We don't want to change the Amazon way of life. We just want to be allowed to live our lives the way we want."

"Not while I live." Reann left her daughter, her angered footsteps in the plains grass quickly fading.

"Don't force that point, mother. You may not like the consequences." Cora continued her slow breaths until her mother called for the Amazons to continue their journey.

Chapter 64

Trees lined the road, some of their branches still heavy with leaves from the summer season. Percival didn't recognize the specific area, but he knew Cora was unconscious from the mage poison when they first traveled this part of the road to Jonquil.

In front of the group, four Amazons blocked the road, their expressions filled with surprise. Behind him, Percival heard Nimbly chuckle.

"Do you think they expected to face Percival alone?" he asked with another laugh.

"Most likely," Tylina whispered in return.

"I don't want to fight you. Just let us pass," Percival requested, stepping closer to them and dropping the reins to his horses.

"You will not pass," one of the Amazons declared, drawing her sword and charging at him.

The Black Hand pulled his own sword, swinging it up to block the Amazon's attack. He fought her recklessly, not caring what injuries he inflicted or suffered. His anger fueled his attacks and left him open for her retaliatory swings. He ignored the numerous wounds that appeared on his arms.

"I think Cora's mother was serious," Nimbly's quip cut through Percival's battle haze.

"Serious?" Tylina asked as she exchanged blows with a third Amazon.

"About not wanting us to follow." He laughed again.

Though he heard Nimbly and Tylina's casual exchange, Percival did not voice his opinion. Blocking a side swing, he pulled a dagger from its sheath at his back with his empty hand.

The Amazon pressed her attack, bringing her sword down against his in multiple overhead attacks. She brought her sword up again, preparing for another attack, but Percival lunged forward and drove his dagger into her stomach. She staggered away from him, looking at the weapon in surprise. A bloodied hand pulled the blade out and she lunged to attack him again, her movements unsteady. Percival brought his sword up, pushing the larger weapon into the wound created by the dagger. The two stared at each other, Percival watching the life fade from the woman's eyes. Finally, the lifeless body fell to the ground and he pulled his sword free.

He turned to see Kalik and Tylina dispatch their opponent. The two remaining Amazons stopped their attacks against Nimbly and Brolin, lowering their weapons.

"If we let them go, they may join another group left behind to slow our progress," Tylina observed, stepping up next to Percival.

"I don't feel like dealing with prisoners, Tylina." Percival's anger and frustration cut at her, as sharp as his sword. He lowered his gaze. He still blamed the others for Cora being taken by her mother. "Let them go. If another group is waiting for us, then let these two join them. I won't kill them in cold blood." He turned from the group and began tending to his horse.

Tylina turned to speak with the Amazons. Percival heard her speaking in their language and waited for her to finish with them before asking what they said.

"They say at least one more group is waiting for us," Tylina explained as the Amazons left after retrieving their horses.

"The queen must not care how many she loses trying to stop us. Have your wounds examined by Brolin, then we need to get moving again." He felt his frustration leave him, an empty space remaining where it had been.

After letting Brolin tend to the others, Percival called for the group to continue without having his own wounds cared for.

Chapter 65

The Amazon army arrived in Glenys in the early afternoon. The size of it had forced a slower pace, the journey taking three weeks. Cora followed her mother through the city, the army following close behind. Her father walked next to her mother's horse. Frustration made her heart thump in her chest at not being able to share her horse with him.

The large group traveled until they reached the docks. Tied to one dock was the same ship that had brought Cora and Satina to Glenys three years earlier. A second ship rested on the other side of the pier. Both ships appeared ready to sail. At the entrance to the harbor, a third Amazon ship waited to dock for those the first two could not carry.

King Kennan and ten soldiers sat astride horses, blocking the dock and patiently waiting for the Amazons. The king lowered his head slightly toward the Amazon queen.

"Your Majesty, you and your people have created quite a stir in my city," King Kennan acknowledged the Amazons' arrival without letting his voice betray the frustration in his expression.

Cora silently praised the king for his attempt to remain strong against her mother's invasion.

"Don't tell me you are unable to handle a small inconvenience such as this. Perhaps your queen could handle it better." Reann's carefully worded insult appeared not to affect the man.

"Perhaps you are right. I will have to ask her to go door to door to calm the crying children you have disturbed." The two stared at each other. The guards on both sides shifted, anxious that neither leader appeared to want to back down.

"What do you want?" Reann finally asked.

"I only want to make sure all your needs have been taken care of, and to ensure you have all your necessary supplies," Kennan advised.

"I have no doubt you made sure of everything my women purchased while I was absent, retrieving my daughter from your lands," Reann said.

"Of course, however I am trying to be polite. I do hope my efforts aren't wasted. You have, after all, come to my land without an invitation or arranging for safe travel." The king's scrutiny traveled over those with the queen, finally coming to rest on Cora. "I am happy to see you are well, Princess Rylannes. I hope your time here was informative."

Cora shook her head, but held back her response. The glare her mother gave her left no doubt anything she said would be punished when they were alone. Cora tried to plead for help from the king with her eyes, but he looked away from her without even a nod.

"Safe journeys, Your Majesty. I hope you will again grace my humble kingdom and city with your presence soon." King Kennan bowed his head again, then rode past Cora and Reann, his men close behind.

Cora felt a bite of anger toward the man for feeding her mother's ego. When the king disappeared amongst the buildings, Cora dismounted and stood next to Dekart on the dock while they waited for the horses to be loaded. Amazons and mounts divided into three groups, with the first two boarding the ships already docked.

The second ship had left the dock to make room for the third ship, when Captain Reesa joined Cora and Dekart. She stepped between them, placing her back to the queen's slave.

"The queen wishes for you to board now, Princeesa. We are ready to launch," she advised, bowing her head slightly.

Cora nodded, stepping past Reesa. "Unless you have an effective plan to get us out of this, Dekart, I would say we are stuck." She took her father's hand in hers, and proceeded up the plank with him.

Once on board, Dekart kissed her fingers. With a small smile, he left her and went to the queen's room.

Cora stood at the rails, watching the ship leave the dock, propelled by oars in the lower decks of the ship. When they reached the mouth of the harbor, the sails unfurled and were caught by the breeze.

Reann approached her daughter, the angered expression she had worn for the last three weeks replaced by one of peace. She brushed strands of long white hair from Cora's face.

"Mother, why aren't we waiting for the last ship?" Cora whispered.

"It will wait for the arrival of the Black Hand," Reann answered. "In case my warriors are unable to stop him."

"Warriors? What have you done, Mother?" Cora straightened and pulled away from her mother's hand.

"I have placed groups to prevent him from reaching you. Like I said, I will do whatever I need to, to stop him."

"And if you are unsuccessful? If he arrives at the islands?" A knot of fear formed in her stomach that pushed away the nausea she felt returning.

"Then I will make him a prisoner and his spirit will be broken, or he will die." Reann's words were stern, leaving no room for argument or discussion.

Her mother left her, every footstep strengthening the fear Cora felt for Percival's safety.

Chapter 66

Two days after the first attack, another group of Amazons attacked Percival and the others. They fought fiercely, outnumbering the companions by one. The Black Hand dispatched two of the women, while the others handled the remaining three.

Frustration at the delays the queen presented him no longer filled the large man. He faced each combatant without emotion or feeling, his need to be with Cora the driving force behind his actions.

As the last Amazon fell, Percival turned to his friends. He wiped the blood from his sword before sliding it back home.

"We can't leave the corpses on the road. Despite the fact they attacked us, there will still be problems with the law," Percival noted, staring at the bodies.

The others nodded in agreement. They spent the rest of the day digging a common grave for the women.

When the darkness fell, the five continued down the road before stopping for the night. Percival stood on the road, gazing in the direction of Glenys when Tylina found him.

"Is everything all right, Percival?" she asked, resting her hand on his shoulder.

"No, Tylina. I promised her I would protect her and I failed, again. I promised I would bring her home if her mother took her to the island. I'm going to fail in this as well." Defeat rang clear in his voice.

"Don't say that. The journey has barely begun and already you are admitting defeat. What would Cora say?" Tylina's disappointment cut through his melancholy.

"If Cora were here, we wouldn't be having this conversation." Percival turned to the half-elf. "That should be obvious, Tylina."

"It is, Percival. I have to tell you, we understand how upset you are, but as a group, we're tired of you taking your frustration out on us."

He stared at her in disbelief.

"That should be obvious as well, especially given the fact we aren't responsible for what has happened. We are with you because we're your friends, but our friendship will only survive so much mistreatment." Tylina glared at him a moment longer, then turned and walked away.

Percival stood in the darkness until he could no longer hear her footsteps. Then he also returned to the camp, her words weighing heavily on him.

Three days later, as the sun reached its midday peak, the group of friends again stood in the middle of the road to Glenys. In front of them, another group of Amazons stood waiting for them to advance. Tylina had placed herself between the four Amazons and her friends.

"We don't want to fight you," she tried to reason with them, attempting to prevent the clash they knew would come.

"But we will fight you. We have orders to prevent the Black Hand from getting near our Princeese again," the tallest woman declared in heavily accented Trade.

"We have fought and killed eight of your sisters already," Percival declared, stepping forward in anger. "Do you really want to die as well?"

The four women stood in silence, the other three deferring to the one who spoke first. Finally, the speaker shook her head.

"If we must die, we will do so with pride, fulfilling our duty to the queen and our people." She leveled her spear at Percival's chest.

From behind him, a circle of green light floated forward and settled over the startled Amazons. They fought the spell briefly, then one by one, the women fell to the ground, asleep. The circle disappeared.

Percival turned to question at Tylina. She shrugged her shoulders and smiled. "It seemed the best way to end their threat without drawing blood," she advised.

"Why didn't you do it sooner?" he asked.

"I learned that spell a long time ago. I didn't have it readied for use until after the last group. Usually those we face in battle are more resistant." She smiled again. "I will keep it available from now on."

Percival nodded. He and Nimbly proceeded to disarm the Amazons and freed their horses. The group continued their journey after the two were satisfied with the delay they had created.

Chapter 67

On the morning of the fourth day at sea, Cora stood outside the cabin her mother was staying in. Dekart had been kept with her and Cora was intent on seeing him.

After knocking on the door, she waited, listening to the movement on the other side. She counted ten breaths before the door opened and one of her mother's guards blocked the door.

"Princeesa, your mother does not wish to be disturbed at this time. She asks that you return tomorrow to discuss your concerns," the guard advised, then moved to close the door.

Cora sprang forward, pushing her foot into the doorway. "I want to speak to Dekart. And I want my mother to know I do not appreciate being ignored."

"I will be sure to give her the message, Princeesa. Please return tomorrow to speak with your mother." Again, the Amazon tried to close the door, this time succeeding after pushing Cora's foot out of the way.

"This is ridiculous, Mother!" Cora shouted at the closed door.

She waited, a small hope that her mother would change her mind keeping her in place. When minutes passed and Reann did not open the door or even send another guard out, Cora turned and returned to the deck.

Since they had started their voyage, Cora fought a constant discomfort, not only from the pain, but also from a sickness that struck her every morning. The days at sea had not helped her sickness, but this day had progressed without any discomfort or vomiting. Cora leaned on the railing, looking out over the water. Always different, yet always the same.

A bright ball of fire landed in the water in front of Cora, startling her. Pushing herself back from the railing, her feet slipped on the wet deck. Reaching out to catch herself, Cora's left arm collapsed under her. Pain shot through the arm, radiating from the mark burned into her flesh. The scar glowed red.

Cora looked up, already knowing demons would be in the air. Five demons flew toward the ship, their bodies glowing the same red as her arm. Without waiting for the Sea Wolves to react, she pointed her hand toward the closest demon. "Soola lancium!"

The ice spear stretched from Cora's fingers into the air. Satisfaction filled her when it pierced the wing of a bat-like demon. The demons following the group on the mainland had not resembled bats. Cora didn't know if the others could fly, but the ones attacking the ship were the size of humans, with wings sprouting from their backs.

She turned to see the Sea Wolves' mages following her example. Ice spears flew through the air. One of them looked at Cora, a question on her face.

Cora nodded. "Ice only. It's all that works," she ordered, then turned to prepare another attack.

More ice struck the demons, shattering and falling to the deck in shards. The four mages focused their attacks on two of the demons, while Cora continued the assault on the one she attacked first. The uninjured demons threw more balls of fire at the ship, forcing the Sea Wolves to put out the burning sails.

Cora focused on her demon. The area around her felt empty without her friends to stand by her in the fight.

The two demons the Sea Wolves attacked fell into the ocean, a final ice spear from one of the mages piercing a demon's head. Cora's final ice spear shredded through the other demon's chest.

With a screech of frustration, the remaining demons flew off.

"What is going on out here, Cora?" Reann demanded from the door leading into the cabin area.

Grabbing for the railing to keep from falling, Cora glanced at the scar on her arm. "We were attacked by demons. I told you things were not going to be easy, Reann." She turned to look at her mother.

"Have you seen them before?"

"Similar demons attacked my friends and me. Do you understand how bad it can be?" Cora walked toward Reann, her steps unsteady while she tried to hide the weakness she felt. "Take me back to the mainland. The demons will continue to come after me."

"You are not going back, Cora. I don't care what creatures your man sends after us. I won't stand for it." Reann reached out and grabbed Cora's face. "You are coming home with me. You will forget about the Black Hand. Or I will kill him. Do I make myself clear?"

Reann squeezed Cora's cheeks until tears flooded her eyes. Cora shook her head, and yanked her mother's hand from her face.

"I will not forget him. And I will not stay with you."

Chapter 68

Ten days after they left Jonquil, Percival and the others arrived at the seaside city of Glenys. Guards they considered friends greeted them at the city gates, relaying the story of the Amazons arrival and departure. After promising to meet with them while the group was in the city, Percival led his friends to the castle.

The guards let the group into the castle without question, their time of service remembered by all. A servant fetched the steward while they waited in the main hall.

The aged steward ambled toward them from the grand staircase. "I am glad to see all of you again. I hope you are doing well." He greeted the companions, his words tense, though polite. "How may I assist you?"

"We were hoping to meet with King Kennan to discuss helping us with a certain problem we are facing," Tylina spoke for the group. "We are in need of a ship."

"His Majesty is unavailable today. I will put you into his schedule for tomorrow. Will you be staying with your father, Mistress Orenda?"

"Yes, we will be at my father's. Please send all messages for us there."

The steward nodded, then made his way down the hall. A moment later, a page ran up to them and escorted them from the castle.

The group rode to Duke Orenda's estate in silence. Percival's mood remained dark and he spent most of the ride grumbling to himself. When they arrived at the estate, the horses were taken to the stable as Tylina led the others into the house.

"Welcome home!" Duke Orenda exclaimed, charging toward them. He grabbed Tylina in a fierce hug, then shook the men's hands with enthusiasm.

The duke led them into the sitting room and ordered food and drink before sitting down to listen to the reason for their return. Finally, after all pleasantries had been exchanged, and the meal delivered and eaten, the duke leaned back in his chair and studied them.

"So, tell me, why have you returned? Does it have anything to do with the Amazons?"

Percival could tell by the duke's expression that he already knew the answers to his questions.

"Yes, Father. The Amazon queen came for Cora. The princess has made it clear she does not want to return home. Percival promised her she could stay and that he would bring her back if the queen tried to force her to return to the islands," Tylina explained.

"Why, Captain Riesun?" The duke turned his attention directly to Percival.

"You would do no different, milord," he answered defensively.

"No, I guess I wouldn't. I have to advise you to be careful. How you handle this situation could affect more than just you and Cora. A war between our nations would not be good. The Amazons have been looking for a reason to attack our kingdom since their first queen was exiled to the islands." Duke Orenda studied Percival for a moment in silence, then turned back to his daughter. "You are all welcome to stay as long as you need. Please make yourselves at home. Tylina, while you are here, we have some family business to handle."

Percival waited until the duke finished his statement, then excused himself. Unsure of what to do while waiting to hear from the king, he went to the estate's garden to try to calm his mood.

Chapter 69

The next morning, word arrived at the Orenda estate that King Kennan would be available to see the group before midday meal. The group returned to the castle, waiting in the antechamber until they were called into the throne room.

The colorful banners that decorated the room the last time the companions were there were gone. Family tapestries, as well as kingdom banners now hung from the ceiling and on the walls. The king sat on his throne and when the group walked through the open doors, he waved them forward.

"Captain Riesun, Tylina, Kalik, Nimbly and Brolin. How nice to see you all again. I hope your journey has been successful," King Kennan greeted them.

"I found some answers, but I am still seeking the one that will free me from my affliction completely," Percival answered.

"Excellent. I am pleased you found at least something."

Percival squinted at his king, unsure if his response was genuine. "Did the Amazons use your harbor for their ships, before they returned to the islands?"

"They did. They left over a week ago." The king nodded, sitting back in his chair.

"Was Cora with them?"

"Why is that important, Black Hand?" The two stared at each other, until Kennan finally nodded. "Yes, she was with them. There was nothing I could do to keep her from leaving. Whatever the princess did to upset her mother, to force her to come here, is between the two of them. I cannot interfere."

"But I can. I need a ship." Kalix cleared his throat and Percival glanced back at him. "We need one." Percival corrected his statement, gesturing at his friends.

"I can't do that, Captain. I will not risk a war with the Amazons for some personal vendetta. Why is this so important?" the king asked.

The Black Hand stood tall against the king's scrutiny. "Cora told me she didn't want to go back to the islands. She wanted to stay with me."

"Were you in a relationship with the princess, Percival? Do you realize how angry the queen will be? Do you know the trouble this could cause our kingdom?" Kennan's voice increased in volume until he shouted, standing from his chair.

"I don't see how our relationship could affect the kingdom. The queen will try to make me pay for any injustice she feels she has suffered," Percival protested, confident he was right. "Cora can handle anything her mother tries to do to her."

"Is that so? Do you think she can handle seeing the harm her mother will do to you? If the two of you have become so close, then you should know… Will seeing you tortured to the brink of death be something Cora can handle?" the king shouted at Percival.

The others retreated from the two men in shock.

Percival ignored the movement of his friends and his king's raised voice. "I just want to bring her back home."

"She *is* home. Those islands are *her* home." The king dropped back into his throne. "Despite the loyalty you have shown me and this kingdom, and despite the rescue of my daughter, I cannot help you. I will not give you any of our ships to use. I can't afford a confrontation with the Amazons. Too many of them are in my city. The princess chose to return to the islands. You must accept that nothing you, me or anyone else can do will change that."

Percival stared at his king in silence, then shook his head. "I refuse to believe that." He turned and left the throne room without waiting for his friends.

Chapter 70

For over a week, Percival and the others tried to obtain passage on a ship to take them to the Amazon islands. With the time for his monthly conflict with Stromas drawing closer, their lack of success made his temper worse. At one point, Tylina forced him from her father's home until he dealt with the demon and could think rationally.

Percival found the cave he had always used when he was with the kingdom's military force before beginning his travels with Cora and the others. The cave provided a safe place for him to deal with Stromas without worrying about harming others or outside interference.

While lost in his thoughts, the familiar darkness heralded the demon's arrival and a respite from the anger Percival hoped would last until a ship could be found.

"What are we going to do about Cora, Black Hand?" Stromas asked, sitting down across from him.

"What does it matter to you?" Percival growled, his anger surfacing again.

"It matters to me, Black Hand. She is important to me, just as she is to you." Instead of basking in the anger as he normally would, Stromas gazed at Percival with sadness and fear reflected in his eyes.

Percival felt his anger peak out of control. "You want her

only for what you think she can do to increase your power," he shouted.

"I want her returned to us because she is the only joy we have had in our lives," Stromas shouted in return. The demon took a calming breath. *"We must work together, Black Hand. I can add to your strength and together we can take her away from the Amazons."*

"No, I will not give in to you. To do it once will make it easier to do again. Cora would never forgive me, even if I did it to have her returned to me." He turned away as if to end the conversation.

"I can give you strength without control. I can enhance the anger you feel and add it to your own strength," the demon said almost gently.

"No," Percival insisted with less conviction.

"All right. I won't force this on you, but should you change your mind, I will be ready to assist against the Amazons." The demon straightened, pride in his offer flowing off him.

After a moment of silence, Percival returned his attention to Stromas. "Why do you care if I have the strength to bring her back? I would think you'd be happy if I failed. You would be free of me."

"Because, like I said, she is the only joy we've had in our life together. Because I know how happy you are with her and because I enjoy the time you are with her," Stromas confided quietly.

"Almost sounds as if you love her, Stromas." The Black Hand turned away from the demon again to hide the momentary jealousy he felt.

"Maybe I do, Percival. Maybe I do." The demon stood and disappeared as quickly as he had appeared.

Percival stood for a moment, contemplating Stromas' words. The demon had called him Percival. It had never used his given name before.

Without a response from Stromas, Percival began to gather his possessions. Maybe now he could focus on finding a ship.

Chapter 71

For nineteen days, the companions searched for a ship to take them to the Amazon islands. Three days after his confrontation with Stromas, Percival, Tylina and Kalik were sitting in The Sailor's Bed, a local tavern and inn visiting sailors liked to frequent. The day passed again with no success in acquiring passage and Percival insisted on remaining in the tavern for a few drinks before returning to the Orenda estate.

"Obviously our post on the harbor master's board is not working," Percival noted as he swirled his ale within his mug.

"Or the destination is enough to scare even the bravest of captains." Kalik's quiet voice was difficult to hear over the raucous sounds of the tavern.

The three had already changed tables once in an attempt to avoid the sailors who tried to convince the tavern wenches to accompany them to their rooms. The group now sat in a corner, watching the night's activities with disdain.

The sounds of the tavern quieted without warning. A squad of the city guard had entered the tavern. The men searched the room, then made their way to the companion's table. Kalik sat in silence, his head turned slightly as if listening to the guards' approach. When they reached the table, Percival gestured for the men to sit after recognizing one of them from his time with the military.

"Good to see you again, Nolan. I see you have adjusted to

your new position. It suits you well," Percival said in greeting.

The man Percival spoke to smirked, then sat after sending the others in the squad to the bar. "I would not be in this position if it wasn't for you, Black Hand, though I would rather be serving under your command than running the guards myself." Nolan signaled to the nearest serving girl for a drink. After she nodded, he turned his full attention to his former captain. "I hear that you are still searching for passage to the Amazon islands. I also hear that some of the captains are thinking of accepting, for a large sum of money. Have any ideas on how you plan to pay for your passage?"

Percival watched the foam in his ale disappear before answering. "I am limited on money, as I'm sure the rest of us are. I do not wish to borrow from Tylina's father, but we have not had any paying jobs recently, what with everyone sacrificing to help me with my personal quest."

"We would all be willing to help pay for passage, Percival. None of us expects you to pay for us. We came because we have a point to make to the queen," Tylina tried to explain.

"Maybe I can help with the money, Black Hand. The princess must have known something like this would happen eventually." Nolan smirked at a private thought.

Percival clenched his jaw. "What do you mean?"

"When your group saved Princess Stepha, His Majesty offered each of you a boon or money. He allowed you a meeting with his mage while giving everyone else a generous sum of money. But he didn't leave you out of the financial part of his gratification. He gave Cora a smaller sum of money for you. She chose not to give it to you." Nolan laughed.

"In case you've forgotten, Cora isn't here," Percival pointed out, sarcasm dripping from his words. Damn Amazon. Always trying to take care of him, even before she admitted she had any feelings for him. He waited too long to tell her and now he let her be taken from him.

"I know. She was—is—an intelligent woman. Though she did not know me well, she must have remembered me from the first time we met, with the bandits and the few times we spoke when you were in the city. She came to me and informed me that she had deposited the money in trust with the city depository for you, should something happen to her." He pulled a bag from within the folds of his tunic and pushed it across the table. "She put me on the paperwork so I could get it for you if needed. Knowing how much His Majesty gave the others for his assistance, I think this should pay for passage easily."

Percival took the pouch and peered inside. "I can't believe she did this."

Kalik chuckled, an unfamiliar sound to everyone at the table. "You and Cora denied feelings for each other for at least the two years I've been traveling with you. Perhaps she did this because, at least in a small way, she could show you that she did care about you, if nothing happened between you," he reasoned.

Percival shook his head, unsure of how to respond. "Thank you, Nolan. I appreciate your help with this. I hope we can put this to use soon." A loud commotion at the door stopped him from saying anything further.

"I'm looking for the Black Hand. This post says he can be found here," a large man in typical sailor attire announced from the doorway. Several sailors in the room turned and pointed at Percival. The newcomer skirted between the tables until he came to theirs with a grace that betrayed his many years upon the ocean. "Are you the Black Hand?"

"Yes. And you are?" Percival stood, his thumbs tucked casually into his sword belt.

"I'm Captain Menos. My ship is The Lady's Clipper. I see you are in need of a ship for passage to the Amazon islands." The captain sat at the table, uninvited.

"Yes, but we are not willing to pay an outrageous fee, so if you are planning on asking for a king's ransom, move along," Percival proclaimed, refusing to sit again until the captain made his case.

Captain Menos waved his hand at a serving woman. "I don't want a king's ransom. I've heard others want to ask for a large amount, but none of them know the Great Ocean like me, and none are willing to make the voyage. Two hundred gold per passenger and the cost of any repairs should be fair enough. Will you be bringing horses? I don't have room for horses."

Percival stared at the man in disbelief, slowly sitting again before responding. "No, we can leave the horses here. You do realize where we want to go, right? *The Amazon islands*. No one else wants to travel there."

"No one else is willing to risk angering the women like I am. I've lost men to those women and if you are going to cause them problems, like you think you are then I'm willing to take you." Captain Menos sat back and downed his ale as soon as the serving girl brought it to the table. "So, are you going with me or not?"

Percival glanced at his friends, noting the agreement in Tylina's eyes and Kalik's brief nod. Nolan shrugged his shoulders and nodded as well.

Percival returned his attention to the captain. "Yes, we are going with you. When do you leave?"

"We launch in two days. I need to resupply and make final transactions to clear out our previous cargo. Be ready to leave in two mornings. If you aren't there, we leave without you. Bring the money with you. I'll collect when you board." With that, the captain stood, shook hands with the men and planted a small kiss upon Tylina's knuckles, then left the tavern.

"Guess you've found a ship," Nolan stated the obvious.

"I guess we have." Percival watched Captain Menos until the door closed behind him. "Thank you, Nolan, for the money. If I can do anything for you when I return, please let me know."

"I don't know that you will return from the islands, but if you do, then I will make you pay me back, somehow. Maybe I'll push this position of responsibility back onto you." The man stood as well, shook Percival and Kalik's hands, bowed to Tylina, then shouted for his men to follow him from the tavern.

Tylina waited until the guards had left, then turned to Percival. "I will inform Brolin and Nimbly of our plans and finalize my own needs. Will you be coming back to the house tonight?"

"Yes, I will be there before too long. I just want to sit for a few more minutes before returning." Percival ordered a new drink, handing the girl the old mug before she could move away.

"We will see you there." Tylina and Kalik stood and left the tavern.

Percival watched the crowd around him, sipping from his new mug of ale. As the number of people began to decrease and the midnight hour drew closer, he paid for the drinks that he and his companions had ordered and returned to the Orenda estate.

Chapter 72

Two days later, as the morning sun broke through the darkness of night, the group of friends arrived at the pier where The Lady's Clipper was docked. Captain Menos stood at the bottom of the gangplank waiting for them.

"Good morn, Black Hand, Lady Orenda." The captain nodded at the others he did not know, not waiting for an introduction. "Are you all ready for this voyage? Are you still sure you want to undertake this?"

"Yes, Captain Menos. We are ready to begin. Lady Orenda's men will take the horses back to her father's estate." Percival indicated the small contingency of men that accompanied them. "I do have one question though. You said we would need to cover the cost of repairs. What repairs are you expecting us to pay for?"

"I don't expect to arrive at the islands easily. I've run into the Sea Wolves before. They are a mean lot. If they are aware of your coming, they will try to stop us. You'll pay for whatever repairs need to be done should they attack us." Percival felt Menos watching him closely. "Do you have a problem with that?"

"No, Captain, we don't. I just wanted clarification." Percival handed the man a pouch filled with the gold for payment. "That is for all of us."

"Excellent. The cabin boy will take you to your cabins. Sorry, but you'll have to double up. We only have two cabins available." He stepped aside to allow them onto the gangplank. "Also, Black Hand, we will be docking only. No one from my crew will be disembarking with you."

"We understand completely. We do not expect you or your men to join us." Percival let the others pass him before following them onto the ship. "Thank you, Captain Menos. I appreciate your honesty and your assistance."

"I'm in it for the money and whatever hardship you're going to cause those women, Black Hand. I'm not in it for you." The two men stared at each other for a moment, then nodded in mutual respect and understanding.

Percival followed the others onto the ship and into their cabins. After making sure Tylina was settled in the cabin she would be sharing with Kalik, he put his bags into the cabin he would share with Brolin and Nimbly, then went on deck to watch the ship slip away from the land. The sounds of the captain giving orders and the unfurling of the sails brought a sense of calm to him. He would not find true calm until he was with Cora again, but being on the water helped.

The next day, after the cook and his assistant served morning feast, the sound of a ringing bell vibrated through the wood of the ship, into the galley. Sailors that had just woken and sought nourishment before taking their positions on deck scattered from their seats and rushed out of the room. Percival and Nimbly watched the sailors leave, then followed, trying to stay out of the way of other men rushing up from the decks below.

"Sea Wolves closing in," the man in the crow's nest shouted repeatedly as the men filed out onto the main deck.

Percival and Nimbly made their way to the castellan and stood next to the captain, listening to him shout orders at his men. Another ship raced toward them, faster than seemed possible with the breeze that blew through their own sails. The flag flailing in the wind warned anyone who saw it—a large wolf carried on a blue wave announced the arrival of the Amazon mercenaries and island protectors, the Sea Wolves. The two friends gripped the railing tight as the captain spun the helm, throwing the ship hard to port and bringing the starboard cannons to bear.

The sailors on the main deck ran to battle positions without further orders from their captain. Below deck, steel rang against steel as cannons balls were loaded into cannons.

"What can we do, Captain?" Percival finally asked, turning to see the other man signaling position changes for his crew.

"Prepare for battle if they should board us. Each time we've met them has been different. No telling what these women are up to this time," the captain instructed.

Percival nodded, looking to Nimbly, then the two went back down to the main deck and watched the Amazon ship come closer. Suddenly, the other ship turned to parallel their path, cannons prepared to on The Lady's Clipper.

The loud booming of cannons deafened Percival as both ships fired. Numerous cannon balls fell into the water near each ship. Water splashed both crews.

Minutes passed in silence as cannons were reloaded. The ships edged closer to each other, carried by the water and momentum from trying to halt with sudden turns.

Cannon fire rang out again. Time slowed for Percival as one cannon ball flew through the air toward him and Nimbly.

With a shout, he threw himself at the elf, forcing both of them to the wooden deck, away from the path of the missile. The cannon ball tore through the wood of The Lady's Clipper. The wood railing was torn from the hull of the ship behind Percival. Another stone ball tore a hole in The Lady's Clipper below the deck. It flew out the other side before landing in the water with a splash.

The cannon balls from The Lady's Clipper flew toward the Amazon ship. One ball tore a mast from the ship, the sails breaking free to flap wildly in the wind. Another broke through the railing and pushed a single woman from the deck.

Percival pulled himself up from the deck, glancing around. More cannon balls flew from the Amazon ship, tearing more holes in The Lady's Clipper. None broke through a level that would sink the ship, but Percival knew it was only a matter of time. The Amazon queen was doing everything within her power to keep him from reaching Cora and the islands. The loss of a ship and its crew was nothing to her if that's what it took to keep him away—or kill him.

"Captain! Get us out of here!" Percival shouted at the other man over the roar of the cannon fire.

Percival watched the captain consider the situation for a heartbeat, then give the order to retreat. He turned the helm away from the Amazons. The anchor, which Percival had not known was lowered, made a loud clanking sound as it was raised. The ship began to speed away from the other ship.

The Amazons pursued for several hours, suddenly turning away from their pursuit near nightfall. Percival breathed a sigh of relief as the other ship grew smaller the farther away it traveled.

"We are returning to port, Black Hand. We cannot continue with my ship like this," Captain Menos advised Percival once the Amazon ship had disappeared over the horizon.

"Cost of repairs, right, Captain?" Nimbly asked, his usual humor returning.

"Yes, Mr. Nimbly. Cost of repairs."

Percival stood on deck, watching the night sky darken. When the full dark of midnight blanketed the ship, the light of Glenys heralded their return to the mainland.

Chapter 73

For a week, The Lady's Clipper underwent repairs so she could sail again. Instead of returning to the Orenda estate with the others, Percival stayed on the ship, lending a hand with the repairs. Though ship construction and repair was new to him, the physical labor provided a distraction. The fatigue he felt at the end of the day gave him a few hours of sleep.

When the ship was ready to sail again, Percival stood at the helm with Captain Menos when Tylina joined them.

"Captain Menos, my father wishes to extend his apologies for the damage to your ship. He also wishes for me to relay his appreciation at your willingness to assist us with our journey." Tylina handed the captain a large pouch. "This should cover the cost of repairs as well as make up for the time lost from your usual trade route."

Menos opened the pouch and poured the contents into his hand. Five diamonds, each the size of an almond, rested in his palm. He studied the gems, holding each up to the sunlight. Finally, he placed the gems back in the pouch and hid it within his shirt.

"This will do just fine, Lady Orenda. When you see your father again, tell him our contract remains in effect." The captain smirked. "Or I will tell him, since I will probably see him before you do." He bowed at the waist, then walked away.

"Their contract?" Percival asked, confused.

"My father employs The Lady's Clipper for trade and other things that normally would be more difficult to accomplish on the Great Ocean. I did not realize that until we returned," she advised him. "It seems my father had a small part in getting us passage upon the ship in the first place.

"Wonderful. Does everyone think I'm incapable of doing what needs to be done to take care of Cora?" Percival threw his arms in frustration and stormed away, returning to his cabin without speaking to anyone.

Within a change of the water clock, Percival felt the ship return to the flow of the water and again start its journey to the Amazon islands.

Three days after leaving port the second time, a storm washed over the ship. Standing on the deck, with the rain falling on him, Percival felt the ship's forward motion stop. Looking around, he realized the sails had been lowered.

"What are you doing?" he asked Captain Menos, who stood firm near the helm. Despite lowering the sails, the ship still rocked with waves enraged by the storm.

"We will wait out the storm. No need for us to lose any more men than we have to. No telling how long this will last," Menos explained.

Percival opened his mouth to protest, but stopped when he saw the stubborn expression on the other man's face and his determined stance as he held onto the ship's wheel. Disgusted, Percival left the castellan and returned to his cabin, ignoring Nimbly and Brolin's questioning glances when he entered the room.

The storm raged over the ocean for three days. During the first night, with the winds and waves tossing the ship violently, two men were lost to the ocean's depths.

Tylina, Nimbly and Brolin spent the days within their cabins, hiding from the ravages of the weather. Percival and Kalik spent their time on the deck, watching and listening to the storm and the few men who remained on the main deck. Most of the men had been ordered below decks to wait out the storm. Percival's growing anger strengthened his body and while

Kalik occasionally faltered in his stance because of the motion of the ship, the other man stood unmoved and unaffected.

Finally, on the afternoon of the third day, the storm cleared. While the crew made repairs, Captain Menos pulled out the map and gestured for Percival to join him.

"We were here," Menos pointed at an obscure point in the middle of the water on the map, "when the storm hit us. Now we are here, approximately." He pointed again, the place he indicated two finger lengths from the first.

"How do you know?" Percival asked, looking out at the water to try to find what could have shown their location to the captain.

Menos pulled out a blue crystal on a length of twine. Percival watched him hold the crystal over the map. Percival expected it to circle and spin, as he had seen others do. Instead, the crystal immediately dropped to the location Menos indicated. The crystal then made a small movement on the map, as if it traveled with the ship.

Percival looked up at Menos, noting the grin of satisfaction. "Fine." He returned to the main deck, assisting with the final repairs before the sails were raised.

Chapter 74

A little over a month after leaving Man's World, Cora and the other Amazons arrived at the main island. Their journey had been delayed due to a storm pulling them off course. The storm had continued toward the mainland after three days.

When Cora's feet touched the dock, the freedom she felt with Percival drained from her completely. She felt trapped again, just as she had before Satina returned to her mother. Compared to Man's World, the Amazon islands were small and restrictive.

A large group of warriors and mages waited for the passengers to disembark the ship. They proudly displayed the colors Cora used to distinguish her private guard. The numbers appeared to have grown since she left and despite her absence, the joy on their faces let her know they remained loyal to their princess.

She looked past her guards and felt an unexpected disappointment when she did not find her sister or even a representative for the heir to the Amazon throne. Her mother appeared unaffected by Rainne's absence as she strode past the younger princess' guard and started toward the fort. Cora stopped in front of the captain of her own guard and grasped the woman's arm in greeting.

"Silva, it brings me joy to see you, my sister," she said, pushing aside her displeasure.

"It gladdens my heart to see you, Princeesa. We were saddened to hear you would be returning against your will." The other woman gestured at the Amazons behind her.

"Do not let anyone hear you say that, Silva. I do not want you to suffer my mother's wrath." Cora glanced at her mother and her guards.

As if she could hear Cora's words, Reann turned to glare at her daughter. "You are not following? Do you not think it would be appropriate for you to get some rest and let Misabel know you need to see her?"

"Yes, Mother. We are coming." Cora squeezed Silva's hand again, then started walking behind her mother's guards toward the fort.

Once inside the fort and in her own rooms, Cora waited impatiently for one of her guards to return with Misabel. Being the oldest priestess as well as the most experienced healer and herbalist on the island, Misabel served the queen and her family. Reann knew the woman's age made it difficult for her to travel to the outlying tribes of Amazons, so she kept the woman close and required her students and lower ranking priestesses to do the traveling.

Cora's private quarters had not changed while she was gone. The colorful pillows filling the sitting pit were as bright as they had been when she left. A table with chairs for meetings and large meals was in an alcove to the left of the main entrance and appeared well oiled and cared for. A set of glass doors across from the main entrance revealed the balcony Cora had loved as a child. From the balcony, she could see the Amazon forest and watch the comings and goings of clans to the queen's fort. Paintings still adorned the walls, depicting the Amazon history and a bowl of fruit had been brought into the room before she arrived. The door to her bedroom remained closed, but she knew the room would be in perfect condition.

"We have had an increase in our numbers while you've been gone, Princeesa. Most of the women who joined us did so *because* of your journey to Man's World. They hope your journey will help show your mother that we can travel to the mainland and still be Amazons," Silva advised, reminding Cora of her presence.

"Reann won't allow that, Silva. She does not feel I have

remained true to our people," Cora whispered, staring at the floor.

"We know. I've read your journals. Shayta required it of all of us before your return. The queen wanted us to know what you saw, so that we would be prepared for any 'corruption' you may show and any desire you may still have to return." Silva leaned closer, nudging Cora's head up so they could see each other. "I know about the Black Hand, all of us do. We all want to know what it would be like to love someone and have them love us in return, instead of being forced to share our beds. After Satina came back, our numbers swelled again with those who do not agree with keeping the men as slaves."

Giving Cora's journals to her personal guard was not something Shayta should have done if she wanted to remain in Reann's good graces. Shayta and Cora were childhood friends, always together except when they were training. Shayta became a warrior and progressed through the ranks quicker than any other Amazon. When Cora left, her friend was preparing to become the second-in-command of Reann's elite guard. Shayta's own mother was still the captain of the guard at the time.

"That is amazing, Silva. Why has my mother allowed this to happen?" Cora finally asked.

"The queen has made her displeasure with your guard quite obvious. But, she was intent on your return to the islands and has stated that it will prove to us that her way is the only way. The Amazon traditions will prevail." Silva stopped at a knock on the door.

The door opened and an old woman entered, wearing a long dress that hid her figure within its shapeless mass. "Princeesa, I have come as the queen requested." Misabel allowed herself into Cora's room, shutting the door behind her. She shuffled her way to the cushions where Cora sat. "Whatever could be wrong? Don't the men have clerics that could care for any problems you may have suffered?"

"Of course they do, Misabel. This is something that came to my attention while on my journey back home." Cora stretched out, unwrapping her capeshal from around her. Her muscular abdomen, made firmer with her travel and frequent exercise, no longer bore the bruises it had when she was last with Percival. Now, however, a slight bulge revealed the product from that last union.

Misabel looked at her uncertainly. "Why would this be a problem?"

Cora remained quiet, waiting.

The older woman began her examination. The two younger Amazons remained silent, listening to the cleric's mutterings. Finally, Misabel sat back and studied the princess.

"You have an injury to your throat," she started the list of injuries Cora had suffered while in Man's World.

"Because Shoshona hired assassins to kill me," the princess explained.

"Be that as it may, it appears you are lucky to still be able to speak as well as you can. You have recently had an injury to your abdomen, crushing your bones and making it very unlikely that you would survive a pregnancy and childbirth." The old woman studied her. "And yet, you *are* pregnant. Didn't the healer that tended to these wounds tell you of the dangers? Didn't she give you something, a tea, to prevent a pregnancy?"

"Yes, she did. I chose to ignore her advice." Cora smirked at Misabel's assumption the healer had been a woman.

"You are going to cause yourself quite a bit of pain."

Cora held her hand up to prevent her from continuing. "Yes, I know. Your job is to make sure I make it through the pregnancy as well as my baby, as best as you can. I am going to have this child and nothing you or my mother says will change my mind," she firmly informed the healer defensively.

"You will regret this, Princeesa, but I will do as you command. I will make sure Silva has some herbs to help with the pain when necessary. Meanwhile, I will also send up some herbs to end the pregnancy, in case you should change your mind." Misabel gave Cora's hand a soft kiss, then left the room, promising to return with the herbs later.

"She is unhappy with your decision," Silva observed when Misabel had left.

"No one seems happy with any of my decisions lately, Silva. I have learned to live with that." Cora spread the capeshal over her abdomen again and lay back, closing her eyes.

Another knock at the door interrupted the quiet Cora sought. She looked at Silva in exasperation, waving her hand to let the intruder enter. The captain of her private guard opened the door, allowing Dekart to enter the room. His eyes were on the ground before him, his head bowed as appropriate for his station as a slave.

"What do you want?" Silva demanded.

"I came only to inquire as to the Princeesa's health." His words were meek and he refused to lift his gaze from the floor.

"Let him in, Silva and give us a moment, please," Cora instructed from her place on the cushions, lifting her head to smile at her father.

The other woman nodded, then left the room and shut the door behind her. Dekart shuffled over to the cushions, still in the appropriate submissive posture of a slave.

"Stop, Dekart. I no longer see you as a slave. That is my mother's way of relating to you." She waited for him to look at her and sighed in frustration when he did not. "Look at me, Dekart," she ordered.

He lifted his head, a wide smile lighting his face. "I am so proud of you. You have finally freed yourself from your upbringing. I always knew you were different from the others, from the first time you snuck into my quarters and asked for a story about my world."

"It wasn't easy and now that I am back on the islands, living my life the way I want is going to be even more difficult. I don't know many who will be happy to find out my opinions about men now," Cora explained. "And, others who will be even angrier about everything when Percival shows up to take me back to the mainland."

He stared at her in disbelief. "You think he will come? Doesn't he realize how dangerous it will be?"

"Yes, I told him, but he will come anyway. I have told him I do not want to be here. He will come to keep his promise to me and take me back to where we've decided home should be." Confidence sounded in her words. "Can you stay for tea? Or do you need to get back to Mother?"

"I need to return to your mother. She will want to have evening meal soon and I am expected to be there. But I will return to you as often as I can." Dekart leaned forward and, for the first time in Cora's life, kissed her cheek. "I wish your return had been under better circumstances." Her father smiled at her again, then resumed his slouched posture and left the room with his shuffling gait.

Cora laid back again on her cushions, waiting for Silva to enter. When the door opened again, she was surprised to see Reann pushing past Silva.

"Now that we are home, you will answer some questions for me." The queen sat across from her daughter. "Shoshona disappeared over a year ago. Do you know where she is?"

"Dead. If you had allowed me to speak to you while we traveled, you would have had all your questions answered already," Cora pointed out.

"What do you mean she's dead? What happened between the two of you?" Reann demanded.

"She hired assassins. On their first attempt to kill me, they injured me with an arrow that poisoned my magic and resisted the magic used to heal me. She killed Reyna. When we were traveling to a mage's tower, Shoshona herself attacked me in a small town where we had stopped for the evening. She was killed instead. Shortly afterward, her assassins tried again, but none survived." Cora felt a chill travel the length of her spine as she told Reann of her rival's death, but she felt no regret.

"Who killed her?" Disbelief calmed Reann's words.

"Percival. He was trying to save me. Shoshona meant to kill me and as my protector and lover, he killed her instead. She gave him no choice." Pride filled her at the memory.

"He killed an Amazon? He killed *Shoshona*?" Reann leaned back against the pillows. "Maybe I misjudged him. Other than myself, no one has ever been able to even scratch her. At least he understood the importance of keeping you safe—once."

"You have misjudged him, Mother. I hope you don't regret it. He will come for me and when he does, I will not help you. You will handle the problems he presents to you without me." Cora closed her eyes, sighing deeply. "Please, I need to rest. I won't be joining you for evening meal. Silva will have it brought to me."

Reann stared at her daughter, then stood. "I will never regret bringing my daughter home where she belongs. But he will regret coming here." She stormed from the room, pushing Silva aside when she did not move out of her way fast enough.

Silva watched the queen, then entered the room. "Do you wish to have your meal here?" After Cora nodded, the other woman instructed the guard still standing at the door to bring a meal for both of them. When she finished, Silva joined Cora on the pillows again.

The two sat in silence until the food arrived for them. While they ate, Cora began telling Silva the long story of her time in Man's World, answering every question the guard eagerly asked.

Chapter 75

Three days after the storm cleared, Percival waited for his confrontation with Stromas in the bowels of the ship. The demon wasted no time in pulling him into their meeting.

The bright desert sky blinded Percival until his eyes adjusted. In the distance, he could hear waves crashing against a beach that he could not see. Stromas stood in front of the boulder he usually sat upon, his arms crossed. He glared at Percival.

"This trip is taking too long," the demon said by way of greeting.

"I can do nothing to speed it up. You need to understand. We have had delays—the Amazons attacked us, the storm," Percival tried to explain, though he did not find his own words comforting.

"The longer it takes us to find her, the less likely it will be that she returns with us," Stromas insisted. *"Make the captain move faster or I will find a way to kill him and do it myself."*

"You can't do anything to him unless I give you control and I don't plan on doing that—ever." Percival laughed, but Stromas had exerted his strength too many times recently. His control of Percival had only lasted for a heartbeat each time, but that was enough to make him afraid.

"You would be surprised at what I can accomplish when I want to, Black Hand. I am stronger than you think." The demon

reached out as if to grab him. *"I am losing my patience. I want to arrive at the island immediately."*

"I want to be there as well, Stromas. I can feel every moment she is from me, like a rock falling on me from the heavens." Percival's words were quiet, filled with the pain he tried to describe.

"Push the captain, Black Hand. Make him understand." The demon buffeted the man with his wings, trying to make his desire clear.

"I will do what I can." Percival stomped away from the demon, ending their conversation. "Leave me alone."

When the darkness lifted, Percival felt the pressure of his anger lift slightly from his chest. It wasn't gone. He could still feel it at the edge of his mind, tugging at him.

He drifted through the ship, listening to his footsteps on the wood as he made his way up the ladder, then stairs to the main deck. Returning to his room, he was surprised to see Tylina and Kalik waiting for him. Tylina's eyes were filled with concern. Kalik stood when Percival entered the room, his staff placed firmly in front of him.

"It's over for this month. What more do you want from me?" Percival demanded. The anger was still too strong within him, more evidence the confrontation did not give him the relief it normally did.

"We are concerned about what damage the demon will cause if we arrive close to your next confrontation. We do not completely understand your connection with each other. Is there anything more you can tell us before we arrive?" Kalik asked quietly.

"Stromas has been expressing feelings for Cora recently." Percival shook his head. "I don't know how honest they are, but he's offered to give me the strength to defeat the amazons. That, however, would require I give him control, or at least open myself up to him more than ever before."

"What will you do, Percival?" Tylina asked, a mix of surprise and fear filling her words.

"I will not give into Stromas, I promise. I couldn't face Cora if I did and this whole trip would be a waste of time for all of us." Percival straightened his back as he made a promise he had every intention of keeping. "Nothing will make me give in to him."

Tylina and Kalik nodded.

"How will we handle the men being held against their will? What will we do if the queen tries to make all of you slaves or puts you into prison?" Tylina's words again revealed her fear.

"We will handle that problem when it presents itself. I hope that Cora will be able to help us with that. Either way, if her mother is as upset as Cora said she would be, I will be made a prisoner until their battle of wills is decided. I hope I can survive the imprisonment until Cora is able to free me." Percival's words reflected Tylina's fears and his own uncertainty of what awaited them on the island.

"We can't give up on Cora before giving her a chance to help us." Kalik informed them. The other two nodded in agreement. "As we have said before, we are with you to prove a point to the Amazons, that their treatment of us and Cora will not be tolerated by those who care about her. But we are also here to support you, Percival, so don't let your anger get the better of you. She needs you to survive as much as you need to be with her."

Percival laughed. "I don't think Cora needs me that much. I make her feel things she never thought possible for an Amazon, but she is a strong woman. Without me, she would survive." He held his hand up to stop them from saying anything else. "I'm hungry. Dealing with Stromas takes too much energy."

He left the room, shutting the door behind him, cutting off any further discussion.

Chapter 76

Six weeks after leaving Glenys the second time, The Lady's Clipper arrived at the Amazon islands. Though Captain Menos wanted to dock immediately to force his passengers to disembark, Percival and Tylina convinced him to sail around the islands. The additional time gave them the opportunity to scout the islands and the areas where the Amazons had built permanent structures.

For a week, the ship circled the islands. Amazons stood on the shore in beach areas, watching them. They made no move to affect the ship's progress.

The black moon arrived again on the fourth day after their arrival. Reluctantly Percival made his way into the cargo hold before Stromas could force their confrontation on the main deck.

As soon as Percival stepped off the ladder into the cargo area, he was pulled into the terrain the demon preferred. Instead of the desert normally used, Percival found himself on a beach. Stromas stood at the water's edge. Before Percival said anything, the demon whirled around to glare at him.

"How long do you intend to float around these islands before actually setting foot on them?" Stromas' anger washed over Percival like a wave, forcing him to take a step back.

"I can never satisfy you, Stromas. We're here. We will dock

as soon as we are back on the main side of the big island. That will just have to be good enough," Percival defended, steeling himself against the demon's growing anger.

"How much longer do you think you can wait to see her? Each day weakens your resolve against me. Your ability to control the anger and hatred decreases with each passing day. You claim that the separation wears on you, yet you take your time in getting to her. Why?" The demon grabbed Percival by the neck. The sudden pressure on his back told him that the boulder Stromas always used had been behind him.

Percival struggled in the demon's grasp, digging at its hand with his fingernails. "The others are worried about landing immediately. The amazons are not normally friendly and we are intruding on them."

"Lies! You are weak and you doubt your abilities, your love. Let me give you the ability to fight them, to free her and return home." Stromas released him.

"No! I will not do that. Cora would hate me, even if I did it for her." Percival slid to the ground, gasping for breath.

"The woman is frustrating and stubborn. She must come to understand my desires will be achieved, despite the resistance both of you give me," Stromas muttered as he backed away from the Black Hand.

Percival stared at the demon. "What plans have you made, Stromas? What do you think is going to happen on this island that will benefit you?"

"You have been such a fool, for three years. The one thing you need to free yourself from me was next to you this entire time."

"What?" Percival charged toward the demon. "What are you talking about?"

"Cora is the only way you will ever be free of me. She is the only one who can free us both."

Chapter 77

Standing on her balcony, Cora watched her mother's personal guard preparing to travel to the docks. The ship she and Reann believed Percival traveled on was expected to complete its circuit of the islands and arrive at the docks in the afternoon. Cora's own guard would follow, though they were under strict orders not to interfere—from her mother.

The sound of footsteps through her room drew her attention. Turning, she struggled to keep from glaring at the queen.

"What can I do for you, Reann?" Cora asked, returning her attention to the courtyard.

"Nothing. Why are you watching them? Do you wish to join them in sending your man back to his world?" Reann came to stand next to Cora.

"No, but I will go to make sure your women don't hurt him." Cora could not stop the mental images of the destruction she thought Percival's demon would cause. Amazon bodies, twisted, bloodied, would be scattered throughout the courtyard. Blinking the image from her eyes, she looked at her queen and mother. "Someone could die and I am confident it won't be him."

"I do not share your confidence in the Black Hand's abilities. I am sure my women can stop him and bring him under control."

The denial and confidence in Reann's voice made Cora shake her head. "Percival has always said I was stubborn. Obviously it is a trait I inherited from you."

Reann laughed, though it lacked any emotional quality. "At least you got something from me. You must have received your propensity for magic from Dekart."

"I don't think having qualities or talents from him is such a bad thing," Cora mumbled, returning her attention to the activity in the courtyard.

"Of course you don't. You have always been inclined to spend more time with him than me." Reann sounded angry at the revelation, though she made no move to leave.

"He was, and still is willing to accept me for my differences. Just like Percival. Neither of them try to make me into something I'm not, or don't want to be," Cora tried to explain, but the displeasure on Reann's face made her stop.

"If you were a proper Amazon, you would do what you are told and would not question the life of our people."

"Maybe it's better for me to be something different," Cora knew her words were ignored.

Reann's attention turned to her guards. "Bringing him under control will remind him of the proper life you should be living."

One of the women in the courtyard turned toward Cora's balcony and saluted Reann. "We are ready, my queen."

"Proceed," Reann gave the order for the guard to move out. "Come, Cora. You will be reminded of how our laws work." She turned from the courtyard and entered Cora's room again.

Cora nodded at her own guards, then followed her mother.

Chapter 78

Percival watched the number of Amazons on the shore increase each day as the ship made its journey around the islands. On the sixth day, unexpectedly the shorelines were empty. Captain Menos had warned him that the women of the islands were most likely preparing for their landing. Percival acknowledged information, then left to find his friends so they could begin their own preparations.

The morning of the seventh day, the ship rode on the current, drifting close to the pier. A white flag of truce flew beneath the colors of King Kennan's kingdom. Percival stood on the main deck with the others close behind him. A large force of women waited for them on the wooden pier, on the land and in small boats on the water. The seasoned warrior felt the excitement of the upcoming battle growing within as he contemplated what waited for him and his friends.

"Black Hand, the Amazons are a formidable fighting force, even for an entire army. The five of you will be hard pressed to stand against them. Is there anything else I can offer that would assist you, other than my men?" Menos asked from behind the group.

Percival felt the fire in his eyes grow stronger. "I have more power on my side than they realize." The boat stopped its motion and the women closed ranks. "Thank you, Captain.

Your assistance and risk has been appreciated." He lifted his backpack from the deck and threw it over his shoulder, the others following suit.

Percival waited for the plank to be lowered, then slowly disembarked from the boat. He pulled his sword from its scabbard a few inches. The sword slid back in place with a solid clack. The others followed him, and readying their own weapons. Three of the Amazons stepped closer, placing spears at the Black Hand's chest before he reached the end of the plank.

"Stop!" the oldest appearing of the three shouted at him.

Percival looked down at the spears, then lifted his gaze to the women holding them. His anger made his blood race until he could hear it pounding in his ears. Driven by instinct, he drew his sword. Three more spears appeared next to the first ones.

"I said *stop*," the Amazon growled, her eyes narrowing.

"I am here for Cora Rylannes. I will leave when she is with me, or I'm dead," Percival spat back, his voice deep with anger.

"Step off the plank and you will be enslaved—or killed— your choice."

Horses arriving at the pier drowned out the sound of crossbows being cocked, the stretching sound of bowstrings pulled taut and swords drawn. Percival pulled his sword completely. The spears were pushed aside in a smooth movement. He brought his backpack off his shoulder. In an underhand swing, he used it to knock up the arms of the Amazon who had spoken. As her arms went above her head, he brought his sword back, piercing her stomach. His mood darkened more as he sliced her abdomen open. Shoving her lifeless body off his sword, he watched it fall to the ground.

Percival swung his sword again, slicing deep into the arm of another woman. He leapt off the plank, into the middle of the five remaining spear wielders. Kalik and Nimbly jumped and flanked Percival.

The Amazons in the boats let loose their arrows, two from each boat. The three men grunted, the arrows piercing their flesh.

Percival sneered when the Amazons in front of him were also hit by of the missiles. With a glance, he saw the horses at the end of the pier move closer.

The sound of spears dropping to the ground drew his

attention. More swords were drawn.

Weapons moving in unison, Percival, Kalik and Nimbly worked to defend themselves. Kalik used his staff to push the Amazon's swords away from him. Nimbly lunged in with his short sword, stabbing at the woman facing him.

A fresh Amazon stepped forward. She brought her sword up to meet Percival's next attack. Two others not occupied with Kalik or Nimbly, took the opportunity to slice into the Black Hand. Pain added to his anger. Percival grabbed one of the warriors by the arm. He spun her around and drove her own sword through her abdomen.

Kalik pushed the sword of his opponent down with one end of his staff, bringing the other end up into her chin. Her head snapped back, exposing her throat. Without losing momentum, he slammed his staff into her neck, knocking her to the ground. He left her struggling for breath as he changed to another opponent.

Nimbly continued pressing his attacks. He pushed his opponent back until he made it past the line of Amazons. More women stepped forward to surround the elf. One punched him in his lower back. Another punched him with a gauntleted fist. He fell to the pier, unconscious.

Arrows flew from the boats again, hitting the two men on the pier. Brolin walked down the plank, grunting when arrows struck him as well. Tylina grabbed the cleric and placed herself over him, trying to protect him with her body.

Percival stumbled slightly, regaining his footing quickly. Kalik fell to his knees with an arrow protruding from where his neck met his shoulder. The sound of Kalik's knees hitting the pier behind him pulled Percival's full attention for a brief moment. Distracted, he did not see the wooden club swing toward his head until it was too late. The blow made contact, turning him and forcing his back toward the Amazons. As he turned, he felt two swords and more arrows pierce his flesh.

Percival looked around, noting the unconscious forms of Kalik and Nimbly. Tylina still tried to protect Brolin. Collapsing to the pier, more arrows thudded into Percival. He glanced toward the shore, and realized the horses still approached.

A sword lifted over his head.

The horses halted their movement.

"Enough!" a woman astride one of the horses shouted.

The warriors turned toward the voice, then backed away from him. When they separated, he could see the horses and their riders clearly.

Before his vision faded, the Black Hand recognized Cora atop one of the horses.

Chapter 79

Reann's warriors picked up the wounded, unconscious bodies of Percival, Kalik and Nimbly. Two of them dragged Brolin from Tylina's protesting hands. Cora's tears flowed steady down her cheeks, blurring her vision, but she could see the queen clearly.

"Why do you cry for him, Cora?" Reann demanded.

The princess stared at her queen and mother. "I don't cry just for him. I cry for all of them. They are my friends. I've told you, Mother. I love him. How do you expect me to act after you tried to kill him?" On the pier, Tylina gathered the bags and weapons of the men, her movements angry. Dismounting, Cora made to run to the pier, but her mother's spear stopped her.

Reann studied her youngest daughter, her eyes drifting toward Cora's growing abdomen. "You still have time before his fate is decided. The child is the only reason I spared him."

"*I* am the reason you spared him. No matter how much you deny it, I am the reason. You did not wish to anger me more." Cora turned to watch while her friends were placed into the bed of a nearby wagon.

"You will not tend to their wounds, Cora. You will leave that to our healers. The other men should not have come with him. They will come to regret that decision," Reann instructed.

"I would not assist you or our people in their care anyway.

You have called down the demon and you will face him without my assistance. You will find out what it truly means to come between us." Cora stared at her mother a moment more, then turned her back and waited for Tylina to push her way past the warriors.

"Why didn't you stop this?" the half-elf angrily spat at her Amazon friend. "You just stood by and watched them be taken away."

"I could not stop this, Tylina. I told you not to come. I asked you to keep Percival from this place." Cora held her hand out to her friend. "Come with me. We will have a better chance of changing this once we reach the fort."

Silva slipped around Cora and gently took the bags and weapons from Tylina. She protested at first, then relinquished everything. Finally, Tylina took a deep breath and faced Cora again.

"Let's get to this fort you call home so we can discuss what we can do for the men."

Cora nodded in agreement, then led Tylina to a horse. After Cora sat in the saddle of her own horse again, the two women followed the wagon to the fort in silence.

When the wagon reached the fort, Cora and Tylina left their horses in the care of the slaves who attended the stables and followed the Amazon warriors carrying the men inside. Brolin followed behind the others, still flanked by the queen's warriors.

Arriving in the dungeons, Cora gave orders as to which cells she wanted the men put in. She stood in silence when Tylina dashed to care for Kalik, her attention on the Amazons putting Percival in his cell and on the cot inside. When the other Amazons left, Cora crossed to the cot and knelt down next to it. She rested her hand on his forehead as the healers came inside and began tending to his wounds.

"Princeesa, we will attend to them. Return upstairs and rest," Misabel whispered, laying her hand on Cora's.

Cora nodded, pushing the woman's hand from hers. She pressed her cheek against his, reveling in the feel of their skin touching, the tingling she had missed since the day they said good-bye. "I'm sorry, Percival. You shouldn't have come," she whispered. After touching her lips to his cheek, she stood and walked out of the cell. "Tylina, we need to go back upstairs.

The healers will handle their care for now." She controlled the tremor of her voice.

Tylina shook her head. "No, I'm going to stay here."

"You can't. This is a prison for the men. The guards won't allow you to stay and we can't fight my mother if you are down here," Cora protested.

Tylina rested her head against Kalik's shoulder for a handful of breaths, then finally stood. "All right. Where am I to stay?"

"In my rooms, with me, until my mother has the rooms across from mine readied for you." Cora took her friend by the hand and led her from the cell and up the stairs leading from the dungeon.

Before they continued down the hall of the main floor, Cora's sister blocked their progress. Rainne smirked at her, crossing her arms. Cora squared her shoulders and held Tylina behind her.

"I hear your man survived, Cora," she said, sarcastic, glaring at the half-elf behind the younger princess.

"Leave me be, Rainne. I don't wish to be bothered by you right now." Holding Tylina's hand, Cora pushed past her sister.

Rainne laughed. "Ever the sensitive one, sister. Your time in Man's World has not benefitted you. It has only hindered you."

Cora turned on her sister, summoning her magic and holding it as a blue glow in her hand. "Don't try my patience right now, sister. I am in no mood for you.'

Rainne's eyes grew wide, the glow from Cora's hand reflected in them. "You wouldn't do anything to me," she breathed, uncertainty making her voice shake.

"Do you know that for sure?"

The sisters stared at each other, until Tylina shifted next to Cora. Without another word, Cora turned and again led her friend to her private rooms. The Amazons they met bowed to the princess, then stared in disbelief at the woman she pulled along behind her.

When they entered the main room of her suite, after a brief introduction to the guards at the door, Cora stopped in surprise. Dekart stood in the room, waiting for them.

"Princeesa, please forgive me." He went to his knees, hands on the floor in front of him.

Cora released Tylina's hand. "Get up, Dekart. This is Tylina, the friend I've told you about."

He stood and pulled Cora into his arms, comforting her in a fashion that was still new to the two of them. "I was saddened to hear what happened at the pier. But you stood up to your mother, again, and for that I am proud of you."

"Thank you, Dekart, but you should not be proud of me. I have allowed the man I love and the men I call friends to be severely injured and captured." Cora pulled away from him and gestured for Tylina to sit with her on the pillows in the middle of the floor.

"You couldn't have stopped Reann, Cora and you know it." He sat next to her. "And, you told me you warned him. He knew the risks when he boarded that ship. Surely all of them knew the risks."

"We did. When Reann came for Cora, we tried to stop her from being taken, but were unsuccessful. We wanted to show the queen that she could not just take a friend by force. We wanted to make a point," Tylina informed them, her voice shaking.

"I did not tell you everything about our island. I don't think Percival realized the force you would be facing when you got here." Cora took Tylina's hand in hers, the other hand resting on her abdomen. "You should have stayed away."

"We couldn't let Percival come alone," Tylina whispered.

"Does he know of the child?" Dekart asked, reaching to touch her hand.

Tylina sat up, startled. "You're pregnant? When did this happen?"

Cora closed her eyes, thinking. "I missed my first cycle shortly after I left with my mother. Four months have passed since we left Larkspur. That was the last time we were together."

Tylina sat back in silence, watching the father and daughter. It was clear that she did not know what to think of everything she had seen and heard since arriving on the island. Her emotions and thoughts played havoc with her eyes. The princess let her have the peace she needed to think.

Dekart glanced at Tylina, then returned his full attention to Cora. "Why did you leave him there, Cora? I've heard you talk about him and I wonder what could have happened that you would leave him behind."

"Percival is no ordinary man, Dekart. I have seen many men react to the heat of battle, some more strongly than the most uncivilized Amazon, but none with the ferocity he has. Within him is a hidden strength that adds to this, but for three days every month, he must fight with this inner strength for control. Some months he stays with me, some months he must leave. Since we became lovers, he had not left me other than a few hours alone outside of camp. In Larkspur, he had to stay behind because it was so bad."

The three sat in silence, listening to the sounds of the people outside Cora's window in the courtyard and in the hallway. Finally, Dekart stood.

"I must return to Reann before she misses me too much. She knows I visit you, but she will only tolerate so much time from her sight." Cora placed her hands under her, preparing to push herself from the cushions, but Dekart reached out to stop her. "No, my dear, don't get up. Stay with your friend, rest. Silva will let me know if I can do anything for you." He patted her hand, then left the room.

Cora waited for the door to close, then lay back on the pillows, her eyes moist from tears. She shifted closer to Tylina, resting on her friend's shoulder for comfort. Her hand pushed the bulge of her growing baby. The pressure helped ease the pain she was feeling, pain that had gotten worse over the last few weeks as her belly had grown and the baby started to move more. After a moment, she pulled herself away from the half-elf.

"What's wrong?" Tylina asked, concerned.

"Bethany said I shouldn't get pregnant, but as you can see, I listened to her about as well as I do to my mother. The growth of the baby has caused quite a bit of pain and the stress of what has happened seems to have aggravated it," Cora explained. "I need Misabel."

Tylina nodded, crossing the room to the door. Outside, Cora's personal guard immediately straightened when it opened.

"The princess needs Misabel," Tylina told them. Silva nodded, then immediately left. The half-elf returned to Cora's side and helped her into the bedroom.

Minutes passed, then Silva opened the door to the room and allowed Misabel to enter. Cora sat up and gestured for the elderly woman to come closer to the bed.

"Princeesa, you are pale. The pain has returned?" Cora nodded. "Then will you let me take care of it this time? I have seen your man. He is quite large. This does not bode well for you."

"No, your solution would rid me of the child and I want to keep it." Tylina rose from her chair, taking a step closer to the bed. "No, Tylina. Misabel will not harm me or the child." Though Cora could see the uncertainty in Tylina's face, she returned to her seat, watching Misabel closely.

Misabel shook her head in frustration. "Princeesa, the pain will only get worse. See what your wild adventuring brings? Child bearing is affected."

"Yes, you've told me that. You've also told me what it was that caused the pain, which I understand. Just give me something to cope with it again and leave more. Silva no longer has any."

Misabel nodded, then set aside three packets of herbs. "Mix a pinch of each with some warm water to make a tea, not more or you will sleep for days. If you use too much, you will fall into the eternal sleep." She approached the bed and laid a hand on Cora's abdomen. "The child grows, despite your issues. But the man's size still concerns me. Bed rest is the best solution I can suggest. I will have Silva make the tea for you." The old woman turned her attention to Tylina. "I have seen to your man. He has responded well to the healing bestowed upon him and you should be able to visit him, with the queen's permission of course, within a few days."

Tylina nodded, and Cora could see her control the anger trying to fight its way to the surface. "Thank you. I'm sure he will be happy to hear that."

Cora stifled a laugh at the sarcasm she heard in Tylina's voice. Misabel frowned at the two women, then left to retrieve warm water for the tea. She returned with a mug, mixed the tea with the water and handed it to Cora when she was finished.

The three were silent while Cora drank the tea. Misabel made sure the entire contents were drunk before taking the mug from her. Cora lay against the pillows of her bed, waving Misabel away as she closed her eyes.

Chapter 80

Every morning for a week, Cora and Tylina received updates regarding their friends. Kalik and Nimbly's wounds were healed the day after arriving on the island. Brolin, though allowed to heal the other two men, was not allowed to touch Percival.

On the fourth day of their imprisonment, Kalik, Nimbly and Brolin were transferred to the men's quarters. They were placed in rooms with constant guards, an unusual move for the queen. The queen's guards never guarded men while in the men's quarters.

Cora knew her mother heard every report regarding the men before she did, and the queen ensured that the information Misabel gave her daughter was minimal. Misabel's reports regarding Percival were always the same—his wounds were healing. The princess-mage accepted the old woman's words without argument, knowing to do otherwise would give Reann the excuse she wanted to hurt him again.

On the eighth day after her friends arrived, Cora and Tylina sat through morning meal without Misabel bringing their daily report.

When midday meal also ended without a visit from Misabel, Cora left Tylina and went in search of the healer. After searching the second floor of the fort, she found Misabel tending to one of the healers assigned the duty of caring for Percival in the room the healers shared.

"What happened?" Cora demanded, stepping into the room.

Misabel leaned away from the bed, revealing the severe wounds the other healer had suffered. Bruises colored Marque's cheek, and her eye was swollen shut. Dried blood caked the corner of her mouth and fresh blood dripped from her ear. Cora could hear the ragged gasps of Marque's breath before she started a coughing fit.

Misabel rose from her stool, standing between Cora and the bed. "What are you doing here, Cora?"

"When you didn't come to my room this morning, I decided to find you." Cora pushed Misabel aside. "What happened to Marque?"

Misabel pulled her away from the bed. "We need to see the queen, Cora. Right now." She called for one of the other healers to tend to Marque, then took Cora's hand and dragged her out of the room.

By the time the two reached the throne room, Cora held her abdomen, pain coursing through her body. She pulled her hand from Misabel's and leaned against the wall while they waited for the guard to open the door. After a deep breath, Cora followed Misabel inside.

Cora had not been in the throne room since returning to the island, instead spending time in her rooms, the temple to Shae and the chambers for the mages. Looking around, she noted the tapestries paying tribute to the history of the Amazons still hung on the walls. Interspersed amongst those tapestries were hangings to the glory of their goddess. A door near the dais, used for the queen to enter and leave the throne room, was closed with a guard standing in front of it. In the middle of the outside wall, a stone fireplace held a fire to warm against the chill of the changing seasons.

Reann sat on her throne, listening to a report from the captain of her elite guard. Shayta stood next to the captain, nodding. The captain was Shayta's mother and seeing the two women in front of Reann concerned Cora, but she remained silent, waiting for the queen to acknowledge her. Reann dismissed the captain and her daughter and turned to the princess and the healer.

"Well, what is it?" she asked, her voice icy with impatience.

"My queen, the situation has worsened. We need her assistance now." Misabel bowed her head as she spoke to her queen.

Cora pushed past Misabel toward her mother. "What do you mean the situation has worsened? You've been hiding something from me regarding Percival and I demand to know the truth."

Reann stared at Cora, her face filled with shock, then pride crossed over her face, quickly replaced with the emotionless expression Cora always knew the queen to wear. "Yes, we have, Cora. We tried to heal his wounds without the use of magic, trying to keep him weak as long as we could, to enable us to learn more and gain control. Instead of his wounds healing from the administration of our herbs and bandages, as a normal wound would, his wounds have only worsened. When he is conscious, he only asks for you and becomes enraged when we tell him he can't see you."

Cora laughed. "Of course he does. What did you expect? He came here to rescue me from you. We have something more, Mother. Something you will never understand." She stepped closer to the throne, a brief moment of satisfaction filling her when she saw her mother bristle at her words. "Percival loves me. I help to ease his pain and keep his anger in check. He needs me as I need him. We complete each other. I told you before you couldn't keep us separated, yet you still tried. See what it has done? Our people have been injured and killed. Was your need to keep us separated worth the loss of Amazon life?"

Reann angrily stood from her throne. "You overstep your position, Cora!"

"I do not, Mother. You're angry because you were wrong in your handling of this and you've been forced to pay a price you didn't expect. Do not take your anger out on me. I know the truth." Cora crossed her arms, her expression smug.

Reann glared at her daughter for a moment, then returned to her throne. "As I said, his wounds have gotten worse. We discussed it and decided that magical intervention would be necessary. Marque was given the task of healing him with the power of Shae this morning. That is all I know, as I have not spoken to Misabel yet." Reann turned her attention to the elderly healer. "What happened, Misabel?"

"It felt as if the spells were blocked. She attempted several minor ones, testing to see if they would work, based on your information that he was touched by magic as a child, which we assume is the reason for his black hand. Your information on all that was rather vague." Misabel glanced at Cora timidly.

Cora smirked, and was graced with a glare from her mother.

Misabel continued. "When the spells did not work, Marque and I decided to attempt a more powerful healing spell. When she laid her hand on his chest and spoke the words invoking Shae's power, a concussive force slammed into her, originating from him. I do not know how. Her injuries are severe, but we will be able to heal her."

The room fell silent while each of the women studied the others. Finally, Cora cleared her throat. "And? What do you want me to do about this?" she asked, knowing only she could help Percival now. She knew she was being difficult, that she should be eager for the chance to help him, but she wanted her mother to know that she had made a mistake. To teach her not to interfere in Cora's life.

Misabel looked at her queen, who nodded grimly at her, then turned to the princess. "Do you know what is causing this, Princeesa?" Cora nodded. "Do you know how to get past it?" Again, she nodded. "Then with the queen's permission, I am asking you to help us heal him."

Before Cora could answer, Reann interrupted. "How will you get past it, Cora?"

"He can resist all magic he feels is a danger, so he resists you. I can convince him otherwise."

Reann laughed. "Then any of our people can do that. We do not need you for that."

Cora scoffed. "You can try. Percival will not listen to you or anyone else from our island, especially not after what he feels Marque tried to do." She reached a hand behind her, rubbing her back. "My back is starting to hurt. I need to lie down. Good luck with it." She turned to leave.

"Wait, Cora." She felt Reann's hand on her shoulder. "Why are you not fighting me more to help him?"

Cora turned back to her mother. "Because I told you the day you captured him that you would have to tend to him yourself. I am allowing you the opportunity to find out what drives him. I have already learned his needs and desires. I already know what needs to be done to save him. Now is the time for you to learn about others than yourself, to learn that you cannot always control what others do, say or feel. Learn about my needs and desires, and what we mean to each other." She breathed deeply. "And because you still hold both us prisoner. As a prisoner, I am not obligated to do anything."

"I could order you to do it."

Cora nodded at her mother's threat. "Yes, you could. But by doing that, how can you be sure I will do what needs to be done? How can you be sure I won't just be making the next attempt to heal him worse and actually kill someone this time?" She pulled her arm away from her mother. "Why do you care if he survives?"

"What do you want, Cora?" Reann ignored the question, countering it with her own. "Why am I negotiating to get your help with him?"

"I know him, Mother. If you do not get my help and somehow he gets better without it, you will still be holding him a prisoner, a slave. You may even make him my slave, but he could never live like that and neither could I. He has fought his entire life to be free of his own enslavement. Why would he easily settle into being a slave? By negotiating with me for what I want, you are making your life easier in the long run, trust me." Cora studied her mother, waiting for her to acknowledge what had been said. Finally, Reann nodded. "Good. While he is healing, I want him up in my rooms. Once he has healed completely, you will allow us to leave the island. You will order the Sea Wolves to take us back to Glenys and you will leave us alone for the rest of your life."

Reann pondered the demands for several moments, the emotional struggle evident on her face. Cora's stomach tightened at the thought of giving her mother such an ultimatum. No one had ever attempted to speak to her mother in the way she had and Cora had done it and lived, for the moment. After a few more heartbeats, Reann walked back to her throne and sat down.

"So be it, Cora. You will go to him and you will do whatever it takes to convince him that he needs to let our healers help him. Once he has accepted the healing, he will be moved to your rooms where you will assist in his recovery. When his healing is complete and his strength returned, you will leave the island, never to return. You will be exiled. Our people will no longer acknowledge you as their princess. You will be regarded as an outsider from the moment you leave the Sea Wolves in Glenys until the day you die. Your child will not be acknowledged by our people as a possible heir if your sister is unable to produce an heir." She leaned forward, making sure Cora heard her next words. "You will no longer be considered an Amazon. Do you accept these terms?"

"Yes, I do." She turned to Misabel. "You may inform him that I will see him soon. That will bring him some relief and begin the healing process."

A sound from the side of the room drew the attention of the three women. Dekart knelt on the ground, his arms in front of him. "Please forgive the intrusion, my queen."

Reann hid a brief smile, then glared at her slave and mate. "What is it, slave?"

"I would beg of you that I be allowed to tend to him until he can be taken to the Princeesa's room. I ask that you allow me to be the one to tell him she will be coming to him. He is already untrusting of the healers and may not accept their words as true." His eyes never left the floor, nor did he stand.

"What is happening in my home?" Reann demanded, a slight laugh escaping her. "Fine, Dekart. You may be the one to deliver the message and tend to him. Now all of you get out of here. I want to be alone." Cora and Misabel bowed, then left the throne room through the main entrance.

Chapter 81

Dekart made his way into the dungeon, every step bringing back memories of his time in its pits. Before his capture, he had been the first mate on his ship. When the captain died in the wreck, the surviving men turned to him for guidance. When the Amazons captured him and his men, he fought against them as fiercely as he heard Percival had done days ago.

The other men had left the prison before Dekart, resigning themselves to their fate, while he continued to resist. Reann had been in charge of breaking him. At the time, her quest to become queen had not begun. Before his spirit had been broken completely, she took him as her mate. Unknown to his daughters and the other Amazons, Reann allowed him quite a bit of freedom as long as he acted the dutiful slave in front of everyone else.

The walls of the prison were damp from moisture. The prison's depth in the island did not allow the clay walls to dry. The musky smell overwhelmed Dekart, but over it all, he smelled the poultices and herbs used in healing Percival. Dekart quickened his pace, hoping the news he wanted to share would help in Percival's recovery.

Reaching the bottom of the stairs, the Amazons guarding the other man blocked Dekart's path. He stared at the ground, placing his hands in front of him.

"What are you doing, slave?" the closest guard demanded.

"I have come with a message for the prisoner from the queen and the Princeesa. It is very important that he receive it." Looking through his hair, Dekart recognized the woman's hatred, but did not change his stance.

"Proceed," the guard finally ordered.

Dekart crept past her, toward Percival's cell, careful not to raise his eyes until he had passed the Amazon.

Cora had chosen well, having selected a cell further back than the others, drier than most and not used as often because it was too far from the door. He glanced around, taking in the damage that had been caused earlier. A stool still lay upended on the floor. Herbs were scattered, now useless. A pot lay shattered on the ground, next to the stool. Dekart looked toward the bed and winced despite the wounds he had suffered throughout his own life, as well as those he had cared for on his fellow slaves.

Percival lay on the cot, pale from loss of blood, his skin glistening with sweat from the fever ravaging through him. His chest rose and fell rapidly, his difficulty breathing evident in his wheezing and gasping. The wounds Dekart could see were dressed, but the bandages were soaked through with blood.

At the sound of the other man entering the cell, Percival's eyes fluttered open, and he turned his head slightly toward the sound. Pain slowed his movements, but he still managed to sit up on his elbow.

"Who are you?" he rasped, looking at Dekart through fever glazed eyes.

Dekart set the stool back on its feet and sat. "My name is Dekart, Black Hand."

Percival studied him for a moment more, then lay back down. "Are you going to tell me I can't see Cora as well? Because if you are, go away. I've had enough of the excuses you people have been feeding me." A coughing fit took his breath for a moment. When it passed, he turned to Dekart again. "I didn't expect to hear them from her father though."

Dekart smiled, warmth filling his chest. "So she told you about me. I'm not here to give you excuses. I'm here to give you good news."

Percival closed his eyes. "What? The girl survived? I don't care."

The older man laughed. "You are as stubborn as the Princeesa when it comes to hearing what needs to be said. Yes, the girl will survive, from what I've heard. Of course, they didn't tell me that directly. But that is not what I wanted to tell you."

"Then what? I'm not in the mood for guessing games, Dekart."

Dekart nodded. "I apologize. I was sent down here to tell you that Cora will finally be allowed to see you." Upon hearing the Princeesa's name, the guards in the room tensed, turning toward him menacingly. He lowered his gaze. "Forgive me. I mean, the Princeesa will be coming down to visit you, of course. I should not have spoken her name without her permission." The guards nodded, then returned to their positions.

Silence filled the prison for a moment, then Percival opened his eyes again. A spark of life filled to them, driving away the fevered haze. "Really?" Dekart nodded. "Finally. What happened to change the queen's mind?"

"The Princeesa can be very convincing and stubborn when she wants," Dekart whispered so only Percival could hear. His quiet chuckle betrayed his pleasure at the news he had shared.

Percival gave him a weak grin. "Yes, she can. I'm glad to hear I'm not the only one she favors with a tongue-lashing when she's angry."

Dekart watched him for a handful of moments. The spark in Percival's eyes continued to grow brighter and his cheeks flushed slightly with color.

"The Princeesa said it might help you just to hear she was coming down here." Percival nodded "In that case, let me tell you what else happened upstairs this afternoon." Dekart leaned forward, not wanting the guards to overhear. "Cora struck a deal with Reann for your release in exchange for her helping with you. But it will cost her everything. She will no longer be considered an Amazon. She will become an outcast from her people. No one will acknowledge her ever again, after the Sea Wolves return the two of you to Glenys. Not even your ch—" Dekart stopped himself. Cora should tell Percival herself about the baby. "I will go see what is keeping her. She should be coming soon." He stood and left the cell, not waiting for a response.

Chapter 82

Cora met Dekart climbing the stairs to the main floor, his steps slow and his eyes down. Stopping in front of him, she waited for him to acknowledge her. He lifted his gaze to hers, then immediately returned it to the floor.

"I'm sorry, Princeesa. I did not hear your approach," he mumbled.

Cora reached for him, lifting his face so she could see his eyes. "It's all right, Dekart. Is he awake?" she asked.

Dekart nodded. "Yes, he is awake and happy to hear that you're coming to see him."

She nodded, then stepped past her father, her personal guard following at a respectful distance.

Cora continued down the corridor, her skin crawling at the moisture in the air. She knew Percival had been imprisoned there too long. "Silva, he will need steam and herbs to clear his chest, I'm sure. The moisture may have already settled within him. We could have avoided the illness if we had taken him out of here sooner."

"Yes, Princeesa," Silva responded.

When she arrived at Percival's cell, Cora stood back a bit, looking at the man who had helped her put a word to her feelings for him. His eyes were closed, but his chest rose and fell rapidly, and she could hear his breath coming in ragged gasps and wheezes. His left hand rested on his chest. The black had progressed farther up his arm, now reaching his elbow. Did the progression mean that the demon had taken over since they were separated?

She motioned for the guards to open the door, her steps determined when she entered the cell.

"Percival," she whispered. His eyes opened when he heard her voice and he tried to sit up to look at her, but she hurried to his side and placed a hand on his chest, applying enough pressure to keep him on the cot. "No, lie down. Don't sit up." Cora pulled the stool closer and sat. "I have missed you."

"I've missed you, Treame." Percival smiled at her, his eyes lighting with a small fire.

Hearing him say her true name felt like magic coursing through her, and she closed her eyes at the warmth.

Before their reunion could continue, a loud explosion shook the dungeon walls around them. Dust, brick and dirt flew down the corridor in their direction, forcing everyone to cover their heads to protect themselves. Cora threw herself over Percival to keep anything from reaching him. As the dust settled, she stood and turned to the guards.

"Silva, find out what that was," Cora ordered, moving to the door. The guard nodded and sent two of the women down the corridor.

Dekart joined Cora in the cell, stepping in front of Percival. Hearing movement behind her, Cora turned to look at Percival and waved her hand for him to stop moving before returning her attention to the approaching commotion.

The sounds of metal striking metal reached them and Cora heard shouting from the direction of the approaching conflict. She glanced at Dekart in shock, then turned once again to Percival.

"It's one of the wilder tribes of my people. They say they want you, that through you they will protect the island and the queen."

Percival stood, gaining his footing after several attempts. She watched him try to take a defensive stance, but he only succeeded in standing with his feet apart.

"They can try," he growled.

The footsteps came closer, and Cora's remaining personal

guard stepped forward to stop their island sisters. She watched in frustration as Silva and the others were pushed back, small wounds on them from the other Amazon's weapons, but nothing that would maim.

Finally, the main force of invaders arrived in front of Percival's cell. Their leader walked between them, stopping to stand in front of Cora. The princess left the cell, reaching back to pull the door shut behind her, locking Dekart and Percival in. From the corner of her eye, Cora saw Dekart turn to Percival, keeping him from approaching the door.

"What do you want, Sovin? Obviously the queen will be unhappy to see what you have done to her home," Cora said in the Trade language so Percival could understand the conversation.

Sovin bowed deep to her princess, then straightened, placing a hand on her weapon. "I have come to protect the queen and her daughters. We were told this man would tear our island apart. We have come to stop him," Sovin replied, the heavy accent in her voice proof of her refusal to speak the Trade language unless forced.

Cora tried to keep her emotions from her face, despite the fear and anger she felt rising within her. "No, you have been misinformed. This man is not going to harm our island. Who told you that?" She forced a tone of comfort into her voice.

Sovin shook her head at Cora's question. "That is not important. When we arrived at the fort today, to present our concerns to the queen, we were advised that you are giving up your position amongst our people for this man. That is more than we can allow. I'm sorry, Princeesa. We do not wish you harm." She motioned for her companions to enter the cell. "Get in there."

Cora pushed closer to the cell door, placing her back against the bars. She grabbed the bars with her hands and blocked their access to the lock. Her capeshal fell from her grasp and waist, crumpling on the ground around her feet. "You will have to go through me, Sovin. I will not allow you to do this."

The other closest Amazons looked to Sovin for guidance, concern written on their faces.

"Please step aside, Princeesa. Again, we do not wish you or your child harm." Sovin's concern for her princess broke through her growing anger.

"What?" Percival exclaimed from within the cell. "Are you pregnant, Cora?"

She heard him struggle with Dekart and the whispered attempts her father made to calm the other man.

"Sovin, I am serious about this. You will only get to him if I fall, and you will hurt my child in the process. Are you willing to accept that risk? Are you willing to risk the life of an heir to the throne?" Cora grinned at Sovin. Turning her head slightly, she nodded to Percival. "Yes, Percival. Standing here, trying to keep Sovin from you is causing me considerable pain. My mother has said this is the price I pay for adventuring in Man's World."

Percival resumed his struggles against Dekart to reach Cora. "Let me go, old man," he spat, strength returning to his voice.

Cora heard Dekart step away from Percival, then three footsteps behind her. She felt the familiar tingle of Percival's touch on her skin. He rested a hand on her lower back, his other reaching around her and caressing the bulge of their unborn child.

"You will not keep us apart, Sovin," he declared.

Cora stood confident, drawing strength from Percival's touch. "Decide, Sovin. What will it be?"

Sovin stood stunned by the unified front the couple presented to her and her warriors. "You are only proving that he has adversely affected you. In turn, you have put our people in danger. His death will protect us all. I accept the consequences of my actions." She clenched her fist, then slammed it into the side of Cora's face, knocking her to the ground.

"Cora!" Percival tried to reach her through the bars.

Sovin placed a key into the cell's lock, opening the door into Percival and pushing him back several steps. "You will no longer speak her name, *slave*." She stepped forward, reaching for him as four of her warriors entered the cell to help her.

Cora stood, her movements slow from the pain throughout her body, and wiped a hand across her mouth, smearing blood on her face and hand. She turned to face the other woman, raising her hand. "Arcanum misi," she whispered, pointing her fingers at Sovin's back.

Sovin screamed as five streaks of blue tore through the skin of her back, forcing her to release Percival's arm. At Sovin's cry of pain, one of her archers fired an arrow, hitting Cora in the shoulder.

"No!" Sovin screamed again, holding a hand out to her archer. "You fool!"

Cora held her shoulder, blood dripping between her fingers from the wound. The arrow shaft protruded from her skin and clothing. Leaning against the bars again, she slid down to the ground, struggling to keep her eyes open, the pain from her abdomen and shoulder overwhelming her.

A roar reached her from the cell. Through slitted eyes, she saw more Amazons step into the cell, stepping between Percival and Sovin as he tried to lunge at her back. She turned to look at him. "You will pay for her injury with your life, Black Hand."

"You first," he spat at her, the other women grabbing him.

Dekart rushed forward, grabbing one of the warriors holding Percival. "Let him go!" he shouted.

Cora struggled to sit up, trying to get her hand under her. She watched Sovin turn a glare on her father, then drive a sword into him. "No!" she cried out.

"You forget your place, slave," Sovin growled, letting his body slide off her weapon. "Get the other one out of here." She motioned for her tribe to leave, following behind the women who dragged Percival out of the cell.

"Percival!" Cora struggled to follow, pain tearing through her body until it pulled her into unconsciousness.

Chapter 83

Once her wounds were cleaned and dressed, Cora went to her mother's private rooms. One of her mother's elite guards told her that the door to the dungeon had been locked and since they could not find the key, the guards had to enter the dungeon through the hole created by Sovin's attack. The healers were still tending to the guards in the dungeon. Cora's personal guard had tended to her injuries, as well as Dekart's, before attending to their own.

The healer promised Cora that the baby was safe and the loss of blood had not been sufficient to cause the unborn child harm. Misabel tended to her father's wounds because he required more attention than Cora did.

Tylina helped Cora to her mother's rooms. Opening the door to her mother's bedroom, Cora found Reann kneeling next to the bed, holding Dekart's hand. With her other hand, Reann ran her fingers through his hair.

"How does it feel, Mother?" Cora whispered.

Reann glanced at her, then returned her attention to the man who had shared her life for so long. "How does *what* feel, Cora?"

The princess shuffled carefully through the room, leaning on Tylina until they reached the bed. "It's all right, Mother, to feel compassion, love and concern for him. He has spent a good portion of his life with you and I know you have had no others in yours. They would call it a marriage in Man's World."

Reann looked at her daughter again. Moving to sit on the bed next to Dekart, she touched his cheek with her fingertips. "He's been with me for almost twenty-five years, Cora. I have always let him have free reign over what he does, except where it interfered with the normal lifestyle of our people and until yesterday, I didn't realize how much I liked seeing his face at my table, moving around my rooms, giving me a smile when no one else was looking. I've never told anyone how he makes me feel. I don't even know how to describe it."

"Your stomach flutters when he touches you and you wake every morning looking forward to that first touch and the first kiss of the day." Cora let her attention wander as she described the feelings she had when she was with Percival.

Reann favored her daughter with a small smile. "I am a bit past the stomach flutters, dear, but I do remember them. Now, I find more enjoyment in just sitting with him, watching the sunset, reading a book by the fire or even listening to his stories for the hundredth time. You should know, Cora, that I never broke your father as the others did with their own slaves. I've always liked that he still has his own opinion. And he has always made sure not to let anyone else know."

"So why did you hurt him, Mother? Why did you use him against me?" Cora whispered the questions she had been longing to ask. "Why are you so against Percival and I being together?"

"I did what I felt I had to, to get you back, Cora. You will never understand how much it hurt me to do that to him. All I can hope for is that he will one day forgive me." Reann turned her face away, but Cora saw the tears on her mother's cheeks.

"Of course I forgive you, my dear one," Dekart's hoarse whisper broke the silence and he raised a hand to wipe the tears from Reann's face.

Reann cried out in surprise, then pulled Dekart into her arms. They began to whisper to each other, ignoring the two young women in the room.

Cora smiled at her parents, then left the room, allowing Tylina to help her again.

"Your mother is full of surprises, Cora," Tylina observed as they made their way back to her rooms.

"Yes, almost like two different people." Cora shook her head. "She didn't answer my question about Percival."

"She will, Cora. You will have to ask her again," Tylina comforted.

At the door to Cora's rooms, Silva again stood guard. She rushed to help Cora inside.

"Silva, are you better?" Cora asked, noting the bruise on her cheek.

"Yes, Princeesa, I am well." Silva narrowed her eyes. "I am ready and willing to pay back my sisters for the wounds you received, as well as the slight ones that mar my own body."

Cora laughed. "Good." The three made their way into the common room and then the bedroom. After making sure Cora was comfortable, Tylina turned to leave.

"I am going to the slave quarters. I want to check on Kalik and the others," she informed Cora.

The Amazon nodded, watching her friend leave. "How many do we have available, Silva?" she asked once the door had shut behind the other mage.

Silva leaned on her spear, her expression somber. "Normally, there wouldn't be such a fuss over a man, Princeesa. You understand?" Cora nodded. "But since he is your man, the one you had your vision of, the one you chose over us, the one that helped you see a different way of life, a life many of us want to live… Because he is *your* man, we have about thirty, between your personal guard, the queen's elite and the regulars. The queen demanded we limit the volunteers from her elite and the regulars. There were too many. Allowing more would have adversely affected the island's protection and the queen's."

"Good. When my mother is available, please inform me. I have numerous questions that she needs to answer and I want to leave as soon as possible to rescue Percival."

Silva nodded and left the room. Cora pulled out her spell plates, and set about determining which ones she would use against Sovin.

Chapter 84

Sovin shoved Percival. He fell to the ground, his feet entangled in the ropes around his ankles. The woman's harsh laughter grated in his ears and he ground his teeth against the overwhelming pain he felt raging throughout his body.

"Are you incapable of walking, slave?" Sovin rested her booted foot on his back, pushing him down further with her weight.

"I am not a slave," he growled through clenched teeth. He tried to push against her weight, knowing if he were healthy, she would not be able to keep him on the ground.

Every morning for the last three days since Sovin took him from Reann's prison, Percival had been tortured. After they traveled for the day, she tortured him again before being allowing him to fall into unconsciousness.

Sovin herself liked to use a knife to reopen his wounds, painfully cutting away the barely formed scabs. She would dig into the wounds, making each one deeper. One of the other Amazons preferred to use a whip on his back. The wounds were left open, exposed to dirt and insects.

While they traveled, Sovin held his ropes. When she decided he was not keeping pace with her, she would spur her horse into a sprint and drag him on the ground for an immeasurable distance before stopping. While she waited for the others to reach them, she would kick him in the ribs until he coughed blood.

The first evening, while Sovin watched her tribe's shaman try to stop the internal bleeding she caused, Percival demanded she set him free or kill him. The Amazon informed her prisoner she would do neither. She planned to keep him alive until the birth of Cora's baby—their baby. If the babe was a girl, he would be allowed to live, but would only return to the princess once his spirit was broken. If he had sired a male upon her, he would be killed, all in the glorious tradition of the Amazon nation.

Percival felt his resistance to the minimal magic the shaman tried to use to heal him, but he wanted to believe Sovin and fought to allow the magic to work. He knew the spell used was a weak one, meant only to stop the bleeding and he had wondered how much internal damage his body could endure before the spell became useless.

Sovin removed her foot from his back. He counted to five before pushing himself back to his feet. The wounds from the arrows when he was captured at the dock ached and he could feel the illness in his chest from being held within Reann's damp prison cell. The wounds on his back ripped open when he moved and he bit his tongue to prevent crying out at the stinging pain.

While they waited for the others to join them again, Percival studied the ground at his feet, for the moment taking a non-argumentative stance with Sovin. He still found it difficult to believe Cora was pregnant. She should have taken the herbs Bethany gave her. They had discussed Bethany's warning that she not become pregnant and he had accepted it. Or so he thought. He smiled at the ground, turning his head away from Sovin so she could not see. He really wanted to hold the child he and Cora had created.

He would survive Sovin's sadistic plan so he could see his child.

"What are you thinking about, slave?" Sovin demanded, grabbing his face and forcing him to look at her.

Percival glared at her, measuring if the beating would be worth the retort he held back. Finally, he decided against the more flippant response and settled for meeting her gaze.

"Nothing you would find important." He set his feet firmly, expecting violence despite his more restrained comment.

Sovin returned his glare, then turned to the Amazons who had finally caught up to them. The one who liked to use the whip on him had already dismounted and stood behind Sovin, the whip stretched between her hands.

"Grace him with additional lashings, Satir. He seems to have forgotten how to lower his eyes properly when looking at his superiors." Sovin stepped aside, watching Satir take his ropes and pull him toward a tree.

Chapter 85

"Cora, we can't just ride into their camp and demand they release him!" Rainne shouted at her younger sister.

Cora took a calming breath before turning from the map she had been studying with Silva to look at her sister. Rainne had been making the same argument for the last four days and the younger princess had grown impatient with her.

"Why not, Rainne? That's what they did to us," she reminded her sister. "Or, is it that you don't want me to go after them? How did they know of a conversation I had with Mother less than a change before their attack?"

"What are you implying?" Rainne glanced around the room, her face filled with worry.

Cora shrugged. "Nothing." She turned back to the map. "Mother has already started an extensive investigation into the incident. I'm sure she will find whoever locked the dungeon door and told Sovin's tribe about our private conversation."

Rainne glared at Cora, then stormed across the room. Before she reached the door, Reann opened it and entered the room.

Rainne bowed her head and backed away from her mother. "My queen," she whispered.

"Rainne, how fortunate I've run into you. Now I don't have to go to the trouble of sending guards to your rooms." Rainne stared at her mother, not attempting to hide her fear. "Shayta has taken over for her mother as the captain of my elite guard. She and Head Priestess Marisa are looking into the reason for Sovin's attack two days ago. You will answer their questions, just as I have done and many others will."

Rainne nodded, solemn. "Yes, my queen, as you command." She turned to leave the room again, but stopped when Reann reached out and grabbed her arm.

"Rainne, one more thing." She grabbed Rainne's chin and pulled her face toward her own. "If I find out that my suspicions about you are right, I will punish you in ways no Amazon has ever been punished. Do you understand?" Again, Rainne nodded. Reann released her oldest daughter's face and watched as she rushed from the room. Reann turned to one of the guards at the door. "See to it that Rainne does not leave the keep and that she speaks to Shayta and Marisa." The guard nodded and left to carry out the queen's orders.

"She knows something, Mother," Cora stated once Reann reached her side.

"Yes, Cora, I know. Shayta has been watching Rainne since you came home and she says there have been quite a few messages between her and Sovin."

"Then why didn't you do something sooner? Why did you allow her to do this?" Cora asked in surprise.

"Why would I stop any man from being disciplined? Even yours?" Reann asked, just as surprised.

Cora failed to find words to express her confusion and anger. Though her mother seemed to understand how she felt about Percival, Reann still did not want Cora to have the happiness they had together.

Reann studied the map for a moment, obviously feeling the conversation was over. She pointed at a spot on the smaller island. "Sovin's camp is here." Cora nodded. "You cannot kill them, dear. Do what you have to in order to free him, but do not kill them."

"I will try, Mother," Cora agreed reluctantly. "Have you figured out yet what they want with Percival?"

Reann shook her head. "They have their own set of rules and beliefs. They are more primitive than the rest of us, despite what the men may think. If they feel The Black Hand has compromised an heir to their throne, or that you are too attached to him, I don't know what they will do."

"They will have more trouble than they realize. In Percival's weakened state, the chance of releasing his inner demon is greater," Cora said.

Reann stared at Cora as she finished her statement. "What do you mean, 'inner demon'?" she asked.

"Exactly what I said, Mother. If they weaken him more, in any way, a demon may walk on our islands and none will survive if he can't be stopped," Cora answered, her arms wrapped around her bulging belly. She returned her attention to the map.

The room fell silent, each of the women lost in their own thoughts. Reann took a deep breath.

"Where is Tylina?"

"She appreciates that you relocated our friends to a room within the men's quarters, but wishes the guards weren't necessary. She is spending as much time with them as she can." Cora frowned at her mother. "How much longer do you plan to treat them as slaves?"

"I am within my rights to treat them as such for as long as I want. It will depend on how they act. They are very argumentative." The brief truce between mother and daughter ended as the disagreement about her friends resurfaced.

"They were not raised to be slaves, Mother. I can't allow this to continue," Cora informed her.

"You can't allow it?" Reann laughed. "What makes you think you have any chance of stopping me?"

"Because you are not the difficult person you pretend to be, Mother. And because I know how you truly feel about my father," Cora advised.

Reann stared at her, shock on her face. "This is a discussion we will continue at a later time. Today, I have to find out who set my own people upon my home and daughter." Reann turned and left the room.

Chapter 86

The second morning after crossing to the smaller island, before the midday sun drove the winter chill away, Sovin's group of amazons arrived at their home. Percival stood in silence, his hands and feet still bound by ropes. He studied the camp, making note of the ways he could escape while the Amazons ate and slept. Large tents made from animal hides surrounded the permanent structure of a longhouse. Pens for animals and the few male slaves they kept were placed within the ring of tents.

When the group arrived, more women came out of the longhouse and tents to greet them. Children, all female, ran among the women, shouting in excitement when they found their mothers. Moments later, slaves brought food and drink and started unsaddling the horses while the women took their meal and sat around the large campfire.

Percival waited for someone to untie his ropes from Sovin's horse. When one of the slaves came to get her horse, he untied Percival's ropes and let them drop to the ground without even looking at the prisoner. The Black Hand hesitated, then, when the slave left with the animal, he turned and ran for the tree line. The ropes slowed his movement somewhat, but the length between his legs had been increased to help his stride while they traveled.

"Stop him!" Sovin shouted from the fire.

A bizarre silence fell over the camp as Percival continued his dash for the trees. Without glancing back, he recognized the sound of bowstrings releasing arrows. Numerous missiles pierced his flesh, forcing him to the ground.

While the Amazons made their way to his side, Percival painfully sat up on his knees. His hands rested on his thighs while he tried to control his breathing and he kept his back to the approaching women defiantly.

"Did you really think you could escape?" Sovin asked from behind him.

He felt Sovin grip one of the arrows in his back. Grinding his teeth together, he attempted to keep from revealing his pain as she pushed it through his flesh. Pain tore through him, and his vision darkened. He leaned forward on his hands, trying to keep from losing himself into the black of unconsciousness. Before the arrow tore into his flesh more, Sovin stopped pushing.

"Keep this up and you won't be worth anything to the Princeesa. A breeder is only good as long as he can perform satisfactorily. You'll barely be alive, if you survive at all." Sovin laughed.

"I am not a breeder for Cora," he mumbled, struggling to breathe through the pain.

Sovin forced the arrow through his flesh again until it broke through the skin of his abdomen. His uncontrolled scream filled the forest, followed by silence. With his left hand, Percival grabbed the bloody arrow and, yanking it from Sovin's grip, pulled the rest of the shaft through his body.

Despite his wounds and the illness ravaging him, Percival stood and faced the woman who tortured him. His vision reddened from his anger, and for a moment, he forgot his pain. With a devilish glee, he saw Sovin take three steps back from him.

"I will kill you, Sovin and I will enjoy it." Even to him, his voice did not sound normal. He heard a second voice combined with his, a deeper voice that sounded like Stromas'. Percival threw the bloodied arrow at her, showering her with his blood. *"One day soon, the blood on my hands will be yours,"* he promised, the second voice now dominating his.

The two warriors glared at each other for uncounted breaths, long enough for the Amazons surrounding them to shuffle from the tension. Percival maintained his anger-fueled stance the entire time he and Sovin stood in defiance of the other, but he felt the loss of blood taking its toll on his burst of strength.

He knew Stromas gave him the strength to stand against the Amazon and that Sovin had seen the demon's power in his eyes. It brought no comfort, however, to learn the demon could so easily infuse his power through Percival. He was too weak to resist the stronger demon. Not even the knowledge that Stromas couldn't do it while he was healthy gave him any consolation.

Finally, Sovin broke the glare she fixed on Percival and turned to search for her shaman. "Take him to the tree and have Satir tie him to it. After he is bound, you may remove the remaining arrows and perform a minor healing."

"That spell will not be enough this time, Sovin. It hasn't been enough for the last three days," the shaman tried to explain.

"I don't care, Torin." Sovin strode away from the others. "He would be better off dead anyway."

Percival watched her leave, Stromas' gift of strength leaving him when she walked further away. He heard the truth in Sovin's last words and wished he would die so Cora couldn't see his current failure. He had already failed her enough in not protecting her from her mother, and doubting their love for each other.

Before he could fall to the ground from pain and loss of blood, Satir and Torin walked him over to the tree near the campfire. Thankful for the relief, he leaned against the trunk and allowed himself to slip into unconsciousness despite his arms and feet being tied to the large trunk.

Chapter 87

"Princeesa, the queen is here to see you."

Cora looked up from the map she had been studying every day since Percival's capture to acknowledge the guard standing at the door. She absently waved her hand in consent and returned her attention to the parchment.

Reann approached the table. "What more information do you expect to learn from that map, Cora? You've studied it so much, you must have memorized every paint stroke by now." She rested her hand on Cora's. "You can't save the Black Hand by looking at the map."

"Don't call him that, Mother. I know what it represents to him and I truly despise that name." Cora straightened and faced Reann.

"What do you expect me to call him then?" The queen clenched her jaw.

Cora knew even this small concession would be difficult for her mother, but she remained determined to force her point. "I realize calling him Percival will be impossible, so I will only ask that you call him Captain Riesun. It is his rank in King Kennan's army."

Silence filled the air between them for several drops of the clock until Reann finally nodded.

"Does *Captain Riesun* realize how much you defend him?" she asked.

Cora shrugged and returned her attention to the map, ignoring the question. "I can feel the pain they are causing him. I can feel a connection with him, even now. I fear in the end they will use me or our love against him." She hugged herself and shivered.

"I'm sorry, Cora, but it is a weakness." Reann rested a hand on her shoulder.

"Then they will break him by taking the one thing away from him that keeps the demon at bay," Cora whispered.

A moment of silence passed between them again, until Reann spoke. "I have news, Cora. We confirmed Rainne was the one who gave him up to Sovin. She wanted to rid you of him, but she had hoped you would become so upset about it, that you would leave the island without him and never come back. She was trying to strengthen her own child's claim to the throne."

"Why does she think I would leave without him? What gives her the right to try and force me to be without the one I have chosen?" Cora's rage poured out of her.

Reann backed away from her enraged daughter. "She feels you are weak and if you should gain the throne, you will weaken our people," she answered.

Cora flung her hand in the direct of a nearby tree. A ray of light left her hand and surrounded the trunk. A moment later, it burst into flames.

"I am not weak," she growled, turning back to face her mother. "I have been forced by you, Rainne and Shoshona, to be something I am not. I am stronger than all of you realize and with Percival at my side, I am a force to be reckoned with." She stormed past her mother, into the common room. "Silva, it's time."

The captain of her guard entered the room. "I will notify the others, Princeesa."

"What are you doing, Cora? Where do you think you're going?" Reann interrupted before Cora could give further instructions to her guard.

"I am going after Percival. They've had him long enough and I need to get to him before the black moon." She handed Silva a folded parchment.

"Cora, Rainne has disappeared," Reann stated, her voice

quiet.

"So send your elite to find her." Cora turned her anger on her mother.

"You need to find her. You know our laws. She has brought an injustice upon you. Bringing her to punishment now falls on your shoulders."

Cora felt Silva's gaze on her and knew her captain was waiting for a response. The woman studied her, gauging her princess' every action. Was she trying to determine how far Cora would go to protect Percival?

"That's an old law, Mother. No one has followed it in years."

"Nevertheless, as the ruling family, we must continue tradition." Reann crossed her arms.

"I've told you I don't hold much to the traditions of our people any longer," Cora tried to remind her mother.

"You will do it, Cora, and you will bring her back to face justice," Reann demanded.

Cora stared at Reann for several moments, then finally lowered her eyes. "As you command, my queen. Silva, have ten guards readied. I will cast a spell for her location before we leave."

"Good. Take care with her, though. I do not want her baby injured." Reann waited for Cora's acknowledgement, then left the room.

Silva followed Reann from the room. Cora returned to the map on her balcony and stood looking over the top of the trees at the moon. Smoke spiraled toward the heavens from the tree she had destroyed.

"I will make sure the baby comes to no harm, but I cannot make that promise for everyone else involved."

The next morning, after using a spell to locate her sister, Cora led eleven of her guard to the caves where Rainne hid. They traveled in the opposite direction from the one Sovin took when she fled with Percival.

Cora felt the distance between her and Percival growing every day. The connection between them felt strained. She could not feel his emotions, or pain—nothing. There was no way to know if he was protecting her from it, or if the distance masked it from her.

The second morning, the younger princess stood outside the cave entrance, flanked by her guards, staring at the darkness the morning sun could not drive away from inside. She had become angry when she realized Rainne had taken refuge within the caves. When she and the others arrived, she had attempted to draw her sister from the depths by shouting at her. Rainne had refused to come out and Cora could not bring herself to enter.

"I will lead the others for you, Princeesa. We all know what Shoshona did. No one will fault you if you do not go inside," Silva whispered, breaking into Cora's thoughts.

"No, I will go in. Stay with me." She shuffled toward the cave entrance, gripping her spear tightly. One of the women behind her lit a torch as she walked into the cave.

Cora felt the familiar fear slowly tighten its grip around her chest and throat. Stepping farther into the darkness, she struggled to breathe. She reached out with her empty hand and rested it against the cool of the rock. The chill helped her to focus and when the torchbearer continued past her, she was able to follow with only a moment's hesitation.

The twelve women progressed through the passages until they arrived at a small cavern. Within the cavern, they found Rainne and her own private guard. Cora stepped out from behind her guards, prepared for the confrontation with her sister.

"Rainne, we've come to take you home. Mother is not amused," Cora called out.

"Mother's amusement is not my concern," Rainne returned.

"Sister, you are to return with us," Cora instructed.

"Cora, how can you come here to do Mother's dirty work? We are sisters, both of us pregnant. How can you return me to her?" Rainne sounded like she was pleading.

"Being sisters means nothing to you. I have learned this. Not only have you hurt me, but you have also harmed the man I have chosen as my mate. In response to the injustice you have caused me, I am invoking my right to bring you to punishment." Cora waved her guards forward. "I am here under the queen's authority. Rainne, your guard is disbanded." She stopped at the angry murmurs from her sister's guards. "I understand your anger, but the queen's word is final. If any harm comes to me or a member of my guard, the offender will be sent to

Man's World, never to return." The complaints stopped and the women retreated from the older princess.

"How can you threaten them with that, Cora? You've been to Man's World, returned and are begging to go back. Why should they fear something you are willing to do to yourself?" Rainne's sarcasm made Cora laugh.

"Because *I am* willing. I've been there. I've learned how to live in that society. I *want* to live in Man's World." Cora addressed the opposing group of guards. "How many of you want to live there?"

None of the women moved to leave. Instead, each one picked up the bags they brought with them and joined Cora's guards. Rainne stared in disbelief for uncounted breaths, then stood and raised her chin in defiance.

"All right. Take me to our Mother."

Silva stepped forward and took Rainne by the arm while two other guards gathered her possessions. The entire group left the cavern, following Cora from the cave system.

When they again stood under the open sky, Cora took a deep breath, the pressure she had tried to ignore finally lifting from her chest. She rested a hand on a nearby tree for support while trying to maintain her composure.

"How did you manage to walk into the caves, Cora? You've not been able to go into an enclosed area since you were kidnapped by Shoshona as a child," Rainne whispered from behind her sister.

"I'm not as weak as you think I am, Rainne. And, I will no longer allow you or Mother to treat me like I am." Another deep breath and Cora felt in control enough to turn and look at Rainne. "Mount up. I want to leave immediately."

Silva directed the guards before she helped Cora atop her own horse. When everyone was in place, the captain ordered the group to depart.

The third morning after bringing Rainne back to the fort to face Amazon justice, Cora attended her sister's trial. The whole process took less than a day before she was found guilty.

Cora sat next to Tylina throughout the trial. Her friend wanted to remind Reann that her daughters were not the only ones affected by Rainne's betrayal. The queen acknowledged the half-elf's presence, but made sure Cora and Tylina understood the discussion about their friends would have to wait for another time.

Reann made her decision regarding Rainne's fate to a crowd of Amazons who were more concerned about the succession to the throne than what would become of Rainne. She would be banished from the island after the birth of her child. She would be allowed to choose five others to travel with her, provided they were willing to live in Man's World. An Amazon of Reann's choosing would raise Rainne's child.

After the trial, Rainne was ordered confined to her rooms and guards loyal to the queen would be posted outside. Cora watched her sister's trial, and then confinement with very little emotion. Before Rainne walked into her rooms, she met Cora's gaze.

"You will make sure my child is raised by a good Amazon, won't you, Sister?"

Rainne's question surprised Cora and it took her a handful of heartbeats before she could find her voice again. "I will speak for you on your child's behalf, Rainne."

"And if it's a boy? What will you do then?" Rainne's question hit Cora as if she was testing her younger sister.

"If I am given the opportunity, I will speak on his behalf as well." Rainne nodded, then walked into her room and slammed the door.

Chapter 88

For Percival the days blended into one, never ending, pain filled experience, since arriving in Sovin's camp. The minor healing spells had stopped working before they arrived. Now, Percival only felt a break in the constant pain when Crista went against Sovin's orders and used a more powerful spell.

Every breath he sucked in hurt, not only from the wounds on his face, but also because of the bruises, broken ribs, and the illness he had begun to suffer from while in the queen's dungeon. He learned to breathe more shallow than normal to keep from expanding his chest too much.

Sovin still enjoyed torturing him herself, but she allowed Satir to do it more often. The other woman found extreme enjoyment in re-opening the wounds caused by the many arrows that hit him when he arrived at the island three weeks earlier.

The winter sun barely warmed the skin of his injured back. Despite the chill of winter, Sovin refused to allow him into the slave building, leaving him exposed to the elements.

The rough bark of the tree he was tied to cut into his cheek and chest. The sounds of the Amazons moving around the camp, taking care of their daily duties, reached Percival even with his back turned to them.

Thoughts of Cora helped him forget his pain, with concern

for her well-being the most prevalent. He hoped she was not stuck in bed because of the pregnancy. He knew Tylina and the others would help her if they could. His inability to help her angered him more than anything that had happened since arriving on the island.

"I'm sorry, Cora," he whispered, his words filled with regret. He shifted slightly, trying to relieve some of the pain he felt, and closed his eyes to rest before Sovin returned.

Chapter 89

Cora stood in the throne room, waiting to speak to her mother. Other Amazons demanded the queen's attention and the princess found it better to wait with the little patience she could muster, than cause a scene and demand to be seen first.

Tylina had interrupted Cora's midday meal with Dekart the day before. After yelling at Cora, Tylina calmed herself enough to insist the princess speak on behalf of the men she called friend to her mother. When Tylina left her rooms, Cora spent the afternoon contemplating what could be done for the men. She realized she had been so involved with thoughts about how to free Percival that she had not spared a moment to think about the others.

Cora knew her mother would be holding court to deal with issues the Amazons presented in the morning.

The sun had started its afternoon journey when Reann turned her attention to Cora.

"What is your issue, Princeesa? Besides the one we are already aware of?" Reann asked.

Cora smirked at her mother's use of her formal title. The queen still surprised her with the cold formality. "My friends, your majesty. They are not given the same minimal freedoms as the other men within our society. I must protest against their imprisonment."

"They came to our island, knowing the consequences. I have yet to decide their fate." Reann glanced meaningfully at the other Amazons in the throne room. "Many of our sisters have expressed an interest in those men."

"And, when Percival returns, will you force me to take him as a slave?" Cora stepped closer to the dais.

"Cora, I am not going to force him into slavery. Do you have such little faith in me?" Reann's quiet words brought her daughter closer.

"Mother, we both know how you feel about Dekart," she whispered. "You know how I feel about Percival. Tylina loves Kalik. Brolin and Nimbly are my friends. I am not asking you to change everything our people believe in. I am just asking you to set my friends free. Silva has already spoken to the members of my guard. I will make sure they do not go anywhere unescorted and that they respect our customs so those Amazons who are unwilling to accept them are not offended." Cora sat on the dais next to her mother and rested her head on her mother's lap. "Please, Mother. Show mercy and kindness to those who did not mean to offend."

The surprised murmurs of the other Amazons filled the silence between mother and daughter. Reann lifted her hand to Cora's head and stroked her white hair.

"All right, Cora. Take Tylina and Silva to the men's quarters and escort your friends to the rooms Tylina occupies." The two women sat in silence for several more heartbeats before Cora stood and smiled at her mother.

"Thank you, my queen." She bowed, turned and left the throne room.

Tylina waited outside. Silva stood behind the half-elf with five members of Cora's guard. The seven women turned at Cora's approach.

"What did she say?" Tylina rushed to her friend and grabbed her hands.

"She said they can be set free." Before Tylina could express her excitement, Cora rushed the rest of her announcement. "All of you will stay in the rooms you currently occupy. Silva will need to make arrangements to have them escorted everywhere they go to make sure none of the older Amazons become offended or try to cause any trouble."

"That's wonderful. Can we get them now?" The princess-mage nodded at the question and followed her friend, gesturing for Silva and the others to join them.

Moments later, the group of women had made their way through the fort and outside. They rushed to the men's quarters, pausing only once to let Cora catch her breath when pain shot through her abdomen.

Dekart greeted them at the door. His position as the queen's slave allowed him the authority to be the first to greet his daughter. Behind him, many of the men who had befriended Cora when she was younger also welcomed her and Tylina.

"Silva, stay out here with the others. We will be fine. Dekart will make sure of it," Cora instructed. Silva nodded and Cora watched the six members of her personal guard take up positions in front of the door.

After greeting the other men, Cora and Tylina followed Dekart to the room Kalik, Brolin and Nimbly occupied. Two Amazons stood outside the room, standing guard because Reann did not trust that Tylina would not try to help them escape.

"My mother has decreed that the men in this room are to be freed. I will be taking them into my custody," Cora informed the women. The guards nodded, then rushed from the building.

Tylina entered the room first, running to Kalik. "The queen has agreed to let you stay in my rooms with me. Cora talked to her today."

Cora and Dekart followed Tylina into the room. She leaned on her father's arm, watching her friends. Brolin looked up when she entered, then approached her, gesturing at the capeshal that covered her swollen belly. Cora nodded and allowed him to pull it off her.

"Tylina says you are having some problems. Lots of pain and occasional bleeding," Brolin whispered. "She says you had a chance to end the pregnancy, but chose not to." He stared at Cora until she nodded again. "What have your clerics said?"

"That it was an irresponsible decision and I could die."

"That's possible, but if I have anything to say about it, both you and the baby will be fine." He gestured for her to sit while the three men gathered their belongings.

When they finished, and Cora had said farewell to Dekart,

the group returned to the fort. Silva left them at the door to Cora's room and went to arrange for evening meal and the escorts for the men.

After they settled onto the cushions in the sitting area, the conversation turned to Percival and what had been done to rescue him.

"I know where Sovin's camp is and I have the people I need to rescue him," Cora answered their question quietly.

"Then why haven't you gone after him?" Kalik's imprisonment did not appear to have had an effect on his usual quiet demeanor.

"I can't. Despite the fact that my mother insisted I attend my sister's trial for her betrayal, I just can't. When I have tried to ride a horse, the pain has almost incapacitated me. No one has found a way to help me."

The men listened to the explanation in silence, then Kalik and Nimbly turned to Brolin. The priest nodded thoughtfully. "I will begin researching a way to help you in the morning, provided your mother will allow me access to any tomes on the island."

Cora took Kalik and Nimbly to the table that held the map of the Amazon islands. Tylina and Brolin discussed Cora's condition and the changes the half-elf had witnessed in the princess since their arrival.

Chapter 90

Two days after declaring he would find a way to help Cora, Brolin rushed to her rooms, his excitement carrying him ahead of his escorts. Reann had allowed books to be brought to the keep's study for him to read, under supervision, of course. One book on potions held what he believed was the answer to helping Cora ride a horse to go after Percival.

When he burst into the common room of Cora's quarters, the others looked up, startled at his abrupt appearance.

"Where is Cora?" Brolin demanded, ignoring their surprise.

"Lying down." Tylina gestured toward the bedroom, then returned her attention to the book she was reading quietly to Kalik.

Brolin covered the distance to the door and knocked, soft at first, then louder when he received no answer.

"Has anyone spoken to her recently?" he asked, glancing at the others.

Nimbly shook his head. "Not really. She said she wanted to lie down about two changes ago."

"You didn't think to check on her?"

"I looked in on her. She was sleeping. I didn't want to bother her," Tylina defended.

Brolin shook his head and opened the door, peering into the dark room. "Cora?" he whispered. He left the door open to allow light in from the common room.

He shuffled through the room to the bed. From his pocket, the priest pulled out a coin that had been enchanted with a light spell.

Cora lay on the bed, curled up with her knees as close to her chest as she could get them. Her eyes were closed, and Brolin could see her breathing, but it was not the slow, steady breath of sleep. Her breaths came in short pants. He reached out and touched her shoulder.

"Cora?" he whispered her name again.

She opened her eyes this time, though she didn't appear to recognize him. Brolin touched her again, drawing upon his priestly abilities. A heartbeat later, his own eyes opened wide in surprise.

"How long has it been like this?"

"I'm in pain every day, Brolin," she answered, her sarcasm lacking its usual bite. She shied away from his hand. Even that brief movement made her face contort more with pain and she struggled to control her breathing.

Without asking for permission, Brolin put one hand on Cora's chest and his other over the bulge of her unborn baby. The glow of his magic flowed from him into the mage and she gasped at the healing flowing into her.

"What did you do?" Cora asked in surprise.

"Helped you some, I hope. I cannot heal a wound that has already been healed, but I can help ease the pain as the baby grows." Brolin grinned. "Do you want to hear my news?"

She squinted at him, uncertainty clouding her eyes. Finally she nodded, pulling the blanket from the other side of the bed over her.

"I have found a potion that will numb your pain and allow you to ride a horse. But we must use it sparingly. I do not know what side effects long term use could cause," Brolin explained.

She stared at her friend, then nodded. "Thank you, Brolin. We can speak to my mother tomorrow. One way or another, we will leave to rescue Percival."

Brolin smiled again, spoke a single word and touched her forehead. Immediately Cora closed her eyes and her breathing slowed as she succumbed to the effects of his spell.

He walked to the bedroom door. "I found a potion that will

help Cora so she can ride a horse to find Percival. She wants to meet with her mother tomorrow to discuss it," he announced, not caring if any of the others found his interruption rude.

When they nodded, he shut the door to Cora's bedroom and made himself comfortable in a chair next to the bed.

Chapter 91

The next morning, Cora and Tylina, accompanied by Silva, went to Reann's rooms. Cora leaned on her guard for support until one of the queen's guards opened the doors to let them in. Reann looked up from the parchments she was reading, then rushed to her daughter's side.

"Cora, you're so pale," Reann exclaimed. She pulled the princess over to the cushions in the sitting area. "What are you doing here? You should be in bed."

"Brolin was able to find a potion that will allow me to ride a horse. I want to leave immediately for Sovin's camp." Cora reluctantly sat on the cushions.

"I do not think that is a good idea, Cora. What if the potion hurts you or the baby?"

"Brolin will go with me. I trust him, Mother. He is capable with his magic." Silence filled the room while the four women stared at each other.

Finally, Reann sighed and sat back on her cushions. "Sovin still has women loyal to her in the fort. She will know when you leave and with how many."

"I know. We will need Rainne to send a message to Sovin. Let them know I am coming. My people are eager to make this journey." Cora glanced at Silva who nodded grimly.

"I do not want Sovin killed, if it can be helped. I expect

her and her clan to resist, but try to minimize the loss of life," Reann requested, glaring at Silva to drive her point home.

"I will defend the Princeesa, her mate and her friends to my dying breath," the guard declared defiantly.

"Are you sure you want Rainne involved?" Tylina asked from her seat.

"Either way, Sovin will find out we are coming for her." Cora shrugged her shoulders. "Have Rainne deliver the message I have left in the morning. We will leave tonight, under cover of dark, so Sovin's spy will have to get past me to reach the camp."

Reann nodded in agreement. With a kiss to her mother's cheek, Cora led Tylina and Silva from the throne room.

At midnight, Cora, Tylina and Brolin met Kalik, Nimbly and Silva in the courtyard. Cora searched the courtyard, looking for the members of her guard and her mother's that would accompany them. Confused, she looked to Silva for an explanation.

"Where are the others, Silva?"

"I sent them into the forest, in groups of five, just in case we are dealing with more than one spy." She gestured toward Kalik and Nimbly. "It's your turn now. Take Tylina. The three of us will join you shortly."

Cora watched her friends leave, then mounted her own horse. "What is the final count?"

"The original thirty, not counting the six of us, Princeesa. We have supplies of food, water and arrows. I have also made sure we have appropriate blankets and tents." The guard stopped when Brolin brought his horse closer to Cora.

"Drink this potion, Cora. It should start to help you by the time we leave." Cora felt their attention on her while she drank the contents of the small vial.

The three waited in silence, until Silva nodded. "It's time. Follow me, Princeesa, priest." The Amazon warrior gently prodded her horse, walking the animal out of the courtyard, the others closely following.

Chapter 92

"Wake up!" A voice tore through Percival's tortured dreams.

He opened his eyes, then squeezed them shut again at the bright light that pierced his vision. His arms and legs ached and he could not remember when his captors forced him to put his damaged back against the rough wood of the tree. His arms were pulled behind him in a painful, backward embrace. His legs were still tied and he was briefly thankful for being tied to the tree that kept him from falling to the ground.

Again, he opened his eyes, squinting against the sunlight. The high position of the sun told him it was midday, but he did not know what day it was or how much time had passed since he last opened his eyes. He tried to blink away whatever dripped into his eyes, so he could focus on the people around him. Fresh blood still worked its way down his legs from the wounds on his back.

"Finally. Now we can begin." Sovin stepped in front of him, a malicious grin on her face.

"Begin? What more do you have planned, Sovin? Haven't you figured out that I won't break? You'll have to kill me," he growled through clenched teeth.

"Eventually. Since you refuse to learn how to be submissive to your superiors, I've decided to take... what would you call it? Desperate measures to break you. If you still resist, I will kill you. You will never see the Princeesa's child, never hold her, and never look into her face to find out if she resembles you. The child will be brought up as a Princeesa of our people and she will assume the throne upon Cora's death." Percival struggled against his restraints at her words, eliciting a laugh from Sovin. "Still have strength enough to try to hurt me? Amazing." She gestured at a woman dressed in blue and red robes.

The new woman came closer, reaching for Percival's head. He shook his head away from her hands, causing her to step away and glance at Sovin. She frowned, then stepped closer to him, bringing her knee up forcefully into his ribs. When his head fell forward from the pain, Sovin slammed her fist into his face, then nodded to the other woman.

"You can touch him now, Crista," she instructed.

Again, Crista approached and placed her fingers on Percival's temples. She held her grip for a few heartbeats, then released him.

Percival watched the mage remove her hands from his head and step away from him. She frowned at him, then turned to look toward the center of camp. He followed her gaze, his eyes falling upon a lone figure wrapped in a dark cloak sitting on a log at the fire. The individual stood and sauntered toward him, hands coming out of the cloak and reaching for its hood. When the material was pulled back, surprise filled him. Cora moved toward him, her upper lip in a cruel sneer.

She finally stopped in front of him. Seductively, she opened her cloak, revealing a red dress. The dress came down in the front, exposing the cleavage of her pregnancy-swollen breasts. The material was tight against her skin, drawing his attention to her belly. She stepped closer to him and ran her fingers over his arm, then chest.

"Oh, Percival, what a pathetic state you're in. Just look at you. Beaten so badly that you can't even move without re-opening your wounds. Your resistance to the magic of my people has been destroyed, all because you wouldn't listen to me. All because you had to use me to free yourself of your demon. So selfish. You claim to love me, but all you really wanted was my magic." She continued caressing his wounded chest while he tried to shake his head in denial.

"No, Cora. I do love you. I don't even know if your magic can release me from Stromas. Both of us searched for a way to be rid of him. Don't you remember?" he pleaded with her.

"You are so blinded by your emotions, that you thought to come to my home in a misguided attempt to save me from my mother," she continued, as if she had not heard him. Laughing, she dragged her nails across his chest. Blood appeared in the fresh scratches, collecting under her nails.

Percival gritted his teeth, then let out his breath slowly. "I came for you, Cora. You said you never wanted to come back here. I came to take you home."

She shook her head, digging her nails into the scratches she just made. "I lied. This is my home."

Again, he clenched his teeth as she made the scratches deeper, drawing more blood. "Why are you doing this?"

"To show you who I really am, Black Hand," she spoke the words she had refused to say since learning what his father did to him. Each word dripped with venom.

Percival stared at her in disbelief, then closed his eyes.

Chapter 93

Cora brought her horse to a stop, forcing the others to pull their mounts to either side of her to avoid a collision. After everyone stopped, Brolin guided his mount closer to her.

"Are you all right, Cora? Is something wrong?" he asked, anxious, while searching through his pouches.

"Look at the moon, Brolin. Do you see what phase it's in?" She pointed at the sky.

The priest looked toward the heavens. Cora watched him, knowing his search would be as difficult as hers had been to find the orb. Just a sliver of light gave any indication of its location or phase. Finally, he nodded.

"What's wrong?" Tylina asked, joining them.

"The black moon. If Stromas gains control, we won't have to worry about any prisoners," Cora whispered, fear in every word.

The Amazons gathered around them stared at the sky in confusion, while the group of friends nodded in understanding.

"Princeesa, we need to continue, especially if you fear the black moon," Silva advised.

Cora nodded, urging her horse forward again. Silva ordered the rest of the Amazons to start moving again and the group resumed their travel at the fastest pace allowed by the trees.

Chapter 94

"Who cut him?" Sovin demanded, pointing at the four wounds on the Black Hand's chest. The fresh blood was the only thing that distinguished them from the rest of the wounds she and her Amazons inflicted during his imprisonment. She studied the wounds, waiting for a response from those around her, but no one stepped forward to accept responsibility.

Sovin turned to stare at the members of her tribe for several heartbeats, then returned her attention to the Black Hand. Tracing the marks with her fingers, she was careful not to touch him.

"They just appeared, my chief." Sovin spun in surprise at the quiet voice behind her. "I was watching him, to make sure nothing happened to him while under my spell," Crista tried to explain. "Sometime this morning the scratches appeared, then became worse. It must have been caused by whatever is torturing him in the spell."

Sovin nodded. "Good. I will assume that means the spell is working. Cast it again. We will continue until he is broken or dies. Either is acceptable with me." She watched two of the tribe's children wake her prisoner and force him to drink water.

"Where is she? Where is Cora?" the Black Hand demanded, after swallowing the water.

Sovin punched him the stomach, relishing the feel of his flesh bending to her strength. "I told you to never speak her name again!" she shouted in his face.

The Black Hand coughed, trying to catch his breath. Blood reddened his lips and he glared at her. "I'll speak her name whenever I wish. I've had enough of your games, Sovin."

"It matters not what you've had enough of, slave." She gestured for Crista to come closer. "Continue, Crista."

The mage reached up, placing her hands on each side of Percival's head. He tried to shake his head from her grip.

"Don't let him loose, Crista!" Sovin warned.

"I know, my chief. I am prepared this time," Crista defended, pressing her fingers harder into his temples. Speaking a few archaic words, she released him when his eyes glazed over and his head fell forward.

Sovin waited for Crista's confirmation. "Watch him from a safe distance. I don't want you close to him."

Crista nodded, then retreated to the distance Sovin indicated.

* * *

Percival watched Crista walk away from him, then searched for Cora. When he did not immediately find her, he rested his head against the tree, closing his eyes.

"Did you miss me?" Cora's breath blew over his ear.

"I miss the Cora I've known and loved." He lifted his head to look at her, and was once again surprised by the wicked sneer on her lips.

"What? No smile for your love?" She laughed. "Maybe you aren't happy to see me after all." She waved her hand, as if brushing away a bug. "No matter. I will get over it." She whistled a single, loud note, then stood with her arms crossed, a satisfied grin lighting her face.

Moments passed in silence, until a large group of people came into his view, Amazons and a few male slaves, none he recognized from the camp. The group stopped behind Cora. She waved her hand at them and they separated to reveal individuals Percival recognized all too well.

Tylina, Kalik, Nimbly and Brolin were dragged through the path created by the Amazons separating. Once they reached Cora's side, they were forced to their knees by spear point. A large, black armored figure separated from the crowd. Cora gestured for the figure to move closer, caressing his armored chest with her fingers.

"Percival, do you remember Exar? I hope you do. I found him skinning an elf. The blood was glorious. I thought, considering our group's history, that he would enjoy some time with Tylina and Nimbly. What do you think?" Cora laughed at Kalik's struggles against his captors and Tylina's cry of despair.

Percival ignored Cora, choosing instead to focus his attention on Tylina. Her wide eyes stared in terror at the man standing next to the Amazon she had once called 'friend'. The half-elf increased her struggles.

"No, Cora, don't do this!" Tylina screamed. She turned her terror-filled eyes to Percival. "Stop her, Percival!"

"I'm so sorry, Tylina." He hoped he could be heard over the protests of his friends.

Cora laughed again. "Have fun, Exar."

The armored head nodded, then he pulled a string from the bag at his waist. On the string were several dried elven ears, as well as a fresh pair stained with blood.

"These are my bounty, Tylina, as you know." The familiar hoarse voice came from within the mask. He fingered the freshest ears. "These two are your mother's. She was very enjoyable. After I cut her ears off, before I killed her, I raped her. I found out what it was like to be between the legs of an elven noble." Tylina stopped her struggles, breaking into quiet sobs. "Now, it's your turn."

Cora stepped closer to Percival, took his jaw in her hand and forced his attention to remain focused in Tylina's direction. Exar put his string of ears away and sauntered toward the half-elf. Loosening his pants with deliberate movements, he made sure the unbuckling sound was loud enough for everyone to hear. He grabbed Tylina by the hair and pulled her away from the Amazons. The large man ignored Kalik's loud protests and threats, laughing when one of the Amazons backhanded the blind warrior.

Unable to turn away, Percival watched Exar force Tylina onto the ground. Three Amazons stepped between Exar and Percival, blocking the prisoner's view, but he still heard Exar's grunts as he forced himself on the woman. Tylina's sobs and pleas for help rang in Percival's ears. Uncounted moments passed, then a high-pitched scream filled the air, followed by another, suddenly cut short. The Amazons blocking Percival's view separated when Exar stood, holding Tylina's ears in his hand. He dropped his bloody trophies into his bag, then straightened his pants.

Defeated, Kalik's struggles ceased and he hung limp from the hands of his captors.

Exar turned to nod at Cora. When he moved, he revealed Tylina's lifeless body, her throat cut. The large man turned to Nimbly and without a word, he drove his sword into the elf's chest. With the dripping blade, he cut off his victim's ears.

"Not as much pleasure with that one. I have no use for males, except for their ears," Exar growled.

"Neither do I." Cora laughed, releasing Percival's face. Her laughter stopped abruptly. "Your passage back to the mainland has been secured. Your services are no longer required."

Exar nodded, disappearing into the crowd of Amazons.

"I can't believe you did that, Cora," Percival whispered in shock, staring at the corpses of his elven friends.

"Why? Because no one you love could do something like that?" she asked, mocking him.

"No, because you've never been that cruel," he answered, his disappointment leaking into his voice.

"Obviously you don't know me, Black Hand." She walked away from him. "Stake the blind one to the ground." The Amazons rushed to execute her command. "Did it ever occur to you, Black Hand, that your life of doing and acting good bored me? That *you* bored me?"

"No," he shouted, feeling his grip on sanity beginning to slip.

Cora flung her hand toward him. "Soola lancium ariy!" A blue ice spear flew from her hand and into his flesh.

"Enough! Arcanum misi linge!" she screamed, her other hand slashing across her chest. Blue streaks appeared on his chest at the same time, tearing open his clotted wounds.

He gnashed his teeth to keep from crying out. The cold of the ice spear numbed the flesh around the new wound, then darkness claimed him.

Chapter 95

In the early morning light, as the red of dawn flooded the land, Crista watched Sovin study the Black Hand. She leaned in close to the new wounds, examining them. Crista knew her chief lacked the skill needed to understand the workings of magic, but Sovin would try to comprehend what was happening to their prisoner.

Looking around the camp, Crista noted the red from the rising sun. She knew Sovin was more superstitious than their more "civilized" sisters were. She wondered what bad omen the other Amazon saw in the morning colors. Finally, Sovin turned toward Crista.

"Again, he is wounded. Explain to me what happens while he is under your spell!" Sovin demanded.

"I told you, it brings out his inner fears and breaks his will by forcing him to lose the battle against those fears," Crista explained.

She tried to control the patronizing patience in her voice. She took a deep breath, thankful Sovin ignored her tone.

"Then why the wounds?" Sovin waved her hand at the Black Hand's unconscious form.

"I believe that if he receives an injury while within the spell, his body receives it in reality." A child handed a bowl of stew to Crista and then Sovin. Crista ate a spoonful before continuing.

"Do the injuries really bother you, my chief?"

Sovin stared at her, then shook her head. "No, they don't. Eat, then cast the next spell."

Crista waited for Sovin to leave, then set her bowl on the ground and approached the Black Hand. She took a skin of water from a younger Amazon who tried to force him to drink, despite his appearing to be unconscious.

"Only when he wakes, child. Otherwise, you will kill him before we are ready." Crista set the skin on the ground, then took Percival's head in her hands. After she spoke the words to activate the spell, his head jerked out of her grip. His head hit the bark of the tree he was tied to, but he did not appear to feel any pain.

"No," he whispered, his eyes pleading with her. Before Crista responded, he was again lost in the magic.

Crista stared at him, counting her shallow breaths between each of his. When he did not appear to have anything further to say, she returned to her food.

* * *

"So, Percival, what do you think I should do to Brolin?" Cora asked, running the handle of the whip she now held over Brolin's armored chest. "What can I do to make you suffer more?"

"I don't know, Cora. Haven't you done enough with Tylina and Nimbly?" Percival's words betrayed the weariness he felt throughout his body.

"No, I don't think I have. I think you deserve more, much more." She shoved the handle under Brolin's chin, forcing him to lift his head, and pulled his mace from his belt.

"They've called you friend," Percival growled with renewed energy.

"How unfortunate for them. This is much more enjoyable than their so-called 'friendship'. I think I will rid myself of Kalik first. Being blind is such a weakness." Cora carried Brolin's mace over to Kalik's prone form. Straddling the blind man, she looked at Percival to ensure she had his full attention.

Without warning, she brought the mace down forcefully into Kalik's stomach. The mace screamed as it arced through the air. Agonizing moments passed for Percival as Kalik's screams and Cora's maniacal laughter filled the air. Finally, Kalik's voice was silenced, followed by the sound of the mace striking flesh one last time.

Cora stood and turned to grin at Percival, the mace she still held dripping with blood. She wiped a hand across her face, smearing blood that had splattered on her skin. "Only one left now." She sauntered over to Brolin again.

"You've desecrated my weapon and insulted my god," the priest declared, venom dripping from his words.

"I've only just begun to insult your god, Brolin." Cora rubbed the mace over his face, smearing the blood on his skin. Then she threw the weapon behind her and began pulling Brolin's armor off him. Once his armor lay on the ground, she reached into his under shirt and pulled out his holy symbol.

"The symbol of your devotion to Garen." She held it up, gazing at the workmanship, then yanked it from its chain.

"Cora, you need to stop this. You are only damning your soul," Brolin pleaded through clenched teeth.

Cora laughed, throwing the holy symbol in the fire. "Your beliefs do not matter to me, Brolin. *You* do not matter to me." She pulled his prayer book from a pocket inside her cloak. With deliberate steps, she tromped over to the fire and held the book over the flames.

"Don't do it, Cora!" Brolin shouted.

"What?" she asked, teasing. "This?" Cora dropped the book into the fire.

"By Garen, Cora, I'll..." Brolin began, stopping when the ground beneath him started to shake. A shaft of light broke through the surface and washed over him. Surprised, the Amazons holding Brolin pushed him to the ground, then released him, stepping away from the light. As he struggled to stand, the ground opened and a man rose from the fissure.

Percival studied the man standing before the gathered Amazons and their prisoners. He appeared to be the same age as Percival, with rugged features the Black Hand was sure would be considered handsome. His black hair almost touched his shoulders, but his beard was short cropped. He wore a dark patch over one eye, surveying the area with his good eye. Black leather covered his legs. The black shirt he wore revealed a well-muscled chest and his broad shoulders strained against the material. The man smirked at Cora, bowing deep before her.

"Daughter of Shae, it pleases me to see you have kept your

side of our agreement." His deep voice echoed in the night.

"Of course, Lord Talos, to do otherwise would not look favorably for Shae's daughters." Cora seductively approached the god. "Perhaps we can work a bit closer in the future, to the advantage of us both."

She was trying to make him jealous, Percival realized, as the woman he loved continued her seductive dance. He had no idea where she learned to do that. She never moved like that for him and often found women who did ignorant.

The deity studied her, then reached out and caressed her pregnant belly. Percival struggled against his restraints. The god rewarded his efforts with a laugh. "Yes, I'm sure we can think of many ways to work... closer, as you called it." With his other hand, he pulled Cora to him, grinning at Percival over her head, and kissed her fiercely.

Percival continued to struggle, grunting in pain, until the two separated. Cora swayed, unsteady on her feet. Percival watched her turn toward him, a dazed look on her face. Finally, she regained her composure and pointed at Brolin.

"Take him, as we agreed. I have no further use for him, and I know how much you have been looking forward to this."

Talos nodded, and after briefly caressing her cheek again, turned to Brolin. The priest had finally made his way to his feet and had tried to back away from the god. Talos pointed a finger at him and chains appeared on his ankles and wrists, stopping his escape. Without another word, the deity grabbed the chains that bound Brolin and disappeared with his prize down the wound in the earth. With a resounding crushing noise, the ground sealed behind them.

Smug, Cora sauntered over to Percival, her hips again swaying seductively. She brushed her lips with her fingertips, as if she still felt the god's lips upon them. "That was very exciting."

"Now what, Princeesa?" Percival growled, trying to ignore the jealousy she tried to incite in him.

"Now, Black Hand, you have my full attention."

Chapter 96

The boats landed on the shore of the smaller Amazon island without interference. The Amazons unloaded the horses first, then hobbled them while a smaller group of warriors set up the camp.

Cora slowly walked down the ramp of the boat she had traveled in. Silva followed closely, her hands held out to support the princess if needed. At the bottom of the ramp, Cora waited for Silva to move in front of her, then leaned on her friend and guard.

"Will my tent be up soon?" Cora asked, panting between words.

"Yes, Princeesa. Yours is the first they are working on." Silva held her friend, but her eyes searched elsewhere. "As soon as the others have finished your tent, I will send the priest to you."

"Thank you, my friend."

"I believe Sovin's spy slipped by us last night. Those on watch reported seeing someone on a horse riding through the trees," Silva advised.

"We expected that. Sovin will have time to prepare for us." Cora sighed. "Unfortunately, she will also have more time to hurt Percival." The connection between them still felt wrong-- blocked. She assumed the demon was keeping them apart.

The two waited in silence until the tent had been completed.

Walking inside, they found the ground covered in blankets.

"The others gave up their blankets for me?" Cora asked in surprise.

"They must be more aware of your discomfort than we realized. I told you, Princeesa, those who follow you do so because they love, respect and believe in you. No one here would go against you, even those from your mother's elite." Silva picked a spot on the blankets and helped Cora lie down.

"I've done nothing to deserve this loyalty, Silva. I left all of you for three years because of a vision, Satina is dead because of me and I no longer follow the true Amazon path." Cora rolled to her side and rested her head on the blankets.

"Satina is dead because she chose to return without you, instead of enjoying the journey. And, the Amazon path you speak of was laid out by a bitter woman with vengeance in her heart and men looking for a way to get rid of their wives without killing them." Silva sat next to her Princeesa.

"Without meaning to, you have exposed us to a different way of life. Those of us who want to live it will support you. I am your protector and always will be, but I look forward to the day I will follow you to the mainland. Besides, your elven friend—Nimbly—he amuses me." The two women laughed, Silva's sounding more like relief from confessing her interest in Nimbly than amusement.

"Sorry to interrupt," Brolin's voice came loudly over the fading laughter. "May I come in to check on you and the baby, Cora?" He stood inside the tent, waiting.

Cora nodded, briefly hugged Silva, then stretched out on the blankets. Brolin knelt next to her and with gentle movements, pulled her capeshal from her belly. After examining her and mumbling to himself the entire time, the priest sat back on his heels, his expression grim.

"The potion has done its job. It's disguised the pain so well, that you have made things worse. You need to rest. I'm sorry, but I cannot let you ride a horse tomorrow," Brolin explained.

"Brolin, we don't have the time for this. With the black moon so close, anything could happen with Stromas," Cora insisted.

"If you get on a horse in the morning, I will not give you the potion. I will not let you risk your life, or the baby, in this mad dash to save Percival," he informed her quietly, yet his voice was firm.

"I've wasted enough time because of my mother, my sister and the pain." Cora sat up, glaring at him.

"I would have to agree, but rushing now will do nothing but harm you and the baby." Brolin stopped when Silva came closer to them.

"Please, Cora, do as he instructs. Your baby is our future. Do not throw it away because of stubbornness," she pleaded.

Cora stared at her bodyguard, surprised that Silva had used her name instead of her title. Finally, she nodded reluctantly.

"All right. If I am to be forced to rest for the day, then I should probably sleep."

Brolin nodded as well, directed her to lie down again, then rested his hand upon her forehead. A moment later, Cora was asleep.

Chapter 97

"The Princeesa and a group of thirty warriors left the fort three days ago."

Crista stood by, silent, as Sovin's scout reported to her. The scout turned spy ran her horse to exhaustion and when it could run no more, she left it and ran the rest of the way on foot.

"How can you be sure she left?" Sovin asked, gazing at the afternoon sun. "Did you see it with your own eyes?"

The scout shook her head. "I did not see them. Rainne told me after they had gone, and I passed them on my way here."

"Good. You've done well. Get some rest." Sovin turned to her mage. "Crista, take him into the spell again. I don't want him out of it until his will is broken."

"That could be dangerous, my chief. I may not be able to pull him out of it. He could be in the spell for days." Crista wrung her hands, nervous.

"Cora and thirty of the best warriors our people have ever trained are coming. They will be here before we know it. If his spirit is broken when she arrives, then she will see him for the weak fool that he is and she will no longer wish to be with him." Sovin gave Crista a malicious grin. "If you have done your work correctly, then he will be too afraid of her to even gaze upon our Princeesa again. She can give him a merciful death."

"But, Sovin..." The glare Crista received ceased further

discussion. The mage finally nodded and rushed over to Percival.

When she touched his head, he opened his eyes. She abruptly removed her hands, stifling a cry of surprise. His gaze held hers briefly, then she turned back to Sovin. For a moment, she thought of calling the other Amazon over to her, but when Sovin waved her hand impatiently for Crista to proceed, she decided against it. With a loud sigh, the mage returned her attention to Percival and cautiously reached for his head again.

"Please don't do this," Percival pleaded with her when her hands touched his skin.

"I'm sorry," she whispered in turn. She took another deep breath, then spoke the words that would activate a more powerful aspect of the spell she had been subjecting him to.

He stared at her for a heartbeat, then his eyes glazed over and his head fell forward, falling from her grasp. She turned from him and returned to her position next to Sovin.

Her chief glanced at her, a frown on her face. "What's the problem, Crista?" Sovin asked, impatient.

"I don't know, Sovin. When he looked at me, it was like looking into the fires of hell." Crista wrapped her arms around herself, a sudden shiver rolling through her. "I think we made a mistake—a very serious mistake."

The other woman laughed. "Nonsense. Shae protects her daughters." Sovin walked away from her frightened mage to talk to Satir.

"Shae may not be able to protect us, if I'm right," Crista whispered, turning to watch Percival.

Chapter 98

"Are you saying you aren't excited to have me all to yourself, Black Hand?" Cora teasingly ran her fingers over Percival's bare chest, beginning the conversation where they had ended.

"Not like this, Treame." He clenched his teeth when she touched his wounds.

Cora laughed. "There was a time when hearing you speak that name brought me joy, then I remembered what I was really in your world for—to learn. Silly me. I had forgotten that, for about a day." Percival's look of anger only made her laugh more.

After a deep breath, she stopped laughing and started to cut the ropes that bound his legs to the tree. He flexed his limbs, mindful of the weakness he felt days before. His arms came free and he rubbed them while searching the camp.

"Percival," Cora sang from behind him.

He turned to look at her and she reached up and slammed a metal collar around his neck. When he brought his hands up to his neck, she shut metal shackles onto his wrists and then, with a wave of her hand, he felt shackles bind around his ankles.

"What!" Percival exclaimed, reaching to grab Cora by the shoulders. "Don't do this, Cora. You know how I feel about this."

She nodded. "Exactly. After I break you, I might make you my slave. I haven't decided yet."

"You swore I would never be your slave."

She laughed. "I lied."

He released her arms and backed up, just as she brought her knee up, missing him. She whispered a few words, then laughed as a chain appeared in her hands and through the loops of the shackles on his wrist. She pulled him close to the tree again and threw the chain into the branches. With a yank, she pulled his hands over his head.

"Cora, stop! This isn't right and you know it," Percival shouted at her as she disappeared from his view. She returned a moment later, the whip in her hand.

"Why? Because you showed me a better way?" With a crack, the whip bit into the flesh of his chest. "I never loved you, Black Hand. I was just using you." Another crack—more wounds. Percival ground his teeth together. "Everything I did, everything I said, was just to learn. Learn how to manipulate the men in your world and learn your weaknesses." Again, the whip cut into his flesh. "You used me as well. You saw me as a way to free yourself from your demon. I was nothing more than a means to an end." She struck him with the whip a number of times without speaking a word before she finally dropped the weapon on the ground.

Percival rested his head against the tree, trying to catch his breath. Pain traveled from his new wounds throughout his body. As he waited for her next move, he closed his eyes, her words echoing through his mind. He did not want to believe it had been a lie. Her touch had been so soft, so full of love. How could a lie have felt so good, so right? But then, she too often said it was hard adjusting to life in his world, that it would take time for her to get used to the ways of Man's World.

The pain settled in his chest, in the hole that once held a heart that loved her.

"Lost in your thoughts, Black Hand?" Cora asked, pressing herself against his back painfully, her arms wrapping around his chest. Her fingers dug into the wounds she made and his breath came in ragged gasps again.

"Let me go, Cora," he whispered. "Just go away." Her presence disappeared from his back. "What about the baby?" he asked after a breath.

Before he answered, she moved him again and placed his back against the tree once more. When he could see her, she smoothed her dress down, the blood from his wounds disappearing in the black of material. As her hands skimmed over her shirt, he could see the swelling of her belly easier.

"The baby, *our* baby." Cora pressed her hands on her belly. "*My baby*. Not something I had figured into my plans. If anything useful comes out of those painfully long nights with you, then the child will be a girl. I will get rid of my sister and then my daughter and I will be in line for the throne after my mother's death."

"And if it's a boy?" Percival asked quietly.

Cora shrugged. "Then I will kill it." She gave him a smile filled with tenderness. "Or, if you still live, maybe I'll let you take him off the island." He lifted his gaze, a spark of hope lightning within him. She laughed again. "You don't know me very well, do you? I'd suffocate the boy myself before I would let you have it." The hope in Percival died, replaced with a low burning flame. "Or even better, I will give the boy to your father."

"You see, Percival, your mother was wrong." A deep voice drew Percival's attention away from Cora to a masculine figure standing behind her.

Percival recognized his father when the figure stepped closer. He felt the heat in his eyes—the fire—grow stronger.

"She should have told you everyone has an inner demon they fight to keep at bay." Marcus reached Cora and put his arm around her shoulders. "Everyone has demons, son. Yours is just more tangible." His father pulled the Amazon closer, forcing her face up to his and kissing her.

Cora stared at the older man for a heartbeat after the kiss. When she looked at Percival again, he saw her eyes were now void of color. Instead, her orbs glowed brightly, her eyes taking on a sinister quality. He watched her skin lose all color, her ears lengthened to a point, more pronounced than an elf's. She looked to the sky, stretching her arms toward the heavens. Large, leathery wings sprouted from her back. She spread her wings out behind her while she filled the air with laughter. The bulge of her unborn child disappeared from her belly and a naked infant appeared in Marcus' arms.

"Her changes are more pronounced than yours will be, but I believe the look of a succubus accents her beauty perfectly."

When she heard Marcus' comments, Cora's laughter became deeper and she locked her gaze on Percival as if to make sure he knew her laughter was directed at him. Marcus watched him, and Percival could see the fire in his eyes reflected in his father's.

The older man's deep, throaty laughter joined Cora's. "Your child will make a perfect vessel for my new demon."

For a moment, their laughter echoed around Percival as their words repeated in his mind. He lowered his head, staring at the ground, until his father's words faded. Cora words lingered a moment longer, but stopped suddenly when he lifted his eyes again.

"It was all a lie," he whispered and his world erupted into flames.

* * *

"He's been under that spell for more than a day," Sovin shouted at Crista.

"I told you it was a possibility, Sovin. You insisted you wanted him broken before Cora arrived. I told you he could be under its influence for an undetermined period of time," the tearful mage explained to her leader, glancing around the camp. "You said that would only help to control him when Cora arrived."

Before Sovin could respond, a loud, animal-like roar echoed through the camp, followed by a rumble and the sound of wood snapping. The two women turned toward their prisoner. Sovin's shocked expression did not match the terror Crista felt.

Percival stood tall in the mid-afternoon sun, flexing his muscles. The ropes that had bound him lay in a pile at his feet. Crista again noted the flames in his eyes, but now they burned brighter, stronger.

As he stretched his arms and legs, she knew he must have felt pain from the wounds on his back and chest as they reopened and new blood flowed down his skin. While she watched, he approached them, ignoring the Amazons that tried to stop him. When he reached the two women, he grabbed Sovin around the throat and lifted her from the ground.

"What do you want, Black Hand?" Crista whispered.

"I am** not **the Black Hand." His voice was deeper and echoed as if two voices combined into one, just as before. ***"And, I want your people to die!"*** He threw Sovin into a nearby tree and turned to Crista. ***"I am Stromas and I am free!"***

* * *

Cora stopped straightening the saddle of her horse as pain ripped through her core, up her spine and into her head. She dropped the reins and fell to the ground. The pain stole her breath and her vision.

The pain increased, reaching its climax as a roar echoed throughout the forest. Silva dropped to the ground next to Cora. "Princeesa!"

Breathing came easier for Cora as the roar faded. The pain faded as well, however she could feel a knot of it in her womb. The baby had felt the disabling pain as well. Would it be harmed?

"What was that?" Silva demanded.

Cora rested her head on her guard's shoulder. "We're too late, Silva. The demon is free."

"Cora!" Brolin bellowed, running toward her.

"I will be fine, Brolin. We need to reach Sovin's camp." Cora stood with help from both of them. She had already drunk the potion for her pain. There would not be another dose despite whatever Stromas had done to her. She climbed on top of her horse and looked around at the people with her. "Mount up and let's move out."

She waited, each moment passing painfully slow. She knew their progress would be slow because of her pain, and she wanted to start moving again to prevent any further loss of time. Finally, everyone sat upon his or her horse and turned their attention to the princess. With a wave of her hand, Cora led them through the moonless night to face the newly freed demon.

Chapter 99

Stromas watched the sunrise through Percival's eyes, breathing deep of the new dawn. Through the night, he had killed a handful of the Amazons. He played with each one, making them suffer until their final breaths left them. To keep the others from escaping, he put them into the pens the slaves had occupied.

He enjoyed finding different ways to kill them, testing the extent of his powers within the constraints of Percival's body. Sovin died quickest, though she survived her initial assault against the tree where he threw her. He should have prolonged her death, but he could not control his anger and she died only a change later. The others were tortured, first with his hands, then with weapons he found around the settlement. His powers were still increasing, although being in the prime dimension kept them from their full potential. His physical strengths were weakest, but his mental powers grew strong.

Early in his release, Stromas had freed the male slaves for the simple pleasure of seeing the Amazons glare at him, helpless to stop him. When the men ran free into the forest, Stromas concentrated his mental powers on seeking out those who served him still, despite the years of captivity in the human world.

Making contact sent a thrill through him. His body trembled

with the near ecstasy of his power throbbing against the confines of Percival's flesh.

Yes, for now, I am free.

I took control once, I can do it again.

She is his weakness. His loyalty to her will be his undoing.

Ahh, yes, she will be perfect to use against the Black Hand.

If there truly is a child, and it and Cora survive the birth, I want them.

Yes, I will contact you again when I am able.

Finished with the games he played through the evening, Stromas again looked to the sunrise for renewal. He expected Cora to arrive soon. Through her connection with Percival, Stromas felt Cora travel all night, coming closer, though her slower pace concerned him.

"Why do I care that she travels slower than I expected? Am I becoming too attached to the Amazon?" Stromas grinned at the surviving Amazons, particularly Crista. *"A better question is, will I give her back to the Black Hand once I have her?"*

Crista retreated from the fence. "The Princeesa is not yours for the taking, demon."

"No? I think she is. If the Black Hand did not want me to have her, he would never have taken her as his lover while I was still part of him." He approached the enclosure. *"See? Everything is the Black Hand's fault. Everything. Cora's injuries, the discord between all the Amazons, the queen exiling her, Sovin's death and your imprisonment. If he had maintained his place, and not gotten close to her, none of this would have happened."*

"I don't believe anything you say, demon," Crista whispered.

"She will be here soon, and we will see what she has to say." Stromas stepped away from his prisoners, searching for Cora's presence again. *"I cannot wait to see her. I will touch her and she will be mine."*

Chapter 100

Cora and the group arrived at Sovin's camp in the darkest time before the sun began its morning journey. While Silva took two guards with her and scouted the outskirts of the camp, Cora waited and the others set up their own camp.

Silva returned when the morning sun bathed the land with its bright light. "Cora, the longhouses are on fire. Opposite from us, a group of Amazons, adults and children, are in one of the slave pens. I don't see any of the men, or Percival."

"Can you tell how many are dead?" Cora asked, standing and preparing to walk into the other camp.

"No, there are bodies everywhere," Silva breathed. "I don't like this, Cora."

"I understand, Silva. But I have to go in there. If there's any chance to save Percival, I have to try." Cora walked past her guard. "The sun is up. Time for us to go," she called to the others.

The group covered the distance to Sovin's camp quickly. Cora saw the longhouse fires Silva spoke of, the tents the men used were strewn throughout the clearing, trees lay in splintered pieces and a particularly large tree lay uprooted on its side near a dying campfire. The children on the other side of the camp huddled against their mothers. A handful of bodies lay on the ground in awkward and unnatural positions.

Cora stopped next to the fire and studied the area until she spotted Percival stepping out from behind a tree.

Dried blood covered almost every part of his bare chest. A wound slashed across his abdomen still appeared fresh. From her position, it was difficult for Cora to determine the extent of his wounds. His steps were slow and within his expression of anger, she could see the pain caused by every movement.

"Cora." A voice that was not Percival's reached her from across the camp. *"My Treame, how nice to finally see you with my own eyes."* He waved his hand and laughed. *"Well, in a way."*

Hearing her true name felt like a dagger being driven into her back. He knew her true name. Everything Percival heard, felt, said, Stromas did as well.

Cora felt Silva push a wooden shaft into her hand. She gestured for the others to spread out, then gave the man walking toward her, her full attention.

"Who are you?" Cora asked, crossing the camp. She ignored the grunts of warning from her warriors.

"I am Stromas. I am the real strength, the real emotions Percival claimed were his. I am free, finally, to show you who I really am."

Cora leaned on her spear, watching her warriors circle behind the demon-controlled body of Percival. "Is that so? What have you done with Percival?"

"Obviously, I have his body. His mind is questionable. I'm sure he's in here—somewhere—not that it really matters. He will never be the same, not after what they did to him." Stromas kicked one of the bodies.

"What did they do?" Cora asked, not wanting to hear the answer, but knowing that there was no avoiding it.

Stromas turned to gaze at the group of Amazons behind him. *"It was her."* He lifted his hand and with a gesture, he pulled one of the Amazons to him. As she floated over the group, Cora recognized her from the few times Sovin's tribe came to the fort seeking an audience with the queen.

"Her name is Crista," Stromas explained. *"Despite her misgivings, she was the one who set me free. Her magic forced Percival to see things that made him question, doubt and then finally give up on the love the two of you shared."*

"No," Cora denied.

"Yes, that is exactly what happened. But don't worry, Treame," Stromas again spoke Cora's true name and again the pain rushed through her body.

Sucking in a breath, Cora tried to keep the concern from her face.

Stromas threw Crista into the holding pen and turned a look full of love, longing and pain toward Cora. ***"I've made them pay. I knew you would be unhappy about what they did to Percival, so I punished them for you."***

"You had no right, Stromas. No right to determine their guilt or serve as executioner." She straightened from the support of her weapon. "No right to call me by my true name. Only three people in this world can call me that and you aren't one of them."

Stromas walked closer to her, stopping when she lowered the spear point to his chest. Guilt overwhelmed her at threatening Percival and the weapon trembled in her hands.

"I can be." He held his hand out toward her.

"Never. I love Percival, everything about him. You are evil, a demon from another plane and you are keeping the man I love from me." She lowered the spear from its threatening position.

"I have his body. I know everything about him. You wouldn't know the difference."

Cora shook her head. "I would know. I knew Percival wasn't really in control as soon as I saw you." She studied the man in front of her, confused. "Why are you saying these things? You knew I would never agree."

Stromas closed the distance between them abruptly and Cora had to struggle to raise a hand to prevent her protectors from stopping him. She studied him, and Stromas studied her in return. She could see the wounds on his chest, still oozing blood. Her fingers tingled from the memory of his skin the first time she touched him, the connection of their magic. The warmth of his breath remained Percival's, even if it was controlled by Stromas. Longing grew within her, born of loneliness during their separation and she fought the urge to beg the demon for Percival's release.

Stromas touched her cheek, his touch tender, bringing the moment back into focus. ***"I want you. I can be everything you want, everything you need. He will never again be as he was*** *before this happened. They took your love for each other and destroyed it.*" He leaned closer, putting his mouth close to her ear. "*I saw the way you looked at me. You want to touch me. You can't love him without loving me. You said so yourself. You love everything about him. I am part of him. But he will never trust you again.*"

"That is for us to decide, an obstacle for us to overcome." Cora slapped his hand away from her face. "I want him back. I came for Percival and I am not leaving without him."

"*I'm not giving him back. I like it in his body. I like the freedom.*" The demon pounded on Percival's injured chest.

"I won't allow this to continue, Stromas. Percival would not want to live like this, with you in control." Cora raised her left hand and made a circling gesture to the warriors surrounding them. Each one drew her bow and readied an arrow. She could see Nimbly and Tylina also drawing their bows and joining the group of Amazons.

"*They will hit you, Princeesa, but I will survive.*" Stromas straightened, confident. He winced from the pain his motion caused.

"No, you won't. Feel his wounds. And if I know my people, then he's gone days with little or no food." Cora paused, imagining the torture Sovin had inflicted. Finally she continued. "He is injured. Our friends and my warriors will fire their arrows and will keep firing until you fall. But, looking at the wounds he's suffered, it should only take one from each to finish him."

Stromas stared at her, his expression filled with shock as she continued. "I will order his death. While you're in control, he's as good as dead anyway. Your attempts to convince me to let you keep control were a waste of time." Cora stepped back and brought her spear up again, pushing it against the flesh of his stomach, near the other wound. "Give up control and give Percival back to me. Do it, or I will kill you both."

Stromas continued looking at her for a heartbeat longer, then took two steps away from the spear. "*Of course, Treame. But I warn you, I won't go away completely. I will always be in here.*" He pointed at his head. "*Just like I have always been. It's going to take more than this to get rid of me.*"

Cora nodded. "I realize that, Stromas. Understand that I will help him find a way to be free of you forever."

"Oh, yes, you are definitely the one." Stromas smiled. *"His child is mine as well, Cora."*

"No. Percival's father gave him to you. You will not have my child. Shae protects us and she will protect our child. My child will not be offered to you for any reason," she spat.

"Not even for the soul of its father?" the demon whispered.

"Not even for the soul of its father," Cora swore.

"Remember your words, Treame. The day may come when you will have to choose between them. Who will you choose?" His eyes rolled up, revealing the whites, then Percival's body collapsed as Stromas relinquished control.

Cora dropped her spear and rushed to Percival's side. Silva ran to join Cora while the others lowered their weapons.

"Percival, wake up. It's me," Cora whispered, tears falling from her eyes onto Percival's face. "Please come back to me. Whatever they told you was a lie."

His eyes fluttered open. "Yes, it was," he croaked, his voice now void of Stromas' tone. He pushed himself away from her, struggling to stand. His movements were unsteady and it took him several attempts before he was finally able to stand. "Everything, the words, the caresses, our love, all of it was a lie."

Cora stood in front of him. "No, that isn't what I meant. Somehow Sovin was able to make you believe something that wasn't real." She turned to Crista for help when Silva brought the other woman over to the couple.

"Yes, Percival. I used a spell to bring your worst fears into being. The spell was designed to make you fail in a battle against them," Crista explained.

He ignored Crista's words as he stared at Cora. "Let me go, *Princeesa.*"

She listened to the emotions in his words, nodding finally. Sadness filled her, but she could not force him to stay if he insisted on leaving. Making him stay would only reinforce everything Crista and Sovin made him believe.

Cora turned to her warriors and motioned for them to step aside and allow Percival to pass.

He pushed past her, his pain obvious in every movement. She watched him go, her eyes filling with tears again.

The other Amazons remained silent while they watched

the large man painfully make his way to the edge of camp. After making his way past the women, ignoring his friends, he stopped. His body shook with exhaustion and pain and Cora could see his legs quaking with the struggle to remain standing.

"Cora," he called for her.

She made her way to him quickly, her own pain forgotten for the moment. He waited until she stood next to him, then turned to look at her.

"Why did you let me go so easily? What do you have planned? I won't allow you to make me a slave, Princess."

She shook her head. "Nothing, Percival. I have nothing planned. I let you go because that's what you wanted. I could never keep you as a slave or a prisoner. Neither of us could live like that."

"Why? Why can't I live like that?" He watched her intently.

"Because you are a slave to the demon your father tied you to," she answered confidently, noting the smile he hid quickly.

They were silent for several moments before he spoke again. "Who am I?" She stared at him in stunned silence. "Who am I!" he demanded.

"Percival Riesun, the man I chose to follow as the leader of our group, the man I love." She lowered her gaze, her hands coming to rest on her belly. "You are Percival Riesun, the father of my unborn child."

"Who else am I? What else am I called?" he demanded again, not yet satisfied.

"No! You will not force that name from me. I hate that name and everything it represents," she angrily stood her ground against his demands.

He gave her a weak smile, then pulled her into a tight embrace. She held him tight, stumbling under his weight as he collapsed against her.

"Silva! Brolin!" she screamed as Percival's weight forced her to her knees.

Silva and several members of Cora's personal guard rushed over to the two of them and pulled Percival's unconscious body from her arms. They laid him on the ground next to her, stepping away so Brolin could move closer.

"We need to get him to the tent, Silva. Brolin can't heal him out here." Cora watched the priest examine the wounds Percival had suffered. The other woman nodded and quickly set about giving her orders to the others. The princess-mage watched everyone for a moment, then leaned over her lover, caressing his face. "Everything will be better now, love. I promise."

Chapter 101

Percival watched the tent begin to brighten from the sunrise he couldn't see. Brolin had been in and out all night so many times trying to heal him, that Percival finally sent him away with the demand that Cora either come in to see him or there would be no more spells performed. Angry, the priest went in search of the Amazon.

When Stromas took over, Percival almost reveled in the loss of control. The spell that Crista had forced on him tortured his mind with a version of Cora that he had never imagined. But she had been so real. The Amazons he met since arriving on the islands showed him that it was simply a choice that kept the real Cora on the more tolerant side. If she had made one decision, maybe two, different, she could become the cruel Amazon of the spell.

It was easy to let Stromas have control by the end. From somewhere in his mind, Percival watched the demon destroy Sovin and the other Amazons and he relished the loss of their lives. The anger he felt from Stromas and the strength that flowed through him intoxicated Percival.

Cora wouldn't be happy if she knew.

Did he really care?

Percival knew the Amazon of the spell was not the woman he loved. He knew the woman he loved would never do the things the other had done. He knew she was capable of mass destruction, but Cora kept her powers in check and did not draw upon them to her full capability.

Mages could destroy cities if they wanted.

His Amazon was no different, except for her self-control and desire to be better.

Or at least, that's what he hoped.

When the demon dogs back in Glenys attacked them, he had seen the look in her eyes. Though she was weakened by her magic, there was a glee as she pulled the magic through her and released it in a spear of destruction.

Or when she held the mage in Jonquil in the grip of her magic, forcing him to endure a pain that she controlled. That surprised him more than the demon dogs.

But then, when Shoshona's assassins attacked them, she cried after using her magic to kill one of the men.

He really didn't know what she was truly capable of. She hid the full power of her magic so well. One day she could grow tired of him and destroy him.

She may destroy him today.

He waited for Stromas to agree, to play upon Percival's doubt, but he received only silence.

Strange. Why was he quiet? Why now of all times did the demon choose to be silent?

Cora had not come to see Percival since she rescued him, and demanded Stromas release control of his body. Now he took the chance that she would come just because he demanded it.

Percival rolled over, lying on his stomach, hoping to relieve some of the pain in his back. The whipping wounds hurt when he laid on them. Despite the blankets and healing Brolin had done, Percival could not stay on his back for long.

A rustling sound from the tent flap reached him and he looked up to see who had entered.

His breath caught in his throat when he heard Cora's soft voice.

"Percival?"

Chapter 102

The second morning after arriving at Sovin's camp and freeing Percival from Stromas' control, Cora stood near the tree he had been tied to for almost three weeks. After treating the wounds Stromas inflicted on her, Crista had given the spell plate she used on Percival to the princess and explained everything she had learned about it.

Cora had listened to the explanation, then spent the evening studying the spell. By morning, she decided magical methods could not be used to reverse the effects. Instead of seeking the sleep she needed, she chose instead to watch the sunrise.

"He asked about you last night, before I left to sleep." Cora turned to see Tylina stepping closer to her.

"I'm sure it wasn't to find out how I am doing. The pain seems to be keeping him within the spell." The Amazon returned her attention to the rising sun.

"Actually, Percival was worried the journey here had harmed you and the baby." The half-elf wrapped her arms around her friend in a comforting embrace. "He needs your help to heal from this, Cora. Percival is a strong man, but it is obvious this will haunt him."

"There have been times when his love did not feel genuine, and times when he has seemed so full of doubt, as if, no matter how happy I was with him, he did not believe he could ever love me. Or that I could love him. Maybe this spell is just the excuse he needs to leave me." She heard the doubt in her words and knew her friend could as well. "I could be wrong. This is all still very new to me."

"As you told Stromas, this is something for the two of you to decide. You will handle this together."

Cora turned to embrace her friend. "Yes, we will. Thank you, my friend. As usual, your insight teaches me where my stubbornness blinds me."

The two stood in silence for several heartbeats, until the sound of footsteps reached them. They separated and turned toward the approaching individual. Brolin nodded at them grimly. He took Cora's hand in his when he stood next to her.

"Cora, he asked to see you."

"Tylina told me he asked about me. I'm tired. I don't feel up to arguing right now." The hours without sleep had finally caught up with her and she tried to leave for the tent Silva had erected for her.

"No, Cora. He wants to see you. Percival's awake and refused to let me heal him more until he does," Brolin explained.

She breathed deeply and released the air from her lungs slowly. Finally, Cora nodded and left her friends standing by the tree.

The darkness of the tent blinded her, until her eyes adjusted to the lack of light. The interior was warm, thanks to the small fire pit and heated rocks placed in strategic locations throughout the two-room structure.

"Percival?" she called out quietly.

Cora found him in the second room, lying on several blankets. He lay on his stomach, though she knew he was in pain no matter what position he slept in. His pain was a constant pressure through their connection. The dim lamplight revealed the healing wounds in his flesh and she saw very little improvement from when they first found him.

She sat on the ground next to him and adjusted the blanket covering the lower part of his body. Her hand stopped in the air above his wounded back. She longed to touch him, but knew it would cause him too much pain. Her skin still tingled at the closeness of him, though not as strong as it would if they touched.

"It took you long enough to come in here. What were you waiting for?" Percival's voice was still hoarse, grating like footsteps in sand. He turned his head to look at her and rolled onto his side.

"The previous times we have spoken since my arrival have not been very pleasant or friendly on your part," she whispered.

"You let that prevent you from being with me?"

She heard his surprise, despite the pain in his voice. Immediately she regretted staying away from him.

"In part. I thought, considering what Sovin and Crista had done to you, it would be best if I spent as little time as possible with you until you were healed." It was a poor excuse for allowing her doubts to affect her judgment. "I'm sorry, Percival. I know you're in pain and you're right. I should have been with you, despite the things you said." She caressed his hand, moving closer to him.

Silence filled the room while they looked at each other. Percival caressed her fingers in return. It was an unspoken agreement that kept their contact only to their hands.

"What are we going to do, Percival? I don't know exactly what you saw while under that spell, but from what Stromas said, I figured prominently in it," Cora whispered when she could no longer tolerate the silence.

"I don't want to talk about it yet, Cora." He paused a moment, then shook his head. "What did Stromas say?"

Cora considered her words before responding. "That our relationship would never be the same and it would be best if I just let him maintain control." She dropped her eyes to the blankets.

"I'm glad you didn't." He reached up and finally touched her cheek. "When will we return to your mother's?"

"In the morning, if you're doing well enough." She pushed her cheek into his hand and had to stifle a yawn.

"Didn't you sleep last night?" Percival asked in concern.

"Not really. I was studying the spell all night. I was on my way to bed when Brolin said you wanted to see me." She yawned again.

"Stay with me, Treame. I don't know if it will help, but I would rather you be with me than elsewhere."

Cora nodded. Standing from his side, she went in search of

Silva to get additional bedding.

While she waited, she watched her guards distribute morning meal to the prisoners. Percival had called her Treame. Why did that surprise her so much? Did she think he would never call her that again after Stromas was freed?

"Princeesa," Silva broke into Cora's thoughts. "I will be nearby if you should need me."

"Thank you, Silva. I am so tired, I am sure nothing will wake me until evening meal." Cora accepted the bedding, squeezing Silva's hand in comfort.

Returning to Percival's side, she situated her bedding, swatting his hands away when he tried to assist. "I am able to do this, Percival." She tried to make her words sound playful, but she was so tired, her voice fell flat.

Percival lie back on his blankets and winced in pain. "All right. Just hurry. I'm tired too."

Cora finished with her bedding and lay down next to him. She tried not to touch him, letting him control their contact through his embrace, as he had done after her injuries. The warmth of his body and rhythm of his breathing lulled her to sleep.

Chapter 103

In the morning, Cora's guards and the survivors of Sovin's clan started their journey to the main island and the queen's fort. Percival rode next to Cora, silent. She knew he was in pain, but he insisted on traveling despite the need for more healing and rest.

Every morning, before they started, Cora took Brolin's potion. She took care to hide it from Percival. She did not like lying to him, but she did not want him worrying about her when he was in so much pain.

Even when Brolin came to her again about taking the potion too many days in a row, she took him aside and they argued alone. Her travel that day was excruciating since she refused to stop for the rest she needed, her need to get Percival to the fort pushing her.

The return journey was slow, allowing for Percival and the larger number of people. Sovin's people avoided the warriors that protected the princess-mage, as well as her lover and friends. Silva frequently counted them to ensure none tried to escape.

Cora and Percival continued to share a tent, but rarely spoke. She didn't know his reasons, but she did not want to discuss his capture more than they already had. Several times she caught him gazing at her, a look of longing in his eyes, but the words to close the gap between them remained unspoken.

Three changes of the water clock after nightfall on the seventh day, the large group arrived at the queen's fort. Reann, Shayta and a small contingency of the elite guard met them at the courtyard gate.

"Sovin?" Reann asked without preamble, in the Trade language.

"Dead before we arrived," Cora answered, dismounting. Pain blinded her and she held onto the saddle of her horse until Silva appeared at her side. "In the morning, please, Mother. We're tired and saddle sore."

"Fires have been lit in yours and Tylina's rooms. Food was prepared as soon as the perimeter guards reported your approach." Reann looked at Percival, then softened her voice. "Shall I send someone to tend to the captain?"

Percival straightened his back at Reann's words and he pushed Brolin's hand away. After he dismounted, he turned to Cora and shook his head. "Brolin can handle whatever needs to be done. I would prefer to leave it that way." He waited until the two guards Silva had assigned him stood nearby, then walked into the fort. One of the women took the lead and the four disappeared inside.

Mother and daughter watched the others go inside as well, but did not speak until the horses and prisoners were taken away. When they were finally alone, except for Silva and Shayta, who waited at a respectable distance, Reann returned her attention to Cora.

"How bad is it?" she asked.

"Silva questioned those who survived. Sovin barely kept him alive. She whipped him, cut open scabbed wounds repeatedly, dragged him by his ropes, and kicked him until he coughed up blood. That was just while they traveled. Once they reached her camp, she continued the whippings until she decided to have Crista use magical means to break his spirit." Cora pulled out the spell plates Crista had relinquished. "This is the spell she used. He won't tell me yet what he saw, but it seems the spell manifests a person's worst fears and uses them to destroy their spirit."

"And what of the demon?" The queen sounded apologetic, though Cora knew she would never say as much.

Cora sighed, tired. The pain was becoming worse and she wanted to end the questioning so she could go to bed. "It was freed. Now it will be even more difficult to control it." She kissed her mother's cheek, surprising the older woman. "I will answer all your questions tomorrow, after I have rested." The two women parted and Cora reached out for Silva's support.

Cora led her friend to her rooms, dismissed her for the night and went inside. The common room was empty, so she went into the bedroom. Brolin was putting his supplies away when she entered, and Percival was already in the bed, his chest covered with new bandages.

"How is he, Brolin?" she whispered when she realized Percival's eyes were closed.

"I'm doing the best I can, Cora. There was a lot of internal damage and the journey back didn't help." He turned and his eyes were filled with concern. "I have no idea what that spell did to him emotionally. I can't heal that damage."

"That spell took everything and everyone I love—that I care about—and destroyed them." Percival rolled onto his side, away from them. "Thank you, Brolin. Sleep well."

Cora followed Brolin into the common room. "Yes, thank you for everything."

"How is your pain?" he asked, looking at her belly.

"It's bad. I am not sure how I am still able to stand right now."

"You don't want him to know." Brolin gestured at the pitcher of water on the dining table. "I will have someone bring you tea. Drink some if you can't sleep. I will check the damage this trip has caused after you have rested. I don't think we have helped anything, but at least Percival is safe. You are the priority now."

Cora nodded, and escorted him from her rooms and across the hall. He spoke to his guard while she returned to her common room. Leaving the doors open behind her, she stood on the balcony and waited for a servant to bring the tea Brolin requested. She heard the servant arrive, but kept her eyes on the trees of the surrounding forest.

Though Cora and Percival were together again, Stromas would fight to tear them apart. And Sovin gave him the strength to succeed.

Epilogue

"I want the baby," the man demanded, his features hidden by shadow.

"There is no baby. The old woman said Cora would be an idiot to try and have a baby after her injuries," Exar growled. "The Amazon is not an idiot."

"Then her time with my son has affected her intelligence."

Lanterns lit the room, the sudden flash of light blinding Exar momentarily. When his vision cleared, he saw a large mirror in front of the man who had summoned him.

The man stood at approximately the same height as Exar's former captain, though Percival was almost a hand's span taller. His dark hair showed the gray of his age, most likely made worse by the excessive use of magic. Dark purple robes dusted the floor with every movement. Exar stood, staring at the smaller man unimpressed.

Within the mirror, Cora knelt on the ground next to the battered form of Percival. Behind her, Exar saw the remains of tents, a partially destroyed longhouse, trees torn from their roots and bodies of women strewn in the dirt.

"My demon was free, though only for a short time. But he was free. Percival is stronger because of that demon, but he won't let me control it. His mother saw to that." The man turned back to study the image in the mirror. "I want that baby.

I can duplicate what I did to my son and this time I will control the demon," he said, affection in his voice. "Bring me that baby!" While he spoke, Cora stood from her place on the ground, with assistance, and the bulge of her unborn child was revealed.

"She won't give it up easily," Exar commented.

"What she does or does not want matters very little to me. Kill her if necessary. Just bring me that baby!" Percival's father shouted the last words at Exar.

The large man stared a moment longer, then nodded and left the room. After stepping into the sunlight, Exar mounted his horse and turned the beast toward the East.

His thoughts wondered through his memories of those he had traveled with for two years. Percival's father had plans for Cora and her baby, and as long as the money was good, Exar would let him have his fun.

About the Author

Micaela Fischer lives in Las Vegas, Nevada with her family and their zoo of animals. As a second generation native of Sin City, she always smiles and nods when "newcomer's" try to tell her about the city she has called home all her life. She has been writing for as long as she can remember and looks forward to every day when her muse speaks to her and her characters agree it's a good day to write.

You can reach Micaela at silvermanewriting@cox.net or visit her website at www.micaelafischer.com

www.ingramcontent.com/pod-product-compliance
Lightning Source LLC
Chambersburg PA
CBHW030808260626
47169CB00001B/241